TEN

Elisabeth's writing caree~~~
Harlequin's *So You Think Yo*~~~
hasn't looked back. She teach~~~
write full time because, unl~~~ ~~~characters
generally do what she tells them. She spends most of her spare
time reading and is a pro at cooking one-handed while holding a
book.

She lives in Cheshire because the car broke down there in 1999
and she never left.

elisabethhobbes.co.uk

 twitter.com/ElisabethHobbes
facebook.com/ElisabethHobbes

Also by Elisabeth Hobbes

The Secret Agent

DAUGHTERS OF PARIS

ELISABETH HOBBES

One More Chapter
a division of HarperCollins*Publishers* Ltd
1 London Bridge Street
London SE1 9GF
www.harpercollins.co.uk

HarperCollins*Publishers*
1st Floor, Watermarque Building, Ringsend Road
Dublin 4, Ireland

This paperback edition 2022

1

First published in Great Britain in ebook format
by HarperCollins*Publishers* 2022

A catalogue record of this book
is available from the British Library

ISBN: 978-0-00-849815-3

Printed and bound in the UK using 100% Renewable Electricity
by CPI Group (UK) Ltd

To Emma and Emma, my Charlie's Angels. Xxx

Chapter One

Paris 1930

'I can almost reach them; I just need to be a little further through.'

'Are you sure we won't get into trouble?'

'Of course we'll get into trouble. That's why we're doing this in secret.'

Anyone familiar with the house hearing the conversation would immediately recognise the two voices as belonging to Colette Nadon and Fleur Bonnivard, residents of the property. They would be unable to see what was occurring, however, owing to the height of the wall at the back of the long garden. From the house itself this small, untended sliver of land at the furthest end of the garden was completely concealed by a thick curtain of rhododendrons.

For two young girls it was a perfect place to explore.

Fleur, who was skinnier, wriggled with her arms out in front of her and succeeded in slipping through the small opening where the bottom of the potting-shed wall had crumbled away. She gave a cry of exultation.

'I was right! The door isn't even locked.'

'Quick, let me through,' Colette demanded. Already sturdier and developing a bust, she could not risk wriggling through the same gap as her friend, and a fear of tight spaces made it impossible to even try.

'It's stiff,' Fleur grunted from the other side of the wall. There were a few loud thumps and then a creak and a door that was almost completely hidden by trailing ivy and nettles opened just wide enough for a body to squeeze through.

'I'll get my legs stung,' Colette said doubtfully.

'Not if you pull your socks up and do it quickly. You really want to see what is here.'

Colette bit the inside of her cheek. Always more cautious by nature, she was Fleur's faithful follower, something which struck neither girl as odd, but over which adults often commented on darkly.

'Count for me,' she entreated, bending down and tugging her socks as high up her shins as they would go. 'I'll do it when you say.'

'Okay.'

'Wait! From five or ten?' Colette asked.

'It really doesn't matter,' Fleur pointed out. 'You still have to jump when I get to zero.'

'I know but it gives me more time to think about it,' Colette answered.

'No, it gives you more time to worry. I'll count from five.'

Fleur counted down and Colette jumped on command, slightly surprising herself. She leapt over the nettles and through the door to land in Fleur's arms. The girls stumbled back giggling.

'Well done.' Fleur hugged Colette then waved an arm around. 'Look at what we've found.'

Colette gazed around. They were standing in a long, narrow space. The Nadons' apartment – one of four tall slivers in the same building – was on a corner and this spot backed onto the side wall of the building on the intersecting boulevard.

'I think it was once a hothouse. There are parts of a roof with glass panes,' Fleur said, pointing them out.

Colette nodded then spotted something Fleur hadn't.

'Strawberries,' she breathed. 'There must be hundreds of them.'

In the furthest corner sunlight streamed down against the wall that marked the end of the property and there were the remains of a planter, now overgrown with plants that spilled across a large area.

Fleur plucked a couple. 'They must have been growing wild for years. I wonder if anyone knows they are here?'

'No one knows any of this is here,' Colette said. '*Mère* and *Papa* don't even know there is anything behind the rhododendron garden.'

They picked handfuls of strawberries and sat on the ground to feast. The long summer had ripened the fruit to perfection and the girls devoured them enthusiastically. The ground was a mixture of pebbles, gravel, weeds and the strawberry plants, which ran wild and tangled among twisted bean plants. After they had finished eating, they lay back and looked at the cloudless sky.

'This is like in the book Edith read to us last year – *The Secret Garden*,' Fleur said. 'Do you remember it?'

Colette wrinkled her nose. She was not very good at English and consequently never very interested in what her English governess read. She had a vague recollection of the book and was fairly sure the garden in that was larger and more impressive than a scrub of land that had been ignored for years.

'Only a little.'

'Well, this can be our secret garden,' Fleur said decisively. 'Just for the two of us. We can come here whenever we want, and nobody will ever find us. Look, there's even somewhere to keep things. We could keep books, paper to draw or write on, *bonbons*…'

She crawled on her hands and knees to a cold frame that was still mainly intact and opened it. Half a dozen spiders scuttled out in protest at being disturbed and Fleur hastily closed the lid with the tips of her fingers and wiped her hands down her skirt.

'Maybe not *bonbons*.'

Colette giggled at her dislike. Insects had never bothered her. She caught a spider and watched it dangle on its thread from her fingertips. 'In a tin they would be fine, and I don't think spiders would eat them.'

Fleur lay down with her head close to Colette's and her feet pointing in the opposite direction, like two hands of the clock pointing to twelve and six. They linked hands, giggling.

'This is our own world. Just you and I. Sisters together,' Colette said dreamily. She frowned. 'I wish we truly were sisters. Wouldn't that be perfect? Then we could play together as much as we liked.'

'I know,' Fleur said.

Colette sat up. 'You don't have a papa. Perhaps you could say that my papa is also your papa.'

Fleur rolled onto her belly, picturing Monsieur Nadon. A tired-looking man in a suit who came home late in the evening from his factory, he was always kind to her, more so than Colette's mother, who was only concerned with her friends and Colette.

'I did have a papa but he died of the *grippe espagnole* before I was even born. *Tante* Agnes told me he was very brave. He was her brother.'

Colette thought for a minute. 'Then we will have to declare ourselves sisters. Perhaps your papa would've been as rich as my

4

father and you might have lived in the apartment next door, with the same entrance archway.'

Fleur said nothing. At eleven years old she hadn't met many people as wealthy as Colette's father. Certainly not any with a grand house and a housekeeper; Fleur's *Tante* Agnes.

A shrill voice punctuated her contemplation.

'Colette, where are you?'

The girls rolled their eyes at each other. It was Edith.

'What does she want? I have done all my lessons today,' Colette said with a frown.

'I don't know. You'd better go and find out,' Fleur answered.

Colette lay back down and popped another strawberry into her mouth. 'I'll just stay here until she goes away.'

'She won't go away, and if you don't go then she might come through the rhododendrons and see the doorway. Then our secret will be discovered as soon as we have found it. You can't avoid going.'

Colette rolled over reluctantly. 'You're right.'

'Colette, answer me at once!' Edith's voice came again.

The girls squeezed through the door. Together they pushed it shut before pulling some of the ivy back down across it. From a distance it was as if it had never been touched. They crawled through the rhododendron bushes onto the neatly mown grass where a fountain stood in a raised pool, then sat side by side behind it, facing away from the house. When Edith called for the third time both girls raised their hands.

'Here we are!' they called in unison.

Edith marched across the lawn towards them; immaculate as always in a pretty, green cotton dress, but with pink cheeks, a fierce expression and the manner of a Général d'armée.

'Where have you been, girls? I have been calling for you,' she said in flawless French. She folded her arms and glared at them. The girls weren't exactly sure of her background, but she had apparently attended one of the best schools in England, which was renowned for producing women who were indomitable. Educating Colette was a temporary step for her until her parents found her a husband she could mould to her satisfaction.

'We know.' Colette gave her a mischievous smile. 'I thought it would be fun for you to find us.'

'Fun for you, perhaps,' Edith said. 'Madame is waiting to see you.' Suddenly, she let out a shriek. 'What have you been doing?'

Both girls looked down at themselves then at each other in horror. They had strawberry juice stains all over the front of their dresses. Fleur's plain blue cotton had fared better, but Colette's peach muslin with embroidered rosebuds was ruined with red smears that would never wash out.

'We were eating strawberries,' Colette explained.

'And where did you find those?' Edith demanded. The girls looked at each other, at a loss to explain.

Fleur was the first to reach for an answer. 'There is a bowl in the kitchen. I didn't think *Tante* Agnes would miss one or two of the small ones.'

Edith darted a hand forward and slapped her arm. 'It's wicked to steal. Now, Colette, go to your mother in her salon. Fleur, go and find your aunt in the kitchen; she will have work for you.'

Edith spun around and strode back up the garden path.

'You didn't have to take the blame,' Colette said.

Fleur shrugged and rubbed her arm. It stung and she wanted to cry but she would endure another slap rather than admit that. 'I don't mind. It didn't hurt anyway. A little pain is worth it to keep a secret.'

The girls parted at the garden door, Colette to go upstairs to her mother's salon and Fleur to the room on the ground floor she shared with her aunt.

'Secret sisters,' they whispered, linking their fingers and thumbs.

~

Delphine Nadon was already tipsy when Colette entered the airy salon on the third floor of the house, though she would deny the fact to her last breath. Fortunately for Colette, this meant that she was surrounded by a fragrance of fumes and perfume and in a good humour. She pouted and gave Colette a look of disappointment.

'That dress was one of my favourites. I assume you have been in company with Fleur Bonnivard. I would never have allowed you to play with that girl if I had known what it would lead to. In fact, I should never have agreed to her coming to live with her aunt. If Agnes was not such an excellent cook, I'm not sure I would have.'

Remembering the way Fleur had taken the blame, Colette flushed. 'It was my fault as much as Fleur's. She didn't lead me anywhere. Don't stop us playing together. She's my best friend. My only real friend,' she added under her breath.

Delphine shifted on her chaise longue and took another sip of the bright pink cocktail she was working her way through. She drummed a glossy red nail against the side of the glass and gave her daughter a long look.

'We do need to solve that problem don't we, *ma chérie*. You do need friends. Proper friends in the right circles. Your papa makes excellent money now, so we should be mixing with the best families Paris has to offer.'

'What about Rachel and Simone Halevy from the other side of the boulevard?'

'Perhaps not the Halevy girls.' Delphine's smile tightened, as did the skin around her eyes. 'Perhaps we should send you away to school. I loved my school. I made a perfect start in life.'

Colette couldn't deny this. Delphine had left behind the provincial Breton town where she had grown up and married an

7

ambitious businessman almost twenty years her senior just before the Great War. Louis Nadon's modest tile-making workshop had prospered, and he now owned an entire factory on the edge of the sixteenth arrondissement, manufacturing beautiful tiles for bathrooms and kitchens.

'What did you want me for, *Mère*?' she asked. Always *Mère*, never *Maman*. She envied the ease with which Fleur and her *Tante* Agnes got on with each other.

Delphine beckoned her across. 'I thought we could look at some magazines together. I have a new delivery from New York that we can compare to *Le Miroir des Modes*. We can pick you a hairstyle and choose some new outfits for the autumn. Would you like that, *chérie*?'

Colette drew up a chair eagerly. For all that she loved playing with Fleur and exploring the garden, there was something about the photographs of sleek women in beautiful dresses that she couldn't resist. One day she would be one of them, and when she was, she would not waste her days lying in a quiet room drinking cocktails. She would explore all that Paris had to offer.

~

The conversation in *Tante* Agnes and Fleur's bedroom was much less amicable.

'Every time you lead Colette into trouble you jeopardise our situation,' *Tante* Agnes raged, whipping at Fleur's legs with her apron. 'How many women in Madame Nadon's position would allow her employee to raise an orphan child in the household rather than terminate their employment? It is only because we grew close when we were younger that she allows it. Do you know how fortunate we are? You could ruin that for us.'

Fleur looked around, not for the first time thinking that the long, thin room with a bed at each end and only a curtain to give a little privacy was not very fortunate. The concierge's *loge* in the entrance archway to the four apartments that comprised the building had more space. Fleur sat on the bed with her head bowed.

'I'm sorry, *Tante* Agnes, but Colette and I like each other. We are friends.'

Agnes Bonnivard sat on the bed beside her niece. 'You cannot be friends. At least, perhaps you can for now, and only in the house. When you grow up you will move in completely different circles. Colette will marry somebody rich, and you will have to earn your living.'

Fleur raised her head. 'But you were friends with Madame Nadon. You just said so.'

Tante Agnes sucked her teeth. 'That was during wartime. Things were different. Usually a woman like her would not grow close to a woman she employed. Thankfully, we do not have to suffer that anymore. France is at peace. Europe is at peace.'

She stroked Fleur's hair and Fleur leaned in towards the comfort. She had only vague memories of being cherished by her mother, who had died when Fleur was three, and Agnes was not the most affectionate of women but her love at times like this felt as solid as a blanket.

'You will not have to work as nurse or become a housekeeper like I did. You are a clever girl, little one. You could become a secretary.'

'I would like to work in a bookshop,' Fleur said shyly. She hadn't ever admitted this to anyone besides Colette but this moment of peace and affection between her and her aunt emboldened her.

'I didn't realise. Your father wanted to be a writer,' *Tante* Agnes said with a smile. 'I think if my brother is looking down from Heaven, he would like that for you too.'

Fleur smiled back. According to *Tante* Agnes, people in Heaven were so busy singing praises to God and Mary and Jesus all day and night that she doubted her father would have the time spare to notice what Fleur was doing. It sounded like very hard work being there.

'Or perhaps I could work in a library. Maybe I could even attend the university one day.'

Tante Agnes frowned. 'I don't think we will have the money for that. But if you turn your mind to behaving well and charm Madame and Monsieur Nadon, who knows. They may be kind enough to let you join in Colette's lessons a little longer.'

Fleur frowned. 'I hate that everything I do must depend on whether Madame will be charitable. I'm much better at my lessons than Colette is.'

'I know, *mon trésor*. But that is how the world is. Now, will you come and help me fold the laundry?'

As Fleur followed her aunt outside she kept the thought to herself that the world wasn't fair. Something needed to change, and hopefully within her lifetime it would.

~

Colette and Fleur did not manage to speak again until the evening. One of Fleur's chores was to close all the windows and water the vases of flowers when the air had cooled. As she passed by Colette's bedroom the door opened and Colette gave a low whistle. Fleur glanced around and seeing that the corridor was empty she slipped inside.

'I have something for you. To say sorry for you getting into trouble.' Colette opened her hand to reveal a scallop shell. On the smooth underside she had painted two letter 'S' side by side.

'For *Sœurs Secrètes*. Secret Sisters. This can be our special sign.'

Fleur grinned. 'I like it. SS. That will never mean anything to anyone but us. We should paint it on the wall and door in the

Secret Garden. After our lessons tomorrow why don't you try to take some paint from the box?'

Colette's face dropped. The thought of lessons reminded her of the conversation with her mother. '*Mère* talked about sending me to a school somewhere. I told her I don't want to go. I think she was persuaded not to, at least for a few more years.'

This did not elicit the response she expected.

'You're lucky. I'd love to go in your place,' Fleur answered.

Colette hugged her. 'You are so strange like that, but I don't care. You're my friend and nothing is ever going to change that.'

Chapter Two

Despite their best efforts, Colette and Fleur's paths diverged. When Edith returned to England, they were enrolled in different schools and Delphine made good on her promise of introducing Colette into society. No amount of pleading on Colette's part secured an invitation for Fleur when young ladies in a festival of coloured skirts and blouses, and handsome boys in well-cut suits, called to spend time in Madame Nadon's salon.

Each time there was a party, Colette devotedly saved Fleur some of the patisseries and fresh orange juice and they shared them in the garden or Colette's bedroom. Colette reported everything that happened at the parties, until Fleur burst into tears one evening and asked her to stop.

'What's wrong?' Colette put down the macaron she was eating and stared at Fleur in distress.

Fleur swallowed a sniff. She looked down at her plain, green serge dress, then stroked the edge of Colette's fringed chiffon skirt.

'I love you for saving me the cakes, but I don't want to hear any more. I haven't seen the films you have, and I don't know the dances. I'm not part of that world and I'll never be part of it.'

'Oh.' Colette flushed with embarrassment. Of course it must hurt Fleur to hear about everything she was excluded from. 'I thought you wanted to know what I was doing. I'll stop being so thoughtless. I'm sorry.'

Fleur hugged her. 'Don't be sorry. I love you for trying to include me. Whatever happens, I'll always appreciate how you tried. We'll meet in the Secret Garden when we can.'

Colette obeyed Fleur's wishes until a warm May evening in 1938 when a party was being held on the terrace at the back of the house.

This was hard for Fleur to stomach. Delphine's afternoon gatherings in the salon were private, and Fleur could ignore them, but the whole garden was in use, and she couldn't pretend nothing was happening. Through the open window, Fleur could hear voices raised in laughter and conversation over the gramophone music. The sweet scent of jasmine blossoms filled the air, and she would have liked to go and sit on the patio with a book, but that was out of the question tonight.

She passed by Colette's door with a pile of freshly ironed shirts and was surprised when it opened and Colette stepped out.

'Come and dance,' she entreated, catching Fleur by the waist.

'I'm a little busy.' Fleur held the shirts out as evidence, but Colette took them from her and put them on a stool outside her father's bedroom.

'Don't you want to come and see what is happening?'

'I have a new book,' Fleur answered. Luckily this was true and she picked it off the sideboard where she had put it.

Colette screwed up her lips and looked sad. 'This should have been my party but *Mère* and *Papa* have invited so many people I don't know half of them. I want a friend to talk to. I think they hope I will find a rich husband with connections in society. Perhaps you can find one too.'

'I don't want one,' Fleur said.

It wasn't quite true. Whenever the hero and heroine in a film kissed, she experienced a pang of envy as well as a quivering sensation inside herself, but she couldn't imagine meeting anyone who would interest her among the second or third tier of Paris society that Delphine and Louis moved in. If they were not as high in society as they hoped to be, Fleur was far lower.

'Then just dance and flirt for an hour. It's great fun. *Papa* has put lights all down the garden path as far as the fountain, but it won't be too bright there.'

'It will still be bright enough to show that my skirt is two years old and I am wearing the same blouse I wore last year,' Fleur pointed out.

Colette looked her up and down then tutted. 'Come with me.'

She took Fleur's hand and pulled her into the bedroom. It was a tastefully decorated room with cream walls and Egyptian motif leaves picked out in turquoise. The carpet matched but was rarely seen thanks to Colette's habit of turning everything out until she located what she had lost. She gestured around at the clothing and accessories, which lay on every surface.

'You can borrow anything of mine. Not dresses though, they would hang off you like sacks – you're so lucky to be slender and not to have filled out at all since you were fifteen – but necklaces or shawls … anything else will be fine.'

Fleur looked down at herself and then at Colette. She knew the offer was kindly meant and the insult was unintentional. Colette was wearing a pale pink silk dress with a halter-neckline. It was tight to emphasise the curve of her waist below full breasts. It would indeed sag around Fleur's barely existent bust, and probably trail on the floor for good measure.

'I don't know any of the people here,' Fleur said, trying one last refusal.

'You never will if you don't talk to them. Now, you're coming with me for at least half an hour,' Colette said firmly. She picked a silk square from a box and unfurled it. 'You can wear this. It's a scarf for women! Isn't that strange? But Hermès have just produced it so it must be fashionable.'

She wound it around Fleur's neck. The light fabric was cool and felt wonderfully elegant. It was nicer than anything Fleur owned. The bright printed pattern of red and blue omnibuses made even the old cream blouse she wore seem fresh and interesting.

'You are so good at choosing clothes,' Fleur murmured.

'Then you have to show it off,' Colette said, her eyes dancing. 'In fact, consider it a gift from me.'

'I couldn't. It must have been expensive,' Fleur said doubtfully.

Colette tossed her head. 'Oh, that doesn't matter. I'd like you to have it.'

How nice it must be to have enough money to disregard the cost of something so easily, Fleur mused. Colette's expression was so hopeful Fleur was persuaded she meant it.

'In that case, thank you. I love it.'

Colette adjusted the folds around Fleur's throat, her face alight with pleasure, and Fleur followed Colette to the terrace, her book still in her hand. They walked side by side through the guests, Colette murmuring titbits of gossip into Fleur's ear that made her giggle. Colette pulled her towards a black-haired young man standing on the edge of the terrace watching the couples dancing.

'This is Serge. Have fun.'

She gave Fleur a discreet wink and walked away. Fleur's stomach plummeted. She had been set up.

Serge plucked the book from Fleur's fingers and tossed it

casually onto a table littered with champagne coupes and half-full bottles.

'I don't want you to read to me,' he purred. He poured two glasses of champagne and encouraged Fleur to drink. The fizziness made her nose itch and sent shivers down her spine, but it was delicious. As soon as her glass was empty, he took it away and whisked her into the steps of a foxtrot, holding her close to his body and singing along with the words to the song. His breath smelled unpleasantly of cigarettes and she held her head rigidly away. He didn't seem to notice and continued to move her around. They passed Colette, who was dancing with a tall, handsome man with extremely blonde hair and startling blue eyes. He was at least ten years older than the girls. His hands were on Colette's lower back and hers were about his neck. From the expression in Colette's eyes, she was enjoying every minute. At least Serge kept his hands in a more appropriate place.

'This is Gunther. He's from Trier but wants to be an actor. Isn't he wonderful?' Colette whispered as they drew close.

Fleur smiled politely, though a flicker of worry made her belly twitch. The Rhineland was something she'd seen mentioned in the newspapers. The German chancellor had marched his troops into the territory two months earlier, causing much consternation, but fortunately it had not led to war. She wondered if Gunther had left Trier before or after that had happened and what he thought of it.

As soon as the music ended Gunther whispered something in Colette's ear and she grinned, her eyes widening. She giggled, then the couple sauntered, hand in hand, down the garden path and into the shadows beyond the fountain. Fleur narrowed her eyes as a stab of possessiveness took her by surprise. It seemed Gunther was about to be introduced to the Secret Garden.

Fleur danced a second dance with a man who told her he was often mistaken for Gilbert Gil the actor. When she burst out laughing, he pouted and expressed surprise that the daughter of the Nadons' employee had been invited to the party. He then dropped her hand and adjusted his sleeves, flashing pearl cufflinks, before walking away. Colette and Gunther were nowhere in sight so Fleur retreated to her bedroom and her books.

∼

She didn't see Colette again until the following lunchtime.

'You were rude to Maurice,' Colette said with a frown, bursting into the kitchen where Fleur was sitting at the table struggling with Maths exercises. 'He was very upset that you didn't agree with him about his looks. He has worked very hard to get his hair to look like Gil's.'

'Well he doesn't look like him,' Fleur retorted.

Colette rolled her eyes. 'Of course he doesn't, but men don't like it when you point things like that out. Gunther still thinks that Frau Riefenstahl will cast him in a movie. I'm not going to point out that she won't because then he'd get into a mood.'

Fleur crossed her arms. 'You do that if it makes you happy, but I don't want to spend my time telling men how wonderful they are. Thank you for inviting me though, I enjoyed the champagne.'

It was the last invitation she received.

∼

Two weeks before Fleur's nineteenth birthday, *Tante* Agnes shook her awake.

'Mademoiselle Colette wants to see you in her room. Go quickly please.'

Fleur rubbed the sleep from her eyes and sat up. Agnes had already disappeared.

She made her way to Colette's bedroom to find Colette

standing by the window looking out over the boulevard. As usual, the room was littered with clothes and magazines.

'*Tante* Agnes said you wanted me,' Fleur said hesitantly.

Colette spun around. 'Yes. I wanted to tell you my news. I'm going to England and staying with Edith. Isn't it exciting!'

'How wonderful for you,' Fleur said. She bit her lip uncertainly.

Colette's eyes were very bright but she did not look as if it was wonderful. 'I wish now I had paid more attention in my lessons. I will hardly be able to talk with anyone.'

'Would you like me to help you pack?' Fleur offered, glancing around the room. Colette shook her head. Her face twisted into an ugly frown.

'*Mère* is sending her maid to pack for me. I won't be taking much. Winter clothes, of course, but I'm sure I will get new clothes for the spring season in London. How different do you think the fashions will be?'

She picked up a glass of water from her dressing table then sat on the chair and drank it in large gulps.

'This is very sudden,' Fleur said. 'When did you decide to go?'

'The decision was made for me,' Colette said. She gave a bright laugh. 'Aren't I lucky? *Mère* and *Papa* told me last night.'

She lit a cigarette, tugging on it defiantly. Smoking was her new affectation; a form of rebellion against her father, who said it was not an appropriate activity for women.

'Does Gunther know you are going?' Fleur asked.

Since the party three months previously Colette had met him regularly to walk around the animal enclosures in the *Jardin D'Acclimatation* and ride on the carousel. Fleur had half wondered whether this morning's summons was to announce an engagement.

To her astonishment, Colette's face grew thunderous, twisting into an ugly mask and Fleur thought for a moment her friend was about to scream.

'Oh, yes, Gunther knows. Gunther is relieved I am going. You see, Gunther…' She took a long, smooth drag of her cigarette then retched and made a face. She tossed the cigarette into the ashtray, her red lacquered fingers grinding the stub into oblivion.

'I don't want to talk about Gunther. He is returning to Trier. I think we will not see him here again, and for God's sake do not mention his name to my mother.'

Fleur began to understand. The love affair must have ended badly and to save Colette's heartbreak her parents were treating her to the extravagant trip. She squeezed Colette's shoulder.

'Of course not. I won't say anything at all. How long will you be gone for?'

'I don't know.' Colette stretched out her legs and put her hands in her lap. 'Seven months at least, if not longer. I'll be leaving this afternoon. I wanted to say goodbye.'

'So soon?' Fleur dropped onto the chair by the door. The girls didn't spend as much time together as they used to, but this was a shock.

'Yes. Aren't I lucky?' Colette began to laugh again.

'Don't you want to go?' Fleur asked. 'I would love the opportunity to travel.'

'Why would I want to go elsewhere when Paris is full of life?' Colette closed her eyes and sprawled back in her chair. Her face looked puffy, as if she had been crying. 'I will go and I will make the best of it. I'm sure I will have a perfectly wonderful time.'

'I shall miss you,' Fleur said.

Colette suddenly pushed herself from her chair and flew across the room with her arms out to embrace Fleur. 'Thank you. I need to know that I won't be completely forgotten.'

Fleur noticed with dry amusement that Colette did not say she would miss Fleur, but then she looked into Colette's eyes and saw they were gleaming bright with emotion, and she could no longer be angry or resentful. She eased into Colette's embrace.

'Plant some more strawberries for me, darling,' Colette whispered in her ear. 'In the Secret Garden. I'll be back by summer when they will be ripe. We'll eat them together.'

'Of course.' Fleur gave a small laugh. 'Goodness me, Colette, you should be in the films being this dramatic.'

'Yes I should,' Colette said. 'Or perhaps on stage. A showgirl doing high kicks and blowing kisses to the audience. I wonder if my parents would be proud of me then?'

'I'm sure they are proud of you whatever you do,' Fleur murmured.

It sounded hollow. She knew Delphine especially hoped for a marriage that would help Louis' business expand or secure them entry into the cream of Paris society, preferably both. Gunther, the hopeful actor from a part of the continent that was now under German authority, was obviously not the son-in-law they had hoped for.

'I will write to you and tell you everything that happens while you're away. Your mother will give me your address, I'm sure.'

～

That afternoon, as Colette climbed into the back seat of Louis' Traction Avant she waved to Fleur. 'Remember to plant the strawberries and I'll be back by the time they are ripe.'

～

Fleur dutifully planted the strawberries but Colette did not return. Nor did she respond to either of the letters Fleur wrote in the first three months of her absence. Delphine was reluctant to give Fleur the address but agreed that if Fleur kept her letter to one sheet of paper, she might slip it in with the letters she herself wrote to Colette.

'It's funny. I did not want you and my daughter to become close friends. I thought you might lead her into trouble,' Delphine said. She looked Fleur up and down and Fleur knew she was comparing the two girls. 'How wrong I was. Yes, I will post your letter, but don't expect Colette to reply. She will have enough to keep her busy.'

Sure enough, a reply never came. Fleur wrote three more times but after that, she stopped. She tried not to resent the lack of communication too greatly, but it stung. After all, Colette was a reluctant writer at the best of times and was undoubtedly enjoying sights Fleur could only dream of. She had books to keep her company and was happy to retreat into the attic room, which Monsieur Nadon had kindly given her as a bedroom. The privacy was wonderful. No more sharing with *Tante* Agnes and listening to her aunt's snores.

Even better, she found work four days a week in a small bookshop in the winding back streets of Montparnasse. It was a convoluted journey to get there, but she didn't care. She caught the Metro at Porte Maillot to Bienvenüe. From there she would leave the wide, tree-lined boulevards and wind through the narrow streets until she reached the modest shop with its wood panelled front. The painted sign named the shop as Ramper et Frère Librarie. There was no sign of the *frère* from the sign and Fleur did not like to ask the remaining Monsieur Ramper what had happened to the absent brother.

Most of the shop contained conventional volumes but Monsieur Ramper had an unashamed passion for *bandes dessinées*, detective novels and science-fiction. Two shelves and one window display were given over to the illustrated exploits of *Tif et Tondu*, *Tintin* and the American *Flash Gordon*.

Monsieur Ramper was an amusing employer, given to long

monologues of a scurrilous nature, though on occasion he would lose his train of thought and grow grave.

'I saw the Great War as a young man, *ma puce*, and I can taste it coming back.'

He smacked his lips as if tasting wine. Fleur eyed him anxiously, waiting for him to laugh and dismiss his words as a joke but he didn't. He shook his head, ran his hand through his chestnut hair, and pushed it back from his temple.

'The Anschluss in spring was the start, Fleur. It is not good. Austria apparently welcomed the Führer, but how true was that?'

He said no more about it, but his words planted a seed of apprehension in Fleur that lay dormant, waiting for the right opportunity to sprout. She did her best to ignore it.

With a thoughtful expression, Monsieur Ramper handed her an envelope of pay at the end of the third month she had worked there. He then poured her a cup of coffee – he insisted the only way to drink it was black and bitter – and patted her shoulder.

'How often do you explore this neighbourhood? You are surrounded by artists, poets and writers. If you wish to be one of them you should go meet others.'

Fleur sipped her coffee before answering, trying not to let her distaste for it show but wishing she had a jug of hot milk to hand. 'My aunt might not approve if I did. I had to argue long and hard to be allowed to work here at all.'

'Then tomorrow tell your aunt that I need to keep you late to inventory the stock. Take an hour and walk around before returning home. See what you find.'

～

The following day, Fleur dressed in her best skirt and pressed her blouse carefully. She folded the Hermès scarf in her bag and once Monsieur Ramper closed the shop she carefully arranged it around her neck, combed her hair and walked from the bookshop to the Metro station a longer way round to normal. The route took her down the Rue Daguerre and through a square filled with horse-chestnut trees, which shaded cafés where groups of both sexes wrapped in heavy coats sat outside around tables. As she crossed a corner her ears were attacked by the most discordant sound she had ever heard.

It was a screeching saxophone, what might have been a clarinet, and definitely drums. There seem to be little rhythm and she wasn't even sure if there was a melody. Still, it pulled to something inside her and she followed the sound to a café. The noise – Fleur could not in all honesty call it music – was coming from inside. The café was single fronted with a door to the right of the window with a ruby-red painted frame and a matching red awning extended over the front. The glass was slightly tinted but Fleur could see figures moving inside.

She read the name.

Café Morlaix.

This was exactly the sort of adventure she should report to Monsieur Ramper so she cautiously opened the door and stepped inside.

Chapter Three

S he was greeted by a fog of sweet cigarette smoke and a spicy, exotic fragrance that made her eyes water but her heart race. There was something old and shabby about the Café Morlaix. The clientele was mainly young and male, with a handful of women seated at circular tables close to the corner where the source of the cacophony was coming from. Three young men were playing; a saxophonist with dark brown skin and tightly curled black hair, a clarinettist (was that the word, Fleur wondered) with pale skin and light ginger hair that stuck up in spikes, and a drummer who looked more like a bank clerk with neatly combed black hair and a Mediterranean complexion. Fleur wondered whether they had deliberately chosen each other for their contrasting appearances as they barely seemed to be playing the same tune.

'Mademoiselle?' A waiter dressed in black with a ruby-coloured apron around his waist approached her. He stared at her through a pair of very thick, round glasses. His light brown hair made Fleur think of an owl.

'A table for one, or are you meeting somebody?'

'For one, please,' she replied. 'But not too near the band.'

The waiter grinned. 'Of course. This way, please.'

He escorted Fleur to a small table with two chairs set against the back wall and handed her a menu. He returned a few moments later with a carafe of water and Fleur ordered a *café crème*, thinking how disapproving Monsieur Ramper would be. One or two of the other patrons looked at Fleur and she smiled back self-consciously. She took a book out of her bag and began reading it, referring occasionally to her English dictionary.

'What are you reading?' the waiter asked when he brought the coffee. She showed him the front cover.

'Jane Eyerer?'

'Eyre,' she corrected. 'It's an English book.'

The waiter pulled up a chair and sat without asking. 'You speak English?'

'A little,' she admitted with pride. 'Not enough to read this without a dictionary.'

'You're a student?'

Fleur took a sip of coffee to delay answering and give herself a chance to observe him. He had a searching face and was probably not much older than she was, though his glasses and a line between his eyebrows – which Fleur was later to discover was the result of a childhood spent squinting at the world without glasses – made him appear older.

'No, but I enjoy reading and I'm trying to teach myself. I work in the bookshop a few streets away.'

This obviously met with his approval because the waiter held out his hand. 'I am Sébastien.'

Fleur shook it and told him her name.

'I am very pleased to meet you, Fleur. I *am* a student,' he said proudly. 'Of art and literature.'

'And a waiter?' Fleur asked.

Sébastien's jaw tightened. 'I need to eat. The café is owned by my second cousin, Bernard, and he gives me as many shifts as I can manage. I don't have rich parents like some of them.'

He waved a hand around the room. Fleur looked around. Thanks to living with Delphine, she could tell many of the patrons were wearing quality garments.

'Forgive me for saying so, but this doesn't seem like the sort of place where wealthy Parisians would gather.'

His eyes grew hard, and she thought she'd offended him but the corner of his mouth jerked into a quick smile. 'Very perceptive. Some of them like to pretend they are not rich. Some have rejected families but kept the trappings before they slammed out of the house.' He leaned in close to Fleur and spoke in a low, drawling voice that made the skin on the back of her neck shiver. 'See Sabrina over there with the black hair? She had a fight with her father and walked out of an apartment just off the Champs-Élysées but went back the next day to pack three suitcases of shoes, hats and bags.'

'Naturally. How could anyone survive otherwise?' Fleur laughed. 'I should bring my friend Colette here. She would find it remarkable.'

She grew sober at the mention of Colette's name. She had never replied to Fleur's letters so she couldn't really describe Colette as a friend any longer and on consideration, she liked the idea of having something of her own.

Sébastien frowned. 'If she would view us as a circus or zoo exhibit, don't bother. I'm afraid I had better get on with work now.' Sébastien picked up her empty cup and gave the table a quick wipe. 'I hope we will meet again, Fleur.'

She looked at his smile and her stomach did a slow flip. 'So do I.'

'If you come on a Wednesday evening, a few of us gather to discuss … the world. You'd be welcome to join us.' He'd paused before completing the sentence, leaving Fleur to wonder what aspects of the world they discussed. Somehow, she could not imagine this young man or his friends listening to this discordant noise while they sat and nodded in agreement at government policies. Her scalp prickled with excitement.

'Yes, I would like that, thank you.'

Fleur walked back to the Metro station pleased that she finally had something she could tell Monsieur Ramper about. His advice had been good and she was glad to have taken it.

~

It was three weeks before Fleur was able to find the time to visit the café again. She dressed in her blue-striped skirt that matched last year's grey cardigan, conscious that her clothes were nothing like some of the elegant but slightly bohemian ensembles she had seen in the café. To think she had been invited to join them made her insides wriggle with trepidation but Sébastien had clearly seen something inside her worth inviting. She added a peach silk scarf that had been a present from Delphine and Louis on her nineteenth birthday, and a touch more mascara than she usually wore, and felt almost bohemian herself as she walked through the door.

Again, there was the sound of jazz, but tonight it was only a recording that sounded even more scratchy and discarded. The café was almost empty apart from a group sitting close to the bar with three of the round tables pushed together. Sébastien was sitting at one, alongside the red-headed man who had played the clarinet. Fleur waved timidly from the door and Sébastien rose to greet her with rapid kisses on both cheeks.

'I didn't think you were ever going to come,' he said, with obvious pleasure at having been proven wrong.

'Neither did I,' she admitted, sitting on the chair he pulled up to the table. 'My aunt is a housekeeper for a family, and we live on the premises. As well as working in the bookshop, I help her as there is often lots to do in the evening.'

'So you have to work twice as hard to be able to live there,' said the clarinet player. He spoke with a clipped accent Fleur could not place. 'I suppose they grew rich off the back of honest workers?'

'Are you communists?' Fleur's voice came out as a squeak, and she clamped her lips shut. Someone pushed a glass of red wine into her hand, and she grasped it tightly.

'If you are asking, are we dangerous men who will forcibly take property, then no,' Sébastien assured her.

'But a few have everything and others have nothing. Does your aunt's employer work harder than your aunt to merit his wealth?' asked another man.

'I don't know, but he does work hard.'

'Harder than his employees?' Sébastien asked gently.

Fleur took a small sip of wine and considered the question. 'He spends a lot of his time at his factory. His wife complains of it.'

But she could not deny that in the evening, when Monsieur Nadon sat with a cognac, reading the newspapers in the late sunshine, *Tante* Agnes was still ironing his shirts despite her arthritis that was becoming a curse. Fleur looked up and caught a glance between Sébastien and one of the others.

'You're thinking, I see,' Sébastien said. 'We are socialists, not communists. We want people to think and then perhaps change a little. Though I am not too sure about Brendan, but he is an American so we will excuse him.'

The red-haired man laughed and raised the middle finger of his left hand at Sébastien. American. That explained his accent at least.

Sébastien refilled Fleur's glass.

'*Santé!*'

The others echoed his toast, Fleur included, and they all drank.

It was a strange introduction into a world Fleur had never imagined. Sébastien's friends were either students or had recently been. They aspired not to own factories or businesses, much less labour in them, but to create art or music or write. Fleur met with approval because a bookshop was the source of knowledge and she was supporting herself.

Sébastien was from a village in Brittany. Brendan's grandparents had emigrated from Ireland to New York decades earlier. He had been travelling to Enniskillen, but had stopped in Paris for a weekend on the way from Chicago two years previously, fallen in love with the city (and a dancer named Celeste), and never left. He shared an apartment with Ike, the saxophonist, whose father had been an American soldier. Then there was Daniel, who was studying to be a doctor as his father wished, but preferred painting, and Pierre, a poet. Odile had dismayed her parents by moving in with an artist who painted her naked in hues of green and purple.

'I think my parents might have been less offended had the nudes been at least flesh-coloured,' she drawled, which made everyone hoot with laughter.

~

'It's wonderful,' Fleur told *Tante* Agnes when she arrived home that evening, her aunt listening to everything Fleur said with a disapproving expression. 'They are men and women from all over Europe and further away who have seen what possibilities the world can hold. If I can't travel, this is the next best thing.'

'God-fearing men and women would not behave in such a way,' Agnes said crisply. 'I thought your friendship with Mademoiselle Colette was unsuitable, but now I wish she was still here to guide you.'

Fleur bit her lip, a little of her joy melting under Agnes' fierce disapproval. Listening to Sébastien describing the work of daring artists, or Ike declaring equality for black men must come before long, she felt swept up in their enthusiasm and passion. She didn't care if Colette, with her love of pretty clothes and vapid men, never returned. She had new friends now. The world was too exciting. Too perfect.

~

That changed in the spring of 1939 when Fleur arrived at the café one evening to discover serious faces and no music playing. Brendan announced he had decided to return to America following the annexation of Czechoslovakia two days earlier. 'I thought about going on to Ireland, but my mam wants me back home.'

'War is growing closer,' Sébastien muttered, pouring everyone a shot of brandy.

'When it comes, I will be ready to fight,' Daniel announced.

'We all will,' said Pierre. He was an attractive-looking man with black curls and dark eyes, whose quick tongue frightened Fleur a little.

From that point on, the talk of war was never far from the surface. Areas of the city that had once been parks had been dug up and were now trenches. The sight of flowerbeds and wide lawns where families used to sit now housing bomb shelters was chilling. Her hand slipped to the box at her side. Gas masks had been issued to all citizens, along with the instruction to carry them at all times, but no one believed they would really be needed.

'My mother and *tante* nursed during the *Grande Guerre*,' she said. 'So did Madame Nadon. I would do the same if it became necessary.'

'You can tend my wounds and give me bed baths,' Pierre said, blowing her a kiss, and they all laughed.

'What about you?' Fleur asked Sébastien.

He gave her a wry grin. 'I don't think they would want me. I have a weak chest and am as good as blind without these glasses.'

'We would have to be desperate if we were relying on Sébastien,' Pierre said. 'He is a philosopher and a thinker, not a man of action.'

'A lover not a fighter,' purred Yvette, a woman who occasionally joined them, to general laughter.

Fleur glanced sidelong at Sébastien. She wondered if Yvette spoke from personal experience and a throb of envy deep in her chest cavity caught her unawares. She wondered what it would be like to kiss him. Sébastien had fine lips and delicate features, with a straight, narrow nose that resulted in his thick glasses constantly slipping down. It was quite an appealing look.

'Now is the time to start a newspaper,' Pierre declared, tossing his drink back. 'We who are articulate and young need to be heard. We have ideas.'

'If you mean your poems, I don't think they will inspire an army,' Daniel said, hooting with laughter.

Pierre threw a balled-up serviette at him.

'You have no printing press,' Brendan pointed out.

Sébastien shrugged. A light had come into his eyes that made them gleam. 'Then we'll buy blocks and print by hand. A single sheet at a time if necessary. Start small. Fleur, you write, I know. Would you write for us?'

Fleur almost choked on her mouthful of brioche. She wrote stories and her thoughts about books she read, but she had never shared them with another person. She'd only confided in Sébastien because they had been laughing about childhood diaries and she had wanted to show him they had something in common.

'What could I write about?'

'Anything you feel people should know,' Pierre said. 'The conditions for workers, perhaps. How the preparations for war are affecting morale in the upper classes. I bet they are only concerned they won't be able to get fresh oysters flown in from the coast.'

'I think you're a little confused. I don't live with royalty,' Fleur retorted, which earned a wink from Sébastien that set her cheeks flaming with pride. She loved that he found her amusing.

'I'll have a think and if I come up with anything I'll tell you,' she promised Pierre. With no printing press or firm idea of how to go about starting a newspaper, she doubted it would come to pass.

Wind and rain lashed at the bright-striped canopies outside the cafés as they emptied. Fleur shivered as she left Café Morlaix and pulled her collar up, wishing she had brought an umbrella. She picked her way through the puddles, trying her best not to slip on the smooth paving slabs.

'Wait a moment, Fleur.'

She looked over her shoulder to see Pierre waving and stopped.

'All this talk of war gets the blood racing. We might be blown up before the month is finished,' he murmured. He grasped her by the hand and pulled her into a kiss.

Fleur was too dazed to resist and when it became clear she was not going to be released immediately, she closed her eyes and concentrated on the sensation. Pierre's lips were full and his chin and cheeks stubbly, grazing her skin like sandpaper. It was quite pleasant in some ways. Cautiously she put her hands on his shoulders, knowing that this was giving tacit approval and moved her lips in a vague attempt to match his. Pierre stopped kissing her then and raised his brows.

'Was that the first time anyone has done that to you?'

She nodded, slightly taken aback and unsure whether admitting it would lessen her in his eyes.

'Ah.' He reached out and dabbed a fingertip on the end of her nose. 'Sorry, *ma belle*, I didn't realise. Were you hoping to hold out for Sébastien?'

'No!' Fleur exclaimed. Her insides shrivelled with embarrassment. Was she so easy to read?

Pierre's face twisted into an amused grin. 'There is no need to look so shocked. No one would blame you if you were. In fact, half of us would turn green with envy. He is a complete dream after all.'

Fleur's eyes widened even further as the implication sunk in. Pierre's grin widened.

'Don't be so shocked, little innocent. Yes, people have done that for centuries. Why, half the men and women in these clubs are in and out of bed with each other, irrespective of body parts. Don't tell me you disapprove.'

'I…' Fleur bit her lip, still throbbing from the kiss.

'I'm only teasing you, Fleur. Sébastien only likes women, more's the pity. But be warned; if you do hope to get involved with him, be prepared for long evenings listening to him talk about art and how the world should change, and don't expect him to offer marriage.'

'Who says I am hoping to get involved with him?' Fleury retorted.

'You do.' Pierre smirked. 'Through your eyes and the way they go large like a calf's whenever he talks to you.'

A buzzing filled her ears. Of course she admired Sébastien. He was a very attractive man and he was inspiring. But Fleur would rather cut her tongue out then admit it to Pierre.

'You're talking nonsense. And, if that is the sort of metaphor you use in your poetry, it's no wonder you haven't yet been published.'

Pierre erupted into laughter. He leaned forward and kissed her on the cheek. 'You are too wonderful, and I would like to kiss you again, but the rain is stopping. I think I will chance going home. I can't persuade you to come home with me, I suppose?'

He didn't wait for her to answer but unfurled an umbrella and snapped it open. 'No, a first kiss is one thing but you don't want to lose your virginity to me, do you?'

'I don't want to lose it to anyone yet,' Fleur called after him.

His laughter sounded over the raindrops as he walked away.

Fleur stomped back to the Metro station, seething with annoyance. What was wrong with her liking Sébastien anyway? Of all the men she had encountered he appeared to be the hardest-working, and if he wasn't the best-looking then he was certainly one of the most intriguing. If only she could find out whether he liked her too.

~

Her opportunity came one Saturday afternoon when Fleur called in after leaving the bookshop. Instead of sitting with Pierre and the others, Sébastien was at a separate table in the corner, his nose buried in a book. Fleur walked over to him, trying to remember how Colette had behaved when she wanted to show a man she liked him.

'You work so hard,' she commented.

He rolled his shoulders back. 'I have to study hard if I want to be a success, and I have to work if I want to eat.'

'But you look so tired.' Hesitantly she put her hand on his arm. 'Can I help?'

'You could fetch me a *vin rouge*. Only a small one.'

She obliged and handed it to him. His fingers touched hers and she felt a jolt like the spark of electricity. The colour rose to her cheeks and she hastily whipped her hand away. Sébastien looked into her eyes and as he held her gaze Fleur held her breath, unable to do anything until she saw a sign. He smiled and touched her cheek.

'I forget how young you are sometimes, Fleur. One day, a man will fall in love with you and be completely lost in how fortunate he is. Now, if you excuse me, *chérie*, I really must read this chapter.'

It was the kindest dismissal and the gentlest refusal he could have given her, but Fleur's throat seized with humiliation. She turned away, feeling her legs growing wobbly. She heard Odile calling her name but only waved a hand and hurried on.

～

When Fleur returned home, she hoped to avoid speaking to anyone, but *Tante* Agnes was upstairs in Colette's room, and called her name as Fleur passed. The windows were wide open, letting in a blast of chilly wind. Agnes paused her task of attacking the carpet with a stiff brush.

'Mademoiselle Colette is coming home. Madame and Monsieur would like her back in France before she is unable to return so she'll likely be back very soon. Won't that be nice?'

Fleur smiled faintly. Colette home after so long would be nice, she supposed, though the circumstances necessitating her return filled Fleur with an even greater sense of foreboding.

Chapter Four

April 1939

'Colette, darling! Pay attention!' Delphine snapped. 'Madame Tourval was telling you about her trip to Alsace last month.'

Colette blinked and focused her attention on the elderly woman dressed in a sea of peach tulle.

'I am, *Mère*, I had a sudden headache. Please forgive me, Madame Tourval, I'd love to hear more about your trip. Are the Alsatians concerned about what the German Chancellor is proposing?'

Madame Tourval's eyes narrowed. Colette could tell that such a topic was both unexpected and unwelcome.

'I am sure I have no idea. My husband and I made a tour of the ancient churches and I also spent time at Baden-Baden and Niederbronn-les-Bains. I have nothing to do with politics, and the sight of the ugly concrete slabs along the Maginot Line are an abomination to the senses.'

Madame Tourval waved a hand dismissively and the rings

she wore on each finger glinted in the afternoon sunlight. Colette dipped her head deferentially, implying that she too had little care for the subject of politics. The thought of concrete bunkers guarding the borders to France was chilling. Hitler's determination to remilitarise Germany had been the talk of nearly every home she had visited in England, and as a Frenchwoman she had been asked the same questions repeatedly.

What will France do? How has the civil war in Spain affected relations between your country and theirs? Are the Jews in France worried about the restrictions in place in Germany?

Colette couldn't answer any of the questions. How could she, when she had barely any contact with her home country beyond the monthly letter from her parents? She probably knew less about the situation in Europe than anyone in the room.

'I visited some beautiful churches in England, as well as a number of health resorts,' she remarked.

'Nevertheless, we were discussing *my* experience,' Madame Tourval said coldly.

Delphine gave a discreet cough. A hush descended over the salon.

'My friends, we are here to welcome my daughter home from England.'

Tante Agnes entered the room just then with a tray of champagne coupes. When everyone had a glass in hand, Delphine raised her glass and smiled fondly at Colette. Her eyes were uncharacteristically clear, given that it was already three in the afternoon, and Colette supposed she should feel honoured that her mother had held off indulging in a cocktail or three until the official reception.

'Welcome back, my darling. I do hope that your time in England has not completely removed France, and Paris in particular, from your heart.'

Colette smiled genuinely. She put her hand over her heart. '*Mère*, nothing could erase Paris from my heart or soul.'

The women all sighed and raised their glasses. Colette felt a frisson of relief at their approval. After such a long absence she needed to be accepted back into Delphine's circle. As Colette smiled around the room at the brightly dressed women, she tried not to think of an aviary filled with middle-aged birds. With immaculately made-up faces, chic hats with feathers and net, and rings and necklaces in a variety of stones set into gold and silver, the women of Paris were stylish in a way English women could only hope to emulate. But their average age must be fifty at least and they were all her mother's friends or acquaintances. None of Colette's friends were present at the party to welcome her home.

Apparently, she didn't have any as not one of the girls she had known from school or outside it had written to her while she was in England.

'Your continued good health, my dear,' Delphine said.

Colette received the toast and looked around, smiling at each of the women in turn.

Delphine rang a bell and Agnes appeared again, carrying two towering cake stands laden with pastries and cakes, glossy with icing and fruits. Colette's mouth began to water.

'England cannot compete with Paris when it comes to pastries,' she said.

'Be careful, *chérie*,' said Madame Brassai; a woman whose face was so wrinkled and folded with fat she resembled a bullfrog. 'If you eat too many you will never fit into your new gown. I remember you looking quite puffy-faced when I last saw you, but I suppose that was long ago and you are no longer an adolescent.'

Colette turned on the spot, posing to show off her dress and biting back a response. Her dress was cornflower blue with a billowy blouse and flared skirt and fitted her perfectly. She had a curvaceous figure with high, full breasts but a shapely waist and, most importantly to Colette, a flat stomach.

'It would take more than a *mille-feuille* to make me fat,' she quipped, to general laughter.

As the women began to nibble at the delights on offer, two of the youngest joined Colette at the window overlooking the garden.

Sophie and Josette Lucienne. Both blonde and pretty. They were twins, two years older than Colette, and daughters of a hotelier who had fought with her father in the Great War. Colette knew them by sight but not intimately. Mind you, as she had not been in Paris for nearly a year, there was no one she did know intimately.

'Tell us about England,' Sophie urged. 'Do they think there will be a war?'

Colette thought for a moment. The younger women seemed a little less vacuous than the older generation. 'The prime minister said not. He signed a peace pact with Germany last year.'

'Good. *Papa* is dispirited at the thought that if there is a war no one will come to stay in the hotel.' Sophie sighed. 'It is a worry.'

'We heard you had been devastated by the end of a romance with a German and your nerves were too fragile to stay in France,' Josette said.

Colette's mouth dropped open. Delphine and Louis had sworn that, if anyone asked, they would say Colette had gone abroad to widen her mind.

Josette continued unabashed. 'Just imagine if you had married a German. We might have been enemies soon!'

Sophie nudged her sister and spoke quickly. 'Tell us about the English men.'

What was there to tell? Colette had stayed closely within Edith's circle and rarely had the opportunity to speak to any young men, much less alone. Not wanting to admit the truth, she smiled and lowered her eyelashes.

'Oh English men are the best in the world. Such gentlemen, but rather dull at times. They all seem to know the same poetry and quote it at any opportunity. Or they know nothing and spend all of their time hunting or shooting things.'

'That sounds dull,' Josette said. 'Did you meet any royalty? Did you have any wild romances with dukes or earls?'

'I'm afraid not,' Colette admitted, relieved at the change of subject. 'I was staying mostly with my old governess and unfortunately she did not move in quite those circles.'

Despite Edith being an 'honourable', as she had tried to explain to Colette, she had married for love to a music teacher and was now plain Mrs Colin Gregg. They lived in a modest house provided by Colin's boarding school on the east coast, and their idea of a good day out involved walking in all weathers along the cliffs. No wonder she had returned home slim.

Sophie pressed her hand against Colette's. 'I know where to find the most exciting men in Paris. Come with us one night and we will show you.'

Colette's heart leaped. This was more like it. 'I don't particularly want a man, but will there be dancing?'

'Oh yes. Dancing and music and drinking. Smoking, too, if you're daring enough.'

Colette wrinkled her nose. She had tried smoking at Gunther's suggestion, but the thought of it now turned her stomach.

'Dancing sounds exciting,' Colette said.

Sophie gave her a wide smile. 'Come on Saturday this week. Take the Metro to Abbesses to arrive at eight and we will meet you there.'

For the rest of the afternoon Colette was bright and sociable with all of her mother's friends. They drank cocktails and talked of fashion and films and she felt invigorated, despite the long journey home. The company Colette had kept in England had been more sedate and serious, and towards the end of her stay every conversation had inevitably turned to the situation in Germany and the Chancellor's ambition in Europe, which Colette had found insufferably tedious. Who were the British, on an island safe across the sea, to worry about land disputes in Europe? This salon with its gaily dressed women exemplified the best of Paris and, consequently, the best of France.

After the guests had departed amid effusive kisses and promises to attend cocktail parties and make visits to couturiers and galleries, Delphine called Colette back.

'Ring for a fresh carafe of water, Colette. It's too stuffy in here and I have a headache.'

Both women knew Delphine's bad head was less due to the air and entirely a result of the number of cocktails she had consumed, but Colette went along with the pretence.

'I'll order some coffee too,' she suggested. 'I'm still tired from travelling.'

The coffee arrived with a plate of finger-size *madeleines* decorated with glace icing flowers. Colette ate one enthusiastically. Delphine narrowed her eyes.

'I see your appetite is large. That's good as I would hate to see you falling prey to any more bouts of sickness. We do not want any more illness, do we, Colette?'

Colette felt a creeping sense of disdain. Her mother's voice was uncharacteristically full of steel but, despite that, Delphine talked in vague hints and euphemisms.

There had been no 'illness'.

There had been a pregnancy and an undignified banishment across *la Manche* so that Colette's shame would never be known among Louis and Delphine's circle. Delphine would never mention Colette's unfortunate condition by name, nor refer to the circumstances under which she had been exiled to England. Colette wondered how any rumours of the disastrous end to her love affair had breached the walls of the house. Gunther had ended the relationship in the same conversation Colette had told him about her condition. Her stomach writhed with fury at the memory.

'No, there will be no more bouts of illness.'

'Good.' Delphine reached out of hand and briefly stroked Colette's forearm. 'I regretted sending you away, but you know it had to be done. I'm so glad you're home now and safe. There won't be a war. There *won't* be. But if there was, I couldn't bear to think you were across the sea from me.'

A chill rippled down Colette's back.

Delphine's cheeks dimpled. 'Now, we must make plans. We need to have you fitted for some new clothes. The English fashions are so sensible. Nothing I would let you wear. I think lunch at Le Procope on Tuesday. A walk through the *Jardin du Luxembourg* on Wednesday morning. A charity event at the Luciennes' hotel to help those poor, displaced Czechoslovakian women who have taken refuge in Paris. On Friday evening we'll dine with Madame Pirolle and her son Georges – he's been married once but his wife died of pleurisy so he is once again looking for a wife. On Saturday—'

'On Saturday,' Colette interrupted, slightly awed by the schedule proposed. 'I am meeting with Josette and Sophie for an evening visit to go dancing.'

Delphine looked approving. 'Excellent. The hotel has a lovely terrace. I believe Josette even entertained the thought of marriage to a count from Brittany until she decided the climate by the sea would not agree with her complexion.'

She reached out and seized Colette's wrist, her fingernails

digging into Colette's flesh. Five red talons. Colette looked up in shock. The movement had been smooth and speedy and totally unexpected.

'Find a good husband, Colette. Your father is rich enough and well respected enough that you could attract a higher calibre than a would-be film actor, especially now relations with Germany are turning hostile. Take advantage of that.'

Colette eased her wrist free. 'I will, *Mère*. Now, if you will excuse me, I am tired. This afternoon has been rather strenuous. I think I shall go lie down.'

'I agree. I shall do the same until my headache goes,' Delphine said, pouring the remaining dregs of a Seapea Fizz into a glass. She ambled over to the chaise longue in the window bay and lay down. Colette turned away, shaking her head. Delphine would be asleep there until Louis returned from the factory. She had not changed in the slightest.

Colette did not get as far as the bedroom before she heard her name being called. It was a girlish voice that she had not heard for nearly a year. She turned to find Fleur standing at the top of the stairs, holding a pile of towels.

Colette walked back along the landing to her, taking time to examine the girl who had once been her closest friend. She was much prettier than Colette was, Colette realised with a touch of envy. She had grown a little taller but was still small-boned and dainty. Her eyes looked incredibly large in her pale face, giving her a young and innocent air.

It was disappointing to see that her former friend was still working here when she had been so ambitious. Colette felt a little guilty that she had not written to Fleur, but then again, Fleur had not written to her, and she had promised to.

'Fleur! I wasn't sure if you still lived here. I haven't seen you since I got back.'

'That was only yesterday, wasn't it?' Fleur asked. She gave a

43

nervous smile that flickered on and off her face rapidly. 'I don't work here all the time. Four days a week I work in a bookshop, but *Tante* Agnes still needs my help.'

'Oh that's good to hear,' Colette said with genuine pleasure. 'You always liked books.'

'Yes, I did. I mean, I do,' Fleur replied. She pressed her lips together awkwardly.

Colette curled her fingers into the cloth of her skirt. This was excruciating. They had once been so close, but now had nothing to say to each other.

'Do you still share the room with your aunt?' Colette asked.

At this Fleur smiled. 'No, your father was kind enough to let me turn one of the box rooms on the top floor into a bedroom of my own. It's small but has everything I need.'

'Then you will be almost above me,' Colette said.

'I'll try to be quiet if I come in late,' Fleur said.

Colette wondered where she went that made her come in late. A bookshop wouldn't be open in the evenings. Did she have a boyfriend? She must have friends. Again, Colette felt a stab of jealousy. Fleur had been her special friend but now they were practically strangers. Fleur had had the freedom of Paris all the time Colette had been away. It was unfair! She silently cursed Gunther once again.

Fleur gave a brief smile. 'We must talk properly at some point. We must have lots of news to share. You must tell me everything you did in England. I want to hear all about it.'

A siren screamed in Colette's head. Once she would have shared all of her secrets with Fleur, but Delphine and Louis had sworn her to secrecy about her shame. She couldn't tell Fleur about vomiting until lunchtime while day by day her belly swelled and she read disappointment in Edith's eyes. Couldn't describe the agony of her body splitting wider over nine hours as a baby sought freedom. Couldn't share the mix of relief and

44

heartbreak that the child had been whisked away as soon as it had emitted its first wail, without Colette even learning its sex.

'There isn't much to tell, I'm afraid.'

Fleur looked disappointed. She motioned to the towels in her arms. 'Well … I had better put these away. It was nice to talk to you.'

Fleur clearly felt she had been rebuffed, and though Colette could never explain why, it filled her with melancholy to do so. Colette nodded.

'Of course. I'll see you soon, I hope.' She walked away but as she reached her bedroom, Fleur called her name again. Colette turned back.

Fleur smiled nervously. 'I planted the strawberries. They grew really well. I was sorry you missed them.'

Colette had no idea what she was talking about, but it obviously meant something significant to Fleur.

'Thank you. I'm sorry I missed them too.'

She went into her room and looked around at the disarray of her luggage that was spread out on the bed and floor. She would arrange things in the morning but now she felt quite overwhelmed. She was a stranger in the home she had grown up in.

~

It was only when she was brushing her hair before bed that she remembered what the reference to strawberries was. The scent of warm earth on baking hot tiles, mingled with floral fruit filled her memory. How simple her life had been then.

Fleur had not completely forgotten Colette if she had planted things in their secret hideaway.

It was good to know.

~

Delphine drove her and Colette to the Luciennes' hotel herself. Not many women in her circle could drive and she prided herself on the skill.

'I met your father when I was chauffeuring a doctor during the Great War,' she reminded her daughter.

Colette nodded, only half paying attention while she looked out of the window. Paris had changed since had been away. Street names that Colette recognised were now accompanied by newer signs indicating the location of shelters.

There was also a level of paranoia there hadn't been before, which echoed what she had seen in England. Everything was overlaid with a veneer of anxious anticipation that things were about to change. Like the British, the French government had issued gas masks, which were to be carried everywhere.

'Are you listening?' Delphine asked. 'You aren't, are you? What are you thinking about?'

Colette dragged her attention away from a huddle of pinched-faced, foreign-looking women and children who stood at the edge of the entrance to the Bois du Boulogne. They had a hunted look about them, as if they were used to keeping one eye always over their shoulders.

'Everyone is anxious here. It was the same in England. Anticipation that things are about to change. Those women there...' She pointed at the group. 'They might have been dancing and choosing autumn hats from fashion magazines only a few months ago and now they are begging for aid on foreign streets. What if the same thing happens to us?'

Delphine grimaced. 'It won't. And don't mention the subject over lunch.'

'But the lunch is in aid of Czechoslovakian refugees,' Colette pointed out.

Delphine shook her head and sighed wearily as if Colette was simple-minded. 'Yes, but who wants to be reminded of that while we're trying to enjoy ourselves? We'll raise money to help them. That's enough.'

∼

The atmosphere at the event was forcedly bright. The guests at the luncheon were women who usually picked slowly at dishes but today they ate everything, as if preparing for future hunger.

Talk of war was consciously avoided until Madame Brassai announced in a voice swimming with irritation, 'My dressmaker has left the city. Jewish, so of course the whole family have simply abandoned the *atelier*. It's very inconvenient.'

The room rippled with conversation as other women described their own experiences of closed shops and departed workers. Colette pushed her spoon around the plate, scraping up the final smear of lemon crème brulée and thinking that however inconvenient it was for the women to have to order clothes from elsewhere, at least they still had homes to return to.

Chapter Five

When Colette accompanied Sophie and Josette to the cabaret that evening, the atmosphere was wildly different. They stopped at the bottom of the steps of Montmartre in front of a modest doorway with a sign that read 'Cabaret des Papillons'. They were admitted into a dimly lit corridor, but when they passed through the heavy velvet curtains Colette discovered she had stepped into a world of vibrant hedonism.

Screeching jazz was blasting out from the band while women wearing barely more than a few feathers kicked their legs and shimmied across the stage. On the dance floor couples held each other more intimately, it seemed to Colette, than she and Gunther had been on the night they had first made love in the Secret Garden.

Josette and Sophie rid themselves of their coats and revealed themselves to be wearing dresses that were short, sleeveless and practically backless.

'I think I am overdressed,' Colette whispered to Josette. She smoothed down her black satin dress. It was calf-length with wide straps and cut on the bias to drape over her hips and emphasise her waist. It was more suited for dinner with her parents' circle than the wild dance floor where couples flung each other around and shrieked with delight in time with the throbbing beat of the bass drum.

'A little,' Josette said, giving Colette an appraising look. 'But you're pretty enough that it doesn't matter and no one will be looking at your dress. You will know next time.'

Sophie took Colette by the hand and wove a path through the tightly packed tables to the front, right beside the band, waving and calling hello to various people. There was a small table with a card bearing the girls' surname.

'I'll find us some partners while Josette finds us some drinks. You wait here and make sure nobody tries to take our table,' she instructed. She disappeared back into the darkness of the room, while Josette waved her hand towards a waiter clad in an immaculate, crisp white uniform and reeled off an order without even asking Colette what she might like. The dance partners arrived before the Dempseys that Josette assured Colette she would adore. Two men and a woman. Colette wrinkled her brow in confusion.

'Victorine is for me.' Sophie giggled, wrapping her arms around the neck of the statuesque ice-blonde woman dressed in a man's tuxedo. They whirled off together into the crowd and vanished.

'Which do you want?' Josette asked, cocking her head towards the two men. Both were similar with slicked back brown hair. One had a thin pencil moustache and the other was clean-shaven. Other than that, there was very little to distinguish between them.

'I don't know,' Colette said.

The man nearest to her – the moustachioed one – reached for her hand and pulled her from her seat.

'You're mine in that case, mademoiselle.' He grinned as he spoke and swung Colette into his arms, breathing a fug of alcohol and tobacco into her face. She almost recoiled, but managed not to. They danced on the edge of the crowd, Colette resisting her partner's attempts to pull her further into the swell of bodies.

'Relax, *ma bichette*, you're too stiff,' he murmured into her ear.

Contrary to his instruction, Colette grew even tenser. It had been so long since a man had touched her and the feel of strong arms around her waist, and his chest pressing against her breasts made her heart thud and blood rush to her throat and cheeks. He had called her a doe, and for a moment her mind filled with the image of a wide-eyed creature she had seen standing impassively on the Yorkshire moorland just before being brought down with a shotgun.

'I'm sorry, it's been a while since I've been anywhere like this. It's all very strange. Everything seems so wild.'

He gave a leering smile. 'Of course we are wild. Nobody wants to miss a moment. The world might end tomorrow and we want to take advantage of it while we can. We can sit and have a drink though if you'd rather.'

They returned to the table. The Dempsey turned out to taste strongly of apples and liquorice. It was interesting, but Colette decided she'd rather have champagne. She sipped it again and thought back to what the man had said.

'What do you mean while it lasts? While what lasts?'

He lit a cigarette and took a drag before answering. 'Peace. I work in the government offices and I can tell you that there is great concern in all departments. We are increasing munitions manufacture and preparing for defence.'

'Of Paris?' Colette's heart leaped to her throat.

'Of course not, silly child. But of the borders. Austria might have welcomed Adolf Hitler's incursion, but France never will.

He says he won't but, just in case he decides to change his mind, we will be prepared.'

He tossed his cocktail down his throat and held his hand out. 'Now, let's dance. That's what we're here for after all.'

He pushed her backwards, taking control of the steps and for the rest of the evening, no doubt thanks to the Dempsey, Colette managed to put all sinister thoughts out of her mind and enjoy herself. By the time the band left the stage, her calves and feet ached.

'Do you still think English men are the most exciting?' Sophie asked as they gathered their coats.

Colette thought before answering. She had danced with a series of men, all more charming and debonair than the last, but no one in particular had given her the internal shivers that Gunther had.

'Perhaps.'

Sophie had spent the evening dancing with Victorine. There had been other female couples and a few male couples dancing together. Seeing them and realising no one else was shocked made Colette feel very unworldly. 'I do think men in general are exciting. Don't you?' she asked.

'Not really,' Sophie said. 'They are a necessary evil if one wants to have children and a home, but I get my kicks in other ways. Did you have fun?'

Colette slipped her sable throw over her shoulder. 'I really did, though now the music is over, I'm thinking about what the first man I danced with told me. He said he thinks war is coming. He said that is why everyone is so determined to have fun.'

'He probably just said that in the hope you would go to bed with him,' Josette scoffed. 'We are determined to have fun because we can. War might be fun though, our mothers seemed to enjoy themselves. Ours nursed in the American Hospital in Neuilly and said it was wonderful to be free and busy.'

Josette and Sophie's mother still enjoyed being busy from what Colette had seen. She oversaw the female staff at the hotel and busied herself with organising charitable dinners and lunches there for various causes. Colette couldn't say whether Delphine had enjoyed her time nursing at Montfaucon during the Great War, but she seemed happiest in the house with a cocktail glass in her hand.

'Anyway, there won't be a war,' Sophie said decisively. She linked her arms through the other girls' and they walked back down the winding streets to the Metro station together.

~

As long as Colette could remember, the family had spent August in a house on the coast of Normandy where the breeze was fresh and clean enough to make the heat bearable. Her stay in England meant she had missed a year and she was devastated to learn the family would remain in Paris. Even so, she did not take the news as hard as Delphine who stormed around with a frown for days.

'All this because your father wants to buy some old houses to turn into another factory. Even if he has to stay in Paris, I don't see why we can't go, or why I can't go myself. I could stay with Max and Aline in their house. They always rent somewhere with plenty of rooms for visitors.'

'You could go and sit in the garden,' Colette suggested, opening the window of her mother's salon and leaning out to catch the breeze. The temperature remained high even into the evening, and however often one bathed it was impossible not to become sticky and dusty. 'There is some shade on the terrace and a lovely breeze by the fountain.'

'I suppose so,' Delphine said with a distinct lack of enthusiasm. 'You don't seem to care that we can't go to Houlgate.'

Her voice was almost accusatory and Colette made her mind up not to admit her annoyance even under torture.

'I haven't been back in Paris long enough to grow bored even though it's hot,' she said airily.

Delphine narrowed her eyes. 'There isn't a man, is there? You haven't heard from Gunther?'

Colette felt a violent stab in her breast. 'No I haven't. And I won't, I imagine. I don't even know if he is still in Paris. He probably returned to Trier.'

'He will no doubt have enlisted in the army or that dreadful youth organisation,' Delphine said, frowning. 'It's just as well that things ended when they did. Just imagine if you had married him. You would have had to leave Paris and join the Nazi party.'

'You're talking nonsense,' Colette snapped in a rare moment of inescapable irritation. 'Gunther is far too old to join the *Hitlerjugend* and I don't think everybody in Germany is a Nazi. Gunther wasn't and he wanted to live in Paris to become a film star.' She dropped her head. 'Besides, he never wanted to marry me, as you well know, and it upsets me to hear you talk like that.'

She stood and walked out of the salon. Even if Delphine did not want to sit in the garden, Colette would take advantage of the cool shade. She went outside and saw Fleur was already sitting on the iron bench at the end of the terrace.

Colette ambled over.

'Hello, Fleur, isn't it warm!'

'Very. But the night stock smell lovely currently. I'd rather sit out here than in the kitchen.'

Fleur was working her way through a pile of mending from the basket at her side and had her feet up, stretching out along the whole of the bench. She didn't move, even though Colette was standing, so it was pretty clear she didn't want company.

'Well, it's nice to see you. I'd better go get ready; I'm going dancing again.'

Fleur snipped off the thread and gave her a quick smile. 'Have a nice time.'

Colette stood for a moment, feeling like the intruder. It was toe-curling. Fleur was friendly enough when they met, but she had her own life and interests and the closeness they had shared was long gone. She walked back to the house feeling like a cloud was filling her stomach. In her bedroom, she pulled out her new dress and felt slightly better. It was emerald-green silk with thin straps and a fringe of silver beads that finished just below her knees. Much better for the club than her old black dress.

She would go dancing and everything would be lovely. She had spoken the truth to Delphine: there was no particular man that she liked, and she was content to keep it that way.

And there would be no war either.

And then came September, and life as Colette knew it changed for ever.

~

On the third day of September, Louis walked into the house at five and requested that everyone, family and staff, gather in the dining room. Michal Drucker, the concierge of the apartment block, was with him. Colette greeted him warmly. Michal had been the concierge for the entire time Colette had lived there and she hoped the rumours of ill treatment towards Jews in other countries would not extend to France. Michal was far too nice to deserve that.

When everyone was there, Louis unfolded a copy of the *Paris-Soir* newspaper. He closed his eyes briefly and bowed his head then began to read aloud from the front page.

'We are waging war because it has been thrust on us…'

As he read Edouard Daladier's declaration of war, Delphine moaned aloud and dropped her head into her hands. Colette felt

Fleur's hand slip into hers and squeeze it tightly. She gave an answering squeeze, intensely glad of the mutual gesture of comfort. Fleur was holding Agnes' hand with her other, and even through her preoccupation with the news, Colette felt a flicker of envy at the closeness of aunt and niece. Across the room, Michal stood white-faced, gazing towards the window.

'What does it mean?' Fleur whispered. Colette was thankful someone else had found a voice as she didn't dare to speak in case she cried.

Louis ran his hands through his hair, massaging his scalp. He looked wearier than Colette could recall him ever being.

'I don't know yet. I hoped… I believed it would not come to this. I am too old to fight in this war, alas. Agnes, would you pour everyone a drink, please?'

Agnes obliged, handing out small measures of cognac to everyone. The bottle was almost empty. Louis eyed it with a wry smile. 'I think perhaps I had better buy another. This one won't last much longer.'

He raised his glass and swirled it in his hand. 'To all of us. We go to war on the side of righteousness. France will never be enslaved. *Vive la France.*'

Everyone repeated his words as if they were echoing a benediction from a priest, then drank. Fleur gathered the glasses and handed them to her aunt. Delphine walked out of the room with her head held high, but her shoulders were rigid. Louis watched her leave, then came over to his daughter. He embraced her, but Colette could feel the tension in his arms and it wasn't much comfort.

'*Papa*, should I be scared?'

'Possibly. I hope not. With luck this will all be over very soon. Perhaps I won't even need a second bottle of cognac.' He kissed the top of Colette's head.

'I think I will be losing lots of my workers. There will be a call to mobilise.'

'But what of the army?' Colette asked.

'The army will need more men than it already has. I must go back to the factory. Take care of your mother for the rest of the evening.' He gave her another quick kiss before leaving the room.

Fleur was lingering by the door. Colette went to speak to her, but Fleur put her hand out and gestured to Michal Drucker. He was standing exactly where he had been, still staring at the window.

'Monsieur Drucker, are you alright?' Fleur asked softly.

He took a moment to notice her. His dark eyes were filmy. 'This is bad for my people. For me.'

Fleur touched his hand. 'Not in France,' she said firmly. 'Never in France. You are French before anything else.'

Colette understood then what they meant. Michal was a Jew, and Hitler had waged a particular war on Jews in Germany and Austria. Many of the refugees coming into France were Jewish.

Michal gave a wan smile. 'Already things are bad. You would not necessarily see it, but I have friends with shops. People don't want their business. They are eyed with suspicion.'

'But not you,' Colette reassured him. 'You haven't done anything to deserve that.'

His eyes flashed to her. 'And the women who work in the clothes factories have? The butcher or his children?'

Colette dropped her eyes. 'I didn't mean that. I have Jewish friends at the cabaret.'

'I know you didn't, *mon sucre*, but it is a dark time to be of my race.'

'You will be safe here,' Fleur said. 'This is France. The German army will never be allowed to come this far. What happens in Germany is under Hitler's authority, but nobody in Paris with Jewish friends will stand by and let anything happen to them.'

She sounded firm, but Colette could hear the uncertainty in her voice and hoped she was right.

Michal took both their hands. 'Thank you, girls, I hope so. You say you have Jewish friends now. How many people will say that in three months' time?'

He left the room and the two girls looked at each other.

'We are right, aren't we? And my friends will be safe too, won't they?' Colette asked.

Fleur wrapped her arms tightly around herself. Already petite, she looked wretchedly fragile.

'I don't know. I don't know anything. It's all too new to think about. I want to ask my friends what they think. They're students or writers and they're better at understanding this sort of thing than I am. We spend a lot of evenings discussing politics but often they lose me.'

It was the first time Fleur had shared anything personal about her life. It made sense that Fleur would be friends with serious types as she was like that herself. They sounded dull in comparison to Colette's friends, but at the moment, they were probably more use than the sisters. She thought of her dancing partners and the bright crowd of men and women who gathered in the Café des Papillons or the other cabarets along the Boulevard de Clichy or Rue Pierre Fontaine. They lived for pleasure and excitement. Only the man she had danced with on the first visit had spoken of preparations for war. He had been right, but Colette had never seen him again.

'If they tell you anything, will you tell me?' Colette asked. 'I don't think mine will know anything.'

'Of course. I'll tell you everything I find out,' Fleur said. 'Try not to worry.'

She patted Colette's shoulder but then she took her hand hastily away. The feeling of closeness ended, but for a fleeting moment it had felt like they were children again, with nothing to worry about beyond getting caught stealing strawberries or swapping exercise books. Colette wished she had confided in Fleur as to why she was going to England. Perhaps then they might have remained closer.

That was behind them now, however, and the future, with whatever it might hold, was more of a concern.

Chapter Six

April 1940

'I think we should start hiding things,' Colette said as she swept briskly into the kitchen one afternoon and threw her gas mask down onto the table.

Fleur looked up from her baking. 'What sort of things?'

'Jewellery. The best knives. Anything the Germans might steal.'

Fleur's throat tightened. It startled her to see Colette so anxious. War had been declared, but war as Fleur imagined it did not arrive. She had expected bombs and armies, but nothing had happened yet. People had started referring to the situation as the *drôle de guerre*, saying the inaction was a joke.

'Has something finally happened? Have the German army moved against France?'

Colette dropped onto the comfy chair and kicked out her legs. She removed her green silk turban and began twisting her fringe between her fingers.

'No, but I was lunching with Josette. Her friend Angelique's cousin was visiting Salzburg when Germany occupied Austria. She said the streets were full of people panicking, and theft. I don't want that to happen here.'

Fleur put down the rolling pin and stared at Colette. The Anschluss had come up in the café and the level of support it allegedly had was hotly debated. 'I thought Austria welcomed them?'

'Not everyone. Besides, once they were there, who would admit they weren't welcome?' Colette gestured to the gas mask case she had dropped beside the chair. 'I hate having to carry this. If the government are confident then why are we being given these horrid things?'

They both regarded the hideous grey contraption with goggles and tubes.

Colette wrinkled her nose. 'They are so ugly.'

'I don't think anyone designed them with fashion in mind,' Fleur said. She had felt like she was going to suffocate when she had tried hers on and was genuinely unsure if she could endure wearing it for more than a few minutes. If Colette's only objection was the offence against fashion, she was lucky. 'You could always go back and ask if they come in turquoise.'

Colette made a valiant effort to smile. 'Not with my colouring. Possibly peach.'

~

She appeared in the kitchen two days later with a cover for the gas mask case made from an old skirt embroidered with pale yellow fleur-de-lis. She had added decorations in the form of silver buckles at each corner.

'Very clever, Mademoiselle Colette,' Agnes said.

Colette preened, looking like a child showing off a first attempt at drawing.

'I didn't think you were being serious,' Fleur said.

'Well I was. I could make one for you both too,' Colette said. '*Mère* has asked for one.'

'Thank you, that is very kind. We would both love one,' Agnes said before Fleur could speak. She caught Fleur's eye and Fleur, long familiar with her aunt's stern expression, agreed. When Colette left, Agnes turned to her.

'You were about to turn down her offer of a case cover, weren't you?'

Fleur shrugged. 'I hardly think it is the most important thing she could be doing. If she wants to fill her days she could come and iron Louis' shirts.'

'It is important to her,' Agnes answered. 'She isn't like you or me. She hasn't been brought up to work so doing that took initiative and her offer is generous. You would have been rude to pour scorn on her efforts.'

Fleur sat back in the comfy chair with a sigh, an unpleasant flicker of shame in her belly.

~

A week later, when she was gifted with a mask bag of her own, in red satin trimmed with blue piping, she accepted it with a smile, praising the careful handiwork, then beckoned Colette into the small bedroom.

'I thought about what you said before. We should make some preparations, but not jewellery for me. I don't have any worth stealing.'

Colette managed a wan smile. 'I suppose you want to say books?'

Fleur sat on the bed. 'I was thinking of food. The ration books worry me and I'm trying to think what might become scarce. Do you remember the strawberries that grew in the Secret Garden?

We could plant some vegetables too.'

Colette looked doubtful. 'I don't know the first thing about growing plants.'

'How hard could it be? Michal will advise us if we ask him. I'm sure that if we keep the snails and slugs away, they would do well. If not then we could eat the snails,' Fleur said, giving a laugh that she didn't entirely feel.

Colette bit her lip and her anxious expression returned. 'It won't come to that, will it?'

Fleur's ribs tightened. 'I don't know what will happen, but I feel better for the idea of having a plan.'

～

Colette seemed to have unburdened herself and had a spring in her step once more. She may have been hiding away valuables, but if she was, she did not share that with Fleur. She spent her days sat in the garden, sunning herself in the spring sunshine, and reading magazines when she was not busy sewing gas mask bags for her friends.

'I envy you,' Fleur told her. 'I wish I could switch my brain off as easily as turning off a light switch.'

Colette narrowed her eyes, possibly suspecting it was a criticism.

'You have to make yourself. Come with me one evening when I go out with Josette and Sophie. Nobody can be sad when they are dancing. *La Jeunesse Coquette* is our favourite cabaret at the moment.'

'I think it will be far too glamorous,' Fleur replied. 'But thank you all the same.'

'Are you sure?'

Fleur couldn't help but notice the flicker of relief in Colette's eyes.

'Perfectly. You have your friends and I have mine.'

Even though Colette had been living back at home for a year, the two women spent little time in each other's company. It was natural of course, as they had different groups of friends and different lives.

'What are your friends like?' Colette asked, sitting up and stretching.

Her breasts jutted forward in the fitted cashmere cardigan. She had a striking figure and Fleur could only imagine the impression she would make on the men in the Café Morlaix group. Fleur didn't particularly want to spend time with Colette's circle and she really didn't want to share hers with Colette.

'Oh you would find them very dull,' Fleur assured her. 'We talk so much about politics and ideas. I don't think your mother would approve.'

'Perhaps I don't care whether or not she does,' Colette snapped.

She pushed herself to her feet and walked away. Fleur watched her go thoughtfully. Sébastien's group were very serious. Given the mood of the country they had every justification in being so, but, all the same, it would be tempting to spend a night dancing as if there was nothing wrong.

~

The unimaginable happened on a stiflingly hot June morning. Fleur had been helping *Tante* Agnes to fold bed linen in the cool cellar room when thunder erupted overhead.

'Ah, the storm.' Fleur passed her hand over her neck. 'Good, we need it.'

Tante Agnes's cheeks had turned ashen and one hand clutched at the cross around her throat.

'That's no storm.' She dropped the sheet on the floor and

walked stiffly out of the room. Fleur followed her anxiously. Agnes would never treat her employer's belongings in such a way unless something serious was happening.

From all across the city rose the wail of sirens. The sky was cloudy, but in places puffs of white smoke billowed.

'They are bombing us!' Agnes' voice rose to a shriek.

Fleur gripped her aunt's hand. It was terrifying to see the usually self-contained woman in such a panic. Colette ran round the side of the house from the garden, her eyes wide with fear.

'That siren! It's the air raid siren. Who is doing this? The Germans or the English?'

'I don't know,' Fleur said in a trembling voice. 'Why would it be the Germans after so many months without fighting? And the English are our allies.'

The two girls looked at each other, mystified, as curiosity temporarily won over the fear Fleur knew she should be feeling.

'Back inside at once. Everyone.' Louis appeared from indoors and seized them both by the wrist, tugging them firmly. Hearing the urgency in his voice, terror swelled inside Fleur.

There was a roaring of engines, the sound of whistling and then an explosion that sounded far too close. All three women gave shrieks of varying degrees.

Louis flinched.

'Now!' he barked.

The women ran inside and met Delphine in the hallway.

'That sound,' she exclaimed. 'I never thought I would hear it again.'

She was trembling and Louis pulled her into his arms. 'Girls, run upstairs and close all the shutters. Delphine, do this floor. Agnes, find oil lamps and matches. Then everyone go into the cellar.'

Within minutes the whole household sat huddled on wooden chairs in the cellar where the sheets still waited to be ironed and folded. *Tante* Agnes muttered continually beneath her breath and Fleur knew she was praying. Louis sat with his arm around his wife's shoulder, rocking Delphine as though she were a child, while their actual daughter paced back and forth across the room. Fleur huddled down into her chair, flinching whenever she heard the explosions. Even in the depths of the cellar the sound was loud enough to penetrate, and worst of all were the occasional vibrations, as if the bombs were close.

Paris under fire. It was inconceivable.

After an age the siren screamed again, announcing the raid was over. Louis commanded the women to stay in the cellar and left.

'What will have survived?' Colette asked.

Fleur could only shake her head. Her stomach growled and she clasped her hand over it to stifle the sound. After the intensity of the bombing the cellar was eerily quiet. She looked at her watch and discovered it was only early afternoon.

'Next time we shall have to bring sandwiches down,' Colette said.

'Next time?' *Tante* Agnes jerked her head up.

'There might not be a next time,' Fleur said hastily.

She looked to Colette for reassurance but received only a shrug in return. Colette looked as close to tears as Fleur felt.

'I'm not staying here any longer. I want a cocktail,' Delphine announced. She walked out of the cellar.

Fleur and Colette exchanged a glance. There was rarely a time Delphine didn't want a drink, but now it seemed a reasonable request.

'So do I,' Colette said as she followed her mother. 'I'm sure you both do too. Please, come and join us.'

Agnes was sitting in her seat and trembling. Fleur linked her arm through her aunt's and led her up the stairs.

'The bedsheets,' *Tante* Agnes murmured, pulling back.

'They can wait,' Fleur said decisively, leading Agnes into the dining room.

Delphine had already opened the drinks cabinet and Colette was finding ice. *Tante* Agnes accepted a small glass of cognac and sat on the edge of a chair, sipping it.

~

It turned out that frivolity was just what Fleur needed. The women spent the next hour inventing cocktails as they went along and when Louis returned, the women were in varying states of inebriation and merrier than he had left them. He poured himself a drink too.

'I can't tell what is still standing. An apartment building only four streets away has been completely destroyed. I need to go to the factory.'

'Not today,' Delphine said, clinging on to him. 'Stay with us.'

He kissed her cheek. 'Very well. For today.'

'I must go and finish the laundry,' Agnes murmured.

Fleur began to follow her aunt out of the room but Colette caught her arm.

'Will you stay and keep me company? We could play cards or something.'

'I should help with the laundry,' Fleur said despondently.

Agnes had paused when Fleur had.

'Stay with Mademoiselle Colette,' she said, returning and patting Fleur's cheek. 'She needs you more than I do.'

'Thank you,' Colette said.

The girls wandered out into the garden. The sun was blinding and Fleur's head ached from the cocktails. Colette fetched a deck of cards but they didn't play and just sat in silence watching plumes of smoke rising over the city.

Usually, *Tante* Agnes served the evening meal to the Nadons then she and Fleur ate together at the kitchen table, but that evening they all ate together. No one had much of an appetite and picked at a platter of *saucisson sec, chevre* and figs without enthusiasm. More than once, Fleur found herself staring at the ceiling, waiting for the thrum of engines overhead but they never came. When night fell, the streets were silent and dark. Louis insisted on switching off the electricity and the house was in darkness.

'Go to bed, everyone,' he said. 'There is nothing we can do. We'll have to see what the morning brings.'

'Goodnight, *tante*.' Fleur kissed Agnes' cheek as she always did. 'Things will seem better in the morning.'

'You are a good girl. I will pray for you.' Agnes nodded absently and trudged away, leaving Fleur slightly embarrassed.

Fleur went upstairs and lay on her bed fully dressed. Waiting to hear the sound of aeroplanes overhead made sleeping impossible. For Paris to be bombed was unimaginable. Who would destroy the most beautiful city in Europe? Had Montparnasse escaped destruction? Were Café Morlaix and Ramper et Frère still standing? Tomorrow she would have to brave the streets to discover the wreckage for herself.

~

She woke to a meagre crack of light struggling through the shutter. The room was stuffy; usually in summer she threw the window wide open all night to let the air in but there had been no question of that last night and all shutters remained closed.

Tante Agnes was not in the kitchen. There was no answer to Fleur's knock on the bedroom door so she opened it. Agnes was lying on her bed fully dressed. Like Fleur, she had not changed into her nightgown.

'*Tante* Agnes, you've overslept.'

Fleur drew closer then stopped in alarm. Agnes' mouth was open with a line of spittle trailing from it. Her eyes stared glassily at nothing.

Fleur dropped to her knees beside the bed.

'*Tante* Agnes! Wake up!'

She shook Agnes' arm, but the cold skin only confirmed what Fleur had tried to deny.

Agnes was dead.

Fleur heard a wail erupting from somewhere. She realised it was herself. The sound was terrible but felt like she was powerless to stop it.

'What's happening?' Louis rushed in. He stopped in the middle of the room, his eyes taking in everything, He was usually immaculately dressed but today his hair was uncombed and he was unshaven. He knelt beside Fleur and opened Agnes' hand to reveal the small bottle of tablets she took to help her sleep sometimes. It was empty.

'She took them all,' Louis murmured.

'Did she do this on purpose?' An invisible fist punched Fleur's stomach; another grasped her throat. She looked from the bottle to Louis and back again. 'Why would she?'

'Perhaps she could not bear the thought of war again.' Delphine stood in the doorway. Her face was made up as always and her hair was immaculate. She looked incongruous at the scene of a tragedy. 'She was so strong throughout the *Grande Guerre*, but it affected her, as it affected all of us.'

'We cannot know that, Delphine,' Louis said sternly. He patted Fleur's shoulder. 'The bombing last night perhaps unsettled her mind. Perhaps she did not intend to overdose but took too many tablets out of confusion.'

'Yes, that must be it,' Fleur whispered, her voice wobbling. 'She wouldn't have deliberately… She couldn't have.'

Her vision blurred. She wrapped her arms around herself,

squeezing tightly to hold in her sobs. It must have been an accident. It *must*. The church viewed suicide as a mortal sin and *Tante* Agnes was deeply religious. She had prayed continually in the cellar while the bombs fell. Fleur's eye fell on the Bible that lay open on *Tante* Agnes' bedside cabinet. Her page was open, marked by a pink silk ribbon. She had been reading the crucifixion of Christ, and with a pencil had marked the verse when he cried out asking why he had been forsaken.

What if she had felt her prayers had been ignored – or worse, denied – and had rejected the church in her final moments? A sob broke free. She gulped it back.

'Why didn't she talk to me about how she felt?' she wailed. 'I don't know what needs to be done. She's left me and I don't know what to do now.'

About the funeral. About the grief that wracked her. About the horrific suspicion that she might never know the truth about Agnes' death.

'A funeral needs to be arranged and Agnes' belongings dealt with.' Louis patted her hand kindly. 'Don't worry, Fleur. I will help you with the legal matters.'

'You must not feel that you should leave immediately,' Delphine added.

Fleur didn't understand at first, then grew cold. Of course the Nadons would need to employ a new housekeeper. Agnes' death had not only robbed her of her last relative but also her home. She muttered her thanks and left the bedroom.

'Fleur, I'm in here,' Colette called her from the kitchen. The room smelled of freshly brewed coffee. The smell jolted Fleur's senses. So normal.

'I was listening, but I didn't want to come in. The room seemed too small. I'm so sorry about *Tante* Agnes. Drink this, you've had a shock.'

Colette poured Fleur a cup of coffee and pushed it across the table to her. It was a small gesture, but the kindness of it meant a lot.

'What will you do now?'

Fleur gripped the cup tightly. 'I'm not sure. I can't afford to rent a room on what I earn at the bookshop even if I can increase my hours.'

'You could become our housekeeper,' Colette suggested. 'Then you could stay living here. I don't like to think of you living somewhere strange without a friend.'

She gave Fleur an eager smile. Fleur's throat tightened. She did not want to become a housekeeper. Helping her aunt with the chores was one thing but she could tell herself it was no more than she would do as a wife or daughter in her own house. Colette was trying to be helpful, but as she didn't have to work at all and had a secure home, it seemed tactless to point out Fleur's lack of options. Fleur's heart already felt too full of shock and grief, but resentment added another level of confusion. At that moment she hated Colette. Hated Agnes too, for leaving her in this position.

'I'll think about it. I'm going for a walk,' she said abruptly.

She left the house and trudged through the streets until she was exhausted. The air smelled of smoke and there were piles of rubble where familiar buildings had stood a day earlier. It was not just Fleur's world that had changed, not just her life that was balanced precariously on the edge of a chasm. She couldn't yet forgive Agnes for what she had done and perhaps she never would. Agnes had said nothing to Fleur. Given no hint that she was in such turmoil. If she had helped with the laundry instead of playing cards would Agnes have felt less alone? She had too eagerly left to go with Colette.

'I could have helped you,' she moaned aloud.

Not just with the washing but by being company and consolation.

An old man stopped and looked at her. His eyes were

bloodshot and stark in a face etched with misery. He clutched a pair of shoes to his chest.

'Did you speak to me?' he mumbled.

He sounded confused, as if he was waking from a dream. Fleur shook her head.

Seeing shock on pale faces made it more understandable. Remembering the thunder of bombs falling and Louis' description of destruction across the city she wondered, would anyone have a secure home for long? How many others had decided they would rather face their end on their own terms than wait for it to trap them unawares?

Chapter Seven

'**Y**ou cannot make Fleur homeless.'

Colette marched into her father's office at the factory without knocking. He was sitting at his desk and his face grew dark when he saw her.

'Colette, what are you doing out of the house? It's too dangerous at the moment.'

'Is it?' She knotted her brows. 'It was too dangerous to be at home for the families who were killed when bombs fell on their houses. Being at home didn't help Agnes, did it?'

Her stomach turned over. Despite her current bravado it had taken all morning to summon her nerve to leave the house. Seeing Fleur walk off alone to take the Metro to work had made her determined to be brave and spurred Colette into action. She sat on the edge of Louis' desk, leaned over and put her arms around his neck.

'*Papa*, I'm scared. I'm trying not to be but whenever I look at the newspapers the stories are worse and worse. The Germans are getting closer, aren't they?'

Louis disentangled her arms and leaned back, looking at her sternly.

'Why are you looking at the newspapers?'

Colette's skin prickled. 'You give them to Fleur once you have finished with them. Why shouldn't I look at them too? I'm not stupid, you know.'

'I know you're not. I just worry for you. Yes, the German army is advancing across the country. I fear for what is to happen. I wish to protect you from that worry.'

'If Fleur can cope with reading what is happening then I can too,' Colette declared. 'And speaking of Fleur, that's why I came to see you. You can't make her leave just because *Tante* Agnes is dead. It's callous.'

Louis raised his brows. Colette recognised her own expression on his face.

'I won't make her leave. At least not for the time being. I know what your mother said sounded heartless.'

'Yes, it did, and you have to understand that Fleur and I, well...'

She paused and drummed her fingers on the table. 'I can't bear to think of her homeless or having to find an awful man just so she could live somewhere.'

'Are those the only options you can imagine?' Louis asked. The scenarios she had imagined for Fleur were what Colette feared herself but before she could answer, her father smiled and patted her hand, leaving her with the impression he was teasing her.

'Don't worry, I won't see her forced onto the streets or into a scoundrel's bed. Does Fleur know you have come to speak to me?'

'No and she mustn't find out. She's so self-reliant she would hate to think I was speaking for her.'

Colette heard the admiration in her voice. Fleur was forced to be independent but was facing her uncertain future bravely. She looked at the world with determination, trying to salvage a future after a dreadful loss. Colette was certain no one viewed her in that way.

Left without a relative in the world, Colette knew she would crumble. She felt close to crumbling most days as it was.

She leaned against Louis, wishing she was a child again without any worries. She caught herself. That was exactly the problem: she wanted to feel safe and while she could, there was no need to be brave.

She walked around the desk, straightening pens and coffee cups. 'What is going to happen to the world? Everything seems so uncertain now.'

Louis' expression was bleak. 'It is. I've lost nearly all my male employees to the army. The women are close to exhaustion trying to work and keep their families going. I don't even know if the business is going to make any money this year. I only thank the Good Lord that the factory survived the bombing.'

'Paris will have to rebuild. There will be plenty of opportunity to sell tiles to the people who have lost their homes,' Colette told him.

He smiled. 'Do you know, *ma petite*, that is what I said after the *Grande Guerre*. And it was true. The timing was exceptionally good for me. But this time I don't know. It is too uncertain.'

Colette drummed her fingers on the desk again. Today, her almond-shaped nails were rose pink and glossy. They were hands that were unblemished by work. She closed her fist, suddenly ashamed of how easy her life was.

'I can help you, if you need more workers.'

Louis frowned. 'I swore that you and your mother would never have to work. Why do you think I toil such long hours?'

Colette returned his frown. 'But perhaps I want to. Not on the machines, as I wouldn't know how to begin making anything, but if you have paperwork, I could do that. Invoices or orders, and so on. I am good at mathematics.'

She lifted her head, hoping to see pride in her father's eyes but seeing only uncertainty.

'Perhaps, if you want something to keep you busy until you find a husband...' Louis said reluctantly.

Colette gritted her teeth. It wasn't what she had meant. It was on the tip of her tongue to ask where she would find her husband, given that most men her own age were in uniform fighting for their country's freedom. Besides, with bombs falling on the city that was the least of her concerns.

'I'm proud of you for showing compassion for Fleur and for thinking to offer your help. After your unfortunate behaviour in the past I am surprised but pleased. Now go home, *ma petite*. The greatest help you can be to me is to keep your mother company. She has fragile nerves and they are becoming increasingly so.'

Louis kissed her on the forehead then, dismissing her, and she returned home, conscious of how little equipped she was for a changing world.

It was to change further before long.

~

There had been no repeat of the bombing attack and it was Colette's view that Paris was determined to act as if nothing had happened, and prove it by drinking more, kissing harder, and dancing later into the night. Colette was more than happy to join in.

She woke at eight with a pounding head and a gritty throat after a hot night of decadence to celebrate Sophie's birthday. She was pondering whether to sleep off her hangover for an hour or two longer, or have a bath and face the day, when Louis burst through the door of her bedroom without knocking. He stared down at her with a frown.

'You are still in bed at this time? Colette, come to my bedroom.'

His urgent tone cleared her head. Colette sat up.

'Is *Mère* ill?'

'Just come.' He turned on his heel and walked away.

Colette kicked back the bedclothes and wrapped her robe around herself. She didn't bother with slippers but raced barefoot through the house, ignoring the banging of her head. Her parents' bedroom was in chaos with drawers open and clothes everywhere. Her mother's jewel case was lying on the bed.

Delphine sobbed. 'France has fallen!'

'*Papa?*' Colette looked to where her father stood in the corner of the room with his hands clasped behind his back.

'Not yet, but the German army is marching on Paris. Our government have declared Paris an open city.'

'What does that mean?' Colette asked.

'It means we are undefended. We have to leave!' Delphine cried. Her voice was a high-pitched wail with a slur to it. A cocktail glass was the culprit, as ever, though it was shocking to see one on the table before noon.

'It will take me days to pack, and the best of my jewellery is in the safe at the bank.'

Delphine had very few valuable pieces and most of her day-to-day accessories were paste gems, but all the same she began fastening necklaces around her neck and shoving multiple rings on her fingers. When she reached for a bracelet in the shape of a snake with rubies for eyes, Colette seized her hand.

'*Mère*, don't be stupid! You can't drive through the streets like that. We will get robbed.'

Her stomach heaved and she tasted vomit. Worse would happen if the Germans found them. Louis stepped in.

'Colette is right. Put everything in the large case and pack that. Take all the clothes you can fit. Colette, go and pack. I want you ready in fifteen minutes.'

Colette ran to her room on shaking legs. The newspapers had

said this would never happen. The Allies would hold back the Germans. She looked at the hangers of silks and linens; light summer clothing at one end, moving into warmer fabrics at the other.

'How long will we be gone?' she said aloud. 'Where will we go?'

Her blood felt hot in her veins, rushing to her head and making her feel dizzy. The hangover intensified. She drank a glass of water and wondered if Delphine had any headache sachets. She leaned out of the window to get some fresh air and saw that the other family from the building were leaving. A long queue of cars edged slowly down the length of the road to turn onto the boulevard at the end. There was no time to waste. She dressed in a green day dress and the shoes with the lowest heels. She bundled six cardigans of increasing warmth and a dozen blouses and skirts into a suitcase and emptied the contents of her lingerie drawer on top. Blusher and lipstick, earrings and necklaces went into a smaller case along with a bottle of scent. The scarlet beaded dress she had worn the night before was lying in a heap on the floor waiting to be laundered. She shoved that in, along with three other evening dresses and two pairs of heeled shoes. She doubted they would get worn, but hoped the world and her unknown destination would still contain the opportunity to dance. What would be the point of fighting if there was not the prospect of fun?

At the last moment she remembered her toothbrush, used it, and added it to the case. She stared around, taking what might be her last look at her room and tears blurred her vision. Downstairs she could hear Louis calling her name. She picked up the cases and her gas mask bag and left.

Delphine had succeeded in creating a tower of four cases and three hatboxes. Fleur was standing in the corner of the entrance hall, one suitcase in her hands and wearing her winter coat.

'You're coming too,' Colette exclaimed warmly, hugging her.

'Of course, it is too dangerous for her to stay,' Louis said.

Beside Fleur was a basket containing three jars of preserves, a punnet of strawberries, five eggs and yesterday's bread rolls. Cutlery poked out of a rolled tea towel.

'I didn't have time to bake fresh,' Fleur said so apologetically that Colette felt ashamed of her own selfish packing. There must be other, more practical, things she could take than scent and shoes.

'You need to leave now,' Louis said.

'Us? Aren't you coming?' Colette asked.

Louis' face was set into a hard expression. 'No. I'm not leaving the factory unguarded. Whatever the government have decided about the city, that is mine and I have workers to take care of. I won't hear arguments. I've already had them all with your mother.'

Delphine gave a sob and Louis kissed her on the cheek then picked up two of her cases and led the way to the Simca 8 that stood waiting outside. Fleur and Colette followed.

The cabriolet was six months old and Louis' pride and joy. Delphine and Colette had often tried to persuade him to exchange it for a larger model like his previous Avant, but he had refused. Now Colette wished they had pressed the point because there was barely room in the back for the suitcases if Fleur was to have a seat. Colette willingly abandoned her case of non-essentials and watched in shame as her mother argued and wept when Louis told her to leave all but the most essential luggage.

'Fleur can carry one on her lap,' Delphine said.

'No she won't!' Colette exclaimed. She turned to Delphine, hands on her hips. '*Mère*, you are being ridiculous! Fleur will be carrying the food basket and her own case. I will take your hatbox but you must leave the rest. None of it matters.'

Fleur's eyes filled with approval and Colette beamed back.

'We should take my bicycle if it will go on the roof,' Fleur said.

Louis nodded. 'Excellent idea. Who knows how easy fuel will be to come by in Dijon, even with the milage this beauty does. There's a coil of rope in the cellar. Can you fetch it?'

She did, and together they attached the bicycle precariously to the roof by passing rope through the rear windows. Colette felt a pang of envy seeing them working together. Louis treated Fleur as more of an adult than he did his daughter.

'Well done in standing up to your mother,' Fleur whispered to Colette.

'Don't patronise me. I don't need your congratulations,' Colette snapped.

Fleur's eyes widened. Head down, she turned away, mumbling an apology. Colette cringed inwardly.

'Wait, I didn't mean that. I'm just anxious and being unfair. Thank you. I surprised myself, in truth.'

Fleur smiled uncertainly. 'We're all scared.'

'You don't seem it. Or you don't seem sad to be leaving, in any case.'

'I don't have much to leave behind. Now *Tante* Agnes is gone I didn't know how long I could have stayed here anyway. It's very generous of your father to give me a space in the car.'

Fleur twisted her fingers in the belt of her coat. Her face was bleak and Colette wanted to hug her.

'Did you think we would leave you behind after you've lived here for so long!'

Louis clapped his hands together. 'You must leave. You are heading for Dijon where my cousin Gervase lives. He will be expecting you.' He kissed Colette's forehead and whispered, 'Look after your mother. I know you will be sensible.'

Despite her terror, a ripple of pride passed through Colette. 'I will. I am. I love you, *Papa*.'

Louis shook Fleur's hand, then took Delphine in his arms.

'We will win this war, as we did the last, and you will come back to me.'

He kissed her passionately and she pressed her body against his in a way that made Colette's cheeks flame. Parents should not behave in such a way!

Fleur tugged her arm. 'Let's give them a moment alone.'

'They really love each other, don't they?' Colette whispered.

'Are you surprised?' Fleur asked, tilting her head.

Colette bit her lip. 'A little. And jealous. I can't imagine being loved so much.'

'Nor me. Where is Michal?' Fleur asked.

Colette looked around. Usually the door to the concierge's *loge* was open and Michal sat sunning himself. Today it was closed.

'I haven't seen him today,' Louis said, unwinding himself from Delphine's arms. 'I hope he has left with his family.'

Colette and Fleur exchanged a worried glance. Michal's family consisted of an aged mother and an older uncle. Leaving would not be easy for them. They didn't even have a car, as far as Colette knew.

Fleur squeezed into the back seat. Colette sat in the front. Delphine, now released from her husband's embrace, climbed in, started the engine and the car purred into life. They were really leaving.

Colette took a final look at her home and father, wondering when she would see either of them again. She had left Paris once before in disgrace, under the cover of a lie. To be running away from the beloved city now ripped her heart to shreds. She wanted to cry, but seeing Fleur's placid eyes reflected in the mirror, she was determined to show the same bravery as her friend.

Chapter Eight

The Simca crawled at an interminably slow pace through streets that were clogged with cars and vans.

'I think everyone in Paris has had the same idea of leaving,' Colette remarked.

'They would be stupid not to,' Delphine answered through gritted teeth as she spun the wheel hard and accelerated, cutting in front of a car coming from a side street.

The pavements too were heaving. Families pushed carts piled high with possessions. Not even carts at times. Some had only prams, others, wheelbarrows. One old woman sat in a bathchair being pushed along, her lap piled so high that the wizened face beneath the hat was barely visible. The pedestrians moved at a pace barely slower than the vehicles and Colette began to recognise the same faces, pinched with fear and weariness.

The swell of people grew larger as roads converged near what remained of *Aeroport Villeneuve-Orly* after the bombing raid, and the cars ground to a halt. The sky was cloudless, offering no respite from the heat and dust. Practically the only thing that stemmed Colette's tears was the thought that losing any moisture would be even more uncomfortable.

She stretched her legs, feeling her hips complaining from sitting still too long.

'I actually envy the walkers a little,' she groaned.

By now it was past eleven-thirty. It had taken almost the whole morning to drive barely twenty-five kilometres.

'We will never get out,' Delphine said wearily. She rolled her shoulders as she gripped the steering wheel with both hands. Ungloved, her knuckles were white and her hands like talons.

'Yes, we will,' Colette assured her. 'Once we get onto the route national it will be easier. It is always slow when the traffic meets.'

She glanced back in the mirror and caught Fleur's eye. Fleur nodded, though there was uncertainty in her gaze. Oddly, it reassured Colette to see Fleur was worried too. Knowing she was not overreacting in her own fear was good.

As if to prove her point, the traffic then began to move again. Colette sat back in her seat and closed her eyes, only to be caught unawares when Delphine stamped on the break with a loud cry of alarm, causing cases and passengers to be flung around.

'She came from nowhere!'

A small girl stood in front of the car, eyes screwed tightly closed and mouth open in a wail. A loop of string hung down from her left wrist.

'Véronique!' A little way along the pavement, a woman screamed. She dropped the cases she was carrying in each hand and began to run towards the car, pushing through the crowd.

Colette got out of the car and held the child gently by the wrist until the mother arrived, then handed the child into the mother's arms. The other end of the string dangled from the woman's wrist, the end frayed where it had broken.

'She isn't hurt. My mother stopped in time.'

The mother clutched the girl tightly and stroked her hair. She

82

looked at Colette with imploring eyes. 'Will you take her with you?'

'Me?' Colette exclaimed. 'But I don't know you.'

The mother's eyes filled with tears. 'You have a car. I cannot go fast enough. We have been on the road since half past five this morning and she can't walk much further. I just want her to be safe. I can pay you.'

Colette choked out a breath. She had given up her own baby willingly – eagerly, even – and felt nothing but relief that the unwanted child was not her problem. Véronique was clearly adored and she couldn't imagine the desperation it took to give a beloved daughter to a complete stranger. Someone, somewhere in Britain, was caring for the child Colette had so easily discarded. For the first time since returning to France, she felt shame for what she had done.

She glanced at Delphine who mouthed 'absolutely not', her face thunderous as she gestured around the inside of the car. Every space was taken up with her and Delphine's belongings. Shame flooded her. She leaned into the car.

'Can't we take her?' she implored Delphine. 'We could leave some of these things. The girl could sit on my knee.'

'Don't be ridiculous. I'm not throwing away my clothes. The child would need to bring belongings and they would take space,' Delphine snapped. 'Besides, how would we ever know where to find her mother when we stop? Get back in the car now and stop being so foolish.'

'I'm so sorry,' Colette said. She couldn't meet the mother's eye. 'We have no room and I don't know how to look after children. On foot you may get further than we do anyway.'

She dug her hand into her purse and pulled out a handful of francs. 'Please, take this. Buy some chocolate for Véronique.'

She pushed it into the woman's hand and climbed into the car.

The traffic in front had moved and now the vehicles behind were honking horns and shouting for them to move.

'I'm sorry,' she muttered again.

She watched in the mirror as the car pulled away down the long avenue. The woman and child receded into the distance, trudging slowly hand in hand.

'Giving her money was kind,' Fleur said.

Colette squeezed her fists. The mother had been neatly dressed but her clothes looked well-washed and mended. They weren't rich and she could have spared more.

'It was very little. Less than nothing.'

'Maybe it will buy them passage in a car with more space. Both of them together. I can't believe she wanted to give her daughter to complete strangers,' Fleur murmured. 'How could any mother bear it?'

'Don't judge her. If it was the best thing for the child, how could she not?' Colette snapped.

She jerked her head round to look at Fleur in the back seat and saw astonishment on Fleur's face. It had been her own guilt that had made her snap.

'But being with her mother is the best thing,' Fleur said quietly. 'That's all any child wants.'

She turned to look out of the window. Sunlight caught her eye and Colette saw tears glinting. Fleur hadn't been much older than Véronique when her mother had died and she had gone to live with Agnes.

'You're right,' Colette said gently. 'Staying together was the best thing.'

'You two are being very dramatic over a stranger's fate,' Delphine said briskly. 'Look up ahead – I can see fields!'

It was true they were at the edge of the city but the traffic was worse than before. There had been many roads leading from Paris to here and now they all converged into one long, stationary ribbon of metal.

'How far do you think it goes?' Colette murmured.

'Let me take the bicycle down and I'll see,' Fleur suggested.

The two women quickly undid the rope and Fleur set off, weaving steadily between the cars and lorries.

The road was dusty, grit invading Colette's eyes and nose, filling her hair, filling her mouth. She paced backwards and forwards, looking at the people surrounding her and wondering where they were hoping to get to.

Véronique and her mother passed on the other side of the road. The mother had bound the little girl to her back with a long scarf, leaving both hands free for the suitcases. The child clung to her mother's back, half asleep while the woman trudged with rounded shoulders, weighed down by the burden. Colette avoided eye contact, too ashamed that she had not helped. She climbed back into the car to discover Delphine peering through the front window.

'See, she has the right idea.'

Colette wrinkled her brow, confused that her mother would approve.

'Véronique's mother?'

'Who? No, that woman in the divine mink.'

A few cars ahead of their Simca, a woman dressed in a silver fur and feathered hat had pulled over to the side of the road. She had laid out a picnic rug beside her Peugeot Eclipse and was drinking champagne. Two young boys dressed in identical sailor-suits bickered and ate cake. Colette's mouth watered, even though the woman must be unbearably hot in the heavy coat. The roof of the car had been folded away, and cases and trunks teetered in a high stack. There was even a gramophone.

'What did you think you were doing suggesting we take that child?' Delphine demanded.

'I felt sorry for her mother. She looked exhausted, and the girl was so small to be walking so far. She couldn't have been more than three or four. Are you sure we couldn't have taken her?'

Delphine gave Colette a long look. 'We don't know them. You don't just offer to help strangers in the street.'

'Perhaps we should,' Colette muttered.

'Why are you so concerned about that child? Are you—' Delphine lowered her voice before continuing. 'Are you with child again?'

'No. I'm not.'

For the first time since giving birth, Colette had nothing to distract her from thoughts of the child she had given up. She didn't even know the sex. Was the baby a blond boy like Gunther, or a darker haired girl like Colette? Had he or she been adopted into a big family or were their new mother and father otherwise childless? Regardless, she was grateful someone had taken the baby she had not wanted. Her life was better for it and she hoped the child's life would be better too. At least in Britain the baby would be safer than in France. If Hitler ever reached the island that would change, but she could not think of that now.

'Do you ever wonder about the baby? Mine, I mean. Your grandchild.'

Delphine's head whipped round. 'I have no grandchild. You have no baby. Believe me, your life will be easier and happier without one, especially an illegitimate half-German brat. One day you will find a suitable husband and then perhaps you might have a child, though don't be too quick to do it. Babies are tedious.'

'Was I?' Colette asked.

Delphine reached out and stroked the side of Colette's face. It was such a tender gesture it took her by surprise.

'Of course not, darling. I made sure you were always dressed in lovely outfits to match mine, and you had the nicest bassinet. You looked beautiful. All my friends loved to watch you.'

Colette grimaced. She had always had the finest clothes but there hadn't been much affection. All her care had come from *Tante* Agnes or Edith.

'You make me sound like an ornament. An accessory.'

Delphine rolled her eyes. 'Your father works hard to earn the money we need to be happy and I work hard to make our lives beautiful with what he gives me. That includes his daughter. Oh, will I ever him again? Will I ever return to Paris? I need a cocktail. Why didn't I tell Fleur to pack something to drink? Boiled eggs and bottled peaches are all very well but I would rather she had made space for gin.'

Colette ground her teeth, though couldn't deny that listening to Delphine's complaints made her long for a drink herself. She couldn't think of anything to say that would not result in a fight so sank lower into her seat and stared at the road ahead. Her mother must have been less self-centred when she married her father because she could not imagine hard-working Louis choosing a wife like this.

It was little wonder Louis admired Fleur who seemed to have the sense the rest of his household lacked. The look of disappointment in his eyes when Colette had admitted her pregnancy was seared onto her mind. If she ever saw her father again, she would double her efforts to become someone he could be proud of.

But what if she never saw her father again? Her guts squirmed and tightened. She pressed her fist into her belly to stop them. They should have forced him into the car with them whether or not it meant the factory fell to the Germans.

Finally Fleur returned. Her dress was stained with sweat patches and her hair was coming out of its usually neat roll. She laid the bicycle on its side and sat beside it with her legs stretched out.

'Do we have any water?' she asked in a raspy voice.

'Only the milk,' Colette told her. She found the bottle and passed it to Fleur who took a sip and licked her lips.

'Drink it all, if you want,' Colette suggested but Fleur shook her head.

'We'll need it later. I passed through a village but the shops are all crowded and people are pushing to get in. By the time we get there the shelves will be empty.'

'What does the road look like?' Delphine asked. 'Are we going to be able to move soon?'

Fleur scraped back her hair with her fingers. 'It's at a standstill for miles. I can't see the end of the queue. Everybody has had the same thought. There are parents begging drivers to take their children. Old women lying by the roadside with handcarts or basket chairs. It's horrible.'

A gust of wind blew dust across the front of the car and from above came the sound of engines in the sky, then gunshots. Rapid punctuations of terror.

The three women shrieked, their voices joining the rising chorus of screams, and Colette seized Fleur's hand and pulled her into the passenger seat, cramming them both in together. Not far ahead, three German planes dived low across the road, releasing volleys of bullets before rising up again.

Colette gasped. 'They're firing on us!'

Fleur clutched her hand. 'Those *salauds*! On women and children! How could they? *Baise-les tous*.'

She let fly a further torrent of obscenities – some of which Colette hadn't even heard before – calling down hell on the pilots. Colette sat stunned into silence. To see Fleur lose her composure in such a way was the most startling part of the day. She began to sob; hot tears burning down her cheeks. She felt

Fleur's arms come about her and she wrapped hers around Fleur. Delphine joined in the embrace and the three women hugged each other and sobbed. For the first time that day Colette felt safe, huddling inside the car, while the world exploded ahead of them.

Whether they had run out of ammunition or merely decided the message had been sent, the planes left then. The women clambered out of the car. All around, others were doing similar, inspecting vehicles and each other. Hugging with relief. Weeping. The woman with the fur and convertible Peugeot Eclipse stood staring at her car.

'We shouldn't have put the roof down,' she wailed.

The sky was growing cloudy and the first hints of evening were starting to show in a subtle change of temperature and a haze on the horizon.

'I don't feel safe after the attack and we're getting nowhere. We should go back,' Fleur said.

'To Paris?'

'Yes. I am even if you aren't.' Fleur dragged her suitcase from the pile inside the car and fixed her hat back into place. She picked up the bicycle and cocked her head at Colette with her brows raised.

It was a tantalising proposition. To be home. To sleep in her own bed. Take a bath. Eat something besides stale bread rolls and boiled eggs. Colette's stomach growled and her mouth filled with bitter liquid. She spat onto the ground beside her, not caring how unladylike the gesture was.

'You're right. I'd rather die there than die by the side of the road. I'll come with you.'

'We can't possibly turn the car around,' Delphine said.

Colette lifted her chin. 'Then we'll walk.'

'But it will take all night,' Delphine moaned.

Colette shrugged. 'Then we had better start walking, Fleur,

will you help me pile as much onto the bicycle as possible? We can wheel it between us.'

The two women roped the cases together and balanced them between the saddle and handlebars. Colette looked at Delphine.

'*Mère*, are you coming?'

Delphine nodded. She picked up her remaining case and hatbox. She bit her lip. 'I don't know what your father will say when we tell him we have abandoned his car. He loves it so much.'

'I hope he loves us more and will understand,' Colette said archly.

'We can worry about that when we're home,' Fleur added.

~

The three women trudged back to the city, arriving long after night had fallen. The streets were silent and dark. The skeleton of a city with no flesh. No beating heart. Nevertheless, it was Paris, and it was home. Whatever happened next, Colette would rather be there than anywhere else in the world.

Chapter Nine

'They are staying in our hotel!'

Josette Lucienne sounded hysterical.

'They just came in and commandeered it. Every room! And they aren't paying either.'

The sound of her wailing had brought Fleur rushing from the dining room to the hallway. Colette stood in the doorway with a look of bewilderment on her face.

There was no need to ask who 'they' were. A glance at the calendar told her the date was June the twenty-third. It was hard to believe it was little over a week since Paris' remaining citizens awakened to the harsh, German-accented voice broadcast through loudspeakers on military lorries that crawled through the streets. The proclamation was seared on Fleur's memory.

The city was now under German control. A curfew would be in place from eight that night. There was to be no resistance. Citizens should stay in their homes.

Fleur and Colette had ventured out when the need for fresh food had made it necessary. Checkpoints had been set up in roads the women had previously crossed without a second thought and the sight of soldiers in German uniforms openly carrying weapons had made her want to run home and hide.

Sophie patted her sister's shoulder. '*Papa* is beside himself and *Maman* refuses to leave her room.'

'Coffee?' Fleur mouthed to Colette who nodded eagerly.

'We'll go into the garden.'

Fleur went into the kitchen and set the percolator on the stove alongside a pan of milk. She sat on a stool and listened to the comforting, ordinary sound of the water spurting and bubbling through the grounds inside the pot. She took a deep breath, savouring the aroma of brewing coffee and trying to concentrate on normal things. That way the constant feeling of sickness might eventually ebb.

Colette and Josette were sitting together on the patio when Fleur stepped outside with the coffee. Sophie was pacing up and down on the grass, smoking.

'Will you join us?' Colette asked.

Ordinarily, Fleur would have declined. She never felt she had much in common with Colette's wealthy and glamorous friends, but now she wanted to hear what Josette had to say. Any news about what was happening in the city was worth having. She fetched a fourth cup and Colette poured, adding only a splash of warm milk where once she would have mixed her coffee equally.

'They say there is going to be a shortage of coffee,' Josette said gloomily. 'I do hope not.'

'I am sure the Germans will ensure supplies still reach the city now they are here,' Colette said.

Fleur reached for the sugar spoon then tipped back half. It might be wise to try weaning herself off sweet coffee. 'Do you imagine that they will share their coffee with us? They fired on women and children who were trying to leave Paris. They will not give a damn about whether or not we have coffee. Or anything else.'

92

The other women blinked and Fleur was taken aback by her own vehemence. 'Perhaps you will be fortunate enough to still get it in the hotel,' she said in a calmer voice.

'Tell us about the hotel,' Colette prompted.

Josette's cup rattled as she placed it in the saucer. 'It isn't only ours. It's every hotel in the city. *Papa* had no choice. An officer appeared three days after the city fell and took *Papa* into the office.'

She squeezed her hands together, though they still shook.

Sophie took a drag on her cigarette and exhaled loudly. '*Maman* thought they were going to arrest him. He had said something loudly in the dining room a few weeks ago about still offering rooms to Jews. She thought someone might have informed the authorities. He came out and told us that the hotel has been requisitioned as accommodation for the army. They are in every bedroom, eating in the dining room, sitting in the salons. We cannot escape them.'

'Oh, I am so sorry,' Colette said. 'Would you like to come and stay with me for a while? I'm sure *Mère* could find you a room. She could turn over her salon perhaps. The chaise is very comfortable.'

Fleur grimaced. Delphine had not left her bed since they had arrived back after the long trek home from the aborted escape. It had placed an added burden on both girls.

Josette sniffed and sat up straighter. 'No, I shall make the best of things. In any case, some of them are quite polite. They keep asking Sophie and I where the best places are to go dancing, how to see the art in the Louvre, which is the best architecture.'

Fleur raised her brows. Being surrounded by Germans sounded terrible but entertaining them was apparently not too dreadful. 'You don't intend to take them anywhere, surely?'

'I don't know what would happen if we refused,' Josette said. Her mouth wobbled.

Sophie rolled her eyes impatiently. 'It would be foolish to anger them, and perhaps there will be benefits to having to associate with them. Who knows how long the situation might last? It might be for ever.'

'It won't be for ever,' Fleur said firmly. 'France will fight back.'

Sophie lit another cigarette. 'France will not fight back. Didn't you listen to Pétain on the radio? There will be no more fighting, not after the Armistice was signed yesterday. You can sneer all you like about not associating with the Germans, but they are in charge now. They control the food, the power supply, our every movement. Everything that makes life worth living. If the only way to get back some of what we have lost is to appear friendly, then that's what we'll have to do.'

'Don't take them anywhere we usually go, would you?' Colette said anxiously. 'I would hate to be surrounded by Germans when I'm trying to have a nice evening.'

'Don't worry, we won't take them anywhere too nice. Maybe to the *Chausson en Soie*. You'll come with us, won't you, to keep Josette company?'

The Silk Slipper was practically a bordello by all accounts and Josette looked as if she was either about to start wailing again or slap her sister. There was clear friction between the two sisters regarding the subject. It was odd that softer-looking Sophie, who was all curls and dimples like a matinee idol from a decade earlier, was expounding such hard opinions, while the more angular and severe-looking Josette was crumbling.

'I'm done with this, thank you,' Sophie said, holding out her cup and saucer to Fleur as if she was addressing a waiter in a café. Taken aback, Fleur accepted it and put it on the tray. There was a flicker of a smirk on Sophie's face.

'Let me help you,' Colette said, taking the cup from Josette, despite it being half full.

Fleur snatched the tray from her reach. 'I can manage.'

She walked to the kitchen, seething with humiliation at Sophie's rudeness. To take her mind off it she began making an inventory of all the food in the house, from dry goods to preserves. She discovered ten glass jars filled with a suspicious brown sludge, labelled in *Tante* Agnes' looping handwriting as courgette pickled in vinegar. She piled them in the back of the larder, considering how short of food they would have to get before she opened one. Maybe she would offer it to Sophie at lunch the next time the sisters came visiting Colette.

As Fleur thought back to happier times spent helping *Tante* Agnes make confitures and cakes, a burst of melancholy overwhelmed her and she swallowed a sob. Agnes always used the time to lecture Fleur on her manners, attitude, and appearance. She would have seen Fleur moping about Sophie's rudeness, laughingly snapped a dishcloth at her and reminded Fleur that she had not been raised to worry about what silly girls thought.

Fleur sighed. 'I miss you.'

Presently, she heard the front door close. A moment later there was a knock at the kitchen door and it opened a crack.

'May I come in?' Colette asked.

Fleur shrugged. 'It's your house, you can go where you wish.'

Colette seized her hands and her face twisted. 'I'm so sorry for what Sophie said. She was so rude to you! I have never heard her talk in such a way or say such things. It must be the tension of everything that has happened.'

Fleur made a non-committal noise. Josette had been polite, and she was living in the same hotel as Sophie.

Colette's brows creased. 'You'd like her really if you got to know her. She's fun.'

Fleur pictured Agnes' expression listening to the sisters' plans to go dancing with Germans. She would have had nothing but contempt for them and Fleur shouldn't either. She pulled her hands away. 'No, I don't think I would. I'm sorry, Colette, but your friends and my friends are very different.'

She sank onto a stool, a feeling of loneliness creeping over her.

'I need to go across the city,' she murmured. 'I don't know if the bookshop is open or closed, or if I'll have a job. I don't even know if my friends are still in Paris. Sébastien and Pierre talked about opposing the German army, but I can't believe they would have. I don't know how they could without risking arrest or being...' She broke off, remembering the sight and noise of the planes diving onto the exodus of women and children. The newspapers said that Paris had been taken without a shot being fired, but was that true or just what Germany wanted the world to believe?

'They sound brave,' Colette said. 'And I'm sure the shop will be safe. Who would destroy a bookshop?'

Fleur gazed at her, trying to hide her disbelief. Sometimes she wondered if Colette lived in the same world.

'The Nazis burned books in the streets. Of course they would destroy a bookshop. Besides, who would want to buy books at a time like this?'

Colette gestured to the table and the copy of *Regain* that Fleur was halfway through.

'The people who like dancing want to dance. The people who like reading will want to read.'

Fleur mustered a smile. 'I hope you're right.'

Colette looked at the table covered in tins and jars. 'Do you think we should hide some of these in the cellar? If there are going to be shortages it might be good to keep some things back.'

'I think so,' Fleur agreed. 'But not the cellar. Do you remember the old Secret Garden? There is a metal trunk in the attic that would be waterproof. It might be a struggle to get it through the door, but I would rather things were not in the house if possible. If we were to be visited by any authorities the cellar is the first place they would look.'

She was surprised by a hug from Colette. 'I adore how practical you are. I'm not sure I will fit through that gap now though.'

'I'll do it,' Fleur said. She smiled. 'Do you remember how we used to hide there from Edith and the grown-ups? Those summers were such fun. I didn't ever think things would change.'

A wistful expression crossed Colette's face. 'That's where I took Gunther…'

Her eyes grew blank as she became lost for a moment in private memories.

Fleur looked away, her cheeks growing hot. She could very well imagine what Colette and Gunther had got up to amid the rugs and cushions. She looked at the cupboard then pulled out a tin of coffee beans.

'We will definitely hide this.'

Colette nodded. 'And we certainly won't tell Sophie we have it. Let her beg her coffee from the Nazis. I would rather drink dishwater than do that!'

She came around the table to Fleur. Her blue eyes were wide, giving her a helpless look that made her resemble Delphine quite startlingly. 'I'm very glad you are here with me. I don't think I could bear this on my own.'

'Of course you could,' Fleur assured her.

Her vulnerability was moving, but also a little pathetic. Fleur hadn't appreciated how much strength Agnes' robust upbringing had given her. Seeing how the other women had responded to the situation made her more appreciative of her aunt than she had been when Agnes had lived. She would not fail her aunt's memory and vowed to herself that no matter what happened, she would never crumble and wail as Josette had, take to her bed like

Delphine, or belittle herself by partying with the enemy like Sophie.

~

'I have bad news,' Louis announced one hot August evening. 'The Ministry of Agriculture and Supply have announced the introduction of food rationing. Tomorrow we must all take our identity cards to be recorded and collect ration coupons.'

Fleur and Colette exchanged a triumphant glance. It had been worth an afternoon of sweat dragging the heavy trunk from the attic to the Secret Garden and filling it with bottled fruit.

'Can't you go for me?' Delphine asked.

'We all have to go in person,' Louis said. 'We leave the house promptly at eight tomorrow morning. Luckily, we do not have to walk far.'

Fleur dropped her head to avoid being caught in the look that Delphine and Colette exchanged. Louis had gone in search of his beloved car only to discover it was nowhere to be seen. He'd put a brave face on it and assured the women they had made the right decision but it must have hurt him.

~

Eight o'clock was not early enough. By mid-afternoon they were still queuing at the *mairie*. Squadrons in uniforms marched in perfect unison down the wide avenues. Their arms swung stiffly at identical angles, while the heavy black boots struck the road as one, creating a thunderclap each time. Seeing them intensified the tightness in Fleur's throat and chest. It didn't feel like she would ever breathe instinctively again. She shrank back as the unit approached and brushed up against Colette. They linked their fingers.

Despite their disturbing presence, the soldiers dressed in their heavy uniforms with high boots and stiff collars looked as if they were struggling in the stifling August heat. Dressed in a cool skirt and blouse, with a wide brimmed hat, Fleur felt quite smug.

'They do look uncomfortable, don't they?' she murmured to Colette.

Colette adjusted her hat brim to the side, better to keep the afternoon sun from burning her face. 'Good. I hope they get headaches and all vomit.'

'We should be in Deauville, drinking champagne, not standing in a line getting grit in our eyes.' Delphine sighed.

'Deauville is full of Germans too,' Colette snapped. 'It would be just as bad.'

Delphine narrowed her eyes. 'But cooler. I hope they all drop dead from heatstroke where they march.'

The woman in the line behind them, steel-grey hair in an immaculate chignon and lips painted scarlet nodded. 'So do I.'

As the squadron passed, the woman gave a carefree sigh and fanned herself idly with a magazine. Colette did the same. Delphine twirled the handle of her parasol and to Fleur's delight, all along the queue, women began to demonstrate how little the heat was seemingly affecting them.

There was no way of telling whether the soldiers were aware of the tiny act of defiance that they were marching past, but it filled Fleur with a glee that sustained her until she reached the front of the line and was issued with coupons detailing the items they could be exchanged for and the days they could be used. The family eyed them dismally.

'We'll be queuing a lot more,' Colette said.

'We'll take turns,' Fleur answered. She looked back along the line that still snaked around the corner. 'I am going to the bookshop. I should have gone weeks ago.'

'Will you be safe?' Colette asked.

The back of Fleur's neck and her armpits grew even stickier. If she didn't do this now, she doubted she ever would.

'Of course. This is my city. I will be back long before curfew and won't let the Germans scare me.'

Before she could change her mind, she walked off in the direction of Montparnasse.

Chapter Ten

Fleur's confidence began to ebb as she walked along Avenue Foch. The wide street was lined with palatial homes and Fleur had always enjoyed dreaming which she would choose if she became rich. Now it was full of soldiers and military vehicles stood in the driveways. She took the Metro but the carriage was full of Germans and she got off after three stops, preferring to face the rest of the journey on foot.

The centre of the city was markedly different to the streets near home. There was a much higher German presence, not simply marching on parade, but walking the streets, sitting outside cafés, passing the time of day under the shade of trees. The occupying army nonchalantly behaving as if their presence was perfectly normal brought her close to tears but even worse was the sight of the swastika flags hanging proudly from the *Arc de Triomphe*. The stark black symbol against the red and white was a blood-chilling proclamation of power and for ages Fleur could only stand and stare at the flags as her limbs turned to ice. She half expected to discover Hitler had given orders to scale the *Tour Eiffel* and fly one from the top in celebration of his victory. The thought made her feel sick and she walked through the streets with her head down, avoiding eye contact.

The blinds of the bookshop windows were down when she arrived and she feared for Monsieur Ramper, but then the blind tweaked aside, and his face appeared briefly. She heard the drawing of bolts and then the door opened, and she was pulled inside. They embraced and Monsieur Ramper led her into the cosy office behind the shop

'It has been a terrible few weeks.' He sighed, wiping his forehead with a handkerchief. 'I have sold barely anything. The Germans do not want my books or *bandes dessinées*, and the French have more important things to spend money on. I am sorry but I can only offer you two days' work every week.'

It was a significant drop in income. Already the cost of food had risen, and she expected it to rise further now that rationing had been introduced. Her wages were necessary, though she would at least be able to earn her keep at the Nadons' house.

'At least I will have time to queue for the shops now,' she said, trying not to show her panic.

Monsieur Ramper patted her hand. 'You are a good girl, my dear. If things change, I will do what I can.'

She shook his hand then made her way to the café. Unlike the bookshop, the cafés and restaurants didn't seem to be lacking in German patrons. Fleur's knees trembled. She couldn't bear the thought of seeing Café Morlaix occupied. She took a series of deep breaths before she dared to turn the corner onto the street where it stood.

The café, like the others in the square, was open, with tables set under the shade of trees. At the tables outside were three groups, totalling ten Germans altogether. She grew cold, while simultaneously feeling hot perspiration beneath her arms. She couldn't pass them so closely and risk their scrutiny.

She turned away but caught herself and bunched her fists. This was her city, not theirs. Unless she was going to spend the rest of her life hiding inside the house she would have to interact with the enemy at some point, so it might as well be now. She clutched her bag a little tighter, took a deep breath and walked towards the door.

'*Fräulein*, stop.'

The speaker sat beside the door. She turned her head towards him slowly, feeling the terror rising to her throat and met sharp eyes of ice blue in a face creased with lines. He was solidly built and his legs were outstretched slightly in front of the doorway, presumably intentionally. His uniform bore an insignia but Fleur had no idea what it meant, or how senior he was. It occurred to her dismally that she would no doubt become familiar with them before too long.

'What are you doing here?' he asked. He spoke the French words accurately, but his accent was thick, and the words rolled around his mouth, making it hard to understand them.

'I am looking for a friend.'

'A particular friend or can anyone be your friend?'

His tone became hopeful, and Fleur suppressed a weary sigh. He wasn't going to question her, only flirt. She had been propositioned before, though never by a German.

'A friend I have not seen since…'

Since your army invaded my city.

She wanted to spit the words at him but held back, knowing how unwise it would be. The question had given her time to consider her answer, however. Perhaps mentioning she had a personal connection to the café was unwise.

'She's called Colette. I don't know if she is still in Paris, so I am asking in a few of the places we used to meet. Is there a reason I cannot go into the café?'

'No reason. Show me your papers.' Now he had realised he was not going to get lucky, the officer's voice became hard. When

Fleur didn't obey instantly he thrust his hand out. 'Your identity papers, *Fräulein*.'

Fleur took her card out of her bag and handed it over, trying to keep her hand from shaking. She had nothing to be afraid of. She had never done anything wrong.

The officer inspected the card in agonising detail, and Fleur's anxiety began to transform into something else; something rebellious. Everything was in order. The paper was neatly folded in her bag as always and was in perfect condition. He was enjoying the power he had over her and the knowledge that she had no choice but to comply. She felt acid curdle in her stomach. He was just a bully intimidating a girl half his age.

This was what occupation would be like. Feeling terrified for even existing in her own country.

'Very good. You may enter.'

He passed the papers back to her. Fleur gave him the quickest of glances, not enough to appear confrontational but enough that her dignity was intact.

'Thank you, monsieur.'

'Thank you, *Offizier-Anwärter Durlich*!' he snapped.

Fleur repeated his name and title obediently, stumbling slightly over the unfamiliar syllables. He waved his hand again and she walked inside.

The café was dark and stuffy, and as a result it was deserted. She wanted to weep at the comforting familiarity. Sébastien appeared from the room behind the bar and Fleur ran and threw her arms around him. He gathered her into a hug. She closed her eyes and leaned against his chest.

Wonderful, strong, safe, Sébastien.

'Let me get you a glass of beer. Take a seat.'

Fleur pulled out a chair well away from the door. She unpinned her hat and used it to fan the back of her neck where loose tendrils of hair clung to the skin uncomfortably. When

Sébastien brought the beer, she drank half in one go, then held onto the glass. It was cool and the condensation on the outside felt refreshingly clean on her grimy fingertips.

'Did the officer outside bother you? I've seen him visiting different cafés in the area and he likes to throw his weight around.'

'Not really. I think he just wanted to scare me.'

'Did he?'

She thought. 'Yes. But now I'm more angry than scared. If he wanted me to cry it didn't work.'

Sébastien leaned his elbows on the table. 'When you didn't come before I hoped you had managed to escape.'

'We tried but had to turn back.'

Fleur poured out everything that had happened since they had last met while Sébastien listened without speaking. As she described the death of Agnes, he covered her hand and a sob choked her momentarily. She described the aborted flight from Paris and the return, Sophie's rudeness and her conversation with Monsieur Ramper.

Sébastien took off his glasses and wiped them on his apron, peering at her closely.

'It sounds like your friend Colette is learning some courage if she defied her mother to come back with you. It's good that you have a friend.'

'Speaking of friends, do you know if anyone else is still in Paris?'

'Odile left on a train the day the government declared Paris an open city. She said she was going home to Dijon. I haven't heard from her. Daniel is now working in the hospital despite not being qualified. I have only seen him once. As for the other regular customers, few are left. Who wants to drink in a café alongside Germans?'

Fleur glared in the direction of the door. 'I hate them. I thought that seeing tanks and flags would be the worst part, but they are behaving as if they own the city.'

'They do,' Sébastien said quietly.

He sounded resigned, but as their eyes met, Fleur saw anger magnified by the thick lenses of his glasses. Fleur leaned back on her stool and stared at the ceiling, watching the blades of the fan lazily rotate. It brought to mind the propellors on the planes that had gunned down the women and children. Her stomach swam with nausea. She slid her glass across the table to Sébastien.

'I must go. I told the *Offizier-Anwärter* that I was looking in different cafés for my friend. If I stay here too long, he may get suspicious.' She shivered and hugged herself tightly. 'I hate this. I feel as if I should look over my shoulder all the time but if I did it would look suspicious. I don't know whether I should ignore the Germans or smile at them. Neither is good. If I had a knife, I fear I would stab as many as I could before someone took it away.'

'This is the first time you have been out and really seen what Paris is like now, isn't it? I can tell. It gets easier, though not any more palatable.'

He patted her hand. 'I wonder...'

A pair of German soldiers came in through the front door, blinking as their eyes adjusted to the gloominess and he stopped mid-sentence.

'Take a seat outside, *mes messieurs*, and I will be with you as soon as I have finished with this customer,' Sébastien called. The men backed out, chatting to each other. As soon as they left, he leaned close to Fleur.

'Many of us don't like what is happening in the city and want to protest against it.'

'How? In the streets?'

'No. Nobody will rise up because everyone thinks they are alone so we want to show people that they are not. You have a good way with words. Would you help us create posters and leaflets, or a newspaper, as we talked of before?'

Fleur dropped her head. Before it had seemed fun but if they were discovered the consequences would be imprisonment or execution.

'I'll think about it.'

'Do. We can use the wine cellar.' Sébastien fetched a paper serviette and scribbled on it. 'Here is the number for the café. I am here until curfew every night and if I have gone then my cousin will take a message. If you need anything you can ask, and if you want to be a part of what we are doing, let me know.'

~

When she got home Fleur found Colette in a state of excitement, standing in front of a display of hats and scarves laid out across the dining table. She ran across the room and pulled Fleur into the centre.

'I've been waiting for you to come home. *Mère* and I have been talking. It was wonderful to see so many women showing defiance this afternoon, wasn't it?'

Despite her weariness, Fleur smiled at the memory.

'We are going to do it again,' Delphine said, walking into the room. She was dressed in a sunflower yellow, floor length evening gown that was at least ten years out of fashion but fitted her voluptuous figure perfectly. Louis arrived home at that moment, raised his brows at the sight of his wife, and listened while Delphine explained again.

'We will not be cowed when we wait in line. We will dress in our best and brightest clothes to show them that Parisiennes are not scared of them. Let them keep their grey and green. We will have every other colour in the rainbow.'

She raised her cocktail glass then wobbled upstairs to her bedroom.

'Is she really going shopping in that?' Fleur asked Colette. She was exhausted from the walk and the horrible feeling of being watched. It didn't seem like bravery, more like stupidity.

'Probably not that exact gown, but I'm sure she will wear something striking.' Colette began to gather the scarves. She gave Louis a worried look. '*Papa*, do you think we are being foolish? You didn't say anything.'

'I haven't seen your mother this happy for such a long time. I didn't want to spoil her fun. Evening gowns won't bring down an army, but if it makes her feel more confident what harm could it do?'

Colette left, bearing her accessories, and Fleur looked down at her dress. It was old and slightly ill-fitting. After the long walk to and from Montparnasse it bore perspiration marks and dirt. She straightened her belt and caught Louis looking at her.

'Fleur, you are the most sensible member of this household by some degree.' He lit a cigar. 'We have not talked properly about your situation since the death of your aunt.'

Fleur's stomach twisted into knots. Before he could tell her she would have to leave, she began speaking.

'Monsieur Ramper has had to reduce my days. I can work for you, if you will let me keep living here.'

Louis smiled. 'I will do better than that. I will pay you what I paid your aunt. If you are willing to combine your ration coupons with the rest of the family and take over the duties Agnes used to do, you will have wages and a home under my roof for as long as you choose.'

Fleur didn't anticipate the weight his words lifted from her shoulders. A sob of relief welled up and she covered her eyes to hide her tears.

'I'm sorry, I know you have more ambition than to be a

housekeeper,' Louis said.

Fleur sniffed and wiped her eyes. She managed a faint smile. 'I'm very grateful, truly, Monsieur Nadon. It is more than I hoped for.'

'Life is going to get hard, Fleur. Not everyone is strong enough to bear that and war changes people. Some for the worst, and some for the better. I believe you are one of the strong ones.' He picked up a scarf that Colette had overlooked, running his fingers through the long fringe. 'I have not told my wife or daughter yet, but my factory is being requisitioned and turned over to the manufacture of parts for the use of the German army. I will actively be aiding our oppressors.'

'I'm sorry,' Fleur said.

He waved his hand to dismiss her words, but his eyes were bleak. 'It is hard to stomach but it was inevitable as soon as our government abandoned us. I hope France will prevail, and this will not last for ever. Will you leave me alone now, *ma petite*? It has been a long day for me, and I will be working late.'

Fleur went upstairs. She hung the scarf over Colette's door handle and her brow furrowed. She had seen the expression on Monsieur Nadon's face and caught the upwards glance as he had spoken of strength and changes.

Monsieur Nadon had confided in Fleur before his wife and daughter. She stared at herself in the mirror, cheeks flushing with pride.

You are one of the strong ones.

She was determined to prove him right.

~

The following afternoon she snuck to the concierge's office, which had been empty since Michal had vanished, and called the café. Sébastien answered.

Fleur licked her lips. Her throat was dry but what she was about to say was important.

'Yes. I want to be involved. I want to play my part.'

~

'What are you going to print?' Fleur asked.

It was the first day of September and she was sitting on an upturned barrel in the cellar of the café, along with Sébastien and Pierre.

'A guide to living in Paris under the Germans,' Pierre said.

'We know how to live,' Fleur interrupted. 'Keeping our heads down and queuing with a constant sense of fear.'

Pierre folded his arms. 'And we shouldn't. Yes, we are living under occupation, but that doesn't mean we have been defeated. I propose a list of suggestions to help Paris rebel in small ways. Things to raise morale.'

They all drank silently, thinking.

'Pretend you don't know where they are looking for if a German ask for directions,' Sébastien offered after a minute or two.

Fleur grinned. 'Or send them in the opposite direction.'

Pierre laughed. 'Excellent. It takes a woman to be vindictive.'

Fleur thought back to the conversation between Colette and the sisters from the hotel. Sophie thought that flirting and being accommodating would be the safest way to behave.

'We should pretend we do not see them. Greet their overtures of friendship with faces of stone.'

Sébastien noted it. 'Water their beer down. They complain that our beer is not like it is at home but drink it anyway. They would never realise.'

By the end of the night they had produced a list of small rebellions or irritations. Nothing that could be seen as outright resistance but enough that anybody following the list would feel a small sense of defiance inside themselves.

'Tomorrow I will set the type and next week we will print them,' Pierre announced.

They clinked glasses and Fleur felt an elation she hadn't for longer than she could remember.

∼

A week later, Fleur left the bookshop an hour before curfew with a sheaf of leaflets tucked between the pages of some old *bandes dessinées*. She walked slowly through the winding alleys, past cafés and nightclubs that were preparing to close. When she was certain no one would see, she slipped a leaflet into letterboxes, vestibules and under doors. Sébastien and Pierre would be doing the same thing in other directions.

They were not alone in this. Walls across the city had become covered in graffiti and posters denouncing the Occupation, and when tobacco was rationed in late September, there was barely a wall that did not have an angry slogan painted across it.

'It is infuriating that our message is being lost,' Pierre ranted, when he discovered in December that a four-page newspaper, named *Resistance*, was being circulated. 'Who will read our words if there are so many others surrounding them?'

Fleur suppressed a sigh at his vanity.

'Surely as long as the message is out there it doesn't matter who the author is?' she asked. Seeing his face, she quickly added, 'Your writing is so eloquent it will stand out.'

Pierre adjusted his cuffs, preening slightly. 'I know that.'

She left him to his vanity. It gave Fleur a sense of satisfaction to know that among the posters denouncing the Occupation, a few of her own words bore witness to the fact that not everyone in Paris had given up hope.

Chapter Eleven

November 1940

The weather was impossibly cold; worse than any winter Colette could recall.

'It feels like the weather is on the side of the Nazis,' she muttered through chattering teeth as she and Fleur joined yet another early morning line for bread in dense, freezing fog, her breath visible in the air. 'I hope the line moves quickly today.'

It wouldn't.

Everything took longer these days. To Colette's amazement, the initial shock of occupation had been replaced by resignation and even irritation. Producing papers on demand at checkpoints with fingers stiff from cold. Queuing daily for food only to discover the ingredients for particular meals were not available.

'At least by spring the cold will be gone, even if *they* aren't,' Fleur muttered, eying the passing detachment coldly.

The soldiers glanced across then walked on, pulling the collars of their heavy greatcoats a little higher to ward off the bitter winds.

The woman behind them leaned round to talk to the one in front. 'Did you see the woman from number seventy-three? She has new stockings, and we all know she didn't pay for them herself,' she said in a mock whisper.

Colette suppressed a sigh. The hours of queuing meant the women had nothing to do but chat and when it didn't turn to mean-spirited gossip it was talk of where it was possible to obtain rationed goods on the newly formed *marché noir*, and which *trafiquants* exacted the least extortionate price for goods.

As she walked home with Fleur after the long morning, she was still thinking about the unspoken accusation.

'Do you think they were talking about the *marché noir*, or suggesting the woman was sleeping with a German?'

Fleur looked sceptical. 'No one would sleep with the enemy just for stockings, would they?'

'Maybe if they were very good nylon or silk,' Colette said, giving a laugh.

'Talking of which, I need to spend tonight darning and mending. Would you like to come join me and listen to the radio?' Fleur asked.

'I can't,' Colette answered. 'I'm going to see Josette.'

Fleur narrowed her eyes. 'Has she started going to the clubs with Sophie? Will you go too?'

'She goes, but I won't,' Colette answered. After her initial horror, Josette had resigned herself to sharing a roof with Germans. Her descriptions of evenings spent listening to music and talking to the soldiers staying at the hotel were hard to resist. Though so far Colette had managed, her resolve was weakening more and more over the dark, rainy months.

'I'm just going to the hotel. I haven't been since it was occupied so I'm a little nervous.'

'Then don't go.' Fleur still looked disapproving but Colette ignored her. She missed their friendship.

~

That night she nervously entered the hotel and was relieved to see Josette was waiting at the reception desk. As they walked through the foyer to the staircase, she tried not to stare too openly at the soldiers who relaxed in the salon and dining room. Some played cards. Some read. One was playing the piano and another was singing.

'They look like normal men,' she remarked.

'They are. They are away from home, some for the first time, and they know no one wants them here. I think some of them are quite lonely.'

'I can understand that,' Colette said thoughtfully. She'd felt lost in England when she had arrived, despite being welcomed by Edith who she already knew.

A young man caught Josette's eye and waved.

'That's Franz. Before the war he used to give tennis lessons.'

She waved back. Franz blushed to the roots of his ash-blonde hair. He had a sweet smile that looked out of place on someone who was currently oppressing an entire country. Colette tried to imagine him goose-stepping past the morning queues at the *boulangerie* but couldn't. Holding a tennis racket, yes, but a rifle, not at all.

'He promises that if he is still stationed here next spring, he will play doubles with Sophie and I.'

'Next year! But surely the war will be over by then,' Colette said. She'd been wondering whether she could be invited to play tennis, but the prediction brought her crashing down with a thud.

'I don't know if the war is going to end that soon but until it does, I'm going to make the best of it,' Josette said, gathering Colette's arm in hers and leading her upstairs.

Sophie was delighted to see Colette. 'I've missed you! You haven't come dancing with me for so long. Say you will come.

They still serve champagne but who knows for how long. Everything feels so much faster paced because most people must be home before the curfew at nine.'

'Perhaps,' Colette said.

Most people.

She narrowed her eyes. That suggested not everyone and she wondered who was exempt and why.

In the warmth of Sophie's greeting it was hard not to be charmed and the thought of cold champagne was tempting. Colette missed dancing. Her evenings now consisted of listening to the radio then watching Delphine mix cocktails while Louis pored over his newspapers. Colette read Louis' newspapers avidly now, from cover to cover. She could name people and places she had never heard of until recently. Thanks to her time in England, she was also able to translate the BBC radio broadcasts for the family. It felt good to be useful, but it was dull.

'You don't sound convinced.'

'The Metro always seems to be delayed nowadays. What if we can't get home again and we're arrested?'

'Don't be a mouse. No one is going to arrest us if the Metro is at fault.' Sophie lit a cigarette and took a long drag. The rationing had not affected her supply, it appeared. Colette darkly wondered what the women in the food queues would have to say about it. 'Some of the senior officers here have a car so we never have to use the Metro, and of course we never get stopped. Did Josette tell you we have some officers now? It's so much nicer. If you come with us next Saturday night, then you will only have to do one station on the Metro from here and then walk home.'

'I'm not sure. I could ask Fleur to come with us,' Colette suggested.

Sophie pursed her lips.

'I don't think that's a good idea. She would disapprove and ruin the fun.'

Colette bit her tongue. Fleur would have every reason to be disapproving. The word *collaborator*, flashed through her mind. An ugly word and an ugly act. But just dancing wasn't actually collaborating, was it? They weren't actually helping the Germans against the French.

'You could ask Fleur if you must,' Josette said, perhaps thinking this was the reason for Colette's hesitation. 'Though she hardly fits in with the crowd at Cabaret des Papillons with her sensible clothes and dull hairstyle. She's probably never even danced with a man, let alone kissed one.'

Colette wasn't so sure. Fleur had male friends and spoke of them in glowing terms. They sounded dull – more interested in poetry and ideas than dancing or fun – but in truth Colette was a little envious. She wondered whether Fleur was in love with either – or both – of them and if she had kissed them. That longing for physical contact hit her like a bolt through her heart and sent ripples flooding down to her groin.

Sophie stretched and gave a bored yawn. 'You don't have to come but really, it is silly not to join in. If the men are happy, they are less likely to complain that the sheets are old, or the coffee is weak. We are stuck with them as guests, so it makes sense to get something out of it for ourselves.'

It was hard-nosed, but Colette saw the logic. Why antagonise the guests in the hotel when they all had to live there? As if to demonstrate the advantages, Josette offered Colette a piece of chocolate. She hesitated before taking it, feeling that by accepting, she was somehow on the first step to collaborating. The small brown square was too tempting though and she slid it into her mouth, letting it melt on her tongue. Her tastebuds sputtered into life, causing her to shiver. Never mind kissing, this was what she had missed!

'I understand it if you are too scared to come, of course,' Josette said kindly. 'They have captured our city after all.'

'I'm not scared of them.' Colette flushed. She was though and it seemed perfectly understandable when they marched in columns with weapons. She thought of the men in the salon downstairs. They hadn't had guns. There would most likely not be any in the cabarets either. 'Alright, I'll come to show them – and you – that they can't frighten me, but I'm not going to dance with any Germans.'

'Fine, you can sit and watch while I do,' Sophie retorted. 'And don't mention it to Fleur.'

Colette wouldn't. Quite rightly, Fleur would be horrified, and Colette didn't think it would take much to dissuade her from going. And she really didn't want to be dissuaded.

∼

When it came to Saturday evening, Fleur was out anyway and Delphine barely seemed interested that Colette was going out. She waved a hand from her salon and carried on talking with Madames Brassai and Delonge. Louis had gone out to a café with friends.

It was disturbingly normal to be entering the *Cabaret des Papillons* again. Despite her previous request that Sophie kept the Germans away from the places they had always gone, she was glad now to be on familiar ground. She knew where the bathrooms were in case she needed a few minutes of solitude. Knew where the exit was in case…

She wasn't sure in case of what, but it was good to know.

The table the women usually sat at was already taken, but the three officers who accompanied Colette, Josette, and Sophie presumably pulled rank, because the other group stood smartly to attention, saluted, and vacated it.

'See, there are advantages.' Josette laughed.

Colette did not answer. She perched uneasily on the edge of

the velvet-covered chair. Everything felt wrong about what she was doing. Her parents would be appalled to know where she was. She found herself wishing they had queried where she was going and stopped her, but of course they had been too busy with their own concerns.

Uneasily, she accepted a glass of champagne. The atmosphere was disconcertingly as gleeful as it always had been. The rhythm of the music was fast and familiar, but the lyrics sung by the ice-blonde woman on the stage were in German and Colette didn't recognise the song. Of course it made sense that Germany would bring its own culture and entertainers but a sour taste filled her mouth. It was another sign that the occupiers had made Paris their own.

She took a small sip of champagne, half expecting it to taste sour thanks to the feeling of guilt, but it was as refreshing as always, the initial sharp bite preceding the fizzing sensation that made her feel more alert. She stared around. Couples danced. Groups laughed and drank. She could fool herself that this was just a normal evening out and these were men who played tennis, and missed their families, and hadn't been responsible for the deaths of French citizens. They weren't Hitler; just men following orders and doing their jobs. It made her feel a little better to believe that, as long as she didn't think about it too hard.

Some of the clientele had subtly changed, as well as more obviously. There were women wearing bright-coloured lipstick and garish dresses that left very little to the imagination.

'Prostitutes,' Sophie whispered in her ear. 'Some of them aren't even bothering to hide it. They're completely shameless. At least in the old days they used to be more subtle about touting for business.'

'Would you like some more champagne?' Kurt, the officer sitting opposite Colette extended the bottle.

'No, thank you.' Colette put her hand over the top of her glass before he could refill it.

'Are you already drunk?' Sophie whispered.

'If we accept this, then how does that make us different from them?' Colette nodded in the direction of the women parading round the room who would be earning their fee on their backs later.

'You don't have to make love with Kurt. Unless you want to, of course.' Sophie raised her eyebrows, an unpleasant smirk on her face.

Colette bit her lip. 'It just feels wrong to be accepting something from them. Is Victorine here tonight? What would she say?'

'The Nazis would not approve of us dancing together.' Sophie's eyes dropped and for a moment Colette caught a glimpse of real distress. 'I don't know where she is. I haven't seen her for weeks.'

'Sophie, I'm sorry.' Colette's heart swelled with pity. She put a hand on Sophie's arm.

Sophie shook it off and her ruby mouth trembled a little.

'Please, just come and dance with us, Colette, and forget about your conscience. I just want things to be as normal as possible. This is the only place I can pretend it is.'

'Alright, but only one dance.'

She smiled at Kurt and let him lead her to the dance floor. He was quite a good dancer and laughed when Colette told him so.

'Does that surprise you, Fräulein Nadon?'

'A little,' Colette admitted. 'I imagined you would dance the way you march. So stiff and correct.'

He laughed again and stepped into the crush of bodies, taking her into a spin. For a while Colette was able to close her eyes and forget reality, understanding more clearly why Sophie craved this feeling so much. When the song ended, and flowed into another more plaintive piece, a cheer went up around the room, followed by a sentimental sigh.

'She is singing about the Motherland,' Kurt explained. 'The words are very beautiful and it makes us feel sad in our hearts. I hope to get home leave but I don't know if that will happen.'

'Perhaps you should all go home,' Colette said daringly. A thrill raced through her that she was openly telling a German soldier he should not be here. Wait until she told Sophie and Josette, then who would call her scared!

His face froze and then he laughed. 'Very funny, Fräulein Nadon, but we both know that will not happen. But see, life is as it always was for you.'

He slipped his arms a little tighter around Colette. Her flesh crawled, but at the same time parts of her body responded to being held. His cologne was fresh and spicy and his frame was broad and strong. He might have made a good lover had they had met in other circumstances, but she would rather remain untouched for the rest of her life than do that. A dance was as far as she was prepared to go.

~

She was silent on the way home as they sat in the black sedan. The men talked in their own language and Sophie dutifully laughed when they did. Her eyes sparkled but Colette had seen behind the mask now. This gaiety was an act and knowing so made her feel a little better.

'Will you come again?' Josette asked. 'It wasn't too bad, was it?'

'I'll think about it,' Colette promised.

~

February 1941

Colette did return, of course. In secret, and no more than once a month, throughout the long, cold winter. She was drawn back to the Luciennes' hotel where fuel was never in short supply and it was always warmer than at home. Back to the clubs where the sisters and men were happy to see her, and the dancing helped her pretend everything was normal. Sophie had been right about that. She kept firm to her resolve to dance with the men, but never to kiss a single German. She could bury her conscience while she danced, but it was in a shallow grave and one she feared could be unearthed at any time.

~

The detachment at the hotel left in February and was replaced by another. There would be no tennis with Franz after all and Colette was surprised at how sad she felt at familiar faces going.

Her monthly cramps had started and she approached the first evening in the company of the new guests with less excitement than usual. An hour later she gave the excuse of a headache and left, saying she would make her own way home from Montmartre.

She emerged from the Metro station into darkness. Streetlamps were extinguished as soon as dusk fell and the sliver of waning moon barely gave enough light to see by. Colette had to concentrate on putting one foot before the other so as not to slip on patches of ice.

She only noticed the presence of the man when he came along side her.

'*Fraülein*, I beg a moment of your time?'

His breath hung in the frosty air, and he smiled at her. The hair at the back of Colette's neck rose. If she had been among a crowd, she might have been brave enough to ignore him, however, as she was on her own, it seemed both rude and dangerous.

'I would like to go for a drink but I must have got off the Metro at a wrong stop to the one I should.'

He waved a pamphlet in front of her. Colette recognised it as a guide to the city for soldiers who were stationed elsewhere and spending their leave there. She noticed with disgust that he had folded it open at a page listing the brothels that were exclusively reserved for German clients.

'I'm sorry, I can't help you.'

He looked her up and down then gestured to her with the pamphlet.

'You are *Strichmädchen*? Yes?'

'No!' Colette's cheeks blazed. He thought she was a prostitute.

'You live close? Perhaps you would join me for a drink? I pay well.'

'No, thank you. I have to get home before curfew,' Colette said firmly.

She turned away and began to walk down the street. The man followed alongside her and caught her arm.

'Why are you so cold? If you come for a drink, I could arrange a special dispensation for you. Isn't Paris the city of love?'

'Not for me.'

Colette pulled her arm away and tucked her bag under her shoulder. By now she was having to fight down the rising sense of panic in her chest. The further she walked away from the Metro, the emptier the streets became. She was torn between wanting to get to the safety of home and not wanting him to discover where she lived. There were always rumours about homes being raided on some spurious pretext thanks to spiteful neighbours informing, or a family coming to the notice of the authorities.

'I am home now,' she said, putting her hand on the first gate she came to. 'Goodnight.'

She closed the gate behind her and walked up the path, rummaging in her bag in pretence of looking for her key. If he followed, she was not sure what she would do other than scream and hope the real residents came out to help. Fortunately, she heard his footsteps moving away.

She waited a few minutes, crouching behind a fir tree in a pot, before exiting cautiously onto the street and turning down a quiet passage, which brought her out beside one entrance to the Bois du Boulogne gardens. To her dismay, she saw another woman being followed by the same German. From the way she held herself stiffly, arms wrapped about the bag she clutched to her chest, it did not look as if she was happy about it.

They had stopped beside some steps that led down to one of the fountains in a quiet part of the ornamental gardens. In summer it would be the perfect place to meet a lover, but now it was remote and dangerous.

'I said no. I'm not interested.'

Colette froze as she recognised the voice. The woman was Fleur.

'But I am. Come here.' The German pulled Fleur towards him and planted a kiss on her lips. She gave a squeak and pushed him away.

Colette tensed. There was a chance that if Fleur kissed him properly, he would go away, but Colette knew deep down he wasn't planning to stop at a kiss. She wished she had just gone to the bar with him. She was much more experienced than Fleur was. She stalked towards them.

'Leave her alone.'

Her voice made the German pause.

'Colette!' Fleur sounded relieved.

'Go away unless you're going to join us,' the German snapped.

'If you hurt my friend I'll report you,' Colette said. She walked closer, heels tapping on the paving stones, and stopped a short distance away, cursing inwardly that Fleur had used her name.

The German gave a dismissive laugh. 'I'm leaving the city in the morning. Who will you report me to, and if you did, who would they believe? Me or a couple of French whores?'

He turned back to Fleur and took her roughly by the shoulders. She shoved him away hard, both hands in the centre of his chest. He staggered back with a cry of fury and raised a fist, ready to come back with a punch. Without stopping to think, Colette ran forwards, swinging her gas mask case at him from behind. It struck him on the base of his skull. He jerked his head round, already off balance from the shove and his foot twisted on the icy step. He plummeted backwards down the steps and landed with a sickening cracking sound at the bottom. He gave one whimper, then grew silent.

Fleur gasped. 'You hit him!'

'You pushed him.' Colette's knees buckled and she dropped to the ground. 'Why isn't he moving?'

Fleur dragged her eyes from the supine body at the bottom of the steps. 'I think he's dead.'

Chapter Twelve

Colette stood frozen, sick with horror. She couldn't look at Fleur. Could only look at the body lying at the bottom of the steps. Her gas mask case was swinging back and forth. She stilled it with her hand and felt wetness on the edge; lifted her fingers and in the moonlight saw a dark smear that could only be blood.

'I didn't … I mean…' She looked at Fleur. 'I thought he was going to rape you. I couldn't let that happen.'

'What are we going to do?' Fleur began to tremble. Her face was twisted in shock.

Colette put an arm around her. She was trembling too.

'We need to go get help,' Colette whispered.

'For him? He's dead. Besides, if we tell anyone what happened they'll shoot us,'

'But it was an accident,' Colette said. 'I didn't think it would hurt him so badly. I just wanted him to stop.'

Fleur gulped a sob. 'They won't care. We've killed a German soldier. I need to think.'

She began to pace backwards and forwards, muttering under her breath.

'Sébastien,' she said eventually. 'We need to find a telephone quickly. Come on. I know where we can go.'

Colette hesitated. 'But we can't leave him here.'

Fleur looked both ways down the road. 'We can't take him with us! It's nearly deserted. If we are quick, it won't matter if we leave him for a few moments.'

She took Colette's hand and led her back the way they had come. Halfway to the Metro station they turned into a quiet street off the boulevard and stopped beneath an arched doorway. Fleur knocked quietly but repeatedly on the door of a concierge's *loge*. It was opened by an old woman dressed in black. She blinked at the visitors.

'Fleur Bonnivard?'

'Did I wake you, Madame Farrier? I'm sorry.'

'No, no. I was just resting my eyes a moment. Is something wrong?'

Fleur pulled a contrite face. 'Not very. May I use your telephone please? I left my favourite scarf at the Café Morlaix and only realised when I got off the Metro, but I won't make it home in time to telephone from there.'

Colette bit the inside of her lip. It was startling to see Fleur lying in such a cool manner.

'Young people are so careless! Can't it wait?' Madame Farrier grumbled. She pulled her cardigan around herself.

'I won't get the chance to go back until next week and I would hate for someone else to claim it. It's one Colette gave me and is made by Hermès.'

'Very well, come in. If only to keep out the cold air.' Madame Farrier stepped back, admitting them into a cluttered room.

'You still have that scarf?' Colette whispered. She remembered the scarf and the night she had gifted it. The party where she had first made love with Gunther.

'It is far too nice to throw out, and of course; it was a gift from my friend.'

Colette had never been inside the *loge* at her apartment block and was astonished by the cramped room. It was an office, bedroom, living room, and kitchen in one. The telephone was mounted on the wall beside the door above a table with notepads and pens so the concierge could take down messages for the apartment residents.

'Distract her while I make my call,' Fleur whispered to Colette.

Colette's eyes fell on a photograph in a plain frame. It was Madame Farrier at least thirty years younger, holding the arm of a handsome man and dressed as a bride.

'Is this your wedding day? You look beautiful.'

'Thank you.' Madame Farrier's face cracked into a smile and Colette briefly saw the younger woman buried inside the older one.

'Your husband was very handsome.'

The smile grew a little fainter. 'He was. He died at Givenchy. We were married only seven months.'

'I'm so sorry,' Colette whispered.

Madame Farrier shrugged. 'It was a long time ago. He would have been appalled to see France now. You are the Nadon girl, aren't you? Agnes Bonnivard spoke of you occasionally.'

'You knew her?'

'Many of the concierges and housekeepers know each other. I was sorry to hear she died. How is Fleur taking it?'

They both glanced at Fleur who was talking quietly into the phone. Colette couldn't answer and shame fluttered inside her breast. She should have asked how Fleur was long before now, but somehow, she never had. She resolved to do so, assuming they had not been arrested by morning.

Fleur ended the call and put a couple of coins into a bowl beside the pot of pencils.

'Sébastien will keep the scarf and label it as mine so no one else tries to claim it. Thank you, Madame Farrier.'

They bade the old woman good night and left.

When they were halfway across the wide road Fleur murmured, 'Sébastien is coming. He has a motorbike but may be half an hour. Let's walk up and down to keep warm.'

Colette offered an arm but Fleur shoved her hands in her coat pocket.

'How long have you been going to the cabarets?' Fleur growled. 'That's where you've been tonight, isn't it? You wouldn't just go to the hotel dressed like that.'

The accusation in Fleur's voice made Colette's stomach tighten. She glanced down at the bottle green skirt that peeked beneath the hem of her coat. No wonder the German had mistaken her for a whore with her high heels and fur stole. She pulled her coat tighter around her, wishing she was not dressed quite so lavishly.

'A few months,' she admitted. 'Not that it is any of your concern.'

'It isn't. But I can't believe you lied to me!' Fleur was pinch lipped. She looked angrier than Colette could remember seeing her. Or was it hurt that had turned her cheeks scarlet?

'I'm sorry. I knew you wouldn't approve.'

'And you're right. For good reason,' Fleur exclaimed. 'Do you want to risk being called a collaborator? A French whore for Germans? Don't you care about your reputation?'

'That's why I kept it secret. The Luciennes aren't good friends with my parents.' Colette swallowed 'Not that I imagine they'd notice I wasn't at home anyway.'

Fleur's expression softened at that. She knew Delphine had always been a neglectful parent.

'Besides, if I wasn't out tonight you would have been raped,' Colette said.

Fleur rounded on her. 'French women dancing with Germans is the reason they think they can have any of us!' She lowered her head and muttered, 'Let's just keep walking. We'll talk about this another time.'

They trudged on but the silence meant Colette's mind kept returning to the body. She sought for something to say that wouldn't cause an argument.

'That old woman knew *Tante* Agnes,' she said hesitantly.

Fleur still looked angry but made eye contact. 'Yes. They were friends for years.'

'Do you miss her?'

Fleur's eyes dropped. Colette chanced putting a hand on her drooping shoulders, offering comfort. Eventually Fleur spoke in a choked voice.

'She was my only family. She was stern and I didn't always like her, but it's strange to think she has gone. With everything else that has happened it's hard to grieve though. Thank you for asking.'

'I should have before,' Colette admitted.

'Perhaps when this is all over, I will find the time. It feels like our lives are on hold, don't you think, and we're waiting for them to start properly but they can't.'

Colette sighed. 'It really does.'

Fleur pointed her hand. 'I think Sébastien is here.'

A motorbike was coming towards them. The engine was off and the rider was propelling it by pushing one foot and then the other. He pulled up alongside the women, kicked out the stand and dismounted. He was dressed in a raglan overcoat and a trilby that shadowed his face.

He and Fleur embraced tightly. Colette looked on in envy, wishing someone would hold her like that. Sébastien tipped the brim of his hat back. The lenses of glasses caught the light, giving him an unearthly appearance.

'Tell me why you need my help?'

'We'll show you.' Fleur led him to the top of the steps and pointed. 'Down there.'

Sébastien peered down into the dark space then swore.

'German?'

Fleur nodded. 'We don't know what to do with him. You were the first person I could think of,' Fleur said.

Sébastien pulled his collar higher. 'Report your find to the authorities and let them deal with it. They can waste their time trying to work out what happened.'

'We know what happened,' Fleur said. 'Colette hit him, and he fell.'

Sébastien looked at Colette as if he was seeing her for the first time. His glasses implied his eyesight was poor but all the same, she felt she was being turned inside out.

'You did this?'

She nodded and drew closer to Fleur.

'*Merde!*'

He spat out the expletive with the force of a bullet leaving a gun and turned to Fleur with anger in his eyes. 'Don't you realise the trouble you will be in?'

'Of course I realise,' Fleur snapped. She folded her arms and held his gaze. 'I told you we need help deciding what to do. We can't move the body alone.'

Sébastien gave a low whistle. 'You are asking me to cover up the murder of a German soldier to save your friend's neck? Why would I do that for some little rich girl I don't even know?'

Fleur lifted her chin. 'Because the *little rich girl* saved me from being raped by that piece of garbage lying there.'

She glanced at Colette and smiled, acknowledging the rescue, and Colette felt warmth spreading through her. She spoke for the first time.

'It was an accident. I didn't mean to. I mean, I did mean to hit him. I didn't think he would die. Fleur pushed him in the chest, then I hit him with the case, and he caught his foot and fell.'

'Take a breath, mademoiselle, before you expire. What is in your case? Bricks?' Sébastien gave a tired grin; the first sign of humour since he arrived.

'My gas mask.' Colette held it out to show him. 'But I edged the box with some belt buckles to make it look interesting. There was a dreadful crack. I think his neck broke when he hit the third or fourth step down.'

'I think you're probably right. Let me go look at him.' Sébastien went down the steps and knelt over the body. Colette and Fleur sat together on the top step, watching.

'Do you think he will help?' Colette whispered.

'Of course he will.'

Sébastien returned to them.

'We are in luck. Yes, his neck has broken. There is a gash on his head, which I assume is from your box, but there are more from where he fell. Even more fortunately, he has a bottle of brandy in his pocket. He reeks of the stuff. I think what happened is perfectly clear. He came down here for a piss. Pardon my language.'

His eyes flickered briefly to Colette, who waved his apology away and he continued.

'He was drunk so did not notice the winding plants and caught his foot. I have unbuckled his belt and opened his flies.'

'You can't leave him here!' Colette exclaimed. 'Someone will come looking.'

Sébastien gave her a patient look. 'If he is never found that will be more suspicious. Look at all these weeds. Help me drag a few more across the steps, Fleur, and can you wind some around the toes of his boot?'

Fleur did as asked. It did look convincing.

'I think that will work,' Colette said.

Sébastien nodded as if he was in no doubt. 'Could anyone place you here? Are there any gaps in your whereabouts tonight?'

Fleur shook her head. 'Madame Farrier knows I was at the café then came back here but she won't know when I left there.'

Sébastien turned to Colette. 'You, mademoiselle?'

Colette leaned back against the wall. After the angry way Fleur had reacted to discovering that she had been dancing and drinking in a club filled with Germans she was reluctant to bring it up again and face further criticism, but what else could she do?

'Dancing at *La Balajo*,' she admitted

'With Germans? Do you always dance with the enemy before you murder them?' She could hear the sneer in Sébastien's voice.

'Your café only serves Frenchmen, does it?' she retorted.

'I swallow my morals to put bread in my belly. Were you earning your keep?'

She swung towards him, finger jabbing out. 'Don't you dare—'

'Both of you stop arguing,' Fleur pleaded.

Colette and Sébastien exchanged a glance. Colette lowered her hand and lifted her chin.

'I answer to my conscience and my friends, not to strangers.'

He folded his arms. 'Then can your *conscience* answer my question? Did anyone miss you?'

'I drove to the club with the Lucienne sisters and three officers from their hotel. We always return there together before I catch the Metro, but tonight I left *La Balajo* on my own more than an hour before we usually go home.'

Her mouth trembled. She clenched her jaw to try stop it.

'Oh god! They will have wondered where I had gone. They

will know it was me. I should just turn myself in to the *Abwehr*. I'll say I was alone. I promise I won't mention you at all Fleur.'

'Now there's no need for that,' Sébastien said calmly. He squeezed Colette's upper arm gently. Reassuringly. It was the first kindness he had showed her and the first touch from a man she genuinely welcomed.

'Where is the hotel?'

Colette swallowed, trying hard not to burst into tears. 'Boulevard Pereire in the seventeenth arrondissement.'

He sucked his teeth. 'Come with me, Mademoiselle Nadon, I think I can help you. Fleur, you go home. Will I see you tomorrow as usual?'

'Yes. I'll take my lunch break around half past twelve and come to the café.' Fleur and Sébastien embraced again.

'You can trust Sébastien. Do what he tells you,' she told Colette then walked off.

Sébastien turned to Colette and folded his arms. He looked her up and down appraisingly. 'Mademoiselle Nadon, have you ever ridden on a motorcycle?'

It was not the question she had been expecting.

'No,' she replied warily.

He led her to the motorbike and bestrode it. 'I think you will have to hitch up your skirt a bit. Climb on behind me and put your arms around my waist.'

'Are you sure?' Colette asked.

'You'll fall off if you don't.'

Reluctantly she obeyed. He started the motorbike and drove slowly. The engine was smooth but in the almost deserted streets it sounded dreadfully loud.

'It's icy. I don't go any faster than this. Close your eyes if you think it will make you feel safer.'

'No, no I will be fine,' Colette assured him. She didn't enjoy the way the vehicle leaned as they went round corners and winced when they passed traffic going the opposite direction. Being sightless and not able to anticipate the motion was a worse thought. She did not want to seem cowardly but held on tighter, pressing her chest to his back. He smelled of cigarette smoke, wine, and vanilla.

'Good girl. Direct me to the hotel if you will.'

Still holding on tight, she directed him. They turned off Boulevard Lannes and wound through streets that were empty of traffic. Colette relaxed a little, though did not dare loosen her grip on Sébastien. They drove past the hotel without stopping. A street further on, he pulled into an alleyway and turned off the engine.

'You can let go of me now. Climb off.'

'What are we doing?' Colette asked.

'We are going to have a lover's quarrel.' Sébastien grinned. 'You left the club because you were secretly meeting me, however our evening has not gone to plan so you have come back to the hotel. Have you ever wanted to be in the movies, Mademoiselle Nadon?'

'Not particularly,' Colette said, 'but I will be happy to quarrel with you. And you had better call me Colette if we are lovers.'

Behind the thick lenses, Sébastien's eyes gleamed. 'Well then, you walk ahead, and I will follow.'

Colette walked along Boulevard Pereire. As she drew closer to the hotel, she heard Sébastien shouting.

'Colette, darling, wait.'

She turned round. He had removed his coat and was dressed only in trousers and a shirt. The shirt was buttoned up wrong: a clever, subtle touch to suggest it had been put on hastily. He must be freezing.

'What do you want, Sébastien? Leave me alone!' Colette raised her voice.

Sébastien held his hands out. 'I didn't expect Monique to show up.'

'Didn't you?' Colette folded her arms tightly. Out of the corner of her eye she saw a razor thin sliver of light as somebody moved aside one of the drapes in the salon window. 'I suppose you were just hoping to let her climb into bed with us, were you? As if you could satisfy both of us at once! Ha!'

Sébastien blinked and Colette wondered if she had gone too far.

'She's just a friend. It's you I love. Please give me a second chance.'

Sébastien walked towards her. Colette step backwards, slightly closer to the door of the hotel. By now there were faces at windows.

'No. You've had too many chances already. This evening was your last. Men are deceitful and worthless! There's nothing you can say to convince me.'

She found she was enjoying this. She hadn't realised how much pent-up rage she still held for Gunther.

'What about this?' Sébastien asked.

He strode forward quickly, took her in his arms, and kissed her.

First, she felt only dark amusement. How like a man to steal a kiss even in this situation. But as their lips collided something awoke within her. She wrapped her hands around his neck and kissed him back, very thoroughly. She felt Sébastien stiffen but then he gave into the kiss too.

It was good.

Very good.

She could see why the imaginary Colette would give this imaginary Sébastien so many chances. He only pulled away when Sophie called from the doorway of the hotel.

'Colette? What on earth are you doing?'

She and Sébastien still held each other. Her breath was coming in hot short gasps.

'Go away, Sébastien,' she said.

Their eyes met. Her hand on his neck could feel the pulse hammering below his ear. Hers thumped equally rapidly. He nodded curtly. She nodded back. The objective had been achieved. No one could doubt that Colette had been streets away from home all night, having a sordid quarrel with a lover.

'You know where to find me if you change your mind,' he said gruffly. He turned and walked away.

The problem, of course, was that she didn't, and as she watched him stride into the shadows, she very much wished she did. A man who could kiss like that was too good to pass up.

She turned to Sophie. 'I'm so sorry I didn't tell you I was leaving the club. I've made a huge mess of everything, and now I think I've missed the last Metro home. Please can I stay here for the night?'

Sophie took her arm with an eager smile. 'Naturally you must. I can see we have a lot to talk about.'

Chapter Thirteen

No one came hammering on the door at daybreak to arrest Fleur. She woke at five, too tense to sleep any longer and watched the sky turn from black to dull grey. She had tried to remain awake but had fallen asleep before she heard Colette come home. At seven she knocked softly on Colette's door but there was no answer and her stomach churned. Sébastien would have taken care of Colette, but what if something had befallen both of them?

She took a cup of coffee back to her room. There was nothing she could do except wait and see what happened. At half past ten she heard the front door and presently there was a knock on her bedroom door. It was Colette.

'Oh, thank the Lord!' She collapsed onto Colette's shoulders. 'When I realised you weren't here this morning I didn't know what to think. Where were you all night? With Sébastien?'

Colette perched on the end of the bed. 'No. At the hotel.'

Fleur listened in astonishment to Colette's tale of a staged fight outside the hotel and the audience it gathered.

'That's ingenious. I told you Sébastien was clever.'

'You told me he was dull.' There was an accusing edge to her voice.

'No, I didn't. I told you Sébastien was serious and politically minded and that you would find him dull.'

'Well I didn't,' Colette said. 'He was very quick thinking. I would like to see him again so I can thank him, even though I don't think he will care.'

'Why do you think he won't care?' Fleur asked, leaning forward.

'He didn't like me. He called me a spoiled little rich girl last night, but he doesn't even know me.' She gave Fleur a suspicious look. 'What have you said to him about me?'

The question caused Fleur's neck to heat. She tried to recall anything that might have led to the judgement, but she had always defended the Nadons against any criticism. She felt slightly stupid now she knew what Colette had been doing for months.

'Maybe he just drew his own conclusions when you told him where you had been.'

Colette gasped. 'That's unkind.'

'Probably. Sorry, but I'm still furious at you going to the clubs and not telling me.' Fleur picked at a loose thread on her sweater. 'Why does it matter what he thinks of you in any case?'

'I don't know.' Colette's cheeks flushed. She gazed at the ceiling and drummed her fingers on her knee.

Fleur had a distinct sense she was missing something and an uneasy shiver ran over her scalp. Sébastien was unlike the men she had seen Colette flirting with, but her experience had been a lot more intense than Fleur's had. Scary, no doubt, but also exciting to be riding off on Sébastien's motorbike and staging an argument. She was obviously not immune to his appeal.

'Was there anything else?'

Colette returned from wherever she had been and shook her

head. She got up and walked around the room in her stockinged feet. Fleur curbed her impatience. Colette would talk, but not if pushed.

'Don't be angry at me. It's quite useful to be going to the cabarets,' she said.

It wasn't what Fleur had been expecting, but they obviously needed to talk about it at some point so why not now. 'I'm angrier you didn't tell me. Why is it useful?'

'Often the men I meet are on leave from other parts of France. Hitler promised that every German will see the city at least once.'

'That's all we are now: a tourist destination for the Nazis.' Fleur curled her lip, tasting acid in her throat but her wrath was mostly directed at the Germans, not Colette. 'How is it an advantage to go spend time among them?'

'Because by talking to the men I get to hear what is happening elsewhere in the country. When they've had a few glasses of champagne they are always happy to talk.'

'That sounds like a very convenient justification for enjoying yourself,' Fleur scoffed.

Colette's eyes filled with tears. 'Actually, it's horrible to hear how far the army has spread and how well Hitler's campaigns are doing. But I'd rather know than not.'

Fleur walked to the window and stared out. 'Why do you think they are telling the truth? Or even that they are told it themselves? Pierre says we shouldn't believe half of what gets printed in the newspapers or broadcast on the radio. It's all propaganda. What they tell you will be the same.'

'It might be propaganda but if it is what the army is being told then at least I'm hearing different propaganda,' Colette said, scowling.

Fleur blinked. Colette had actually made a good point, but Fleur was feeling too injured to acknowledge it.

'Unless you plan to do something with the information, it's not actually helpful and it sounds like an excuse.'

It struck her that Sébastien and Pierre would love to hear what the Germans thought was happening, but that would mean introducing Colette to them properly, and explaining to Colette what she was involved in. Neither were things she was prepared to consider.

'I don't want to end up like her,' Colette said after a while.

'Like who?'

'The concierge last night. Living in one room all alone with no one who loves me.'

Fleur turned, confused at sudden change of subject. 'You won't. You are rich and beautiful. Well, richer than most people nowadays anyway. Of course you will meet someone.'

'So will you,' Colette assured her. 'You're far prettier than me.'

'I haven't really thought about looking as I don't have the chance to meet anyone.' Fleur frowned. Anyone besides the group in the café. 'That's what I meant last night, about our lives being on hold. Isn't there anybody you have met when you go out dancing? I don't mean Germans, of course.'

'Of course not!' Colette sounded genuinely horrified and Fleur wanted to believe she meant it. 'No, there's no one. Is it too much to ask for a handsome rich man to fall into my lap?' She raised her eyes upwards as if expecting one to fall from the sky.

Rich. Of course. Fleur let out a breath. Colette wouldn't be interested in Sébastien in that case.

'I would just like someone I can talk to, who loves me,' she said. 'I don't really care how handsome he is as long as he is kind.'

'I would like mine to be a little bit good looking. I know I am shallow, but I can't help it.'

Colette grinned disarmingly and Fleur found it hard not to be charmed. That was one of Colette's talents, of course.

'I know you can't. But I like you anyway.'

'Do you?' Colette looked at her in surprise.

'Yes. I know we aren't as close these days, but I am glad you are here. I'm very glad you were there last night, too. Thank you for saving me.'

Colette blushed. She pressed her lips together then looked up with a guilty expression.

'I didn't tell you everything about last night. Sébastien kissed me. It was all part of the pretend quarrel, but I enjoyed it and I kissed him back. I'm sorry.'

Fleur's stomach twisted. She forced a smile she didn't feel. 'You did what you had to do. Thank you for telling me.'

'Do you like Sébastien?' Colette asked.

Fleur gave Colette a sidelong glance as her heart tugged in two directions. She could say she did. Colette, for all of her selfish ways, had a streak of kindness so it was probable she wouldn't show any further interest in him. But wouldn't that be worse? Knowing that she only had a chance because Colette gave up her interest? And did she even have a chance? Sébastien had let her down when she had tried flirting, though when he hugged her as he had the night before she couldn't help but wonder if one day…

'Do *you* like him?'

It wasn't an answer, but of course it gave Colette the opportunity to talk about herself.

She flicked her hair back from her forehead.

'I've only just met him. How could I possibly form any opinion of him? I'm just pleased that he came to help us. He will keep it secret, won't he?'

'Of course he will. That's one secret you do have to keep. For ever. We all do.'

The enormity of it frightened her and her eyes filled with tears. 'We killed someone. It was an accident but someone is dead because of us. He must have had a mother somewhere.'

Colette curled her lip. 'I don't care. He wouldn't have died if he hadn't done what he tried to do. He deserved it. I bet he would have behaved like that with German women too.'

Fleur gripped Colette's hand. 'You sound so hard.'

'I can be hard if I have to be. You just don't ever see me have to be.' Colette jutted out her jaw. 'I think if we are going to survive this war, we need to become harder.'

Fleur absorbed her words. Colette was not hard and would never be. When had she ever had to make difficult choices? It was all bravado but made her feel a little better knowing Colette was trying.

'I'll try,' she said.

Colette squeezed her hand. 'We both will. Now, I need to change and go say hello to *Mère*. No doubt she'll think I was out all night with a man – if she noticed me missing at all.'

She left, yawning against the back of her hand.

Fleur waited until she heard Colette's bedroom door open then knelt by her bed and pulled out the bag from where she had kicked it the previous night. Inside were thirty paperback-book-sized leaflets.

She broke out in a cold sweat just thinking of what would have happened if the German had discovered these. She had intended to post them through letterboxes and pin them to trees early this morning but that would have to wait. She could not do it in daylight. She heard the door open again and Colette walked in without knocking.

'Fleur?'

Fleur froze, leaflets still in her hand. She raised her head from the other side of the bed.

'I'm here.'

'What are you doing down there?' Colette asked.

'I lost a stocking. I was seeing if it was under the bed.'

'Do you want me to look from this side?' Colette offered.

'No! No, don't trouble yourself.' Fleur slid the roll of leaflets between the bag and the wall. 'It probably got put back in the drawer with some other laundry. What do you want anyway?'

'I wanted to see if you fancy coming out shopping with me this morning. I heard a rumour that Babineau's *épicerie* might have some rillettes.' She glanced at her wristwatch. 'It's probably too late now anyway.'

She retreated and closed the door.

Fleur sat back on her heels. Colette's slightly pained expression had made Fleur feel a little contrite. She felt a little closer to Colette after what they had shared, and of course they were now bound by the secret of what had happened, but she couldn't explain what she had been doing under the bed. Colette's visits to the cabarets and the hotel meant she must never learn what Fleur was involved in. It would be too easy for her to let slip something unintentionally – Fleur was fair minded enough to know it would be unintentional because Colette was not a traitor to France – and then the lives of everyone involved would be in danger.

She had been so hurt by the revelation of Colette's nights out dancing but her secret was not of the same magnitude and she felt no guilt at keeping it.

~

April 1941

'You now walk with more confidence through the world,' Monsieur Ramper remarked one morning when Fleur arrived at the bookshop.

He was boarding up the front window, through which a brick had been thrown overnight. Fleur looked at the destruction in despair.

'Do I?'

She knew the answer. After she had cried for the lost life, she had taken Colette's advice on board. She would be hard. Someone had tried to hurt her and she had stopped him. She felt no remorse for it, nor should she.

She never discovered if the German authorities accepted the scenario they had created, but no one came to arrest the women and there were no black cars with smoky windows slowly purring through the streets. The only change of note was a new checkpoint being erected between the Metro station and the entrance to the pleasure park at the Bois de Boulogne, though that might have been coincidental.

Neither she, Colette, or Sébastien ever referred to what had happened. It was another secret she had to keep but knowing this one was shared was more comforting than she expected.

She tucked an empty paper bag into her pocket. She had discovered that if she ate her baguette and butter as she walked, she didn't notice how meagre her breakfast was.

'I'm sorry I'm late. I forgot to wind my watch last night and it ran down. I can stay late tomorrow instead if you want me to.'

'It does not matter. We had no customers yesterday.' Monsieur Ramper beckoned her inside to sit down on one of the two chairs beside the cash register.

'Fleur, I am leaving Paris.'

Fleur's legs turned to water. 'Why?'

'I have thought long and hard about it. The other shops in this street are closing, perhaps for good. My grandfather was Jewish so in the eyes of the Nazis I am tainted. It is now against the law for my people to own businesses.'

He gestured to the boarded-up window. 'I do not wish my shop to fall into the hands of the Nazis, so I am selling her to you, Fleur. I have prepared the legal documents for you to sign.'

He had fired so much information at her with the precision of a

Fokker's gunner and she could barely take it in. One fact stood out.

'Monsieur Ramper, I can't afford to buy it.'

He smiled. 'The price is five francs. There is no one else for me to give it to. I have no family in France. Perhaps none anywhere. I know you understand how that feels.'

He bowed his head. He looked older. Smaller.

'The shop and the small flat above it are mine. If you wish to keep the bookshop open, do so with my blessing. If you wish to sell what you can then close it, do that.'

'I will keep it going as long as I can, but you can't give it to me. Not to keep,' Fleur protested.

He gave her a gentle smile. 'When – if – the war comes to an end and France is victorious, I hope I may return to Paris. Then, if you wish, we can discuss who owns it.'

Fleur's eyes filled with tears. What if Hitler continued his conquests and the war never turned in France's favour? What if Germany won decisively? The rationing and hunger, the ever-present anxiety and checkpoints might be here to stay. Impulsively, she hugged Monsieur Ramper tightly.

'Thank you.'

'You have been a treasure to me. There is one other thing I ask of you. In the room upstairs you will find a shelf with some books that would not survive Nazi purges. If you can save one or two, my heart will be glad.'

'Of course. I promise I will take care of your shop and everything in it.'

~

Monsieur Ramper left that afternoon, strolling out of the shop as if he was only going to a café. He carried the shabby briefcase he often did. His suitcase, he told Fleur, was at the house of a friend in the twelfth arrondissement, ready for him to collect on the first leg of his journey.

'There are good people who help those of us who need to vanish,' he told Fleur. 'A line of men and women stretching the length and breadth of the country, I am led to believe.'

Fleur tried to picture what he described. Threads of bravery and trust spreading like spider webs across the country. Could such a thing really exist? She hoped so with all of her soul.

'You will come back one day,' she assured him as she gave him one last embrace.

'I hope so,' was all he said.

As she walked home that night her heart was leaden. The bookshop wasn't the only premises to have been vandalised. Shops had windows smashed. Others were daubed with obscenities and, more ominously, yellow stars and the word '*juif*' scrawled brutally over glass and brick. Paris was becoming ugly.

She forced herself to walk with her head up, swinging her large bag and humming instead of scurrying with her head down or looking behind her. It wouldn't do to seem shifty when she carried three slim volumes of poetry by Jewish authors in her bag. Eyes were everywhere and paranoia was entirely justified. The sooner she was home and the books were safely stowed in the Secret Garden, the easier she would be able to breathe.

∾

The door to the Secret Garden looked even more dilapidated and unused, and it was with some difficulty that Fleur pulled it open. Her eyes fell on the letters – SS – that she and Colette had carved in such innocence. It made her feel slightly sick to see them. They had stood for Secret Sisters, but now the initials took on a much more sinister meaning. How could she and Colette, two girls of eleven, imagine the horror that those two initials would wreak on the population of Europe? As she crawled inside the hiding space, she promised herself that soon she would bring a knife and obliterate the letters from existence. The rugs they had once lain on had rotted, but the glass cold frame was still in a good condition. She put the books inside and covered them with waxed paper, then put three shallow pots of soil on top. The books could lie in safety, possibly for ever.

～

The following morning she and Colette went shopping. They wore sturdy shoes and nibbled on yesterday's crusts as they walked. Queuing for hours was no fun on empty stomachs.

'It's a shame Monsieur Ramper did not sell you a food shop,' Colette mused as they edged slowly closer to the front of the line that snaked outside the *Épicerie Babineau*.

Monsieur Nadon had been full of congratulations at learning Fleur's good fortune and had poured out small measures of brandy for everyone to toast the new businesswoman.

'You deserve it. You work hard and that has been rewarded,' he had said.

Was Colette jealous of Fleur's luck or Louis' praise?

'I'd have to sell the food if he had. It isn't like books where I can read them and they still exist.'

'That's true. Food that never ran out no matter how much we ate would be incredible,' Colette said.

There was trouble inside the *épicerie*. A stout matron with hair piled high began trying to elbow a young mother from the front of the queue. Three young children looked on, crying, while other shoppers stood uncertainly by.

'It wasn't yours,' the mother was screaming. 'I was here first.'

'Leaving a child to queue does not count,' the stout woman shouted back. 'Take your grimy brats to the back of the line.'

The mother bared her teeth. 'You don't need it. You're fat enough, you old sow!'

'Ladies, please!' The shopkeeper, Madame Babineau, stood ineffectually behind the counter waving her hands, one of which held a palm-sized piece of sausage.

Fleur leaned back wearily against the wall at the end of the queue. This sort of thing was happening more and more as food was becoming scarcer. This would add an unwelcome delay to the day.

'Neither of them should have it,' muttered an old woman halfway along. 'Give it to me instead.'

The woman in front of her turned round and snarled. 'I'm before you.'

The atmosphere congealed into something altogether more hostile then and Fleur and Colette exchanged worried glances. There were five people in the queue in front of them and all could have a claim. It could very easily become one of the riots that were becoming all too common. Realising their prize was slipping from them, the mother and matron fell on each other with loud shrieks. The children began to cry.

'Get them out of here! This is a respectable shop, for respectable customers. I'll have no trouble here,' shrieked Madame Babineau.

Customers moved in to separate the two women and pull them into the road, where they continued to scream. The noise had attracted a patrol of passing soldiers who efficiently took charge and sent both women off in different directions.

Fleur dropped to her knees by the children who were looking horror-struck.

'Don't worry about your *maman*, I'm sure she will be happy later.' The children continued crying.

'Do you have any *bonbons*?' Colette called to Madame Babineau. She grinned at Fleur. 'They always make me happy.'

Actual luxuries meant more than words of comfort, something Colette would know better than Fleur of course.

'I do, but they're not free,' Madame Babineau said.

'I wasn't expecting them to be,' Colette said smoothly.

'You'll have to use a coupon,' Madame Babineau muttered.

'Take one of mine,' Fleur said. It didn't seem fair to make Colette bear the whole burden.

Three small boiled sugar lollipops were duly purchased and one given to each child.

'Do you know where you live?' Colette asked. The oldest child, a girl with scrawny plaits and a snotty nose, nodded.

Colette patted her hand. 'Take your brother and sister home.'

The children trudged out of the shop.

'Poor things. I hope their mother gets the food she needs,' Fleur said.

Madame Babineau wiped her hands down her apron. 'Those two have been at each other's throats for months. If there was enough food this would not happen.'

Fleur looked longingly at the piece of neglected sausage that had started all the uproar. The meat was dark and marbled with peppercorns and white veins of fat that glistened tantalisingly.

'If you've got the coupons and the money it's yours,' Madame Babineau whispered.

Fleur and Colette exchanged a glance. 'It doesn't seem right to profit from the situation,' Fleur whispered.

'It doesn't seem sensible to ignore the offer!' Colette exclaimed.

Colette handed over the coupon and payment – exorbitant, as everything was nowadays – and Fleur slipped the parcel into her bag. Her fingers brushed against the leaflets she had been planning to secrete in other women's baskets. They would have to wait. Fleur and Colette left the *épicerie* and joined the queue at the *boulangerie* further down the street.

'See? Being hard works and now we have sausage,' Colette

said. 'I worry though. Where will this fighting among ourselves end?'

Fleur rubbed her eyes. The answer to that was beyond her. As she queued, she composed another leaflet in her head.

The women of Paris needed to band together, not let themselves be torn apart.

Chapter Fourteen

The answer to the question of where arguing would lead, came a week later, on the last day of April. Fleur was at work in the bookshop, so Colette went shopping alone.

The line was already past the entrance of the shoe shop next door when Colette joined it. She idly listened to the gossip as she gazed at the display in the window with longing. She had beautiful pairs of shoes she no longer wore now she walked everywhere and needed something more substantial and comfortable.

When the war was over and France was free once more, she would buy a new pair each month and dance until they were worn through. She was absorbed in her daydream and barely registered the ripple of anger that went through the queue until someone nudged her. She looked up, her body tensing in preparation for some fresh horror.

The cause was the stout woman who Fleur and Colette had seen fighting with the young mother. As she approached the queue a couple of women hissed under their breath. She grew pale and stopped dead.

'I know what you are thinking, but it was not I who did it.'

The hisses turned to murmurs of anger then and a couple of the women further down the queue curled their lips. When the stout woman caught their eyes, they dropped their heads.

'I do not care what you think. Righteous citizens have nothing to fear.' The stout woman stalked past the queue to the front. No one objected.

'What happened?' Colette whispered to the woman behind her who was holding a baby on her hip.

The mother leaned close to whisper. 'There was a fight last week between that woman and a widow with three children. The next day, the widow was arrested for prostitution and selling stolen food on the *marché noir*. When she was returned home, she could not walk. She is still bedridden.'

'That's awful!'

'That woman's husband is a gendarme. Rumours say people have disappeared before if they have upset her.' The mother glanced towards the women who had hissed. 'I wonder if the queue will be shorter by two next week?'

Colette tasted bile in her throat. It was bad enough that the Germans were inflicting terror on the population without the French turning on each other.

'That's horrible. So vindictive.'

'That's life nowadays.'

Colette chewed her fingernail. Life felt constantly hazardous. She had a sudden longing for a friendly face. Not the Luciennes though. The idea of visiting the hotel swarming with Nazis sent a chill through her. She wanted the one person who would understand what had upset her today.

As soon as she had completed her purchases she travelled into Montparnasse and searched out Fleur's bookshop. This part of the city was new to her, and she gazed around with interest at the unfamiliar bistros and cafés in the wide, tree-bordered streets.

She wondered idly which café Sébastien worked in. Despite her intention to thank him she hadn't sought him out. In the end, it had seemed wiser to pretend the incident had never happened and put it behind her. Now she was close to where he might be the fluttering of the skin on her neck caught her by surprise. It had been a very good kiss.

The bookshop was shabby with one boarded-up window and garish books with covers showing starlets being menaced by trench coat-clad men displayed in the other. Colette suppressed a smile. She'd been surprised by – and ashamed of – the burst of envy she had felt that Fleur was suddenly the owner of a business, but it wasn't as grand as she had expected.

A bell rang as she opened the door. Fleur was standing on a three-stepped stool, dusting. She turned round, recognised Colette, and her expression grew anxious.

'Is something wrong?'

Colette intended to tell Fleur the whole story, but all that emerged was, 'The mother has been arrested!'

'Your mother? Whatever for?' Fleur dropped her feather duster and clambered down from the steps.

Realising her error, Colette burst out laughing, though she felt far from amused.

'No, not my mother. The mother from the *épicerie* last week. Do you remember the two women fighting over sausage? She was suspected of being a *trafiquant* and prostitute.'

Her face felt dreadfully hot, and she knew she was gabbling. She looked for somewhere to sit down and settled for leaning against the desk on which the cash register stood amid piles of books and loose sheets of paper.

'Oh that's dreadful.' Fleur's voice cracked. Colette's nerves threatened to do the same. 'It must have been that horrible old woman, don't you think? I bet she informed on her. I bet it isn't even true.'

'That's what everyone thinks but they are too scared to say so,' Colette said. 'Those poor children! They were left alone for days! The oldest child was only nine or ten. How terrified they must have been when the house was raided and their mother ripped from them.'

The thought of their plight twisted a knife in her already churning belly and she began to sob.

'Oh, Colette! This isn't like you to cry.' Fleur bundled her into a hug.

'I know. It's just … a home should be a sanctuary and now they'll never feel safe. Ours always has been, but at any time someone or something could cause that to change.'

'It's horrible, isn't it? That isn't the first rumour I have heard of that sort of behaviour.'

Colette shivered. 'Really?'

Fleur frowned. 'Oh yes. People are encouraged to inform the authorities if they suspect any laws are being broken, however small, and so people are using the authorities to get revenge for petty grudges.'

Colette sagged. 'So as well as having to watch out for the German authorities, everyone is now suspicious of friends and neighbours. How have I managed to miss this happening?'

'You don't know that you don't know something until you learn it.' Fleur shrugged. 'I need to go wash my hands. Those shelves haven't been dusted for months and I'm filthy.' She vanished behind a curtain.

Colette dropped her head, feeling stupid. She had been reading newspapers so how could she be so unaware of what was happening close to home? She stared at the desk. Fleur usually kept everything at home tidy but there was no order to the mess here. Fleur appeared once more, pinning a loose curl onto the back of her hair. Her mouth twisted.

'I don't know what I'm doing. Monsieur Ramper doesn't seem to have kept any sort of records. Receipts were scribbled on bits of paper and put in a box. His ledgers make no sense. I don't know where to start working out how much profit he has made in the last five years, if any.'

'Would you like me to have a look?' Colette offered, seizing upon one area she had an advantage over Fleur.

Fleur's eyes gleamed. 'Would you? That would be wonderful. You were always better with numbers than I was.'

'I know. I offered to help *Papa* back when the war started, but he turned me down.' Her jaw tightened at the memory. 'He didn't want me to have to work. He said that wasn't what he'd raised me for. It's hard not to believe he just didn't think I would be of any use.'

Fleur leaned beside her on the edge of the desk. 'Oh, Colette, your father loves you.'

'Oh yes, he loves me, but he thinks I am like my mother. Only good for being decorative while I wait for a husband. But if you want my help, I would be glad to provide it.'

'I would. Come with me tomorrow. We can go for a walk in the sunshine and a drink at lunchtime. It isn't far to the Café Morlaix from here and Sébastien is usually good for a free glass of wine. He keeps a special barrel for French customers that he doesn't water down.'

'That would be nice,' Colette said as casually as she could manage.

Her scalp prickled and she suppressed a shiver, this time of an entirely different cause. She was not sure whether to attribute it to the thought of tackling the accounts, an afternoon in the sunshine, or seeing Sébastien again.

~

The following morning she dressed in what she considered an appropriate outfit for a working woman; a light wool skirt and a white cotton blouse printed with tiny cornflowers. She rolled her hair into a low bun at the nape of her neck and put on her sensible walking shoes.

Fleur was in the kitchen, reading a sheet of paper. She laughed when Colette appeared at the door to the kitchen, but it was kind.

'You look very smart. It will go nicely with your silk hat.'

Colette pursed her lips. The item in question was a flamboyant creation that she had decorated with artificial flowers and a peacock feather.

'I am not wearing that again. It feels wrong dressing like a fashion mannequin when many women in the food queues can barely afford to feed their children.'

The defiance through vibrant clothing had been fun at first but the Germans didn't appear to notice or care what the French women wore to go shopping.

'You not wearing a hat won't change that,' Fleur said.

'No, but the Germans don't care and it must look bad to the other women when their children are dressed in clothes that are too small. I don't want anyone to think I am like that horrible woman who informed on her neighbour.'

Anyone, or one person in particular?

Sébastien had dismissed her as a silly rich girl. He hadn't been the first, and undoubtedly wouldn't be the last, but it had stung. If she might see him today, she wanted to prove she could be as serious-minded as Fleur.

'What do you have there?' she asked, trying to read the piece of paper in Fleur's hand.

'Nothing.'

Fleur shoved the page into a basket of carrots. Colette pulled it out. It was a leaflet, block printed by hand by the look of the smudges and uneven letters.

Statut des Juifs.

It proclaimed that since Jews were no longer allowed to own businesses, the public should boycott shops that had been forcibly taken from them.

'Where did you find that? Do you think it is true?' she asked.

'It was pushed under the door of the concierge's *loge*. Yes, it is true.' Fleur gave her a long stare. 'Why do you think Monsieur Ramper left? The glove shop round the corner from the bookshop had its windows smashed then boarded up. When it opened again the owner, Madame Boch, was gone.'

Colette digested the information. She held the paper between forefinger and thumb, feeling slightly soiled, as if the page itself were somehow responsible for the situation. 'What is the point of writing this sort of thing?'

Fleur snatched the paper from her hand. 'People need to know this is happening. Another I saw said people should refuse to buy from shops displaying signs saying German is spoken.'

Colette bit her lip. Standing in line daily for food was bad enough and if there were going to be restrictions on which shops were acceptable it would get even worse.

'It seems like the French are making life worse, not the Germans.'

Fleur scowled. 'At least the people writing these leaflets are doing something. Imagine what would happen to them if they were caught.'

'Is it worth the risk?' Colette asked. 'It isn't going to make any difference other than making life harder for ourselves. There are enough Germans buying things. The cabarets won't shut if the French stop going, for example. What is the point?'

'They'd sell less champagne if you weren't there to drink it!'

'I haven't been since...'

Their eyes met. It was the closest they had come to acknowledging the events of that night.

'I just haven't, and none of them have closed.'

Fleur's mouth twisted into a grimace. She ripped and twisted the page into spills to light the gas. 'Boycott your hat if you think it will help.'

She stalked out. Colette followed.

～

Given the inauspicious start, the morning was more fun than Colette had anticipated. Her ability with numbers proved to be just what was needed. Fleur arranged books and Colette spread the papers and account books out until the whole desk was covered, then started the process of ordering them.

'I think, though I am not sure, that Monsieur Ramper was selling books on account and never collecting the payment,' she said incredulously.

Fleur stepped down off the stool. 'He said he could not bear to let someone who wanted a book leave without one. Most of them paid within a week or two – they have a green tick next to them in the brown leather ledger. I'm just going upstairs to see if I can find something to fill this shelf.'

Colette opened the accounts book and ran her finger down the entries, wondering why he had picked green ink, which barely contrasted with the blue he wrote entries in. As the entries became more recent, there were fewer and fewer ticks, and the entries stopped abruptly two weeks before Fleur had been given ownership of the business.

'I think if we went to these people and demanded payment the bookshop would suddenly be a lot better off,' she called to Fleur, though the doorbell partially drowned her out.

'Collecting payment for goods, what a novel idea.'

Colette raised her head as a prickle ran down her back. Sébastien had come in. He grinned at his feeble jest, and Colette was reminded that the last time she had seen him, that mouth had been pressed against hers.

'Is Fleur expecting you?' she asked.

'She isn't expecting me. I was hoping to speak with her, but it doesn't matter. This is the last place I expected to encounter you, Mademoiselle Nadon, but I suppose the clubs aren't open yet. Are you bored of shopping?'

Colette pouted. 'There's no need to be rude. I'm helping Fleur with the accounts.'

'Really?' He raised his brows and his grin grew wider.

She walked round the desk and his eyes followed her. She was glad she had worn something sensible but also that the skirt and blouse gave her a shapely silhouette.

'Does that surprise you?' she asked, folding her arms beneath her breasts and meeting his eyes. Her pulse jumped. She was seeing him for the first time in daylight and hadn't expected how very deep blue they would be. Magnified by the thick lenses of his glasses, they were hypnotic.

'A little,' Sébastien admitted. He folded his arms too, mirroring her pose, and leaned slightly forward. 'Does that offend you?'

'A little,' she replied. She thought and rubbed her nose. 'Actually, it depends. If you're surprised that I'm able to do it then yes, I'm offended because you're making assumptions. If you're surprised I'm working at all then I'm not sure I have the right to be offended.'

Sébastien unfolded his arms and gave her a genuine smile. 'Let's go with whichever offends you least. So, how are you helping and why? I didn't realise Fleur was struggling.'

Colette hesitated, then realised that a serious man probably genuinely wanted to hear.

'I offered to help with the accounts. I'm better with numbers than Fleur is, which is just as well.'

She walked back to the desk and he followed her, standing close. She pointed to the ledger. 'Look, all these books sold but the bills were never settled, and the debts go back years in some cases. Some of the names crop up five or six times. I think we'll have to go and demand payment.'

'You might struggle to collect what you're owed in some of these cases,' Sébastien said quietly.

She wrinkled her nose and he pointed.

'Read the names again.'

Colette skimmed the column and let out a low sigh.

'Yes, I see what you mean.'

At least a quarter of the surnames were Jewish. The owners might not even be in Paris any longer.

Sébastien's expression was bleak. 'I knew some of these people. They lived in the area and one or two of them used to come drink in the café, but they're gone now. A couple of them were artists who went to fight and never came back.'

Colette felt a numbness creeping up her legs. The ledger had stopped being an account book and had become a list of the dead and missing. She closed it and laid her hand on top, as if that could keep the information from seeping out.

'I wish I had never started looking. I don't want to think about what has happened to everyone in the book.'

'Yes, it's upsetting to think of it,' Sébastien said. He sucked his teeth. 'Shall we change the subject? Have you been dancing recently?'

He sounded so condescending Colette spun round to face him, anger sputtering in her belly.

'I'm not a child. I don't need shielding from reality. And no, I haven't been dancing for weeks!'

Sébastien's eyes were hard. 'But you don't want to think about the truth you're faced with?'

'What can thinking about it do?' She dropped her head.

Sébastien touched her cheek. She looked up and saw his expression was kindlier.

'Even the bravest of us feels despair at what is happening. We can't hide from it though.'

Colette thought back to the leaflet she had found. Fleur had been right; doing anything, no matter how small, seemed important.

'I wonder where Monsieur Ramper is,' she said.

Sébastien took his hand from her arm and shoved it into his pocket. 'Who knows. Safe, I hope.'

His manner had changed abruptly. Colette barely knew him but got the distinct sense he was hiding something.

'Do you know where he is?'

He jerked his head up sharply. 'No, I don't. And it is best not to ask that sort of question. The people who are involved are risking a lot.'

'People involved?' Colette bit her lip. Were there really people who could help someone disappear? 'I just assumed Monsieur Ramper had left on a train or in a car.'

'Yes, Colette. Men with Jewish heritage carrying suitcases are known for being able to drive straight through checkpoints,' Sébastien said dryly.

'Will you stop being so unpleasant?' Colette snapped. 'I'm sorry I don't know everything there is to know. I'm sorry I'm not Fleur!'

'I'm not.' He ran his hand up her arm and she shivered. He stepped closer. 'Not sorry that you aren't Fleur, I mean.'

The fabric of her blouse was thin enough that she could feel each fingertip individually and it sent her skin fluttering. She was convinced Sébastien did know something and the logical voice in the back of her head told her she was being distracted, but when his fingertips were slowly but firmly spreading out over the sleeve it was hard to remain focused on intrigue. She parted her lips then closed them. She was being played as surely as if she was a piano.

'You don't have to do that. I won't say anything about what you told me,' she murmured.

Sébastien lowered his hand and coughed. 'I should go. Please tell Fleur to drop into the café before she goes home. I want to ask her something.'

'I'll tell her.'

He walked to the door and gave her a nod.

'Is it true you have two barrels of wine, one for the French and one for the Germans?' Colette called after him.

He laughed. 'I couldn't possibly confirm or deny such a thing. I will say that the Germans don't appreciate a good *vin rouge* when they get one, so I don't waste the best vintage on them.'

'You should poison their drinks,' Colette suggested.

Sébastien blinked. 'I can't tell if you are joking or not, but tempting though that is, I don't think so. It isn't an efficient way of freeing France and I'm not prepared to go to the guillotine for a handful of deaths.'

'If I can think of a more efficient way, I will let you know,' Colette said, grinning to show she was joking.

Sébastien walked back and took her hand. He lifted it to his lips and kissed it. 'Good morning, Colette. I have enjoyed our conversation and I hope we will see each other again another day.'

He left the shop and Colette leaned back against the desk. What a strange experience that had been. She wasn't sure if she had enjoyed being mocked and judged. She wiggled her fingers. The back of her hand felt warm, as the sensation of Sébastien's lips lingered long after it made any sense for it to do so. She lifted her hand to her mouth and pressed her lips over the spot he had kissed.

'Was that a customer?' Fleur walked back from behind the curtain with laden arms.

'No. It was Sébastien. He wants you to call in and see him before you go home.'

Fleur paused, then dropped the stack of books onto the table. 'You should have called me.'

'I don't know why I didn't.' Colette smoothed her sleeve and gave Fleur a smile.

'Don't you?'

Fleur's eyes flickered over Colette and it occurred to Colette, far too belatedly, that she had never got a straight answer from Fleur about her relationship with Sébastien. She had a horrible feeling she might have done something wrong.

Then again, Sébastien had said he was glad she wasn't Fleur. It was too confusing.

'He did point out something that is bad news, I'm afraid. Look at this.'

With relief, she turned Fleur's attention to the ledger. She wasn't in the mood for sharing her private thoughts. She wanted to figure out why she found Sébastien so diverting and she wanted to do it alone.

He was passionate about the world and Colette wondered if that passion extended to the bedroom too. Despite his glasses, he was handsome. He had been good at kissing after all, and when he touched her, it made her skin burn with excitement.

How lucky he obviously wasn't rich because otherwise she might be in danger of actually becoming attracted to him.

Chapter Fifteen

Colette walked home with a spring in her step, not having felt so happy or useful for a long time. She had succeeded in making some sense of Monsieur Ramper's filing system and had tallied one box of receipts with the ledger and a list of stock.

Fleur had recognised a name that appeared three times and who still lived only a few streets away. She intended to go pay a visit to ask for the payment before she went to meet Sébastien in the café.

Colette did her best to ignore the flashes of jealousy that reared up as the two women had parted. Sébastien did know something about helping people hide. The way he had practically started to seduce her to change the subject had her convinced. She wondered if Fleur suspected too, or even knew for definite. She had called on Sébastien to help with the soldier after all. Lucky Fleur to have a man in her life who was so dependable and trustworthy she could risk involving him in covering up a murder. Colette could not think of a single man she had known who she could have turned to.

Colette slowed her pace. Sébastien. She needed to think about the odd effect he had on her before she encountered him again because there was an intensity to him that grabbed her attention and wouldn't let go.

He had been rude and dismissive of her on two occasions now, and she had come close to losing her temper with him but he hadn't seemed to mind. If anything, he had seemed to enjoy the result of provoking her, and when she had managed to win a point herself, she had felt triumphant. She was glad she had been working when Sébastien arrived. He was forced to admit that she was not just the useless socialite he had decided she was. Yes, they had argued, and she had ended up feeling naïve, but she didn't feel she had lost entirely.

The afternoon was warm with an intermittent breeze that seemed to arrive just as the air was getting too stifling yet left before it could make her chilly. This was her favourite time of year to be in the city, before summer descended and made the crowded boulevards too hot to tolerate. How lovely it would be to sit on a terrace surrounded by trees with a cool glass of sirop and nothing to worry about. In the distance, the white domes of the Sacre Coeur rose above the city on the hilltop of Montmartre and seeing it chipped away at the peace she had been feeling.

She had only been dancing once since the night of the German's death. He had not been anything distinctive, but for one horrible evening she saw echoes of him on the faces of too many of the blonde, bland young men she danced with. Anyone of them could have behaved the way he had. Sophie had at first cajoled then outright sulked when she declined further invitations but she had remained firm.

'I feel too sad over what happened with Sébastien to spend time dancing,' she had said eventually, forcing out a couple of tears.

Sophie and Josette had accepted that as an excuse and grudgingly agreed to meet Colette for afternoon coffees instead, but it had led to a coolness between them. She missed the sisters and she missed the dancing but being able to say to Fleur and Sébastien that she had not been with a clear conscience had now made it worthwhile.

She crossed the Seine at the Pont de Passy and took a turn down an alley. The road twisted back below the level of the bridge, down to where a slipway led into the water beneath the arches and a small boat was tied. She hesitated at the sight of several vagrants huddled under an archway, sunning themselves. They were a shabby bunch dressed in ragged clothing. She turned to go back in the opposite direction. Stupid, she thought, to put herself in a vulnerable position, but the men barely lifted their heads to notice her. She turned sharply down the road to the right hoping to find her way back to the way she recognised and once out of their sight she quickened her pace. She thought she heard footsteps behind her but wasn't sure. Her stomach clenched and she felt a rush of anger. Wasn't it bad enough having to live in fear of the Gestapo, without also having to worry about being accosted by vagabonds? She wished she still had the gas mask case with the buckle that had been so effective previously but after what she had used it for, she couldn't bear to see it and had replaced it with another, less dangerous one.

'Mademoiselle Colette!'

She hesitated at the sound of her name. The voice was familiar. She slowed but did not turn.

'Mademoiselle Colette, it's a friend. Please, you have nothing to fear.'

She turned cautiously. The man who had spoken had long, straggly hair and a beard but Colette recognised the eyes in a face which had almost – but not quite – changed beyond recognition.

'Michal Drucker? Is that really you?' she asked, aghast at the state of the previously immaculate concierge.

He raised a finger to his lips. 'A name like mine is not good to say out loud in these times.'

His voice was raspy and he licked lips that were dry and cracked.

Colette walked towards him. 'Oh, Michal, we have missed you. We hoped to hear from you, but you never came back. Why are you living here?'

'I am a nameless person now and it is better that way.' His answer was interrupted by a hacking cough that lasted a full minute.

'You are not well! You should come home,' Colette exclaimed.

He shook his head weakly. 'If I go back, I'll be taken to work.'

Colette nodded slowly, fighting the rising anger in her breast. Everyone knew Jews were rounded up and transported to workcamps to help the German war effort. Many, like Michal and the names in the ledger, had vanished overnight.

'I'm so sorry to bother you, but do you have a few spare centimes?'

'Of course, let me see.' Colette opened her purse and pulled out a five franc note. Louis was still generous with his allowance and the little luxuries she used to buy were no longer so readily available. She could do without her chocolate ration this week but it seemed a paltry offering.

'Here, take this. But I want to help you more if I can. Come to the house tonight at about seven and wait in the little alcove under the archway by the *loge* door.'

She could see the internal struggle in his eyes and feared he might refuse, but then he clasped her hand.

'Thank you.'

He slipped back into the shadows beneath the bridge. Colette walked on, wondering how best to help. All day it felt as if she had been bombarded with misery, from the unjustly accused widow to the grim inventory of absent customers. Now she had the opportunity to do something to help at least one person. Let Sébastien try to patronise her when he learned what she had done!

No. Even if it didn't carry a risk, this wasn't something she wanted to tell Fleur or Sébastien about. She wasn't doing it to prove anything to them, but to help a friend.

~

A little before seven she slipped out of the house and waited in the courtyard. Michal edged along the pavement, clutching a knapsack to his chest protectively, and slipped into the archway. Colette's plan was to give him some of her father's clothes and a blanket, but he looked close to collapse.

'When did you last sleep properly?' she asked.

He smiled weakly. 'I am not sure.'

'The concierge's *loge* is not used. You weren't replaced. You could sleep there tonight.'

'No. That is too much of a risk to us both…'

He broke off, leaving the rest of the sentenced unfinished. They both knew what he meant: the risk of him being discovered. Of Colette arrested for harbouring him. The thought terrified her, but she could not let him walk back into the darkness and uncertainty of the Paris streets. She bit her thumbnail, feeling helpless, searching her mind for a solution.

Was there anywhere in the house itself? The cellar? *Tante* Agnes' old room? Fleur didn't use it after all. Thinking of Fleur, the solution struck her. They had spent years hiding together, after all.

She glanced at the house. Louis had only arrived home half an hour earlier and always bathed as soon as he returned from the factory; a symbolic cleansing himself of the taint of assisting the German war effort. Delphine would be absorbed in one of her magazines, lounging with a cocktail and pretending nothing had changed. She wasn't sure where Fleur was, but if she spotted Colette and Michal, she would surely not protest.

'Follow me.'

Michal looked astounded when Colette showed him the Secret Garden.

'All this time and I never knew it was here!'

'No one knows. Fleur and I discovered it and played here for years. No one will discover you, and as the weather is getting warmer you can sleep here for as long as you like. Please say you will.'

'Of course I will. This is wonderful, thank you.' He lowered his knapsack to the ground.

'I will bring you food and some blankets. I'll be back as soon as I can.'

Colette went to the kitchen and looked around. Food was so scarce now that there was very little that would not be missed. Four eggs sat in a bowl on the window ledge to keep cool. The precious eggs Fleur had been saving to make an *omelette aux herbes*. Michal could have one. Colette would pretend she had dropped the egg and go without her share of omelette. She set one to boil, along with a pot of the horrible tasting chicory that they used instead of coffee, while she raided the linen cupboard for blankets. She wrapped the hot egg in a napkin, cut a slice of bread and poured the coffee into a flask. As she was passing the dining room another thought occurred to her and she went stealthily to the drinks cabinet. There was a small bottle of cassis that had grown dusty since Delphine had grown bored of using it in cocktails three or four years previously. No one would miss it.

Michal was standing in the furthest corner of the Secret Garden. His frame was tense, and he glanced past Colette to the entrance when she squeezed through.

'It's just me.'

She thought of how she grew cold and clammy whenever she

passed a patrol or saw the black Citroens belonging to the *Abwehr* or Gestapo. Michal's fear must be ten times that. She felt nervous enough just helping him, though a little proud at doing some good for once.

'Whenever I come, I'll whistle *Dame Tartine* so you know it is me.'

He accepted her offerings with quiet thanks. She had expected him to devour the food immediately but instead he carefully peeled the egg and broke it into small pieces, picking up one at a time and chewing it slowly. Colette felt a sense of shame. Although she had a constant uncomfortable feeling of never being fully satiated, she was far from starving, and it was an inconvenience she had learned to endure. Michal had once been sturdy but was now emaciated. There were days when she could go without her breakfast to share with him instead.

'Where is your family?' she asked.

Michal swallowed the piece of bread he was chewing. 'I do not know. When the city fell, we tried to leave. My mother and uncle found spaces on a train, but I did not. I have not seen or heard from them since. I was staying in their home until a neighbour told me Jews were being hunted. I did not want to go to Germany so I left. I have not been back since.'

He spoke in such a matter-of-fact way that Colette's eyes filled with tears. She blinked them away, not wanting him to see her pitying him.

The sky had grown dull while they were talking and nights were still chilly once the sun dropped. Colette left Michal making a bed with the blankets, went to her room and wept.

For him. For the names in the bookshop ledger. For the widow at the *épicerie*. For the child she had encountered on the road leaving the city.

She had said Fleur needed to grow hard, and had been so proud of letting nothing affect her, but today it was beyond her.

~

Fleur received the news of the smashed egg with dismay and Colette felt like weeping again.

'I'm truly sorry. I was going to start preparing the omelette and it just slipped when I tried to crack it.'

Fleur sighed kindly. 'It doesn't matter. It was kind of you to try and help.'

She cracked the remaining eggs, deftly parting the shell into two with her thumbs, and separating the yolks and whites into two bowls. She began to whisk the whites into frothy peaks. She was not as good a cook as her aunt had been, but as food was becoming scarcer and more expensive it barely seemed to matter if the pastry was too thick or the sauces too thin as long as it was edible.

Colette watched Fleur move around the kitchen, fascinated and impressed. Fleur had learned things Colette didn't have the first idea about. She was almost as useless as Delphine. Now she had a secret mouth to feed she would need to be in the kitchen more.

'I want to learn how to cook. Could you show me what to do so I can be useful?' she asked.

'Are you sure?' Fleur tilted her head on one side, staring at Colette as if she had said she wanted to learn how to perform the can-can naked atop the *Arc de Triomphe*.

'Yes. I should learn how to wash clothes and clean the house too.'

Fleur gave her an odd look. 'Did you get a knock on the head today?'

'No.' Colette pouted, then collected herself. It was a fair question. She debated rapidly whether to tell Fleur about Michal, but the more people knew, the riskier it became 'I felt good about untangling the accounts today. It made me realise how much more I could do.'

Fleur looked surprised but still she handed the whisk over. 'Omelette is easy. Get that as fluffy as you can.'

While Colette whisked, Fleur chopped tarragon and mixed it with the yolks and a grind of pepper and salt. She heated the omelette pan with a little butter, held her hand over it, and when it was hot enough, stirred the yolks into the whites and tipped the mixture into the pan. Colette inhaled longingly as the mixture fluffed up and began to turn golden at the edges, spreading the sweet scent of aniseed throughout the kitchen. Her stomach growled and she hugged herself to stop it. Fleur took four plates from the rack in the cupboard and put them on the counter.

'You don't need four,' Colette said, trying to hide the regret in her voice. 'I broke my egg. You three eat it.'

Fleur flipped the omelette over to cook the top. 'Don't be silly. It was an accident. You need to eat.'

'But that isn't fair on the rest of you,' Colette protested. 'You'll go hungry because of my clumsiness. I'll be fine with some bread.'

By rights she should go without bread too but the smell of omelette made her mouth water and she couldn't be that unselfish. She hoped Fleur wouldn't notice the loaf was smaller than it should be.

'We're going hungry because the Germans have rationed our food and taken almost everything to feed their troops. One less egg isn't going to make much difference, and you need some food.'

Colette's eyes prickled. Really, she seemed to be ready to burst into tears at the slightest opportunity today. She did a quick calculation and, yes, her monthly visitor was about to arrive. That would explain why she was so tearful over the smallest things.

'Thank you. That's very generous. And thoughtful.' In Fleur's place she would have divided the omelette three ways as planned without even thinking about it. She needed to think more.

'Sébastien and Pierre say Karl Marx was one German who spoke sense. And talking of Sébastien…'

Fleur walked to her bag that was hanging behind the door and returned with a small bottle containing a deep red liquid. She held it out to Colette with narrowed eyes.

'He said to give you this to celebrate your first day as a productive member of society, and to tell you it isn't poisoned *or* watered down. He said you would understand the joke.'

Colette laughed as she looked at what Sébastien had sent her. Red wine. She'd been given much more expensive gifts, but this was the nicest one she had received for a long time.

Fleur began to wipe the countertop down with brisk strokes, sweeping up crumbs as if she had a vendetta against them. She gave Colette a sideways look. 'I didn't realise the two of you had been chatting for long.'

'It wasn't a chat as much as a lecture on how I'm naïve and spoiled,' Colette said, wrinkling her nose.

Fleur nodded and gave a slight smile. 'I'll carry the omelette. You bring the plates.'

~

After dinner, Colette shared the wine with Fleur while they washed up. She rinsed the bottle and put it on her dressing table beside her bottles of scent and pots of make-up, straightening it with a dreamy smile.

The conversation she'd had with Sébastien hadn't just been full of criticism. It had been fun and flirtatious. It had made her realise how much she missed talking to men since she had stopped visiting the clubs with the Lucienne sisters.

She was slightly hurt that Fleur hadn't contradicted what she had said Sébastien's judgement of her had been.

When Sophie telephoned her the following day and invited her to a birthday party, she didn't immediately refuse. She missed the sisters too and their easy-going, uncomplicated manner. They were nice friends to have and it felt like she would never be serious enough for Fleur and Sébastien's approval.

She could at least pay a visit to the hotel, even if she did not go dancing again. She had told Fleur that learning about what was going on was useful but it hadn't been really. Now she knew someone who might be interested in what she said. Being able to drop the names of important places or people into conversation would show Sébastien she was not as frivolous as he believed her to be.

Her eyes were open to how dreadful the world could be. She was different now.

Chapter Sixteen

Colette had been behaving oddly all night. Distracted enough to drop an egg. So overly grateful that Fleur still shared the omelette with her. And to have decided that she wanted to be more useful…

Could it possibly be Sébastien's influence? Fleur had watched Colette's face transform when she received the wine from Sébastien. She had blushed, her expression a mixture of delight and coyness. Fleur burned to know what had happened between them while she had been upstairs. Colette seemed far too happy if she had been called naïve and spoiled. What else had she missed?

Actually, Fleur mused as she sat at her dressing table, she was glad she had the gift to bring because it meant Colette had not asked what had happened when Fleur visited Sébastien. She closed her eyes as she brushed her hair, trying to conjure as much of the conversation as she could remember.

'I've been thinking,' Sébastien had said. 'That apartment above the bookshop isn't used for anything, is it? Could we perhaps meet there sometimes instead of at the café? Being on a smaller street, the entrance is a little more discreet.'

She'd been so eager to help. 'Of course. I'll give you a key. That way you can use it even if I'm not there.'

'That's good. I think Pierre has a few ideas about changing the content of what we write and a bookshop would be a more natural place to find printing materials than the cellar of a bar.'

'What changes is he wanting to make?' Fleur had asked with interest. Sébastien claimed not to know and she was eager to find out.

Colette's reaction to the pamphlet she had come across had stung Fleur. It may only be a small thing they did, but it meant something to Fleur to be doing anything. What was Colette doing after all? Making omelettes was hardly going to change the course of the war. She had even announced that she would stop wearing the attention-commanding hats that she and Delphine had so proudly created. Fleur drummed her fingernails on the dressing table, a sudden burst of irritation at Colette catching her unawares. Yes, the reason was fair, and the damage done to the morale of French women outweighed the insult to the Germans, but it felt as if Colette was becoming more reconciled to life as it now was and was burying her head in the sand. She probably wasn't even aware of half the dreadful things that were happening. If that was what being hard involved, Fleur would prefer to remain soft.

~

She arranged with Sébastien and Pierre to meet them after the shop closed on the following Saturday afternoon. She was slightly apprehensive in case Colette decided to spend the day at the shop but needn't have worried.

'Please don't judge me but Sophie invited me to the hotel for dinner tonight. It's her birthday so I couldn't refuse.' She gave

Fleur a guilty look. 'We might go dancing for an hour or two afterwards.'

'It isn't for me to judge,' Fleur said curtly. 'You do what you feel is right.'

Colette looked pained and Fleur felt a flicker of remorse. Only a flicker, mind, because Colette brightened almost immediately. 'I imagine there will be cake. Would you like me to bring you a slice?'

Fleur's mouth watered at the thought. It would be good cake, as the hotel was well supplied with rations. She blinked to clear her head of the temptation. She could hardly disapprove of Colette spending time at the hotel and then benefit herself.

'No, thank you,' she said firmly.

'It's only cake,' Colette said with a slight eye-roll.

Fleur couldn't be bothered to argue. Just when she had thought Colette was starting to change, she proved she wasn't all that different.

'Then go and enjoy it with a clear conscience.'

'Yes, I will.' Colette rammed her felt hat firmly onto her high roll of hair and tossed her head. 'I don't have enough friends to offend the ones I have.'

She stalked out of the house leaving Fleur with a sense of contrition that didn't seem at all fair. She hadn't done anything wrong, and there was nothing stopping Colette trying to make new friends.

～

For once, the shop was busy. A party of young Germans in uniform appeared at half past one. They discovered the brash covers of the crime novels with cries of enthusiasm and spent time, and eventually francs, among the shelves. When the clock on the desk rang two o'clock with a shrill trill, Fleur ushered them back into the street, and closed the front door. Fortunately, the Germans had been too absorbed with their good-humoured chatter to notice the two French men idly thumbing through volumes, who had not been asked to leave.

Fleur wrote the purchases in her ledger, which was already much neater and more organised, (she told herself to compliment Colette about it later) then led Sébastien and Pierre up the stairs.

'This is a large flat,' Pierre said, gazing round with interest.

'You should move here,' Sébastien suggested. 'It would save you from having to travel all the way from Passy.'

Fleur stared around. It was a good size but the presence of Monsieur Ramper was still there, in the choice of carpet and drapes at the windows. Bookcases lined two walls, all filled with volumes, photographs, and bibelots. The furniture was terribly old fashioned, heavy and dark. One large window overlooked the street and another at the other end looked over an alleyway. What passed for a kitchen in one corner was quite filthy with dust, and the crockery was old and fussily ornate. There were two bedrooms, but Fleur had never been in them. She opened the rear window, struggling slightly with the heavy sash.

'I have considered it, but I don't think I would like to live alone. The four of us pool our rations and somehow that seems to go further than if I had to cook for myself. I pay no rent and Monsieur Nadon does not ask me for any money for the bills.'

She put her basket of shopping on the table and sat.

'That reminds me, I don't know what you said to Colette the other day, Sébastien, but when I got home, she asked me what she could do to help. She wanted me to teach her to cook.'

She watched him carefully, not knowing exactly what she was hoping to see at the mention of Colette's name, but he just lifted his hands in a shrug.

'Nothing I can think of. Is she any good?'

'Why, are you looking for a wife?' Pierre guffawed. Sébastien shot him a dirty look.

'She doesn't know the first thing,' Fleur said. It wasn't quite true. The previous day Fleur had talked Colette through instructions in *Tante* Agnes' well-thumbed volume of *Le Livre de Cuisine* by Madame E. Saint-Ange. Fleur had learned to bone and fricassée a rabbit, while Colette made a pepper sauce that the whole household agreed was excellent. 'That is, as long as I keep an eye on what she's doing, she doesn't burn things.'

Pierre gave a contemptuous snort. 'She has no other occupation. She should do everything. Women like her are a waste of time and space. They care only for their own comfort.'

Fleur's neck grew hot at the hatred in Pierre's voice. It was one thing for Fleur to judge Colette's behaviour, but old loyalties bubbled to the surface.

'Colette has a good heart when something reminds her to use it. She gave money to a mother and child as we all tried to leave the city, and she bought lollipops for some children when their mother got in a fight.'

'Oh it's easy to have compassion and do charity when you are rich,' Pierre said.

Fleur looked away, unable to disagree. Nothing Colette did required effort or risk. At least she hadn't mentioned the defiant hats and given him even more of a reason to despise her!

'If she lived as we have to, I'm sure things would be very different. Suffering changes people.'

'Talking of changes, what changes are you proposing to what we write?' Sébastien asked, smoothly changing the subject before Pierre continued ranting.

Pierre helped himself to one of the apples from Fleur's basket. She eyed him indignantly.

'Nothing we write makes a difference to the situation we are living in. Nothing anyone has written has changed the course of the war or encouraged Paris to rise up.'

He took a knife from his trouser pocket and began to peel and quarter the apple as he spoke, the sharp blade slicing the fruit he cupped in his hands. His manner was savage, and Fleur shivered a little. His words echoed Colette's judgement on the leaflet she had discovered, and she was dryly amused at the thought of telling Pierre so.

'We are giving people hope that they are not alone,' she commented.

'Alone in waiting for something that will never change,' Pierre spat. He used the point of the knife to gouge out a chunk of apple and ate it from the blade.

'I am not exactly sure what you have in mind,' Sébastien said.

'We tell people to go on the offensive. Throw bricks through the windows of shops that serve Germans. The window here had a brick through it when it was owned by the Jew. Every establishment that caters to the Germans needs to be shown exactly what patriotic French men and women think of them.'

Sébastien and Fleur exchanged a worried glance. Pierre had always been hot-headed, but this was uncharacteristic behaviour. Fleur didn't like the way he had referred to Monsieur Ramper either.

'Will you put a brick through my window?' Fleur asked quietly.

Pierre paused with the knife halfway to his mouth and gaped as if she was stupid.

'I sold books to the Germans this afternoon. You were there just now. Do I deserve a brick through the window for permitting them to spend money in my shop? If I didn't, there would be no apples for you to help yourself to.'

He had the grace to look slightly ashamed; his fingers digging into the flesh, juice squeezing up around his nails.

'And what about the Café Morlaix? Does Sébastien deserve to be sweeping glass each morning?'

Pierre looked nonplussed. He cut another slice of apple. 'Obviously not. We are friends. I know you don't do it through choice, but under sufferance. And I'll buy you another apple when I see some.'

Sébastien took the knife from Pierre's hand. 'Fleur is right. Yes, of course there will be those who have taken the opportunity to actively profit from the Occupation, but how do you distinguish those from the people who are just trying to make a living?'

Pierre exhaled loudly. 'I don't know. The ones who immediately displayed signs saying German was spoken there, or that Germans were welcome. You are both being wilfully obtuse in my opinion.'

'You are being short-sighted,' Fleur retorted. 'Monsieur Nadon is guilt-ridden at his collaboration.'

'I have already said I know that,' Pierre said.

'Yes, I know that you know. But will the recipient of a leaflet you push under a door in the seventh arrondissement know?' she retorted.

'Well done, Fleur, Plato would have been proud call you his pupil,' Sébastien said, his voice warm.

She beamed at him, looking up into his eyes and hoping to see the same approval in them that she heard in his voice, but there was nothing out of the ordinary she could grasp onto.

'Perhaps Nadon's business would be a necessary sacrifice,' Pierre muttered.

'You are being rude and unpleasant,' Sébastien said.

'I am feeling rude and unpleasant,' Pierre snapped.

The atmosphere in the room congealed.

'I am frustrated and angry. Nothing is making a difference. Nothing we do. Nothing the army does. My neighbour's mother was arrested two days ago. She is sixty-seven years old and all she did was speak sharply to a couple of German sluts who pushed in front of her at the lingerie shop.' Pierre walked to the window and hurled the apple core out. There was a crashing of dustbins, followed by the indignant yowl of the black tomcat who had sired half of Montparnasse's feline population. 'Can you imagine that? A respectable mother of four hauled off in handcuffs, all because a couple of grey mice didn't get their stockings quickly enough. People are being arrested on the slightest pretence.'

Fleur told them about the woman arrested over the *épicerie* fight. 'People are becoming nastier. If we write anything we should write a paper encouraging Parisians not to denounce their neighbours for petty acts.'

Pierre looked slightly mollified. 'I suppose that will do for the next one. But do not expect me to be satisfied with inaction for much longer. I'm going for a walk to clear my head.'

'I'm sorry about that. I don't know what came over him,' Sébastien said once Pierre was gone.

Fleur closed the window.

'I do. I understand his frustration. I feel it myself sometimes. I don't know what the answer is, but I have a feeling that bricks through windows are not the answer. I suppose we should leave too.'

'I wonder…' Sébastien was looking thoughtful. He walked to the window and stared out at the narrow alleyway between the buildings. He leaned back against the frame and folded his arms. 'My cousin is going to be passing through Paris in a couple of days. Could she stay here for one night? She won't leave a mess and will be gone first thing in the morning. Certainly before you get here to open the bookshop.'

'A cousin? Aren't your family all in Brittainy?'

'They used to be. Since the start of the war people have spread out.'

There was something cagey in his manner.

'Is she really a cousin?'

'What else would she be?' Sébastien gave her an innocent look, but his shoulders were tense.

'I'm teasing,' Fleur said. 'I thought you might have a secret lover you don't want to take to the café.'

'Oh.' His expression was neutral.

'Do you have any lovers at the moment?' Fleur asked idly.

It was none of her business but if Colette did like Sébastien, as Fleur suspected, then she wanted to know if it was reciprocated.

Sébastien's shoulders dropped. 'No. There is no one I am involved with at present.'

'Is there anyone you would like to become involved with?' Fleur asked quietly. She held her breath, heart in her throat. If he was to say Colette's name, she would hate it.

He scratched his chin then ticked his finger at her.

'I'm not going to incriminate or embarrass myself by answering that question. Francine is not my blood cousin, but she is somebody I grew up with in the same village and that makes her as close as. I swear to you – and to anyone else who might have a passing interest in knowing – that she isn't and has never been my lover. So, please can she stay here?'

'Of course.' Fleur felt a little embarrassed at having pressed him. 'I am sure Monsieur Ramper would be delighted to know his home is a shelter for others.'

He left. Fleur pottered around the apartment, tidying the shelves and dusting, not happy at the thought of visitors coming in and seeing the neglect. She investigated the bedrooms and turned back the counterpanes on each bed in preparation for Francine's visit. The rooms were good sizes and she considered for a few moments whether she was being silly not to move in. She remembered the promise she had made to Monsieur Ramper and before she left, she selected four of the volumes from the bookshelves that might be risky to leave around. She would hide them in the cold frame in the garden where no one would discover them.

She was in the process of unlocking her bicycle wheel from the drainpipe next to the shop when someone touched her shoulder from behind. She cried out in alarm, her immediate thought of the books she had wrapped in a dishcloth and put at the bottom of her basket of shopping.

'Why so jumpy? It's just me.'

Pierre. She sagged with relief and turned to face him.

'You took me by surprise. Why are you creeping up like that?'

He looked disgruntled. 'I brought you this to replace the one I ate.'

He held out an apple, then leaned forward and dropped it into her basket where it lay innocently on top of her contraband. She expected him to move away but instead he caught her up in his arms and kissed her. She pushed him away and glared at him.

'Why did you do that?'

'Because you are charming. Because I wanted to apologise for being rude earlier.' He tilted her chin back with a fingertip and leaned close. 'Because I am in an odd mood and can't help but think every day might be our last. You and I are the same, Fleur. We are both poor and trying to make our way in the world.'

He whispered the words against the side of Fleur's neck, playfully tickling the sensitive skin. 'We are the workers. The people who keep things going. Paris should belong to us and we need to take it. This is where we belong.'

His words broke the spell that his tongue had been writing over her flesh. She wriggled free.

'I don't want to just belong here. I love Paris – it's my home – but I want to travel. I want to see the world. Colette has been to England. I've been nowhere.'

Pierre twirled a lock of Fleur's hair. 'What were you to her while she was there? Your friend, Colette. I don't say there is anything wrong with her, but what use is she to the world compared to you? I would rather a hundred Fleurs than a single Colette.'

Fleur flattened against the door. What had she been? Colette hadn't even written to her. 'What are you hoping to achieve by saying this?'

'I think you're still pining for Sébastien and he's pining for your friend. That's clear from what he says. Forget him. Be with me.'

He put his hands on either side of her face, his body leaning against hers to keep her still. He began to kiss the side of her neck. His moustache was coarse, but it wasn't exactly unpleasant. Her body responded even if her mind and heart were less enthusiastic. He worked his way round to her mouth, tugging at her lips with his and when she didn't reciprocate, he leaned his head back.

'Do you want me to stop?'

'I don't know. Maybe not. Pierre, I don't love you.' She wasn't sure after his outburst earlier that she even liked him very much.

He laughed but it sounded bitter rather than amused. 'Love? What do you think this is, Fleur? A romantic two-reeler with a happy ending of marriage and children, or one of those books from fifty years ago where letting a man fuck her ruins a woman's reputation? You don't have to love me. I certainly don't love you. I just want some fun.'

Fun. When had Fleur last had fun? Colette had fun; flirting and laughing with men in nightclubs. Eating birthday cake. Did Colette...?

Fleur blushed to realise she couldn't say the word Pierre used, even in her head. Did Colette want to do that with Sébastien? Colette wouldn't hesitate to kiss him, that was certain. After all, Colette had kissed Sébastien when she had only just met him. And Sébastien had kissed her first.

Fleur's stomach twisted. What the hell, she didn't have to like

Pierre, he just needed to give her some fun. Let her feel something other than anxiety and watchfulness. It was only a kiss. She wasn't going to go any further.

She reached her arms around Pierre's neck and kissed him for a longer time. She only stopped when he began wriggling his fingers under her skirt towards the top of her stockings. His thumb brushed against her thigh and she felt a ripple of revulsion.

'That's enough,' she said, pushing his hand away gently and looking up at him with a smile.

Pierre's face was flushed. 'You're an ice-cold bitch, aren't you? Getting me heated up and ready to burst.'

'I'm sorry. It felt strange. It is my fault, not yours.'

He frowned. 'Still a virgin after all this time?'

She nodded, feeling like a child. Wishing she was as ice-cold as he thought she was. If that was how she reacted to being touched intimately it looked like she would remain one too.

Pierre adjusted his trousers. 'Alright, we'll stop this time. If you would like some fun at any point, you know where I am, but don't be such a little tease again. It's not fair on a man to make him stop like that.'

He sauntered off. Fleur waited until he had turned the corner then wheeled her bicycle the other direction. She would take a longer route home rather than risk bumping into Pierre again. It was only as she began to cycle against the breeze that she realised she had tears running down her cheeks.

Pierre had been so kind, stopping even when she had made him think she wanted him. What was wrong with her? She envied Colette's ease around men. She could ask Colette for advice; how to stop being a tease without even intending to be, but Colette and men wasn't something she wanted to think about. Whatever advice Colette gave, Fleur would be picturing her carrying it out with Sébastien. She clutched the handlebars tighter. Better to say nothing, avoid the subject and do her best to avoid Pierre until she worked out what she should do again.

~

Fleur carried two books home each time she returned from the shop. She'd initially planned to take them to the Secret Garden, but decided she might be spotted wandering in and out of the bushes if she did it too often. There was no reason to think the house might be raided by the authorities so she waited until she had a large bag taking up space in her wardrobe. By mid-June she decided it was safe to take them to the Secret Garden to hide with the volumes of poetry. She made her way down the garden, pausing to take a moment to smell the sweet scents. Some of her plants were starting to grow and might bear fruit when summer and autumn came. Courgettes, tomatoes, and beans would be a welcome addition to the repetitive menu. She crawled through the door into the Secret Garden and stood.

A hand went over her mouth and she was pulled backwards against the wall, the blade of a knife glinting in the late evening sunlight.

Chapter Seventeen

Fleur couldn't scream. She could barely breathe. Blinded by terror she flailed her arms and then as quickly as the pressure over her mouth had started, it eased, though the hand remained.

'Mademoiselle Fleur, don't fear me.'

She recognised the voice, though she hadn't heard it since before the Occupation and she sagged. Michal Drucker.

'Do you promise me you won't shout again?' he whispered in a desperate voice. Fleur nodded and he released his hand.

She relaxed and leaned back against the wall. Her legs wobbled and she slid down until she was kneeling with her knees tucked beneath her. Michal was still holding the knife but on seeing her staring, he tossed it onto the blanket that he had discarded. Beside the blanket was a knapsack. A pair of socks were draped over a hook in the wall, drying. He had made this his home.

Michal sat beside her. 'Do you have any food? When I heard the door, I thought it might be Mademoiselle Nadon.'

'No, I'm sorry, I don't.' Fleur digested his words. 'Colette brings you food? She knows you are here?'

'Yes, when she can. It was Mademoiselle Nadon who brought me here and let me hide.'

He told Fleur of how he had slept on the streets until Colette had chanced upon him. How one night of promised rest had turned into many.

'How long have you been hiding here?' she asked weakly.

'I am not sure. I planned to mark the days but I decided after a week that I would rather let time pass without counting.'

Fleur could scarcely believe what she was hearing, her world inverting itself into something completely new and confusing. She had assumed Colette's only form of defiance had been parading in front of the soldiers in her best clothes. Now it turned out that Colette had been doing something not only braver, but infinitely more compassionate than Fleur had ever dreamed of doing. She had never breathed the slightest hint to Fleur even when Fleur had made withering comments about her visiting the hotel. Or maybe because of those comments. Would Fleur have trusted someone so critical with a secret that could see her executed? Not if she had any sense!

'I'm sure Colette has explained that our ration coupons barely give us enough to feed ourselves but we can be creative. I bought a Toulouse sausage this morning so I could make a cassoulet that would last us all for a while.'

Michal's eyes took on a worried expression. 'That's very kind of you, but I cannot.'

Of course. Fleur felt very stupid. People of his faith did not eat pork. 'Not even to save yourself from starving?' she asked. He looked unhealthy and close to starvation.

Michal spread his hands out. 'If I abandoned my faith, it would be as good as abandoning my life, but I thank you for your generosity.'

'Let me think of something else then.'

She wondered whether to broach the subject with Colette. They could take turns giving Michal their breakfast, which would be fairer. But she would have to explain to Colette what she had been doing in the Secret Garden in the first place. She took the books out and showed them to Michal.

'I need to put these safely away before I go. Monsieur Ramper has so many boxes that it has taken me months to find what looks important.' Compared to breaking the law by sheltering Michal, her actions felt paltry. What did paper matter compared to a life? To her surprise, Michal snatched the top one up eagerly.

'Brecht. I know the name. This is a very good thing you do. May I read this?'

It shouldn't surprise her, of course. If Fleur was prevented from reading, she would be unhappy. 'Of course. Please, read anything you wish. Let me show you where the others are.'

She lifted the lid of the cold frame and pushed aside the clutter to reveal the stash of books. Michal's smile broadened.

'Thank you, Mademoiselle Bonnivard. My mind has been too free to imagine what is happening in France. These will help me forget for a while. Now you should go before anyone wonders where you are.'

Before Fleur could pick up her bag there was a scraping sound as the door was dragged open. Both she and Michal tensed, eyes meeting in shared panic. Then there was a low whistle of the first two bars of a child's nursery rhyme. Michal's shoulders dropped and Fleur's heart rate slowed to something almost sedate as she realised they had not been discovered. Colette emerged from the tangle of plants. When she saw Fleur, she froze and grimaced.

'*Merde!*'

'It's alright. I'm not going to tell anyone,' Fleur assured her. 'I found him by accident.'

'And now she has found me I must go,' Michal said.

Colette looked at Fleur, a flash of anger in her eyes. 'What did you say?'

Fleur shook her head. 'Nothing!'

Michal coughed. 'It's true. Now both of you know, both of you will be in danger if anyone finds me. I will not do that to your family.'

'I promise I can keep your secret as well as Colette has.'

Fleur had known him long enough to recognise his mind was set, but there was still hope he might be persuaded.

'Don't leave now while you have nowhere in mind to go.'

'I have imposed upon you for long enough, Colette,' Michal said. 'I don't want to put either of you in more danger. I was only ever going to stay for one night but this has been a magnificent respite from the world.'

'Where will you go?' Colette asked.

He shrugged. 'I will try to go south. Perhaps I will be reunited with my family. There are a few sentimental items in the *loge* I would like you to bring me, if you could.'

'Oh!' Inspiration struck Fleur. 'When Monsieur Ramper left the bookshop, he said there was a network. He described it like a piece of string stretching across France. People helping those who needed to leave and go somewhere safe. Would you do that?'

'Do you know how to contact them?' Colette asked.

Fleur frowned. She suspected who might, but didn't want to name Sébastien. 'Not directly. Michal, give me a few days to see what I can do.'

Colette had brought Michal a wedge of cheese and a flask of coffee. After securing a promise that he would stay until they found a way for him to leave safely, they left him to eat and returned to the house.

'When you broke the egg and we made an omelette, you didn't really break it, did you?' Fleur asked.

Colette gave her a guilty look and shook her head.

'So, you discovered my secret.' She sighed. 'I thought it was such a safe place too.'

They were at the edge of the bushes. The garden below the fountain had long since been turned into a vegetable patch but the fountain remained in place. Fleur sat on the ground and leaned against it as they had done in childhood.

'You could have told me,' Fleur said. 'I could have helped you.'

Colette scraped at the moss on the stonework with her fingernail. 'I didn't need you to. What were you doing poking around in there anyway?'

Fleur took a deep breath, relieved the decision had been taken out of her hands.

'I have a secret too. As I have discovered yours, it is right I should share mine. I've been hiding books from the shop in the cold frame. Books that would not be looked on favourably by the Nazis.'

She could stop there and it would be enough to explain her presence, but she was tired of deceit. 'But do you remember the leaflet that you came across and said was silly? I have been writing and printing them with Sébastien and Pierre. We glue them to walls or slip them through doors.'

Colette let out a low whistle. 'For how long?'

'Since the first autumn after France fell. We had to do something. It was Pierre's idea originally but all three of us played a part in composing and distributing them.' Fleur laughed as something occurred to her. 'In fact, the night that you and I...' She looked around furtively, reluctant to speak of it even here. 'When we encountered the soldier in the park, I had a bundle of them in my bag ready to circulate. All the time you were worried about him raping me I was more concerned that he would discover them.'

'You've kept this from me for all that time. Even after *that* happened. Didn't you trust me?'

There was genuine hurt in Colette's voice and Fleur felt a stab of contrition.

'It wasn't just my secret to keep. I know you thought what we are doing is silly, but would you tell something like that to someone who went dancing with Germans?'

Colette drew a sharp breath. 'Dancing is one thing but informing on people is totally different. You know I'm not a traitor.'

She looked up and Fleur saw the glimmer of moisture in her eyes. 'But yes. I … I see why you didn't.'

Fleur folded her arms. 'We didn't tell anyone. The fewer people who know, the safer it is for everyone.'

Colette bit her lip. 'I'm sorry I said it was silly. I would never have thought it of you or Sébastien. He seemed a man of words not action. You are so daring.'

'Not really. Compared to what you have been doing it is nothing. You were right as well. It hasn't made a difference to anyone. There hasn't been a great uprising and France is as oppressed as ever.' Fleur leaned against Colette and sighed. 'I thought I was being brave hiding things in a box. I never expected you to be concealing a whole person.'

Colette giggled then put her hands quickly over her mouth, as if she thought it was the wrong thing to do. Fleur felt like laughing too even though the situation wasn't remotely funny.

'Only for a short while though. I couldn't let him stay sleeping on the streets when I saw how ill he looked. Oh, I wish you hadn't discovered him. All the bad luck that we should both use the same hiding place!'

Fleur squeezed her hand consolingly. 'It just proves what a good hiding place it is. It also proves how good we are at keeping secrets.' She sat up straight. 'Let's say from now on there will be no secrets between us anymore. It might mean a little more danger, but I would rather be in danger with a friend than in safety alone.'

Colette hugged her. 'Oh me too. It means a lot that you know I'm not as shiftless as you think I am.'

Fleur was about to protest that she didn't, but it wouldn't be entirely true so she just hugged Colette back.

They walked back to the house together. Delphine had come out onto the terrace along with Louis and they were sitting in the wicker basket chairs positioned to catch the last rays of sunlight. Delphine was flicking through a fashion magazine and Louis reading the newspaper.

'Hello, girls. What have you been doing in the garden?' Louis asked with a smile. He looked old and tired. Fleur was quite anxious for his health.

Fleur tensed but Colette didn't seem worried. She kissed Louis' cheek.

'Good evening, *Papa*, good evening, *Mère*. Isn't it beautiful weather? Fleur and I have been checking the vegetables. I think we may have succeeded in growing something edible! Ooh, is that a cocktail? May I have one?'

She indicated Delphine's glass.

'There isn't any left,' Delphine said, casting a regretful look at her glass.

'Oh, well, it doesn't matter. I can live without it. I think I will go and do my nails. They're dirty after touching the plants. Come along, Fleur, we'll do yours too.'

She swept her arm through Fleur's and whisked her off into the house.

'I don't know how you can be so cool,' Fleur remarked, full of admiration.

'Lots of practice fibbing when they asked where I was going in the past.' Colette giggled. 'I'd better go do my nails. Shall we do yours too?'

Fleur looked at her fingers. Shorts nails and cut square across the top.

'Why not.'

She followed Colette to Colette's bedroom.

'Do you really think you could find someone to help Michal, or did you just say that so he didn't leave?' Colette asked as she filed Fleur's nails.

'A bit of both.'

Colette paused her buffing. 'Is it Sébastien?'

Fleur stiffened. She tried to pull her hand away but Colette held on.

'That means yes, doesn't it?'

Fleur nodded and Colette smiled triumphantly.

'I knew he was hiding something when I spoke to him. Men are so easy to see through.'

Were they? A flash of annoyance passed through Fleur. She didn't have Colette's practice and couldn't see through Sébastien at all.

'I'll ask him on Wednesday night. I know we can trust him. Tomorrow, you go speak to Michal and tell him we are trying to arrange some help for him.'

Colette opened the nail polish. 'I hope we can. My heart broke when he told me everything he had been through. It doesn't feel like there will ever be an end to this misery. I want to come with you when you ask Sébastien. I want to be there.'

Her eyes had widened at the first mention of Sébastien's name and now they grew uncharacteristically demure.

'It might be safer if I go alone.'

'It's my secret and my responsibility,' Colette said. 'I should be there.'

Fleur suspected Colette's insistence had less to do with the secret and more to do with seeing Sébastien, but she could hardly raise that objection. 'I suppose so,' she agreed, slightly reluctantly.

'Good.'

'Colette, can I ask you something personal?'

Colette looked startled then nodded. She paused in painting her nails and leaned forward a little, eyes widening with interest. 'You can ask, but if it is too personal I might not answer, even though we said no secrets.'

Fleur bit her lip. 'I mean personal about me. When you kiss a man, how do you know whether what you're feeling is good or bad?'

Colette laughed lightly. 'Goodness, I don't know. I don't think I've ever kissed a man and not liked it.' Fleur felt redness filling her face. Colette's eyes grew serious. 'But you have, haven't you? Has something happened?'

Fleur related the confrontation with Pierre, leaving out his disparaging remarks about Colette. 'I think I should have liked it, but I didn't really. I think there is something wrong with me.'

Colette pursed her lips. 'No I don't think so. Pierre sounds quite horrible so I'm not surprised you don't want to kiss him. I don't think I would want to. Maybe you just haven't found the right person. Have you kissed many people?'

Fleur shook her head. It was embarrassing to admit that at her age she had so little experience. As for finding the right person, well, she had a terrible feeling she had found the wrong person, but wanted him anyway.

Colette put the nail polish brush down and looked directly at Fleur.

'Did you want to kiss Sébastien? Because I would quite like to again.'

Fleur felt sick. She followed the movement of Colette's scarlet nails as she wiggled and blew on them. Little red daggers. Colette had an elegance that was quite breath-taking and which Fleur could never hope to emulate. Of course Sébastien would find her intoxicating. If it came to making a choice, she had a dreadful certainty Sébastien would choose Colette. She couldn't bear the humiliation of losing a competition before she had even entered it.

'No,' she lied. 'He's my friend and he's very serious.'

Colette pursed her lips into a bud. 'Yes, he is serious, isn't he, but I don't want to kiss him for the conversation. And even though he'd gladly kiss me, I don't think he likes me very much. He thinks I'm a silly rich girl, after all.'

Fleur couldn't deny it; she'd been guilty of misjudging Colette too. She consoled herself with the thought that if her friends did kiss it would be a fire that quickly burned out. Perhaps it was best to let it rather than trying to stop it igniting at all. She smiled back.

'Well, when we speak to him on Wednesday, he won't be able to say that any longer.'

Chapter Eighteen

Wednesday felt a long time coming. Fleur left a note at the Café Morlaix asking Sébastien to meet her in the apartment above the bookshop later that afternoon. As the time drew near Colette paced the room, unable to settle. She straightened bookshelves and ornaments, washed and dried every piece of crockery and cutlery, and rearranged the furniture so that the comfy chairs were in front of the window. Fleur sat at the dining table, working her way through a bag of darning and mending she had brought.

'I don't know how you can be so calm,' Colette told her, more than once.

'I'm not,' Fleur replied. 'I'm just tense sitting still.'

'Will we hear the doorbell from up here?'

Fleur bit off a length of thread between her teeth. 'Sébastien has his own key. He can let himself in.'

'Oh.' Colette felt a tightening in her ribs. 'What does he need that for?'

'A cousin of his stayed here a couple of nights ago on her way through the city.' Fleur wrinkled her nose. 'At least, he said she was his cousin.'

'Don't you believe him?' Colette asked sharply. 'He isn't using it to conduct an affair, is he?' Although she had assured Fleur she was not serious about Sébastien, she didn't intend to share him with another woman. Her affairs might be fleeting but she intended to be the only object of her lover's attention.

'I teased him about that.' Fleur twisted a half-darned stocking around her fingers. 'I actually wonder now if she was someone using the methods we are hoping to make use of.'

'I wonder.' During the conversation over the unpaid book bills Sébastien had mentioned people risking themselves. Did he have first-hand knowledge of the process?

He arrived ten minutes later and greeted Fleur with a kiss to each cheek. After a brief hesitation he did the same to Colette, holding onto her shoulders slightly longer than was necessary. Fleur had prepared a pot of what passed for coffee and they sat around the table.

'How did your cousin find her stay? Frances, wasn't it?' Fleur asked.

Sébastien paused for slightly longer than he should have needed to before replying,

'Francine. Yes, I think she was comfortable. She didn't leave a mess, did she?'

Fleur didn't answer. She laced her fingers together on top of the table and caught Colette's eye. She raised her brows questioningly. Colette nodded. Now there was no going back.

'I need to know if I can trust you with a life-or-death secret,' she said.

'You already did,' Sébastien replied. His eyes flickered to Colette and back to Fleur, including them both in his answer. 'Of course you can. When have I ever proven untrustworthy?'

'You haven't.' Fleur drummed her fingers on the table.

Colette leaned forwards, watching carefully. She was not a part of their secret life though she longed to be included, not only because it would draw her closer to Sébastien. While she had been fooling around with accessories and pretending that dancing was bravery, they had been defying the German authorities. They had courage that she lacked. She wanted to be fearless but still, she felt a sense of terror at what Fleur was about to say.

'If I wanted to help a person leave the city, how would I go about it?'

Sébastien leaned back in his chair. He removed his glasses and rubbed the lenses on his shirt, peering at Fleur. 'This person cannot leave by their own devices?'

'Sadly not,' Fleur said. 'If we knew of somebody living in a location who could not leave and must not be discovered, do you think it would be possible for them to be helped?'

Colette suppressed a sigh. This careful dancing around the subject could go on all afternoon.

'We are looking after the man who was the concierge from my family's apartment building. He is a Jew. He needs to get out of the city. Do you know how we can contact someone who can help him?'

'You are sheltering a Jew?' Sébastien's eyes widened and he put his glasses back on to stare at Colette closely. 'Are you insane? Do you realise how dangerous that is for you both?'

'Of course we know it is dangerous. That's why we're asking for help in confidence,' Fleur answered.

'We have known him all our lives,' Colette said defensively. 'It is all my doing. Fleur didn't know anything about it. If anyone should get into trouble, it should be me.'

Sébastien picked up his coffee cup and drank it in one go. 'Why ask me?'

'I remembered you talking about people risking their lives to help others leave the city. Do you remember when we spoke in the bookshop?'

'Yes, I remember that conversation.' Sébastien nodded slowly. Colette's heart thumped in her chest, the pulse heavy enough to reach her belly.

'I didn't know that,' Fleur said, giving Colette a sidelong glance that made her feel slightly rueful. 'Was Francine someone who might have been in a similar situation?'

Sébastien looked from one woman to the other, then abruptly pushed his chair back and walked to the window. He stood with his hands clasped behind his back and stared out for a long time. Colette moved to go join him but Fleur's hand on her arm made her pause. Slightly chafing, she sat back down.

'You make a formidable pair of detectives,' he said with a slight laugh in his voice. 'Yes, I know people who know people who help people move around discreetly. Francine – I don't know her real name but that is the one I was given – is a member of a resistance group. She needed to leave the town she was living in and I was asked to find her a place to sleep before another contact took her onwards.'

'Then you can help us?' Fleur breathed.

'Possibly,' Sébastien answered. 'Tell me everything, but before you do, find something stronger than coffee. I think we are all going to need it.'

They moved to the comfortable chairs. The only thing Fleur could find in Monsieur Ramper's cupboard was half a bottle of sickly Chambord liqueur but they drank it anyway. Sébastien sat in the middle chair, with Fleur on his left and Colette on his right. He sat twisting the glass in his hand, only moving to turn his head to look at whichever woman was speaking.

'I encountered Michal on the afternoon we talked,' Colette said, 'when you asked Fleur to meet you and I went home by myself. I think it was hearing you talking about the people who had to leave that made me want to help Michal.'

'Was it? I commend you, mademoiselle. You have compassion and bravery. It is a rare combination but an admirable one.'

Sébastien looked at Colette and there was a new light in his eyes that she had not seen before. She was used to seeing desire or flirtation, or even pity or scorn, but this was something else entirely. She thought it was respect. It felt good.

She gave him a sweet smile. Her head felt a little fuzzy. The Chambord had tasted nicer the more she drank of it and she wondered if Delphine might have a bottle at home somewhere.

'Where is he now?'

Colette slid her eyes to Fleur who shook her head almost imperceptibly.

Colette cleared her throat. 'We'd better not tell you. Not yet. It isn't that we don't trust you, but the fewer people who know, the safer it will be.'

'Very wise.'

Sébastien patted her arm, allowing his fingers to rest lightly on her left wrist. Tiny butterflies danced up her bare arm and around her belly. Fleur was sitting forward, and Colette could see her eyes drop to where Sébastien's hand rested. Her lips were pressed together tightly. Reluctantly, Colette drew her arm onto her lap.

Sébastien turned to Fleur. 'I can make no promises but let me speak to someone and I will see if we can find a solution.'

'Thank you!' Fleur said. She leaned forward and kissed his cheek.

'Yes, thank you!' Colette impulsively leaned over and hugged him. She heard Fleur cough. Sébastien stiffened and she drew back, mumbling apologies and mortified that she had been so obvious.

'Now might be a good time to tell you that Colette knows about the leaflets,' Fleur said, refilling her glass.

Sébastien raised his brows.

'And if you don't object, I would like to help with them.'

'What?' Fleur leaned forward. She looked unhappy. 'You didn't tell me that.'

Colette felt a little burst of guilt at having surprised her but had suspected that her offer would be met with resistance. 'I only just thought of it,' she said, mentally crossing her fingers at the lie.

'Do you object?' Sébastien asked. Fleur shook her head.

'No, but Pierre might need persuading,' she replied.

Colette didn't like Pierre, even though she had never met him. Fleur's account of their kiss had already prejudiced her. If only Fleur could find a nicer man.

'I'm sure between you both he can be talked round,' Colette said.

Sébastien pushed his glasses further up his nose. 'It might be irrelevant. Did Fleur tell you that we are currently undecided about what to write next, if anything?'

'No I didn't,' Fleur said. 'I should have mentioned that Pierre thinks we should be doing something more direct and productive.'

'More violent,' Sébastien added. 'I'm not happy about it so we're trying to think of alternatives.'

'I can help find things out about how the Germans think the war is going,' Colette said.

'How?' Sébastien leaned forward, looking interested.

Colette sat upright. 'By going to the cabarets and dancing with the German soldiers who are visiting the city. Do you remember when you left me at the Luciennes' hotel? The guests there are from all over France, spending their leave in the city. People talk to me.' She beamed at the other two. 'Men talk to me, I mean, in particular.'

'I bet they do,' Sébastien muttered. His voice was hard and

when she looked at him questioningly his brows were drawn together in a frown.

'What's that supposed to mean?' she asked.

'Nothing really.' He poured himself another glass of Chambord. 'Just that of course men will talk to you. But it isn't really talking they want.'

'That doesn't matter if talking is all they will get to do,' Colette snapped.

She tugged the bottle from his hand and refilled her glass. His words stung and she couldn't help remembering that the German they had killed had thought she was a whore. Clearly Sébastien had his opinions too.

'I want to be helpful. I don't have a way with words like Fleur does but I can find out information. Then you, Fleur, and Pierre can use it however you choose.'

She felt her eyes begin to prickle and she sniffed to clear the impending tears. She hated arguments and avoided them as much as possible. Aside from the horrible afternoon she had tried to convince Gunther not to leave her, it was the first time she had ever argued with a man. That had been so significant but now her pride was injured and it felt essential that her contribution be accepted and acknowledged.

'I don't see why you don't want my help.' She turned to Fleur who had been sitting silently while they had argued. 'Fleur, what do you think?'

Fleur folded her arms. 'You know my opinion already, but you are a grown woman. If you choose to do it, we won't stop you.' She fixed Sébastien with a hard stare. 'Will we, Sébastien?'

It wasn't a question. He threw his hands up. 'No, we won't, but your reputation will be in shreds.'

Colette rolled her eyes. 'For goodness' sake. You sound like my father! I don't think wartime is a time to be worried about reputations. I haven't let it worry me so far and I don't intend to start now.'

The corner of Sébastien's mouth twitched then turned down. 'In that case, do what you like. I look forward to hearing your reports in great detail. Have fun dancing with the Nazis.'

He got up abruptly and walked out, slamming the door behind him.

'What is the matter with him?' Colette asked.

Fleur walked to the window and looked down at the street. Colette joined her. Below them, Sébastien appeared in the bookshop doorway. He leaned against the wall opposite and lit a cigarette.

'Don't you know?' Fleur asked.

Colette shook her head. 'Does he think I'm a collaborator? That I enjoy spending time in German company? I'm doing it to prove to them that they aren't intimidating us, and to find out what I can.'

Fleur gave her a sharp look. 'You do enjoy going out, Colette. You've always loved dancing ever since we were little. Don't pretend not to.'

'I suppose I do, but it's the dancing I like, not the company. You know that.' Colette leaned against the windowsill. 'Sébastien was horrible, wasn't he?'

Fleur glanced out of the window and her eyes shone with fire. 'He feels strongly about what he believes is right. He doesn't always hide his emotions well. If you intend to get to know him, you'll have to be prepared for that.'

Colette looked down at the road. Sébastien was slouching against the wall, his lean frame all angles. He cupped the cigarette in his hand and stared up at the window. Fleur and Colette ducked back out of sight, but Colette knew he had seen her. Her heartbeat sped up.

'Are you saying he is jealous of me going out dancing with other men?'

Fleur rolled her eyes. 'No, I didn't say he's jealous. I said he thinks it is wrong. You're going to have to put in a lot of effort if you want to convince him otherwise, whatever the look on his face when you hugged him.'

The look on his face... Colette hadn't seen it and wished she had seen whatever Fleur had. Her pulse grew faster as she digested the possibilities. She risked a peek out of the window. As she watched, Sébastien pinched out the cigarette and put it back in his pocket, rationing half for a later time. He glanced up at the window and this time Colette didn't bother to hide. She held eye contact until he thrust his hands in his pockets and strode away, though later she wondered how sharp his eyesight was and if he had even seen her after all. He had an odd way of showing admiration, if that really was the case, as half the time he seemed contemptuous and the other half mocking.

'Do you think he's attracted to me?'

'Colette, it's safe to say that most men who meet you are.'

'But do you think he likes me?'

'I don't know enough about men to comment on that.' Fleur looked Colette directly in the eye. 'Perhaps you should spend some time considering why his being angry upset you so much.'

'I don't love him, if that's what you mean.' Colette blinked. Where had that word slipped out from?

'Of course not. But that doesn't mean you don't want him to be in love with you.' Fleur stalked into the bedroom and returned with her cardigan and hat. 'It makes me very relieved that I'm not in love with anyone myself. You are circling around each other like a pair of mating cats.'

She sounded so self-righteous. Colette grabbed her bag and stabbed her straw hat into place with a pin. 'I hope you meet someone very soon and fall over yourself with adoration. It would serve you right.'

Fleur turned on her heel. Her footsteps pounded in Colette's ears from down the stairwell.

~

Irrespective of whether Sébastien was attracted to Colette, approved of their hiding Michal, or otherwise, he came up good. Two weeks after they had met, a knock on Colette's door woke her. It was Sunday morning and Colette's parents had long since given up demanding she join them at church so she wasn't sure why anyone was interrupting her sleep. She sat up blearily and raked her fingers through her hair.

'Come in.'

Fleur entered. 'I thought you'd be awake by now. It's half past ten.'

'I went out dancing with Sophie and Josette. What's that?'

She gestured to an envelope in Fleur's hand, ignoring the twinge of disapproval in Fleur's lips.

Fleur passed it over. 'It was left this morning.'

Colette didn't recognise the writing. She opened it curiously and pulled out a folded piece of paper.

Dear Colette, I would be honoured if you and Fleur would join me for a picnic in the Jardin des Tuileries on Sunday afternoon. I will be waiting by the Grand Bassin Rond at 2.45. We could resume our conversation about vacations we might wish to take once this war is ended. I have grand plans for a journey I am keen to tell you about. My cousin Francine sends her regards. With deep affection, Sébastien.

'Does that mean what I think it does?' Colette asked.

'I think it means he has found someone who can help Michal,' Fleur confirmed.

They exchanged a smile.

~

The *Jardin des Tuileries* was a popular spot for French and Germans alike to enjoy the weekend. The *Grand Bassin Rond* was a large pond on which children sailed boats while their parents basked in deck chairs around the edge. Groups of Germans, French, and in some cases both, strolled along the gravel paths or lounged on the grass. Colette eyed them with contempt. She might dance with the men in clubs but she would never actually entertain a relationship with one. French women who held hands or cuddled up to the enemy were worse than whores and French men who escorted the drab, blonde German women were unfathomable.

Sébastien was waiting beside a statue of a naked Roman lunging with a sword. The contrast between the sculpted abdominals of the marble and the slightly weedy bespectacled human waiting for her was quite amusing. He tipped his hat in greeting. There were no cheek kisses this time and Colette wondered whether Fleur would have got one if Colette hadn't been present.

'Tell me,' Fleur began but Sébastien held his hand up.

'First let's have something to drink.'

He led them to an isolated spot beneath a magnolia tree that he had claimed with a picnic blanket and a basket. It was a little way from the main pathway that ran the length of the gardens.

'White wine seems appropriate for a warm afternoon.'

He produced a half litre bottle and three glasses from the basket. He had also brought a quarter wheel of ripe camembert and half a baguette that he had cut into rounds. Fleur produced a jar of the odd courgette pickle that had been in the cupboard for years. They sprawled on the blanket as they ate, looking like any other group enjoying the sunshine. The bread was stale but the pickle was sharp and the cheese oozed delightfully across the surface when it was spread, compensating for the dryness. Altogether it was a successful meal.

That was nothing compared with when he produced a small bar of Cote d'Or chocolate.

'No!'

'How did you get this?'

The women cried out in delight at the sight of the elephant proudly lifting its trunk on the wrapper, causing a couple walking past to stop and laugh at their reaction before carrying on.

Sébastien grinned and broke it into squares. 'Don't ask.'

Fleur frowned but took a square and popped it into her mouth. Colette drew her hand back. '*Marché noir?*'

'Let's just say I know someone who doesn't have a taste for chocolate but enjoys his wine. Take it, please. Consider it an apology for my rudeness the other day.'

He held the square between forefinger and thumb. Such a small thing, but so enticing. Colette felt her opposition weakening and it collapsed entirely when Sébastien brought it level with her mouth.

'I accept.'

Sébastien leaned towards her. 'The apology or the chocolate?'

'Both.' She parted her lips and he placed the square between them, keeping his eyes on hers. She drew it onto her tongue and let it melt, enjoying both the creaminess and the expression of satisfaction on Sébastien's face. The quality had declined thanks to the difficulties of getting ingredients, but she would not have exchanged it for the largest box of *bonbons* in existence.

Fleur coughed loudly, breaking the moment, as she had presumably intended to. 'If you have finished feeding each other, can we get to business? I want to know what is happening before the grass gets more crowded.'

Sébastien and Colette exchanged a guilty look that was nonetheless tinged with the promise that the flirting would continue later. Sébastien sat up and reached across to refill the women's glasses. As they came close, he lowered his voice.

'It will be another week, but tell your friend to be in the alley beside the Cinema Gaumont at curfew on the fourteenth.'

'Bastille Day,' Fleur said.

Colette winced. There would be no parades this year and the Germans would no doubt be increasing patrols.

'It is the only day that could work. He will be asked if he can help carry a trunk to a van. He should ask if it is for Claude and when the answer is yes, he should get in the back of the van.'

'Thank you.' Colette felt a rush of gratitude and relief. Once again, she had the urge to hug him in thanks but held back. She looked at Fleur who had a thoughtful expression.

'Where will he go?' Fleur asked.

Sébastien shook his head. 'I don't know. From there on his journey is in the hands of others.'

Fleur smiled. 'To one of the threads of string all over the country. I've been thinking a lot about that. Those people who helped Monsieur Ramper and Francine aren't alone. They're part of something bigger.'

She took a sip of wine and her eyes slid sideways to where a party of two couples were setting up their deckchairs close by, amid shrieks of laughter. Even in the privacy of an open park it was right to be wary.

'All the leaflets in the world don't change anything. France hasn't fought back as a result. All that happens is more and more people disappear or turn on each other. Where did they all go? Not just the Jews, the soldiers who are captured in battle. I want to help them. I want to become more involved in this network.'

Chapter Nineteen

Colette realised she hadn't exhaled all the time Fleur had been speaking. 'Do you really mean that? It sounds dangerous.'

'Dangerous, but important. I know there are groups of people out there who are more active, striking at the Germans in a way that will hurt them and help our soldiers. You know people who know people who know people.'

She fixed her eyes on Sébastien. The expression of ferocity in her eyes was at odds with her petite, slight appearance. Colette could not imagine her striking at anyone. 'That sounds so tangled, doesn't it? But I want you to tell them I want to become one of them.'

Sébastien dipped a leftover slice of baguette into the jar of courgette paste. He chewed it slowly before answering. 'Let me ask.'

'What?' exclaimed Colette. 'I don't want Fleur to do that!'

Sébastien reached for her hand and pressed it gently while flicking his eyes to the other group. 'It isn't your decision. It's Fleur's.'

'Well I think it's a stupid decision, and far too dangerous,' Colette said.

'You were the one who invited our guest to stay,' Fleur muttered.

Colette slammed down her glass. 'That was different. He's a friend. These will be strangers.'

'He is our friend but strangers will be helping him. The people I want to help will have friends too and they will be relying on strangers.'

It was hard to disagree with Fleur's logic. Impossible, even. Colette stood and began pacing back and forth. It wasn't fair to announce something so important without any warning. Without even discussing her plans with Colette. Stifling a sob, Colette walked away. She ignored the quizzical looks from the people she passed as she stomped down the path towards the Musée de l'Orangerie. She'd worn nice shoes for the first time in weeks, and she caught one of the heels in the edge of the grass. She swore aloud, then glared at the black-clad old couple who tutted audibly. The explosion had calmed her down a little and she stopped to sit on a bench.

'If you break your ankle, I'm not carrying you home.'

She looked up.

Sébastien had followed her. He approached cautiously, as if he was trying to capture a pedigree cat that had climbed onto a roof, and sat at the other end of the bench. Colette ignored him and busied herself looking at the tulips in a flower bed. There was a sickening humour in the fact that among all the destruction, there were still gorgeous displays of pink and yellow. But why not? They weren't there for the French but for the occupiers.

'Don't be angry,' Sébastien murmured. He reached for her hand, but she snapped it away. It caught the attention of a couple German officers and the dowdy-looking blonde women they were with. The women passed a look between them and Colette stared back. Let them think they were witnessing nothing more than a lover's quarrel. She began to walk slowly down the gravel path, concentrating on not falling again. The heels made a muffled crunching sound. She didn't look back but heard Sébastien's tread following. When she reached the wall of the orangerie, she stopped.

'Colette, why are you so furious with me?'

He genuinely sounded and looked perplexed.

'You really don't know? Our friend asks you to help her put herself in danger and you are going to assist her. You should refuse and try to talk her out of it.'

'Why?' Sébastien held his hands open, palms upturned. 'Fleur is an adult. Moreover, she is brave and determined. I can pay her a compliment of respecting her wishes. Why can't you?'

Collect jerked her head up, incensed at the criticism. 'Don't pretend I am at fault here!'

'There is no fault. I want Fleur to be safe as much as you do, but you can see how much she cares about doing this. If someone had told you not to help Michal, would it have stopped you?'

His voice was low and earnest. How could Sébastien, who had known Fleur a few brief years, say he felt the same about Fleur as the friend who had known her since childhood? Unless his feelings ran deeper than friendship.

Colette's heart twisted.

'Do you think you care for her as much as I do?' she asked.

Sébastien stepped closer to Colette, his hands now reaching for hers. 'I'm not going to argue about who is the best friend to Fleur. We are both her friends.'

Colette allowed his fingers to twine between hers. She raised her eyes to meet his. There was no judgement gazing back at her. No attempt to mock. 'I'm not as brave as she is. I'm quite easily persuaded.'

'Then let me persuade you not to be angry,' Sébastien

murmured. He put his hands on her shoulders and drew her a little closer. 'Yes, it is dangerous, but people have to do these things. Fleur will do it anyway, with or without my help, and I would rather she was with people I trust and vouch for. Wouldn't you?'

Colette thought of Pierre and how Fleur had described him forcing himself on her. Was Sébastien too trusting?

'I know you're right,' she said. 'Just please make sure whoever you put her in contact with will look out for her too.'

'I wouldn't do anything else,' Sébastien said.

He smiled at her. He was still holding her shoulders. She reached her hands up and laid them over his, scraping her fingernails lightly over the back of his wrists. His eyes widened as hunger filled them. The same hunger that Colette was feeling. She gazed into his eyes and then, without the faintest glimmer of a suspicion that it was going to happen, she leaned forward just as he did.

Their lips met. Pressed. Parted. It was the briefest of touches before Colette hastily pulled back.

'No,' she said.

Sébastien stood straight. 'Why not? Don't tell me you didn't feel something just then.'

Colette drew her bottom lip inwards, biting it and wishing it was Sébastien's mouth in place of her teeth.

'It doesn't matter what I feel. You don't even like me. Why would I want to kiss you? I have more self-respect than that.'

She was half expecting him to mock her so-called self-respect, but his expression grew sober.

'I do respect you. What makes you think I don't?'

Colette leaned back against the wall. 'You don't ever seem to. The first time we met you called me a spoiled little rich girl who was barely worth risking your life for.'

Indignation rose inside her at the memory and she scowled.

'Did I really say that? I am so sorry, Colette. I don't remember.'

'Yes. You were furious and told me I was stupid and reckless.'

Sébastien removed his glasses and rubbed his eyes. Without the thick lenses he had to peer at her. In the bright sunlight myriad colours danced over his irises. Chestnut and coffee and chocolate. Colette felt a pang of hunger.

'I did think you were reckless,' he admitted. 'But now I appreciate your bravery too. You did it out of love for Fleur. You sheltered your other friend. You have one of the kindest natures I think I have met.'

'You got angry with me for suggesting I go to the club,' Colette said. She narrowed her eyes, wondering if Fleur's conclusion about the reason behind his anger was right.

'I am afraid that was purely selfish. I have many faults and jealousy is one. Even though I have no right to dictate what you do, I didn't like the thought.'

'Fleur was right,' Colette said smugly.

'Fleur is often right,' Sébastien said, grinning.

She manoeuvred his hands down so that they were on her hips, then slipped hers round his waist beneath his open jacket. His lips twitched.

'What are you doing?'

'What do you think?' She had to stand on tiptoes to reach his mouth, and in doing so her balance faulted. She felt his hands tighten, steadying her and at the same time he stepped closer so they were brushing against each other. When she had kissed him outside the hotel it had been a show of defiance and the passion had been brought on by the heat of their performance and the emotions of that evening. Now she was kissing him because she wanted to kiss him. Wanted to kiss *him*.

It was unlike any kiss she could remember. Tender and sweet. She drew back and opened her eyes. She looked at him, wondering if he had closed his. She always did and it struck her for the first time she had no idea whether men did that too or if they watched their woman's face.

'I want to go to bed with you,' Sébastien said.

His voice was deep and slightly strangled. A tingle spread through Colette, working its way down her limbs.

'I want to go to bed with you too,' she murmured. She glanced around but no convenient bed appeared.

'I'm not making love to you hidden in a bush up against the Orangerie wall,' Sébastien said, grinning as he followed her eyes.

'There is something to be said for that.' Colette giggled. Her humour evaporated as she remembered the frantic sex in the Secret Garden with Gunther. It had been exciting and certainly informative, but what had it led to? An unwanted child and rejection. It had meant nothing to her in the end. She very much did not want it to be like that with Sébastien. She was glad now that Delphine had forced her into secrecy as it meant there was no way of Sébastien discovering her shameful past.

'We should get back to Fleur. I need to apologise for storming off.' She brushed her lips against his jaw and whispered. 'I would like to go dancing one night, but I'd like to go with you, not Sophie and Josette. Do you know anywhere interesting?'

She had no doubt that if she started the evening dancing with Sébastien, she would finish the night in his bed.

He looked thoughtful. 'I know lots of places, but I'm not sure they would be the quality you are used to. Give me time, though, and I'm sure I could think of somewhere. I'll let you know.'

They walked back to Fleur and the blanket. Colette untwined her arm from Sébastien's as they approached, doing her best to conceal her anticipation.

Fleur had packed away the picnic while they had been gone. She was absorbed in a book – she carried one everywhere, Colette suspected – and she looked up as they approached. Her eyes were wary and she looked vulnerable. Colette couldn't imagine her involved in dangerous operations, but maybe that would work in her favour and the Nazis would assume the same thing. She knelt beside Fleur and kissed her cheek.

'I'm sorry for all that. I don't like it, but I can see why you want to do it.'

'Thank you.' Fleur leaned briefly against Colette. 'We should go.'

Sébastien helped her to her feet then reach his hands out for Colette. She took them. Even that simple touch, completely innocent, sent flames dancing along her arms. Goodness, she was quite infatuated it seemed. It was unusual for her, and she wasn't sure she liked it. It was one thing deciding to go to bed with him but quite another to risk actually falling for him. They parted at the Luxor Obelisk.

'Will you be there at the cinema?' Fleur asked Sébastien.

'No. I've passed on the message; that's all I am meant to do. Neither of you should go either. Say goodbye to your friend as he leaves your house.'

Colette stiffened. 'Why do you think he's at the house? We haven't said where he was.'

'No, you didn't,' Sébastien said. 'It was just a guess, but it looks like I am right. Be careful with what you say and who you say it to.'

He tipped his hat and walked off, swinging the picnic basket. Fleur and Colette walked home in silence. There was not much to say that had not already been said.

~

At the appointed time they bid farewell to Michal. He carried his knapsack and a small case containing the few belongings he had asked Colette to get from his *loge*. His eyes were wary as they darted either way down the boulevard, but he looked healthier and Colette felt the budding of hope in her breast. He had a better chance of survival now than when she had met him.

'Thank you. I have no words for what you have done.'

'Please take care,' Fleur said. She gave him a parcel wrapped in brown paper; a sort of *pain perdu* she had made using stale breadcrumbs and a little dried fruit, which he stowed in his knapsack.

Seeing the cake reminded Colette that they no longer had to share rations. It was hard not to feel a twinge of relief, even if that relief was rapidly followed by embarrassment at her greediness.

'I hope when this is all over we will meet again, Michal.'

She held out her hand. Michal shook it.

'I hope so too.'

He walked purposefully away without looking back, keeping close to the line of buildings.

'We did something good,' Colette murmured.

'Yes, we did.' Fleur looked round. Her eyes bore a determined light. 'And there is more to be done.'

She went back inside. Colette remained in the street alone, watching the figure growing smaller and Fleur's words leaving her with a sense of foreboding.

∼

September 1941

As autumn arrived, Colette started to believe Sébastien had forgotten his promise to put Fleur in contact with members of the escape network. He had also made no further mention of taking her dancing until he strolled into the bookshop one morning when Fleur was out delivering a parcel to a customer.

'Ah, the working woman! Be ready at eight on Saturday, I'm taking you dancing.'

'Oh, are you?' She folded her arms and met his eyes. 'How do you know I'm not already going out?'

He tilted her chin up with a fingertip and held her gaze. 'Because the only place you go is to that damned hotel and a patriotic Frenchwoman would cancel any plans involving Germans to spend time with me. So you'll be ready, yes?'

She swallowed. 'Yes.'

He arrived at the front door exactly on the clock-chime of eight. When Colette opened it hurriedly so her parents did not intercept Sébastien, he handed her a thick, dog-eared envelope.

'Give this to Fleur, please.'

'Is that a name?'

'An address. Tomorrow, you can bring her the name. I thought it best to keep them separate.'

'Tomorrow?' Colette tipped her head on one side.

'Tomorrow. Let's not pretend we will be separating at the end of the evening,' Sébastien whispered as he helped Colette into her coat. His matter-of-fact attitude was arousing in itself, even without the way his fingers brushed against the nape of her neck, causing the small hairs to rise.

'Of course not,' Colette said. She ran upstairs and gave the envelope to Fleur who was lying on her bed reading.

'Sébastien sent this for you,' she said.

'He's here?' She put her book down and her face lit up.

'He's taking me dancing,' Colette said.

Fleur's smile became brittle.

Colette's stomach began to curl in on itself. She told herself Fleur was put out at not being invited, but couldn't really deny what the expression meant. Fleur had never said she wanted Sébastien, but she had never said she didn't. It had just suited Colette to tell herself the path was clear but faced with clear evidence, Colette was flooded with regret.

'Have fun,' Fleur said quietly.

Colette would once have seized on the instruction, but something stopped her.

'I won't go if you don't want me to. I didn't realise you cared,' she said. It was only half a lie. She had known Fleur liked Sébastien, but had never been sure of the extent.

'Go,' Fleur said. She brushed her hair behind her ear then pressed her hands together. 'Don't pretend you don't want to. It's something we both knew was going to happen. One of us should have fun.'

'But…'

'I said go!' Fleur held aloft the envelope. She smiled, and while it wasn't as genuine as normal, it was less fragile-looking. 'I've got something else to think about now.'

Reluctantly, Colette backed out of the room.

~

She didn't say anything to Sébastien but as they took the Metro into the city centre, she examined her conscience and was slightly surprised to discover her consideration was all for Fleur's feelings and none for Sébastien's. She didn't have any loyalty to him. Yet.

The club was quite unlike any of the ones that Colette was used to. It was in the cellar of a restaurant and there was only whisky or brandy to drink. The music was played on a Thorens record player while couples – no Germans in sight – danced. Sébastien led Colette to the dance floor and took her in his arms. The song was slow and intimate, sung by an American in English. Colette leaned her head against Sébastien's chest as he held her close, their feet travelling through steps that she was barely aware of. His cologne was earthy with overtones of cloves. Breathing it in, Colette's imagination drifted to cool autumn afternoons in front of a warm fire.

They danced three times before Sébastien took her chin in his hand and tilted her head up to look at him.

'I think it's time to go now.'

Colette slid her hand down his shoulder blade and circled her fingers in the small of his back. 'I think so,' she agreed

They left the club without speaking and walked hand in hand through the dark streets.

In Sébastien's bedroom they undressed each other slowly, standing beside the bed. When Colette stood only in her bra and panties, Sébastien stopped.

'Have you done this before? I don't want you to feel pressured.'

She had a sudden urge to deny it. To pretend this was her first time and that he was her first. There would never be any lies between them, she decided.

'Yes, I have, but not for a long time.'

'So you know what that is?'

He flicked his head to the bedside table and a small tin of Ramses *preservatifs*. With a sense of shame she realised it hadn't even occurred to her. Just like all the times she had been so careless with Gunther. Thank goodness Sébastien was an adult.

'You were very confident about this evening, I see!' she remarked to cover her awkwardness.

'Not confident, but hopeful.'

He kissed her. Whisky was horrid, but lingering on Sébastien's tongue, it became the nectar of the gods. He slid his hands around her back, undoing the clasp on her brassière. She ran her hands down his waist and slipped them inside the waistband of his shorts to ease them off. Her hands shook, despite the heat of the evening. She stood on tiptoes and ran her hands through his hair, then pressed her lips onto the spot between the base of his earlobe and his jaw and whispered against the sweet-scented skin.

'Take me to bed, Sébastien.'

~

Much later, they lay together under the sheets. Colette's head rested in the crook of Sébastien's arm and her leg was slung over his. Basking in a post-coital fug of exhaustion was a novelty that Colette could grow to like. Whenever she and Gunther had finished, they had dressed quickly and parted with the sole intention of not being caught.

She knew this would not be the only time, and it would mean a difficult conversation the next morning when she returned home.

'I wish Fleur could find someone to make her happy.' She sighed as the memory of Fleur's expression popped into her head. If Fleur could find a lover, Colette need not feel so bad at having Sébastien.

Sébastien craned his head down to look at her. 'Were you thinking about Fleur while I was working away down there?'

Her skin grew hot at the memory of an experience that had been completely new to her.

'Not at all. I'm only thinking about her now because I want her to be as happy as I feel. She deserves someone nice.'

Sébastien grinned and put his finger to Colette's lips. 'Don't worry about Fleur. You told me to find someone trustworthy to put her in contact with. I did one better than that and found someone I think Fleur will find very interesting indeed.'

He refused to elaborate, no matter how much Colette tried to persuade him, until he began to distract her in a manner that put all thoughts of Fleur firmly out of her head.

Chapter Twenty

'**H**ave you seen my daughter today?'

Louis' question caught Fleur unawares. She had barely noticed him sitting behind a newspaper in the corner of the dining room. Her belly lurched. So Colette had stayed out all night with Sébastien, as Fleur had suspected she would. She was sure Louis wouldn't like that answer any more than she did though.

'I haven't,' she said. 'Is she not in her bedroom? I know she doesn't always get up very early.'

'Perhaps.' Louis laid down his newspaper on the table. Fleur stared at the upside-down pages. News of battles, news of conflict, news of places in parts of the world she couldn't even picture. Who knew if any of it were true?

'You normally don't see her because you have left for the factory by this time,' she remarked.

Louis rubbed his fingertips through his hair. It had thinned around the ears. 'I am finding it hard to summon the willpower today. I'm sorry, my dear. I don't need to burden you with my troubles.'

'I don't mind.' Fleur poured a cup of coffee from the pot and handed it to him.

'This does not quite invigorate me as proper beans do, but thank you,' he said with a gentle smile. 'I worry about Colette. I had hoped she would be married now. Perhaps a mother even, but alas, in these times…'

He left the sentence unfinished and drank his coffee, suppressing the grimace they all gave on tasting the bitter ground acorns and chicory. 'I do not know how a young lady goes about meeting a young man these days. Do you, my dear?'

'No.' Fleur dropped her eyes, knowing one way to do so – through a friend who should have had more sense than to introduce them.

At that point the front door slammed, and the sound of heels tapped across the hallway floor. It could only be Colette. She had gone out in heeled shoes the previous night. Day-to-day shoes were now soled with cork in an effort to make them last longer.

Colette breezed into the dining room.

'Good morning, *Papa*! I didn't expect to see you.' She swept down on Louis and gave him a kiss on each cheek. She saw Fleur and had the grace to look slightly awkward.

'Good morning, Fleur. I beat you to the shopping this morning. I have already been out and returned. Look, I have fresh bread and butter! Isn't that wonderful.'

Louis folded the newspaper. 'Well done, my dear. Make sure you save me some for dinner tonight. What will we be eating?'

Fleur answered.

'Vegetable soup, but it is made with chicken bones. I saved them from last night.'

'Excellent.' Louis patted his stomach. 'In this heat it is easier to eat lightly, don't you agree? I find I have adapted to the change in diet well.'

Fleur nodded. It was true that the hot summer weather that

had arrived suddenly meant she did not crave big meals as much. Louis was a large man, however, and had always had a hearty appetite.

'I will help you clear the breakfast things,' Colette said. Together they carried the tray to the kitchen.

'Is there any coffee left?' Colette asked. 'I'm going to struggle to stay awake today, I think.'

Fleur filled the sink. 'Is that because you stayed awake late last night?' she asked.

Colette turned to the table, avoiding Fleur's eyes. That was answer enough.

Fleur began to wash the plates. Oddly, now that Colette and Sébastien had clearly spent the night together she felt calmer and less upset than she would have expected. Colette would soon grow bored of Sébastien's seriousness, or he would grow tired of her flippancy, and the romance would peter out. Once Colette had lost interest, Fleur would still be friends with Sébastien and could offer him a shoulder to cry on.

'Sébastien said to give you something.' Colette rummaged inside her blouse and pulled a folded slip of card out of her bra. Fleur raised her brows, the speculation flashing through her mind whether Sébastien had put it there with his own hands. Seeing her expression, Colette smiled faintly.

'I thought it was safer not to keep it in my bag in case anyone stopped and searched me. I felt like a spy. It is to go with the paper he gave you last night.' Colette's fingers tightened on the paper as she held it out. 'I assume they're to do with what you asked him.'

'I assume so,' Fleur agreed, tugging the card from Colette's unwilling fingers. On brief inspection it was a torn beermat with a scrawl of handwriting on one side.

'Will you tell me what it says?' Colette asked, eying it.

Fleur put it into her pocket. The girls hadn't talked of Fleur's plans since the uncomfortable scenes in the *Jardins des Tuileries* but Fleur suspected Colette hadn't changed her opinion. If she didn't support Fleur, then Fleur didn't want her involved. It might be petty but this was something for her alone, which Sébastien was helping her to do. She shook her head.

'No, I think it would be safer for us both if you knew nothing.'

She took it back to her room. It bore only a handwritten name.

Laurent Renou.

It meant nothing to Fleur. She put it on the dressing table and took out the envelope Sébastien had sent her the day before and opened it. It contained a business card for a mechanics workshop, along with a small, sealed envelope bearing the message:

Take this to him. Think of a hiding place to get it there. The more ingenious the better.

Until this morning she hadn't known the identity of 'him', but now she had a name. Her body felt electrified with excitement and trepidation.

If she went to the address her life would change in ways she could not even contemplate.

Of course there was no question in her mind that she was going to go. The war seemed no closer to ending. Any part she had played so far had been paltry. She drew her knees up and hugged them as she gazed contemplatively at the information she had. A name and a place of work. They should be easy enough to find. How to safely take the sealed message was something that absorbed her.

She could use Colette's method of putting it in her underwear, but an image of a grease-covered fat old man in overalls flashed up in her mind. The thought of having to rummage and produce the note in front of a strange man didn't appeal. Inside her shoe would be better, though not very ingenious.

A mechanic…

What reason could she have to visit such a person? She would give it some thought. There was no hurry.

❧

It was only when she was cycling home from the bookshop a week later that an idea occurred to her. She almost squealed aloud before she caught herself.

'Have you gone yet?' Colette asked as they sat in the garden on deckchairs drinking iced water that evening. 'Sébastien was asking if I knew.'

Fleur could almost hear Sébastien's name from Colette's lips without a pang of jealousy. Compared to the endeavour she was about to undertake it seemed such a little thing to be concerned about.

'I need to go almost to Versailles to meet him. I'm going tomorrow once I close the shop.' She drained her glass. 'So, you have seen Sébastien again.'

Colette wriggled her bare toes. 'Yes. I'm sorry.'

'Don't apologise,' Fleur snapped.

'But I didn't realise quite how much you like him.' Colette looked genuinely tense.

It was one thing knowing they were meeting without having to field Colette's conscience. Fleur flicked her hand as if brushing away a fly and affected a smile.

'I was never as serious as you think I was. I just haven't met many men to compare him to. I dare say I will survive the heartbreak, but I don't want your guilt on my back. Enjoy yourself and just make sure you don't hurt him.'

Colette looked relieved. Fleur took the glasses back to the house, thinking how odd it was that her happiness was such a concern to Colette. She was definitely becoming more considerate as she grew up.

~

The following day, Fleur cycled west towards Versailles. She had consulted a map of the city and was reasonably confident that, even though the outlying buildings of the palace were occupied by the German War Ministry, the address she was looking for was far enough away that she would not encounter too much opposition.

The journey took an hour, which felt double in the last burst of September heat. She was hot and perspiring when she dismounted at the end of the Avenue de Saint-Cloud and dropped her bicycle beside her under a tree. Her luck had held because the checkpoint was a hundred metres or so down the avenue, closer to the palace itself and she would not have to cross it.

She flapped her blouse to cool herself then set to work. She released the air from the valve and deflated the front tyre of her bicycle, then prised the tyre off the rim of the wheel using a couple of dessert spoons that she had brought. Once done she folded the note from Sébastien and inserted it between the inner and the rim and put the tyre back in place using the spoons.

It was fiddly work and she was hot and irritated by the end of it. She would not have to act to appear frustrated. She pushed the bicycle down the avenue, took a right turn into a smaller street and at the crossroads stopped on the other side of the road to observe her destination

The Citroën garage, like many similar businesses, made use of the lower floor of an apartment block. This one had the extra advantage of being on a corner of a quiet side street. Cars were not used by the general population of the city, either because they had been commandeered by the occupying Germans, or the price of what fuel was available was prohibitively high. A Rosalie van with one wheel missing was on a jack down the side street, partially blocking the road for anyone else who may wish to drive out. Fleur wondered if that was intentional. If Laurent was involved in Resistance activities, it might suit him to make access to the premises difficult.

Two men in oil-smeared overalls sat outside the front of the open garage door on small stools. They were playing a card game and drinking from shot glasses. Between them on the floor was a bag of tools and sundry bits of debris. Which one of these men was Laurent? she wondered. Both looked to be in their late fifies, both looked wiry and tough. She could imagine either of them staring down an officer of the Abwehr fearlessly.

She wiped her palm across her brow and smoothed her hair back. It came away gritty and moist. This weather was appallingly stifling, and the buildings kept the heat from leaving. This was her last opportunity to back out. She gripped the handlebars tightly, took a deep breath and crossed over the road.

'Excuse me, *messieurs*,' she said hesitantly.

'Wait,' said one man, lifting his hand to her without looking. He drew his cards close to his face and peered at them, muttering under his breath, then smiled, selected one and placed it on top of the pile.

'*Merde!*' The other man slammed his own cards down with a laugh. The two men clinked glasses and knocked back the opaque white liquid.

'Mademoiselle, yes?' asked the man who had won. He turned to look up at Fleur. He had a grizzled face and one eye partially closed. His grin might have been intended to look welcoming, but it made him look grotesque, like one of the gargoyles on the buttresses at Notre Dame.

'I am having trouble with my bicycle,' Fleur said.

'This is an automobile garage,' commented the man who had

not spoken yet. He was even older than his companion but with a friendlier demeanour. 'You have come to the wrong place.'

'My friend told me that you also mended bicycles,' Fleur said. Sébastien had told her most firmly to avoid mentioning his name to anyone but Laurent if possible. She still didn't know which man it was.

'Does it have an engine? A carburettor? No? Then I am not interested,' said the second man. He scooped the cards towards him and began to shuffle them.

Fleur bit the inside of her lip. She had not expected it to be too easy. If this was a cover it would naturally be hard to penetrate it. 'Perhaps one of you might take a look,' she asked hopefully. 'I've come a long way on foot.'

She fanned herself. Her back was clammy with perspiration, and she was thirsty. 'If you can't help me, may I at least beg a glass of water before I have to walk all the way home?'

The first man stood and looked at Fleur's bicycle. 'I believe this must have served in the trenches in the *Grand Guerre*, from the age,' he commented.

'It may well have done,' Fleur admitted. She shifted her bag on her shoulder. 'Are you Laurent? I'm sorry if I have taken your time.'

The two men exchanged a glance. 'Laurent is inside,' the man replied. 'He may look at your bicycle. It is something of a hobby to him.' He leaned back on his chair and craned his neck. 'Laurent, a woman for you,' he shouted.

'Women are his other hobby,' The second man said, then began laughing at his own non-existent witticism.

'Go inside then,' said the first man.

He picked up the deck of cards and began to deal them, seemingly having lost interest in Fleur. With a rising sense of anticipation she wheeled her bike inside the garage.

Chapter Twenty-One

I t was dark and musty inside the workshop. The sun was behind Fleur, but thanks to the height of the buildings its light barely penetrated more than a metre or two into the gloom. She blinked a couple of times to help her eyes adjust, then looked around her.

Her first impression was that if this was the base of covert activities there could be nowhere better. The floor was littered with cables and parts of machinery. The entire back wall was covered with shelving that was full of assorted boxes, as well as more cables, gears, and other sundry tools. A workbench was laden with half an engine and a box that could even have been an old radio. The Gestapo could easily waste an entire morning looking for evidence of Resistance activity and never find it.

What was abundantly missing however, was Laurent.

'Hello,' Fleur called. 'Is there anyone there?'

A door she had not previously noticed opened a crack and a man stepped through. He was tall and wide, but there was not a scrap of fat to spare on him. Every muscle on his arms and chest was toned and taut and he carried a heavy wrench the length of

Fleur's arm. He resembled a statue of marble or bronze. If Greek gods had worn overalls he would have not disgraced the Louvre. Fleur gulped and a shiver ran down her spine, though she did not believe it had been caused by the contrast of the heat outside and the cooler workshop.

'Who are you and what do you want?' he asked.

'I was sent by a friend. He said you may be able to help me.'

'Oh yes?' And how could I do that, *chérie*?'

He walked forward with a swagger, idly swinging the wrench. Clearly he had the impression of himself as being a cinema idol. Women were a hobby to him, the men outside had said. Well, if he thought that she would be an hour's pastime then he would be mistaken.

'You are in silhouette. I can't see you,' he said. 'Come in a little further.'

It was like the wolf beckoning *Petit Chaperon Rouge* into Grandmother's house, Fleur thought. However, mindful that she needed his help, she obeyed.

'Are you Laurent?'

'I am.'

He stepped closer to her. Fleur swallowed. Until that point his muscles had been the most striking thing about him, but now they fell into second place behind his eyes. They were so blue that her mind immediately went to the cliché from cheap thrillers of topaz or sapphire. He fixed her with a level stare as she immediately re-evaluated her decision not to let him charm her into bed.

'My friend sent me. The front tyre is flat.'

'Which friend would this be, *chérie*?' he asked.

'My friend Sébastien,' she said.

Laurent stiffened. Every muscle tensed, reminding Fleur of a panther about to spring.

'Your friend Sébastien?'

'Yes,' Fleur confirmed, wondering if she had made a mistake and this still was not Laurent.

'He sent you to me for help?'

'Yes.'

Laurent sucked his teeth, then cocked his head. 'Bring your bike to the back,' he said.

He picked up a cloth and wiped down his arms and torso, then ran it over the back of his neck. Fleur wished she could do the same. The air inside the garage smelled of engine oil and dust. It made her eyes and nose prickle. It was far too hot.

'Show me the problem,' Laurent said, holding his hands out.

Fleur passed the handlebars into his hand and, as she did, Laurent covered her hands with his and held them tightly.

'Mademoiselle, tell me how you know Sébastien.'

There was always the danger that Laurent may be Gestapo and that she was walking into a trap. But Sébastien would not have sent her into danger willingly, so if he believed this man was Resistance, Fleur was prepared to take the chance.

'We have known each other for a few years. From the café where he works.'

He narrowed his eyes.

'If you are from Sébastien you must have something for me to prove it. Give it to me.'

Fleur slid her hands out from beneath his, belatedly realising he was still holding them.

'I think you should examine my bicycle.'

His eyes flickered and then he grinned. 'Very well. Is there anywhere in particular you would like me to look?'

'There is something wrong with the wheel,' Fleur said. 'I think the tyre has something caught in it.'

His eyes narrowed and he looked at her intently before his lips twitched to the side. Quite thin lips, Fleur noted, but well defined with a deep indentation at the top.

'Very well, mademoiselle. While I look at your tyre, why don't you make us a couple of drinks. It's pretty hot today, don't you agree?'

'What should I make?' Fleur asked.

'How brave are you feeling?' He gave a bold grin. 'There is water in the tap on the wall and blackcurrant sirop in a carafe on the shelf in the back room, but personally I would like a drop of what you'll find in that oil canister there.' He indicated with his head to an unassuming-looking metal jerrycan.

'Not engine oil, I assume,' Fleur said suspiciously.

His lips twitched in amusement. 'The glasses are there.' He cocked his head to one of the shelves. Fleur picked up two tumblers and walked to the jerrycan. She unscrewed the cap and the smell hit her. It might as well have been petrol from the way her eyes watered.

'How strong is it?' she asked.

'Strong enough to put hairs on your chest,' Laurent called. He had bent down and begun fiddling with the tyre.

Fleur laughed. 'What a strange expression.'

'It was one my mother used.' He looked over his shoulder at her. 'Don't worry, it is not meant literally. A chest as fine as yours would be ruined by becoming hairy.'

A slow blush began to creep round Fleur's neck and across the aforementioned chest. From what she could see beyond the cotton vest and overalls, Laurent's own chest was smooth. Hairless. She poured two measures, one larger than the other, and took the glasses across to him. He stood, wiped his hands down his trouser legs, and took the fuller from her. 'To your health, mademoiselle.'

'And to yours,' she replied.

He held the glass up to his lips but did not drink. Fleur paused, having been about to take a sip.

'And to the health of France,' he said.

'To France,' Fleur agreed warmly.

Laurent upended the glass into his mouth in one. Fleur took a swig. Immediately she began to cough and splutter as liquid fire seared her throat. Laurent leaned over and patted her heartily between the shoulder blades.

'You have guts, mademoiselle, I'll give you that. Please try not to cough them all over my workshop floor though.'

She glared at him through tear-filmy eyes.

He walked to the tap and filled her glass with water, then handed it to her. She sipped it gratefully until the burning in her throat subsided.

'Now, let me have a look at your problem tyre,' Laurent said. 'Sit there if you wish.' He indicated the workbench.

'I'll stand, thank you,' Fleur replied, staring at the mess of nuts and bolts that littered it. 'I don't have enough nice dresses to ruin them with engine grease.'

Laurent grimaced and turned his attention to her bicycle. He muttered, reached into a large tool-box and produced something small and metal. He had the tyre free of the rim in a fraction of the time it had taken Fleur. For such a large man he had very deft fingers.

He located the envelope and raised an eyebrow, then slid his thumb under the flap to open it. Inside was one sheet of paper. He read it silently then looked up at Fleur. She realised she was holding her breath. She wished now she had opened the note Sébastien had given to her so she might be prepared for what Laurent might be about to read. If she had done that, however, he would know she had broken the seal.

She wasn't sure whether to smile. His expression gave nothing away as his blue eyes raked over her appraisingly. He walked past her to the front of the garage and pulled the double doors closed. The workshop was plunged into darkness and the noise from the street grew muffled. Fleur tensed. She was now cut off from the world outside. She understood the need for secrecy and caution, but as well as preventing anyone overhearing their conversation, it meant she would be unable to call for help if she needed it. She sucked a breath in through her teeth. She was here to volunteer for dangerous acts so if she was frightened of being along with a man, what sort of *resisteur* would she be?

Laurent walked back and stood opposite her, then held the note between the thumb and forefinger of his left hand.

'Do you know what it says?'

'No.'

'Would you like to?'

'Of course.' She held her hand out to take the note, but he snatched it away.

'It says you are very good in bed and that Sébastien thinks I should try seducing you to see for myself.'

'No it doesn't,' she said calmly.

'Oh, and how do you know that, *chérie*? Because you haven't slept with him or because he is a gentleman and wouldn't betray a confidence.'

'Both!' she snapped. 'That is, he wouldn't betray a confidence *and* I have not slept with him.'

'But you would like to?'

'No.'

She paused, considering how the answer had tripped off her tongue instantly and easily. She had spent so long denying her attraction whenever the subject had come up with Colette, and she was surprised to discover it was not as much of a lie as it had once been. Sébastien was not available (for the time being at least) and, in truth, he had never looked at her the way she had seen him look at Colette in the *Jardin* the day they had picnicked together. The hunger that oozed from the pair of them had been something she could only imagine. She loved Sébastien, admired him and craved his affection, but did she actually lust after him?

'He is in an affair with my friend.'

Laurent cocked his head to one side. 'Which precludes you from wanting to?'

Fleur narrowed her eyes. 'Are you going to tell me what he said or just fool around with me?'

Laurent grinned and the sparkle in his eyes grew brighter. 'I would very much like to fool around with you, *chérie*, however I don't think that is what you meant. Here.'

He handed her the note. She scanned the few lines of Sébastien's cramped handwriting quickly.

She wants to be of use and she will be. I trust her absolutely. If you use her badly or let her come to any harm, I will twist her testicles off with your biggest spanner.

Fleur grinned at the colourful threat. She looked up to see that Laurent was not smiling. He was standing with his arms folded, feet planted apart and gazing at her with a concentration that made the pulse in her throat gallop.

'You want to be of use?'

'I do. I want to do more than post graffiti that makes no difference.'

'And do you think you can be of use? How?'

Fleur frowned. 'I know there are people trying to escape France or evade capture.'

'We do more than that. Could you wire a bomb? Kill a man? Have you ever fired a gun?'

'No,' she admitted. 'I mean I've never shot a gun.'

'You fire a gun to shoot a target,' Laurent said, arching his brows. 'A man, in most cases. To kill him. Could you kill someone?'

'I can learn. And I would use one if I needed to.'

'You can learn? How quickly? You come here in your pretty yellow dress that you won't even get dirty and declare you could kill.

Forgive me for doubting you, mademoiselle. We do not want the war to be prolonged simply because you want to play at getting skills.'

His voice was hard and tinged with scorn. It rankled. Fleur handed the note back to him.

'If you do not want the war to last forever then you should not be so quick to reject help. I don't care what I do, but I want to do something. If I have to learn to kill, I will, whether that be by shooting, stabbing, or setting explosions.'

She stopped and took a breath, aware she had begun to rant. She leaned back against the workbench, then swept her hand over it to move the debris and jumped up to sit on it. What was one ruined dress after all?

Laurent tipped his head on one side. He turned and walked back to the jerrycan and refilled his glass. He sipped it slowly, his eyes never leaving Fleur's, then he crossed to where she sat. 'Very well. Let me speak to the people I know. I'm sure we can find work for you. I will be in contact. Give me your address.'

Fleur hesitated and he smiled. 'Very wise. I do need it, of course, because otherwise how would I contact you? But I can see that you think before answering, *chérie*. It's a very good habit to get into.'

'Yes, I know,' Fleur replied. She was dammed if she was going to acknowledge a compliment. He might be handsome, but he was infuriatingly cocky. She wished Sébastien had sent her to someone else.

'Mademoiselle, do you know of the Café Broderie in the old square near the Jewish quarter? The one next to the clockmakers?'

'The one with the red sign? Yes, though it isn't really the Jewish quarter any longer, of course.'

'No,' Laurent said quietly. 'No, it is not.'

His voice was bleak, but his eyes flashed with anger. He had perhaps also had friends who had vanished. For a moment their eyes met in mutual understanding. This was a man she could work with.

'I wanted the world to change before the war, but not in this way,' Fleur said quietly.

Unexpectedly, Laurent took her hand and squeezed it tightly. 'It can change again, mademoiselle, if we have the courage to make it. I think you have the courage.'

'Thank you,' Fleur said. She smiled and Laurent's lips pursed slightly. She thought wildly that he might be about to kiss her and she ran her tongue around the inside of her lips to moisten them, but instead he broke eye contact and turned away. He knelt by her bike and re-fixed the tyre.

'Here you go, *chérie*. As good as new. Meet me at the café a week today. Two in the afternoon. Sébastien can come if he wishes. By then I will have spoken to my contacts and we will have a better idea of whether you might be of use.'

Seven days seemed an age to wait, but the second anniversary of Hitler's invasion of Poland had recently passed and a week was nothing on that scale.

'Thank you. Goodbye, Laurent.'

She took hold of the handlebars and began to wheel the bicycle towards the front door when Laurent called out.

'Wait!'

She paused. He swaggered towards her in that manner that made him look like a Hollywood film actor.

'You haven't told me your name.'

'It's Fleur.'

'It's good to have met you, Fleur.' He reached out unexpectedly and brushed his thumb over her lips firmly enough to smear the lipstick she had applied so carefully. When she cried out in indignation, he grinned.

'I need to keep my reputation intact, mademoiselle. Auguste

and Marcel, that old couple on the stools, believe me to be a modern-day Casanova and I would hate to disappoint them.'

It was an odd thing to do but at least he hadn't helped himself to a kiss to achieve the effect.

'Oh, I see.' Fleur twisted her finger in the curls at the side of her head and pulled the hairpins slightly askew. 'There, that should help too.'

He chuckled. 'Thank you, Fleur. I can see you understand what we have to do. Until next week.'

'Until next week,' she replied, pushing the door open.

The sunlight blinded her. She walked out past the men who were still playing cards. One of them muttered something to the other, who chuckled as she mounted the bicycle and pedalled away. She felt euphoric.

Exhilarated.

What a strange man, and what an odd encounter. It had been more like a fencing match than a conversation. She smiled to herself, thinking that at least Laurent's reputation as a lothario was intact, even if he sadly hadn't done anything to merit it.

Chapter Twenty-Two

Fleur agonised over what to wear for the meeting for much longer than she usually did, much to Colette's amusement.

'Why does it matter so much? Just pick a pretty dress.'

'I don't have any pretty dresses!' Fleur pointed out with increasing irritation.

To her dismay, the grease stains from sitting on the workbench hadn't come out of her yellow one and her wardrobe, which had started the war full of already well-worn items, had been diminishing and becoming shabby as items were forced to last longer than they should. Most of Paris was in the same situation, though women like Colette who had started with a fuller wardrobe were suffering less. Fortunately, the weather would soon be getting cooler and she would be able to change the cotton dresses for sweaters and heavier cotton twill skirts.

'I want to make a good impression. I want Laurent to think that I am capable and sensible.'

'In which case, why are you spending so long picking out earrings and scarves?' Colette asked. She was lying on Fleur's bed, feet dangling over the end. 'I wish you would tell me how the

241

first meeting went. Sébastien keeps asking me how you liked Laurent and I have nothing to tell him.'

The customary spams of covetousness Fleur expected was immediately submerged beneath a squirming, fluttering feeling inside her belly.

'I wasn't there long enough to form an opinion of him. You'll meet him today and you can make up your own mind,' Fleur pointed out.

Once Colette had discovered that Sébastien was accompanying Fleur, she had invited herself along.

'We spoke. I gave him the message from Sébastien. I left.'

She didn't consider it lying, merely omitting unnecessary details … such as the buzzing in her lips whenever she remembered the touch of his thumb, and the blue of his eyes when a beam of light had caught them.

'It doesn't matter what I wear, does it? Men barely notice these things. I'll just take this one.'

She picked out the scarf Colette had given her when they were younger. She smiled at Colette as she arranged it around her throat. 'It's still my favourite.'

Colette clambered from the bed. 'Then it's a good choice. Come on, we will be late and that will make a bad impression.'

They arrived at Café Broderie before either of the men. It was already bustling despite the weather being cooler.

'We are waiting for friends,' they told the waiter. He indicated a table outside on the pavement and returned shortly with a carafe of water and two glasses.

'Do you think they will arrive together?' asked Colette. 'This is supposed to be a relaxed meeting.'

'They won't do anything that might look suspicious,' Fleur said.

'Yes, we can think of it as a date.' Colette examined her fingernails. 'How exciting.'

'It isn't a date. It's more like an interview,' Fleur pointed out.

It wasn't a date at all in fact, at least not for her or Laurent. What Colette and Sébastien called their meetings was up to them.

She sipped her water and looked around. As usual, the clientele was mainly in German uniform, but with occasional pairs or groups where it was harder to tell the nationality. Before too long a man stopped by the table, casting a shadow over it.

'May I join you?'

His voice was recognisable, but when Fleur looked up, it took her a moment to connect the man before her with the one she had previously met. Before, Laurent had been dressed for work in overalls. Now, he wore a well-cut suit of dark blue, unbuttoned to show a matching waistcoat and a cream shirt. His sandy hair was neatly combed back under a fedora set at a rakish angle.

'Of course you may,' she said in a slightly fluttery voice. From the corner of her eye she saw a smile form on Colette's face.

Laurent laid down a newspaper on the table. 'Excellent. I must just make use of the facilities. If you would like to read my newspaper, you are welcome.'

He pushed it towards Fleur with the tip of his finger.

'Thank you.' It was the previous day's edition, and she had no real wish to read it, but for some reason he thought it was important. While Laurent sauntered between the tables and made his way inside the café to the toilets, Fleur unfolded the newspaper.

'You complete minx. You didn't tell me he was so handsome!'

Fleur looked up from the paper to see Colette staring at her, leaning forward with her eyes wide and her mouth wider.

'Is he? I hadn't really noticed.' Fleur laced her fingers together. 'The last time I saw him he was covered in engine oil and needed a wash.'

Colette rolled her eyes back in her head theatrically and

sighed. 'Oh, my dear, it just gets better. Hot soap and water! If I were you, I would get him into bed as soon as you can!'

'You are appalling!' Fleur blushed furiously.

Colette looked unconcerned. 'I know. But if you don't, somebody else will, assuming someone isn't already.'

'You, perhaps?' Fleur looked sharply at her.

'No. I don't think Sébastien would like that.' Colette bit her fingernail, either missing Fleur's meaning or choosing to ignore it. She pursed her lips, looking worried. 'It's funny. I think I would mind very much if I upset Sébastien when I didn't expect to. I wonder where he is.'

Colette looked around. Fleur studied her, taken aback by the admission. It seemed unlikely that Colette would feel the same stirring of emotion for someone in his position but stranger things happened, especially during wartime.

She opened the newspaper and something fell onto her lap. It was a folded sheet of paper. Intrigued, she put the newspaper on the table and unfolded the page. Before she could read it, however, a hand fell on her shoulder and she gave a cry of surprise.

'Lesson one: be discreet.'

She had not noticed Laurent's return. Now he stood behind her chair looking over her shoulder with a smile. 'Discretion is the key to survival.'

Fleur lowered the note onto her lap and flipped it open discreetly.

You have beautiful eyes.

Tall, angular handwriting in black ink.

She raised the eyes in question to Laurent, narrowing them suspiciously. 'Should I assume this is a code? Do I need to translate it?'

He laughed. 'No, you don't.'

'Oh, well… Thank you, I suppose,' Fleur said.

She avoided looking at Colette, imagining the expression on her friend's face. The note flustered her. She wasn't used to compliments like that.

'If you had mentioned discretion earlier it would have been helpful. I didn't know there was anything inside the newspaper to be discreet about.'

She refilled her water beaker and slipped the note into her purse. Fortunately, at that moment Sébastien arrived. He was in good humour and whistling. He walked up to Fleur and kissed her cheek then sat beside Colette and kissed her thoroughly on the lips.

'What a shame you are here, Sébastien,' Laurent said, shaking his hand across the table. 'I was hoping to keep these two beauties to myself. Well, now you are here, I suppose we should all have a drink. Four *Weissbier*, please,' he called to the waiter.

'It's German,' he explained, pulling out a chair and sitting beside Fleur. 'One of the things the bastards actually do quite well.'

Four tall glasses arrived, containing a pale liquid with bubbles and a small head of white foam.

'*Salut!*' Laurent raised his glass and gestured to the others to do likewise. They all drank. It was quite unlike anything Fleur had ever tasted. Light and fizzy, but with a fruitiness that was quite delightful. She put the glass down hurriedly and looked at it suspiciously.

'Don't feel guilty for enjoying it, Fleur.'

Laurent turned his head to the person sitting at the next table. A handsome young man wearing an impeccable uniform. What he did next was almost beyond Fleur's comprehension. He addressed the man rapidly in German. Fleur gaped in astonishment as the man answered and Laurent laughed. He turned back to the table. Fleur dropped her eyes. Across the table she could see Colette frowning.

'Don't look at me as if I am some sort of traitor. I drink here on a regular basis and as they know me, the regular patrons trust me. I find it useful to be able to speak to them in their language. Emil is expecting to become a father any time in the next fortnight.'

'You must have learned it very quickly,' Colette said, in an accusatory tone that left Fleur quite breathless at the hypocrisy. She was no one to judge anyone's relationship with the invaders.

'I've been able to speak a little for years. I visited the Black Forest as a child and again as a youth. It was a beautiful area. I wish my opportunity to practise it had not come under such dark circumstances. It is tragic what happened to the country. I wonder sometimes if any of these men and women regret putting their trust in the Chancellor and wished they had heeded the warnings.'

Laurent sounded genuinely heartbroken. Fleur put her hand on his forearm. He blinked and shook his head, and his smile returned.

'Why don't you ask your friend?' Colette said.

'Even if he did, do you think he would admit that to anyone?' Laurent said. 'It was only a thought. As you see, Sébastien and I share a love of philosophising.'

'But not beer.' Sébastien laughed. 'I can drink it but give me a good wine or Breton cider any day.'

'I prefer champagne,' Colette added, pushing the glass away.

'Fleur?' Laurent looked at her, head on one side.

Under his scrutiny she felt self-conscious. 'More than anything, I would like a cup of proper coffee. With cream.'

'We have a winner,' Sébastien declared, clapping.

The atmosphere had been threatening to grow dark, but now the tension dissolved. For a while the conversation kept to inconsequential matters while the men emptied their glasses and Fleur sipped her beer. A whole glass would be too much and she was slightly worried that she would belch inadvertently. Once they had finished, Laurent suggested they take a walk along the banks of the Seine. It seemed natural to split into couples and Fleur found herself walking side by side with Laurent. He was much taller than she was and although she was able to loop her arm through his, she was conscious that he was stooping slightly towards her. It was touchingly considerate.

'Have you really been to Germany?' she asked.

'Of course. I don't lie. I've been to Spain too.'

'Have you been to England?'

He raised his brows. 'Yes. I've been to Britain.'

'One day you must tell me about it,' Fleur said. 'Colette went for nearly a year but I haven't had the opportunity, and I would love to.'

'About Colette: can we trust her?' Laurent asked. He slowed as they came to the Pont Marie leading onto the Ile St Louis. Colette and Sébastien were walking ahead, browsing in the *bouquinistes* stalls for books.

'Yes, I believe so.' Fleur didn't hesitate before answering, if only because Colette was as implicated in the secrets they shared as Fleur. 'She's my oldest friend. My closest friend. We've done things together since childhood and some of the things we have done since the Occupation have brought us closer than sisters.'

She sighed dreamily, reminiscing. 'We used to pretend we were sisters when we were children. We don't have any secrets.'

'It will be necessary for you to keep some from her,' Laurent cautioned. 'She knows what you are becoming a part of. That is regrettable, but cannot be helped. However, she must not know the specifics of what you do. That will be safer for her and for all of us.'

'What will I be doing?' Fleur had suppressed the question for long enough and couldn't wait any longer.

Laurent turned left and they crossed the stone bridge onto the island.

'Have you heard of couriers?'

'People who take things from place to place?'

'Exactly. Information or materials intended for the Resistance that would have the bearer arrested and executed without question, and sometimes not only things but people who need to be guided to a location.' He leaned against the bridge and looked out along the river, elbows resting on the parapet. 'People such as British airmen trying to make their way to safety while evading capture. Jews. Other *undesirables*.'

He lifted his head and fixed her with a piercing gaze, his nose wrinkling as he said the final word, leaving Fleur in no doubt that the phrase was not his own.

'I understand.' Fleur shivered and stood beside him, fixing her eyes on the waves beneath. To think this was going on around her while she had been completely unsuspecting. But, of course, if they aroused suspicion, that would ruin the whole point. 'Do you know, when I first went into your workshop I wondered if some of those parts lying around might be used in making bombs or other weapons.'

Laurent grinned. 'I could tell you were thinking something. It was one of the first things I noticed about you. You were observing everything. It was quite impressive to see. Anyway, back to my point, sometimes it is necessary for these people to spend a night in one location before moving on, sometimes more than a night. Most of them don't know Paris and would find it impossible to be where they need to be without help. Many of the British have only rudimentary phrases of French. I'm proposing you act as a courier and a safe house.'

'I'm not sure we should involve Colette's family,' Fleur said. 'It doesn't seem fair.'

'Not there. The bookshop. Sébastien says you have space, the door is not easily observed, and it is close enough to other locations. It would mean meeting your guests at a location in the city when they arrive, offering a bed for the night on occasions, and handing them on to the next link in the chain.'

Fleur broke into a smile. 'That is exactly what I hoped to be doing.'

Laurent faced her. He ran his hands from her shoulders down her arms and squeezed her hands gently.

'Believe me, it will take courage. Often you will be walking through checkpoints in the company of men and women with fake papers or carrying packages that would almost certainly see you detained, tortured and executed. You will need to be brave and you will need a cool head.'

A finger of ice traced a path down Fleur's spine. She suppressed the shiver. She'd carried leaflets around the city that plainly bore criticisms of the regime and incitements to resist. They would have carried the same penalties if she had been found with them. What was this but another foot on the same path? Was she being foolhardy, and if so, why did it matter so much to convince Laurent?

'I think I can do that,' she said. She hoped the slight tremor in her voice was only audible to herself.

'I know you can. I would not ask it of you if I didn't.' Laurent's voice exuded confidence. Fleur looked up at him and saw approval on his face. Warmth spread through her. 'I have every confidence in you. Now, we must give you a code name that I or others will use to communicate with you. If the name is not used, the message must not be trusted. My name is Augustine. What should you be?'

Fleur shrugged. 'I have no idea. You choose for me.'

He studied her before speaking. 'Roxane. The heroine in *Cyrano de Bergerac*.'

'Oh yes, I like that.'

He nodded, satisfied. His hands moved back to her shoulders and he paused. Fleur stood immobile. Laurent's eyes widened, the pupils swelling. He leaned a little closer and Fleur drew a deep breath. He was going to kiss her. When Pierre had surprised her with sudden kisses, she had not really known what was going to happen but now she brimmed with anticipation. The only part of her capable of moving was her lips. She parted them slightly, feeling her heart beginning to race.

He dropped his hands and took a step away.

'I'm not going to kiss you.'

His words crushed her. Stupid Fleur! He had been, until she revealed she was aware of it.

'I want you to,' Fleur said. Her pulse drummed in her ears. To be so close then have the promise snatched away was unbearable.

'Oh I know that, *chérie*. It is written all over your face.'

'And yours too, I think,' Fleur said, putting her hands to her cheeks. Sure enough they were warm and she knew they would be pink.

'I expect so.' Laurent's mouth twitched into a wry smile. 'However, it would not be right.'

'Why not?' Fleur demanded. She was starting to feel agitated, her pulse racing but not in a good way. It made her feel itchy all over.

Sébastien hadn't wanted her and now Laurent didn't. Or rather – and she belatedly saw with clarity the difference between the two men – he did but wouldn't.

'What's wrong with me?'

'Nothing is wrong with you, my Roxane. You are perfect. It's just very complicated. I can't explain but you will have to trust me.'

He cupped her face in his hands, tilting it back slightly. 'Will you trust me?'

His voice was deep and urgent. It was clear this meant a great deal to him. She needed him to believe she was reliable and sensible enough to work with.

'I will trust you,' she said, suppressing a sigh of frustration.

'Thank you.'

He released her, removed his hat, and wiped his forearm across his brow. 'I have to go. I'll send a message to the bookshop or via Sébastien at the Café Morlaix. Remember, if it isn't from Augustin or Elouard then don't trust it. Make my apologies to the others for not saying goodbye.'

He walked off across the bridge, hands in his pockets and head up, whistling as he went. Fleur walked back in the direction they had come from and met Colette and Sébastien. She said Laurent's goodbyes for him. Sébastien then bade the two women farewell and left, carrying a paper bag of books. Fleur and Colette walked back to the Metro together.

'You're very quiet,' Colette remarked, when they hadn't spoken for four or five streets.

'I have a lot to think about,' Fleur admitted.

Colette patted her hand. 'I can see that. I think you're in love.'

'Don't be an idiot,' Fleur said, much more snappily than she intended. She ignored the self-satisfied smirk on Colette's face because she had a sinking feeling in the pit of her stomach that Colette might be correct.

Chapter Twenty-Three

February 1942

'Fleur is so infuriating!'

Colette threw herself back onto the bed and sighed loudly to emphasise her point. Sébastien looked over from the window where he kept a bottle of wine. He gave her a quizzical look, or at least that was how she interpreted it given how short-sighted he was without his glasses. He obviously wasn't going to ask her to elaborate so she continued anyway.

'It's completely obvious that she is head over heels in love with Laurent and yet she absolutely refuses to do anything about it. They've wasted nearly half a year when they could have been doing what we've been doing!'

'How do you know?' Sébastien walked back from the window. He put two glasses of red wine on the nightstand and climbed back into bed, pulling the nest of blankets around them both.

'How do I know she is doing nothing, or how do I know she is in love with him?'

'Both, I suppose,' Sébastien said.

Colette ran her hand down his front, tickling the thatch of hair below his belly. He squirmed and trapped her hand beneath his own. His skin was warm and slightly damp from their recent exertions but his fingers and feet had already turned to icicles. There was never enough fuel to heat apartments adequately anymore and the winter dragged on, milder than the previous one but still bleak and bitter.

'I know she's not gone to bed with him because I ask her. She says they have only met a few times since she started working for him and more often than not it is someone else who gives the messages to her.'

Colette raised herself up onto her elbows, becoming animated. 'I know she's in love with him because whenever I mention his name, she does her best not to blush. I can see her trying as if she could stop her cheeks going red by willpower alone.'

'That doesn't mean she's in love though,' Sébastien pointed out. 'I would agree with you that she is infatuated, but there's a big difference between that and love.'

He looked at Colette intently. She gazed back, unblinking, as small flames danced around inside her. For the past months, they had been meeting two or three times a week to go to bed, sometimes in the evening but most often in the afternoons. Together they had developed quite an interesting repertoire of positions that had never crossed Colette's mind in the brief affair with Gunther. As much as the sex, she enjoyed the lazy times afterwards when they lay and chatted about nothing in particular. It was the longest love affair Colette had ever had, but it definitely wasn't love. She would recognise that when it swooped down on her, shocking her with a bolt of lightning.

Sébastien handed her a glass of wine and drank half of his in one gulp.

'Careful, I don't want you incapable.' Colette laughed, wagging a finger at him.

'Oh, *mon trésor*, if you think a glass of wine is enough to cause that you don't know me at all.' He put the glass on the nightstand. 'Why are we talking about Fleur when I have to go to the café in an hour?'

'Because she is our friend and we both want her to be happy,' Colette reminded him. She did still have occasional guilty feelings that Fleur liked Sébastien more than she had initially let on, but she salved her conscience with the fact that Sébastien had never given the slightest indication he felt the same about her. If he had, that would have made things altogether more complicated.

'True, but I can think of much better things to do with our time.' He rolled over, pinning Colette beneath him.

'And our mouths,' Colette added, gently biting his shoulder.

Sébastien moaned and she giggled. Yes, making love to him was exhilarating and she intended to enjoy every moment before the affair inevitably ran its course. He was not a man her parents would ever approve of, so at some point she would have to find someone suitable to marry.

It was just as well she didn't love him.

~

When Sébastien finally reluctantly dressed and left for the café, Colette made her way to the bookshop walking slightly gingerly with aching leg muscles and thinking how fortunate it was that she didn't have a long walk home. A smartly dressed man was talking to Fleur with his back to the door. He was the same height as Laurent, but over his shoulder she could see that Fleur's expression was slightly strained. When the doorbell clanged, she smiled at Colette.

'Colette, hello! How lovely to see you. Let me just finish with this customer then we can talk.' She smiled back at the customer. 'Colette helps me with the finances. She's invaluable.'

Colette tensed. The Gestapo had eyes everywhere and Germans who weren't in uniform were to be feared. Mistrust was the order of the day and no one spoke to strangers unless they absolutely had to.

'I'll go up to the flat,' Colette said. She strolled through the curtains and did her best to conceal her curiosity. She cut some bread and buttered it and brewed coffee. Shortly afterwards, Fleur joined her.

'Was there a problem?' Colette asked.

Fleur lounged on the comfy chair, nibbling the bread. 'Not in the end. I was worried at first though.'

Colette shivered and reached for the shawl that lay over the arm of the chair. There was a small oil heater in the flat, but they never used it.

'Can you tell me why?' she asked.

Fleur looked away then back again. 'You know I can't.'

Colette nodded, hiding her vexation. It was torment not to know what Fleur was doing. She had never seemed so confident or vibrant as she had over the last half year, and it wasn't just because she enjoyed spending time with Laurent. She seemed to thrive at being useful. Colette had even idly considered whether she should become involved just so she was party to the secrets.

They finished eating and went downstairs. It had started sleeting and the bookshop was gloomy.

'I hate these dark evenings. I can't wait until spring arrives again,' Colette groaned.

A silhouette of a figure fell across the door, blocking the little light there was. Colette felt a cold shiver as if fingers had clutched her neck. The previous visitor had been innocent but there was always the underlying apprehension that at any moment one might attract unwanted attention from the authorities.

Fleur unbolted the door cautiously and opened it.

Laurent stood before them. 'I'm sorry to disturb you, and I

would not normally come here like this, but I need to speak with you.'

'Of course, come in,' Fleur said, smiling at him.

Colette snuck a covert glance at Fleur. Her eyes had the glow of someone who was in love. Laurent stepped through the door. His eyes never left Fleur, which told Colette that her friend was not the only one who had been caught in Cupid's volley of arrows.

'Can we speak privately?' Laurent asked, glancing at Colette.

'Of course. I'll go upstairs,' Colette said. She walked back upstairs but instead of going inside the apartment, she stood in the doorway to listen. Laurent's voice was low but his deep tones carried up the narrow staircase, which funnelled the sound.

'Are you free tomorrow night?' Laurent said.

'Of course,' Fleur answered. 'Is there someone who needs a place to stay? I cleaned the apartment after last night but the sheets aren't washed.'

So that was the secret. Colette suppressed a smile. Anyone fleeing the Nazis would probably not care about who else had slept in their bed.

Laurent's voice came again. 'It isn't that. I have a mission tomorrow. Late. A drop. The man I should have been taking has been struck down with a gastric flu. Can you come?'

'Of course.'

Fleur's answer was quick and keen. Colette wondered if Laurent realised how infatuated she was.

'Perfect. I knew I could rely on you, *chérie*. Wear something dark. Trousers, if you own any, otherwise a sensible skirt, and a big coat. It will be very cold. Come by bicycle to the Pont de Levallois and wait for me on the far bank at half past six.'

He added something else in a murmur that Colette couldn't catch, then a few moments later came the sound of the door closing, followed by Fleur's footsteps. Colette tiptoed inside the flat and went to the sink where she began rearranging the plates.

'I assume you were listening?'

Colette turned, trying to radiate innocence but Fleur was leaning against the door, arms folded, with a knowing look in her eye.

'How did you know? Sorry.'

'No you aren't. I didn't hear the door closing, and I know the floorboards in the middle of the room creak. It doesn't matter. I don't think you know anything of value. I'm not sure I do, in honesty.' Fleur's eyes were wide, making her already fine features look even more delicate.

'Are you scared?' Colette asked.

'A little.' Fleur pressed her lips together, whitening them. 'It's one thing carrying or passing on packages, or even being used as a safe house. It's something quite different to be going out into the countryside. I'm stepping into the unknown.'

Colette pulled her into a hug. 'You aren't doing it alone, though. Laurent will be there. He'll make sure you are safe.'

'I know he will.'

Fleur's expression softened and Colette's heart flipped over at the vulnerability she saw.

'Sébastien chose well when he put you two in contact,' she said.

Of course he had, she thought. She suspected he had deliberately chosen Laurent with the purpose of engineering a love affair. Cunning devil.

'Will you tell me about last night?' Colette gave a guilty smile. 'I heard that too.'

Fleur scowled. 'I wish you hadn't. It might endanger everyone. This time I will, as I don't know enough to be a risk but you mustn't keep asking.' She sat back on the sofa. 'Last night I had a guest overnight in the apartment. An English woman. She is part of a network who are working with the Resistance. British spies in France, can you imagine such a thing? When the customer appeared earlier, I was terrified that he might be asking after her.'

'To see if she was safe or to try and catch her?' Colette asked, a shiver running the length of her spine. She sat beside Fleur and threw the blanket over both their laps.

'I don't know. Luckily, he was just a boring man who wanted to talk for a long time about the books he was buying. Old histories of the ancient Greeks that cost quite a lot so I did well out of it in the end.'

Colette sat forward, absorbed in the previous story. 'Tell me more about last night.'

'I had to meet her at the Gare de Lyon and if anyone asked, I was to pretend she was my cousin. Our papers were checked twice as we crossed the city. Hers were forged, obviously, but they were so perfect that no one spotted it.'

It sounded terrifying, but Fleur talked as if it was a great joke.

'We stayed up half the night talking. She operated a radio – did you know that a lot of the silly messages on the BBC nightly broadcasts are actually codes meant to tell the agents who is leaving or arriving? I'll have to listen more closely to see if I can work them out. Anyway, her signal was picked up by the Germans almost immediately after she arrived and she had to abandon it and leave. This morning we walked halfway across the city and I left her at a bus stop going north. I wonder if I'll ever find out if she gets home safely.'

'Weren't you scared?' Colette asked. She was almost envious of Fleur.

Fleur hugged her arms around her chest. 'I felt invigorated. I was actually doing something that might help change the course of the war.'

'I'm so proud of you,' Colette said, leaning against her.

Fleur's face lit up. 'Thank you. It feels good to be useful. And talking of useful, will you go and strip the bedsheets in the second room please? I am going to sweep the rugs. I need to make sure the flat doesn't look used.'

Colette did as asked, folding the knitted blankets and putting them on top of the wardrobe. She even crawled under the bed to check nothing incriminating had been accidentally overlooked. Her hand came out dusty, and when she mentioned it to Fleur, her friend grinned.

'I know. It's deliberate to make it seem that no one uses the room. Let's go home.'

'I was thinking,' Colette said. 'Do you think the men and women you are helping could use some extra clothes? I have far too many and I'm fairly sure *Mère* and *Papa* wouldn't miss some of their old ones.'

'I think that's a wonderful idea,' Fleur said. 'That's very generous of you.'

Colette shrugged the compliment away. There were clothes she hadn't worn for years now. Far from feeling a sense of defiance in wearing elaborate outfits, most of the women in her mother's social circle proudly wore the same handful of skirts and dresses, displaying their solidarity with the poorer Parisiennes.

They left the apartment for the second time and walked home, talking of any subject except the one that occupied both their thoughts.

Fleur didn't own any trousers so Colette spent the following morning altering a long wide skirt of her own into a split-skirt so Fleur could at least cycle easily. As Fleur's time of departure grew closer, Colette's stomach began to fill with butterflies.

'I don't know how you can eat,' she marvelled at Fleur, who was working her way through a bowl of chicken and barley broth and the end of a baguette.

'I don't know when I'll next get the opportunity,' Fleur replied. She went upstairs and returned in her going out outfit. Colette regarded her appraisingly. The calf-length split-skirt with black stockings underneath for extra warmth, a claret blouse with a dark blue cardigan on top, and a larger sweater Colette had liberated from Louis' wardrobe in her basket for when it grew chilly. With a dark blue headscarf tied behind her ears and her winter coat, she looked as warm as she could possibly be.

'God speed you,' Colette murmured, kissing her cheeks. 'And Laurent keep you safe.'

Fleur nodded. She slipped out of the house, leaving Colette wondering what sort of upside-down world it was where the closest a woman might get to a romantic encounter was skulking around the city in the dead of night.

Chapter Twenty-Four

Fleur and Laurent met as planned on the furthest bank of the Seine. Laurent led her on a route to the north-western edge of the city. He cycled ahead, stopping occasionally to check that she was following but at no point did he make eye contact with her, or indicate they were acquainted.

They crossed the river twice, queuing with others to pass over small bridges where the guards barely glanced at papers as they waved the travellers across. It was bitterly cold and no one wanted to be there, the Germans included.

The densely packed boulevards of apartment blocks and offices gave way to spacious roads with factories and low buildings, and gradually they segued into farmland as the city became villages. Laurent turned left at a crossroad, a sharp right shortly after that, and dismounted. With a quick glance behind him, he wheeled his bicycle down a narrow lane between a churchyard and a barn. Fleur followed, excitement and trepidation rising.

They emerged in a small village square, almost identical to hundreds across France. Laurent leaned his bicycle against the

261

wall of an old stone building and went inside, ducking his head to avoid the low doorway. Fleur followed and found herself in what appeared to be a village hall crossed with a restaurant. A dozen people sat at two long tables, all sharing benches. Laurent was seated at the furthest end of one.

'Roxane, over here.'

He gestured to Fleur to join him.

'What are we doing, Augustin?' she asked, climbing over the bench to sit opposite him.

'Eating. It's too early to do what we need to do but I wanted to be safely out of the city. It's always easier to avoid notice when the checkpoint guards are facing a queue of tired people trying to get home for their supper. Madame Pontoise does a very good cassoulet with leeks and meat that I'm almost certain is rabbit rather than rat. Don't bother asking for a menu, there isn't one.'

Fleur looked around. Sure enough, every diner had an earthenware bowl and a glass of red wine. Plates of dark brown bread were set at intervals. Fleur doubted anyone would take more than their entitlement. Laurent produced ration tokens and money, and handed them to the waitress, who returned shortly with a tray bearing the cassoulet.

It was good. The white beans well flavoured with thyme and leek, and whether it was rabbit or rat (a fact upon which Fleur chose not to dwell), the small nuggets of meat floating in the broth were nicely browned and tender.

The tables filled up with villagers and farmers. Friends greeted each other. Couples squabbled or canoodled.

'They don't seem to mind us being here. I would have thought they would be suspicious of strangers,' Fleur observed.

'I'm not a stranger here,' Laurent answered. He rested his arms on the table and leaned towards Fleur confidentially. 'I have worked with many of these people over the past months.'

'They are Resistance?' She whispered it, leaning close so he could hear her.

'Some of them. *Maquis*, they are known as. They do the roles I mentioned to you before. Setting explosives. Ambush. Sabotage. Dangerous activities.'

Fleur swallowed. Her mouth was dry all of a sudden. 'Will we be doing that tonight?'

'No. I wouldn't subject you to that for the first time you are out here. We are merely collecting supplies.'

He reached across and squeezed her hand reassuringly. 'There will be people watching our progress and if it looks like we are about to be exposed, they will deal with it.'

A middle-aged man entered the restaurant. He was obviously popular as loud greetings hailed him. The reason became clear when he picked up an accordion and began to play. His song was a slow, mournful chanson that was slightly old fashioned to Fleur's ears, with melancholic lyrics about a man pining for the woman he had lost to another man. The next song followed a similar story, with the sexes of the lovers reversed.

'Everyone would be happier if the two forlorn lovers from each song found each other,' Fleur remarked.

Laurent smiled. 'That spoils the point of the song. Imagine if it was so simple to give everyone a happy ending. There would be no great literature and opera would only last half an hour.'

'Ballerinas could wear the same pair of shoes for an entire season.' Fleur giggled. She grew serious. 'Don't you think life is already complicated enough, though? It would be much easier if everything was simple.'

'Yes, it would.' Laurent's eyes met hers. They were warm but wary. 'It is complicated indeed, and I would rather not make it more so.'

He reached across and briefly brushed the back of her hand.

'We need to leave. We have a little further to go. Come on.'

Together they left the restaurant and as Fleur watched Laurent nod to people – both men and women – she wondered if they were part of the group he had referred to. They returned to their bicycles and Fleur discovered that while they had been inside, someone had attached a trailer to the back of Laurent's. It was the first hint that whatever they would be retrieving would not be small.

~

They cycled along quiet, twisting roads, going deeper into the forest until they reached a small barn. They left the bicycles and, taking knapsacks, continued on foot. The moon was full, casting shadows across the barely distinguishable tracks as they walked silently into the depths of the woods. When Fleur remarked on their good fortune, Laurent turned back with a grin.

'It isn't a coincidence. The pilots need moonlight to fly by. They can't use lights for obvious reasons. The RAF boys are some of the best in the world.'

After perhaps ten minutes of walking, Laurent dropped his knapsack against a tree.

'This is where we wait. The Lysander will fly over those fields. It'll drop and leave. That's when we go.'

Fleur put her bag beside his and took up position beside him, kneeling in the undergrowth. The thick tree covering had at least provided some shelter so the ground was merely muddy not a slurry. Occasionally they shifted position but tried to keep movement to a minimum. They spoke rarely and in whispers, usually instigated by Laurent who checked that Fleur was comfortable, not too cold, not too nervous, not hungry or thirsty, understood what to do and other sundry queries.

After trying to ignore it for long enough, she had to admit the pressing need for a trip to find a bush, glad that there was not enough light for him to see her blushing. She crept off and returned to find Laurent had unearthed a hip flask.

'It's getting colder. This will warm you up.'

She accepted silently. Brandy, she thought. It was too strong but warmed its way through her stomach. She sat beside him, shivering as she settled. He put his arm around her, so much bigger than she was that she felt engulfed. Protected.

Neither spoke. It was so quiet. Cold too, far beyond what Fleur had expected. Her teeth chattered audibly. Laurent leaned back against a tree for some support and pulled her against him.

'You can't get too cold,' he said.

She relaxed her form against his, wondering if he was as aware as she was of the way their bodies pressed into each other as they sat. It was comforting in a way nothing she had experienced before had been. She was content to stay like that for ever.

She kept watching the skies. The moon cast a gentle glow over the fields, with only the occasional cloud to obscure it.

'How are you feeling?' Laurent whispered.

'Chilly,' Fleur answered. 'And nervous, if I'm honest. What happens if we're caught?'

'Then we'll make the best of it,' Laurent said. 'If I think that is likely to happen, we abandon the drop. Better the Germans get the equipment than get us as well.'

Fleur flexed her frozen fingers. It was a worrying thought. She was starting to get tired, eyes closing, and finding herself leaning her weight against him when Laurent clutched her upper arm and she started fully awake. With his other hand he was pointing to the sky.

'There.'

At first there was nothing to see, or at least nothing Fleur could see, just a quiet purring sound coming from somewhere ahead of her in the open. As she followed the line of his finger, she thought she noticed something silhouetted against the horizon but when she blinked it had gone. The only proof it had been there at all was that something began descending slowly from where it had been.

'Come on.'

Laurent reached for her hand, grabbing both knapsacks in the other and pulled her with him across the fields towards the falling object. The ground was uneven and going at such a pace Fleur stumbled. Laurent's arm went around her back as he stopped her from falling and he pulled her upright. She put her arms around him and he drew her close. His breath was fragranced with brandy and warm on her face. He loosened his grip and stood her upright.

'Take care. I can't be carrying you back with a broken ankle.'

He slowed his pace slightly.

From the other side of the field there was a muffled thud, followed by a whispering sigh, like a bird closing its wings. Fleur followed Laurent's path wishing she had better eyesight. Adjusting to the darkness was hard. The temperature had dropped and clouds covered the moon and there was nothing for her to see by. Laurent crouched beside a bundle of white. A parachute covered a box, approximately a metre long. It made Fleur think of a small coffin. She stared at the sky.

'I didn't even see a plane.'

Laurent grunted. 'That's the idea. Quick, help me release this.'

They freed the box from the cradle it was bound in and Laurent cut the cords from the parachute with a knife that had appeared in his hand.

'What do you think is inside?' Fleur asked.

'Right now I don't care.' Laurent's answer was brusque and Fleur felt implied criticism.

'I was only wondering aloud,' she whispered beneath her breath.

'Ponder later when we are safe,' Laurent said, his voice slightly kinder. 'Stuff the silk into your bag.'

Fleur did as he told her and put the bag over her shoulder. Laurent curled the ropes and put them in his.

'Help me with this. It's very heavy.'

He was right, and lifting the box was definitely a job for two of them. Stumbling and slipping in the mud, they made it back across the field and into the shelter of the hedge. It took them almost half an hour to reach the bicycles and Fleur was so hot and sweaty, she almost longed for the time when she was cold. They loaded the box into the trailer and covered it with a tarpaulin.

Side by side they cycled along the road. Fleur assumed they would be returning to the same village but they carried on towards Paris, Fleur following Laurent's lead without comment. She already sensed that her questions had put strain on him.

They turned into a larger collection of buildings. What would once have been a village had, like so many others, been amalgamated into the suburbs. Laurent stopped outside a bar on the corner of the main road and a quiet side street.

'Time for a drink,' he announced.

'Really?' Fleur frowned. She had lost track of time, but her body told her she should have been in bed by now.

'Definitely. I need a beer. First, let's rid ourselves of our cargo. We'll take it around to the cellar.'

'Ah.' She should have trusted Laurent that it was not just a random impulse to get a drink. Together they dragged the crate down a ramp into the cellar beneath the bar. Laurent shut the door behind them and turned on the lightbulb. There was a tyre iron leaning against a barrel. They had been expected. Laurent heaved the lid off and turned on a torch, which Fleur had not noticed him carrying before. He shot the beam onto the contents. Fleur inhaled sharply, drawing her hands back from the box.

'Are those guns?'

Of course they were. Small ones that could be carried in a bag or deep pocket, rather than the heavy, arm length ones the

German patrols carried. They were the ideal-sized weapon for people who were not supposed to have weapons at all.

Laurent looked amused. 'What did you think we would be collecting? Bars of chocolate? There are bullets too, and putty explosive, fuses, wires.'

'Chocolate. That would be delectable. Can you ask the British to send us some next time?'

'As much as I would love to grant your wish, they are even shorter of food than we are here,' Laurent said.

They worked quickly to package up the weapons and ammunition. Seven packages. All but two containing at least two revolvers. Laurent pocketed a few items including a box of small glass bulbs that looked like the sort of thing he had lying around in his workshop, and a small box that looked like something from a pharmacy.

'What do we do now?' Fleur asked.

'These will be collected.' Laurent indicated the three largest packages. He put them under a tarpaulin in the corner of the cellar. He gave a fourth to Fleur – one that did not contain a weapon.

'You need to take this one to the art gallery on Carré Rive Gauche tomorrow afternoon. Tell them it is for Pablo.'

'Picasso?' Fleur blinked in surprise. 'He is involved in this?'

Laurent laughed. 'No, it is a codename, but rather an apt one I think.'

'Come on, let's go get a drink.' Laurent stood and slung his knapsack containing the remaining packages over his shoulder. He held out his hand to Fleur. She took it, expecting him to let go when she was on her feet but he held on. Hand in hand, they walked up and into the bar via a staircase in the corner.

Chapter Twenty-Five

There were very few customers in the bar. As it was after curfew there should not have been any, but establishments did stay open for selected customers. It was widely believed that the German authorities turned a blind eye if there was no trouble, and this far out of the centre of Paris it was unlikely they would be checked. A young couple sat entwined in one corner, pausing between kisses to drink. Two old men played a game of backgammon in another. A third man lay with his head in his arms on the bar, snoring loudly. The bartender was a middle-aged woman who brought over two glasses of red wine without taking an order.

'It's what they have,' Laurent said as he passed a glass to Fleur. 'I am not sure it has ever seen a grape so be careful. It's very strong.'

'My *Tante* Agnes used to make wine from elderberries,' Fleur told him.

'I can beat that. My grandmother used to make it from nettles,' Laurent said, pulling a face that suggested it wasn't a pleasant memory.

They clinked glasses and drank. It was strong but welcome after the long hours spent crouching in the bushes. Fleur was glad of something to warm her limbs again.

'I will be good for nothing tomorrow,' she said. A fresh worry occurred to her. 'We've broken curfew now. What if we get stopped on the way?'

'The plane was later than I expected. I don't think we should risk it. The owner here rents rooms above the bar. Usually by the hour.' Laurent paused and indicated the couple who now appeared to be trying to eat each other.

'She's a prostitute?' Fleur stared at the woman, open-mouthed. 'How do you know? Have you ever…?'

'No. I've never been the sort of man who likes to sow my seeds then leave. I have to care for a woman before I go to bed with her.'

Fleur narrowed her eyes. 'That's not what the men at your workshop said. They told me women are your hobby.'

He grinned. 'They don't know half as much about me as they think they do. Let me go and have a word with the owner.'

He left Fleur and walked over to the sleeping man, prodded him awake and had a rapid conversation while Fleur digested the information. Laurent planned to spend the night here. He intended Fleur would spend it with him. She pursed her lips, wondering if this had been his intention all along. The wine. The hand-holding. The solicitous questions. Had they all been leading up to this? She should be furious at the thought he was planning to seduce her and the presumption she would go along with it, but all she could feel was rising excitement.

Laurent returned smiling. 'Yes, we can have a room for the night. There is only one bed, but I can sleep on the sofa.'

Fleur narrowed her eyes and crossed her arms, doing her best to look forbidding. He halted in front of her, looking uncertain.

'What's wrong?'

'Are you planning to seduce me?'

'Not in the slightest!' He looked genuinely taken aback.

'You aren't? Oh.' Humiliated at being so wrong, a prickle of heat began to climb up Fleur's neck. He had to care for a woman. He had told her so only minutes before.

He slipped back into his chair. 'Oh, I very much want to, however, I'm not planning to do it.'

'Why not?'

Laurent gave her a sideways look. The blue eyes appraised her far too closely.

'A number of reasons, not least a concept called honour. I don't believe that seduction should involve situations where neither partner can back out. Finish your drink. I promise you're completely safe in my company.'

He drained his glass and waited while Fleur did likewise. This time he didn't offer his hand when he stood. When they had sat, Fleur had spotted Laurent push the bag containing the final three packages under his chair. He did not take it with him. Clearly one of the other patrons would take in when they left. She considered asking who it was, but he probably wouldn't tell her. In any case, she was too embarrassed to speak after her awkward accusation.

They walked side by side through the bar and to the same staircase they had emerged from, this time turning up rather than down. Laurent led her to a room at the end of a passageway, which contained a narrow double bed and a washstand with a wooden chair in front of it. No sofa. They stared at each other, understanding clearly without the need for words. Laurent cleared his throat and kicked off his shoes.

'I've slept on enough floors in my time. One more won't hurt.'

They took turns washing in the sink and Laurent gallantly paid a visit to the lavatory down the corridor while Fleur removed split-skirt, cardigan, and blouse. She was about to move the knapsack off the bed when a thought struck her. She pulled the parachute out. Metres of smooth, soft fabric with a bright sheen to it in the lamplight. She was holding it at arm's length when Laurent returned.

'Are you performing the dance of the seven veils?'

'I don't know what that is. What should I do with this?'

Laurent leaned against the door and scratched his chin thoughtfully. 'Usually it gets burned to hide the evidence, but that seems a waste. How good are you at sewing? You could make yourself some blouses or slips.'

His eyes flickered over her and belatedly Fleur realised she was clad only in a bra, panties and stockings. Ah well, it seemed too late to worry about that now.

'I'm not very good at sewing but Colette is,' Fleur said, her imagination creating flowing gowns and nightgowns. 'I'm sure she could make something for us both.'

Laurent strolled across the room, a glint in his eye that made the muscles in Fleur's thighs tighten. 'I'd love to see you clothed in the finest Macclesfield silk.'

'Is that what it is called?' Fleur ran her hand over the cloth.

'It's where it's made. A little town in England.'

'You've been to England. Have you ever been to Macclesfield?' she asked.

'I haven't. Perhaps when all this is over I should go and pay my respects.' Laurent took the silk from her, lay on his back on the floor and threw it over himself as a makeshift blanket. It billowed then settled over him. Fleur could see the contours of his large frame swathed in the silk, reminding her of a figure on an ancient tomb.

Fleur climbed into the bed and pulled the counterpane up under her arms. 'I was always jealous of Colette going to England.'

'Then maybe I'll take you with me,' Laurent remarked. 'Goodnight, Fleur.'

Fleur closed her eyes, listening to the sounds of an

unfamiliar room. It was by far the least comfortable bed she'd ever slept in, but at least it was a bed. She leaned over and looked at Laurent. The window shutters were ill-fitting and let moonlight in. His eyes were open and he was staring at the ceiling, his arms crossed over his chest. The floor looked very uncomfortable.

'Laurent?'

'Hmm?'

'The bed is quite big. If you want to, you can sleep in it with me. Just to sleep.'

He cocked his head at her.

'I mean it,' she said. 'It's very cold.'

He didn't need inviting a second time. Fleur moved over and he climbed in beside her. The springs creaked and sagged, and they found themselves rolling face to face. They grinned at each other.

'It isn't much better than the floor,' Fleur said apologetically.

'Oh, it is.'

Their eyes met. The air grew heavy around them. For one dizzying moment Fleur thought – hoped – *ached* – that Laurent would kiss her, but he only reached his hand up between them and pushed the hair back from her forehead. He sighed heavily.

'I think it would be very easy for me to fall for you but there are too many reasons why it would be unfair to both of us.'

A cold weight settled in her chest where warm tendrils had been spreading.

'Are you already married?' she asked.

'No. I don't have a wife hidden in the workshop attic, if that is what you are thinking.'

Fleur couldn't help but smile. '*Jane Eyre*. You know the book?'

'Of course.'

'It is my favourite. I don't know many people who have read it,' she admitted. She leaned on one elbow and looked down at him. 'Knowing you have heard of it and can make a reference to it makes it even harder to resist you.'

'Then it's just as well I have enough self-control for both of us.'

She regarded him seriously. 'You are very strange, Laurent. I don't understand you.'

'It's probably best you don't try. At least for the time being. Perhaps when the war is done it will be possible we have the opportunity.'

He patted the pillow. She put her head beside his. Now she was lying down, Fleur realised how physically exhausted she was. She yawned and rolled onto her side so her back nestled against Laurent's warm side. The frozen core of her body began to thaw. As she drifted off to sleep, she felt his arm falling across her torso as he rolled over and drew her close. He smelled of earth, wine, and brandy. It was delicious.

'Tell me something about yourself,' Laurent whispered.

'What do you want to know?' she asked, turning to face him.

She could make out his smile in the darkness. 'Anything you want to tell me. Tell me what you would eat if you could eat anything. Tell me what you plan to do when the war ends. Tell me why *Jane Eyre* is your favourite book.'

She closed her eyes. 'I would eat chocolate ice cream with marron glacé sauce and Turkish Delight.'

'A sweet tooth,' he remarked.

'Not always but sometimes. If you asked me in a week or so I might say rillettes and cornichons.'

'That's one question answered. Now, why *Jane Eyre*? When I admitted I knew it you seemed very pleased.'

Fleur pursed her lips. It was true she adored the book but had never told anyone why. In the dark and to Laurent she found herself willing.

'Promise you won't laugh at me?'

He made the sign of a cross over his heart. 'Cross my heart and—'

'Stop there.' She seized his finger. 'Don't finish that. I know how it ends.'

She did not want him to die. She didn't want to die herself. He nodded solemnly then turned his palm round and laced his fingers through hers, clasping tightly.

'I like it because Jane had to make her own way in the world. I do too. She also lives with an aunt, as I used to before she died.'

'And there are cousins, weren't there? Cousins who are cruel to her.'

'They are. I've been lucky there. Colette has never been cruel to me in her life. She's selfish and can be thoughtless but if you ever met her mother you'd understand why. She's trying not to be.' She wriggled down a little further, getting comfortable in the warm space beside Laurent. 'I don't think I've always been kind to her. I think because I've had to manage on my own, I've always wanted to. Colette has always had people to help her.'

'Jane wasn't alone, was she?' Laurent pointed out. 'She had friends and her nice cousins eventually and of course Mr Rochester. Is that what you hope for too? A grand house of your own? Is that what you want after the war is over?'

Fleur turned her head away, even though it was dark enough that he would not be able to see her expression. Of course she had fantasised about an English country house – or even a spacious apartment like the Nadons' – of her own, but it would never happen. Laurent presumably lived above the garage and workshop. She laughed.

'Oh, I would like all kinds of things, but I don't think any of them will happen. I might as well long to eat ice cream on the moon as hope for that.'

He laughed.

'Now answer the questions yourself,' she commanded.

'I'd eat trout, preferably one that I have caught myself from a river. I don't have a favourite book. I want to build and race fast motor cars all over Europe. Maybe a little two-seater, with space for a passenger.'

He lapsed into silence, then yawned and shifted his weight, drawing Fleur close.

'You did well tonight, *chérie*. Sleep soundly.'

And, in his arms, she did.

~

They cycled back to the city as soon as curfew lifted, paused for coffee and warm bread rolls, then parted at the Pont de Levallois. Neither mentioned the conversation from the previous night.

'You know where to take the package?' Laurent asked.

Fleur's eyes flickered to the shopping bag in her bicycle basket. A coil of wire, some metal clasps, and a large packet of the odd putty that Laurent said was explosive. An art gallery was a good place to take it. Anyone looking would hopefully assume it was modelling clay.

'I do. When will I see you again?'

Laurent adjusted his sleeves. 'I'm not sure. It depends what we are asked to do.'

'You could come and see me anyway. Join us at the café, or call into the bookshop,' she said.

'Perhaps. I'm supposed to keep a distance from other operatives. For security reasons.'

'Of course.' Fleur pushed her hair behind her ear. It felt grimy. He had said he could grow to care for her, but that it was unwise. Maybe that was his way of ensuring he didn't. She fought down the urge to cajole. She had more dignity than that, but she didn't like the way seeing him had become almost as necessary as eating for her happiness.

276

'Take care, Augustin.'

She turned to go but he caught her by the arm and tugged her towards him. He wrapped her in his arms and buried his face in her hair then very gently kissed her left temple.

'Take care too, Roxane.'

He mounted his bicycle and had gone before she really knew it had happened.

She cycled home and was surprised to find Colette already dressed. She had made a hot tisane of lemon verbena and poured Fleur a cup. It was warm and she held the cup between her fingers to warm them.

'Can you tell me?' Colette asked.

'Not really,' Fleur said.

She felt her cheeks growing warm. There was plenty to tell but some she was forbidden from sharing and the rest was too personal and private.

'But come upstairs to my room in a couple of hours and I'll show you something.'

She bathed and washed her hair then dressed in the warmest pyjamas she could find and climbed into her bed. She felt cold again and desperately tired. She slept huddled into a ball and wishing she was back in Laurent's arms.

She awoke later to the knocking on the door and let Colette in.

'What did you want to show me? Do you have a bomb or a revolver?' Colette asked.

'Don't be silly. I wouldn't bring anything like that into the house,' Fleur said, thinking of the parcel she had to deliver later in the day. She opened her basket and pulled out the voluminous cloth.

'Look, I have a whole parachute of silky material. Laurent said we should use it to make new clothes. Slips or underwear.'

'Did he?' Colette raised her brows. 'I suppose he asked to see the finished product too.'

'What are you trying to say?'

Colette smirked. 'I'm saying he would probably like to see you wearing only a few wisps of silk.'

'I'm sure Sébastien would feel the same,' Fleur retorted.

Laurent's recent rejection had stung. He could talk of honour and the wisdom of it as much as he liked, but when he also said he only went to bed with women he cared about, well, it was hard not to feel spurned.

'I'm sure he would too,' Colette said, smiling like a cat who had discovered an unguarded salmon. 'When the weather gets warmer I'll find a pattern. There's no point making something if it is just going to be hidden under layers.'

It was only as Fleur cycled to the art gallery later that it occurred to her that she had not minded the thought of Colette titillating Sébastien in silky slips in the least.

Chapter Twenty-Six

May 1942

I t was the start of summer before Colette finished her parachute creations. She had intended to complete them earlier, but, in a rare fit of public-spiritedness, Delphine had announced that the trunk of drastically out-of-date outfits were to be altered to fit the children of refugees who were pouring into the city. To Colette's surprise, she even helped with the sewing, suggesting that the three women spent the evening in her salon where the window caught the best light.

Just in time for the summer, Colette produced one short and one long-sleeved blouse for Fleur (who had flatly refused to entertain the idea of suggestive underwear) and a short nightgown and camisole for herself, knowing exactly what effect she intended to have.

Sure enough, when Sébastien came home from the café to find her lying on his bed, wearing her new ensemble with her hair loose about her shoulders, he was rock hard before he had even removed his trousers.

Afterwards, he brought them both a glass of wine and lay back, pulling Colette between his open legs to rest against him. She sipped it and pulled a face.

'Did you leave the cork out? It tastes nasty.'

Sébastien swallowed a mouthful. 'It isn't the finest vintage, but it isn't sour.'

Colette took another cautious sip. If anything, this one was worse, making her feel slightly queasy.

'Not sour. It tastes like someone stirred it with a spoon and somehow the flavour of the spoon came off into the wine. I don't think I want any more.'

'Spoons don't taste of anything, but I'll drink it if you don't want it.' Sébastien took the glass and tipped the contents into his own. He began to massage her shoulders then work his way down and round to her breasts. She ran her hands down the inside of his thigh and felt his cock jump awake in the small of her back. She reclined against his chest, leaving her neck exposed for a kiss and forgot all about the wine.

～

The solution to the mystery was revealed a week later when Colette walked to the bathroom, caught the scent of the geraniums standing in a vase and promptly vomited. Fortunately, she had the presence of mind to turn to the sink before the stream of liquid erupted from her throat. She clung on to the edge of the porcelain lip, trembling, as a cold wash of perspiration soaked her lower back. When the feeling subsided, she drew a glass of water and left the tap running to wash away the vomit while she sipped it. It must have been something she had eaten. Her health had always been excellent, with barely a day feeling off colour since childhood. She could only remember one time when she had vomited in such a dramatic fashion.

'Oh no. Surely not,' she moaned aloud.

She cleaned her teeth and went back to her room on shaky legs. She hadn't needed a diary since the start of the war. Social engagements were so rare that they did not need noting down. In the back cover of a book she wrote down the date, counting backwards. The nausea increased, but for a different reason.

She closed the book. They had been so careful. Hadn't they? They had used the preventatives that Sébastien kept in his nightstand, and on the few occasions he had run out he had made sure to withdraw when he was close to finishing. It must have been something she had eaten that was making her sick.

She tried to keep telling herself that, but the same thing happened on three subsequent mornings. For the next two weeks she walked around the house in a state of anxiety, waking each morning hoping that she would be greeted with the smear of blood that was overdue. It didn't arrive.

After a particularly nasty vomiting episode she undressed and stared at herself in the mirror. She looked pale. Since food shortages had reduced her diet, she had lost weight, but now her cheeks were slightly plumper and her breasts were regaining their fullness. She had never bled particularly regularly and the reduced diet had meant she often went a full five weeks in between. Now she was up to seven.

Colette could no longer deny the probable truth that she was pregnant. She was about six weeks gone by her calculations. It was almost June now so the baby wouldn't be due until December, but she would only have another three months at most before she couldn't hide the bulge.

She leaned over the bath and sobbed. She couldn't bear to burden Sébastien and definitely couldn't admit it to Delphine and Louis. She couldn't even begin to plan what to do. Every time she tried, her thoughts became tangled and she wanted to cry again.

She avoided Delphine and sat on the patio in a deckchair

where the breeze helped her nausea and the morning sun was making a valiant effort to appear when Fleur approached her, carrying a jug of lemon verbena tisane, and two glasses.

'I saw you out here and thought I'd join you. What on earth are you doing outside? I'm still trembling inside from this morning.'

Colette gave her a wan smile. Fleur hadn't come home the previous night. It would be good to have something to take her mind of her own troubles.

'Were you and Laurent doing something together?'

Fleur put the tray onto the table. 'Not what you are thinking. Stop teasing me. I didn't see him. I haven't for a week.'

Her eyes grew slightly dreamy and Colette smiled for the first time in a few days. A distraction was what she needed. 'I wasn't teasing, I was asking. Can you tell me what you were doing?'

Fleur looked around her. They were alone in the garden. Louis was at the factory and Delphine had set off for a lunch engagement with a friend.

'I had to take someone from one safe house to another but the checkpoint guards were being extra careful. Fortunately, the man I was with thought quickly and we pretended to be a couple having an argument so they pushed us on quickly.' Her hair had come loose at one side and she blew upwards to move the strands out of her eyes. 'You know I shouldn't be telling you anything about what I do, but it's good to have someone to confide in.'

She poured two glasses of water and gave one to Colette who drank it eagerly. The hint of lemon verbena was sharp and fragrant and went a little way to slake her thirst and settle the nausea. She raised her head and realised Fleur was staring at her with a serious expression.

'Colette, will you consider joining me in what I do? Laurent says there are many roles and so much to do.'

Colette's stomach tightened. She feared for one moment she

was about to vomit again. The timing couldn't have been worse. If Fleur had asked a week earlier, she might have considered it.

'I can't.'

'Can't, or won't? I know you're brave enough.' Fleur drew close to Colette. 'You killed a man, Colette. You could do anything if you put your mind to it.'

She sounded so full of belief.

'I can't,' Colette repeated. Tears began to prickle.

'Why not?' Fleur asked. Colette could sense the exasperation budding in her voice. 'I don't understand. You're brave and I know you care. You would not have helped hide Michal otherwise. Why won't you now?'

Colette had intended to keep her condition secret for as long as possible but now she was consumed by the urge to share the news. Delphine had expressly forbidden her from telling anyone the first time, but Delphine was not here and Colette was no longer a child. She clutched her water glass tightly and looked Fleur in the eye.

'Because I am pregnant.'

Fleur gasped. Her face contorted into an expression Colette couldn't read. Disgust or contempt, most likely.

Colette gulped a sob. She pushed herself to her feet and lurched down the garden, tears swimming in her eyes. She pushed through the bushes and into the Secret Garden. She hadn't been there since Michal had left and she struggled to open the door. Maybe she could hide here until the baby came. She buried her face in her hands and tried to drown out the world.

She wasn't sure how much time had passed but eventually she became aware that Fleur was standing in front of her, holding out her glass.

'Thank you.' Colette sipped it gratefully.

'Who else knows? Sébastien does, I assume?' Fleur paused, then asked uncertainly, 'The baby is his, isn't it?'

'Of course it is,' Colette snapped, glaring at Fleur. 'What sort of slut do you take me for?'

Fleur looked mortified. 'I don't! I'm sorry. Of course the baby is Sébastien's.'

She sat heavily on the cold frame beside Colette.

'I haven't told him yet. I'm very early on. Part of me hoped...' Colette tailed off and gave a sob.

'Hoped that it would come to nothing?' Fleur's eyes flickered.

Colette nodded. 'Not all pregnancies continue past the first couple of months. I am a dreadful person for hoping such a thing.'

Colette waited for some reassurance but Fleur bit her lip and looked at the ground. Her lack of contradiction was mortifying. Colette felt she deserved every arrow that struck her. Fleur stood and began walking around. She had the same expression she did when she was organising the larder or the bookshop and Colette began to feel a rising relief that she was not alone.

'Well, you cannot bury your head and hope it will go away. I mean if it doesn't *go away* you won't be able to hide the bump for long. You will have to admit it eventually. What will you do?'

'Before the war I might have gone somewhere and had the baby in secret then given it up,' Colette said slowly. The idea had been floating in the back of her mind but now she gave voice to it and realised how impossible it was.

'Well you can't do that,' Fleur said. 'Even if you could think of somewhere to go, people would ask questions about where you are.'

Colette looked at her friend. How could Fleur be so close and yet so far away from the truth?

After so many years of concealing her secret, Colette felt giddy at the thought of unburdening herself. In a few seconds Fleur would discover what sort of woman her friend truly was. She might turn from Colette with more disgust on her face. Colette dreaded it, but she was tired of keeping secrets.

'They didn't before,' she said slowly.

Fleur wrinkled her brow in puzzlement. 'Didn't what?'

'Didn't suspect why I had left Paris. That's why I went to England. I was pregnant with Gunther's baby.'

'No!' Fleur breathed out the word in a long exhalation. 'You never told me!'

She sounded pained. Betrayed. It hurt Colette to hear it.

'*Mère* forbade me from telling anyone. I lived with Edith and her husband until the baby was born. Then a woman came and took it away. I don't even know if I had a boy or a girl.'

'Wouldn't they tell you?'

'I didn't want to know anything about the baby. I couldn't have kept it. I didn't want to know where it went, or who it would live with. I was relieved to be rid of it. Edith promised *Mère* she would never try to find out in case I asked. As far as I know, she kept her word.'

Colette pursed her lips. She looked sideways at Fleur who was rooted to the spot with an expression on her face that Colette couldn't read. A sob broke free.

'Don't condemn me. I made my choice. What child would want me as a mother? It was better for both of us.'

Fleur dropped to Colette's side and put a comforting hand on her arm. It was more than Colette thought she deserved and it almost broke her.

'I'm not going to condemn you, you poor thing. I feel sorry for you. And now I understand why you didn't write to me.'

'But I did!' Colette exclaimed. Her anxiety about Fleur's reaction and the pregnancy was momentarily forgotten. 'At least, I did until I realised you were never going to reply.'

Fleur's mouth fell open. 'But I wrote to you too. Your mother said she would put my letters in with hers.'

Colette sagged. 'She never wrote to me at all until I confirmed I had given birth and the baby had been taken away. She was too angry. My father did, but there was never a letter from you. Oh, the devious bitch! How could she be so unkind?'

Her cheeks flamed with the injustice. Luckily Delphine was out otherwise Colette might have marched inside to confront her. She turned her head back to Fleur. Much to her surprise, Fleur was smiling.

'There's nothing to be happy about,' she said irritably.

'Yes there is. Don't you see? We both thought the other had not cared enough to keep in touch. I can't speak for you, but I resented it. Now I know it wasn't your fault at all. That's why I'm happy.'

'Oh.' Colette sat back, thinking it over. As was so often the case, Fleur was speaking sense.

'I'm still furious, but now when I tell her about the baby, I think I will be a bit braver. Last time, I was barely more than a child and I thought she was doing the best for me. Now I'll do the best for myself.'

'When will you tell them?'

'*Mère* will be home in a couple of hours and will have had a couple of cocktails so hopefully her mood will be good. I'll tell her then. Will you be there when I do?'

Fleur sat back, crossing her arms and stared frankly at Colette. 'I think this is something you should do alone but come and find me at the shop if you need to once you've told her.'

'Thank you. I will.'

Fleur patted her hand. 'And what about Sébastien? When will you tell him?'

Colette closed her eyes. 'I don't know. Soon. He's a good man and he doesn't deserve this.'

'Did you do it on purpose?'

'To trap him? Or do you mean did both of us plan to have a child?' Colette's mouth twisted into a grimace but seeing the way Fleur pulled away she put her hands over her face and shook her head. She wasn't angry at Fleur. She exhaled slowly.

'Neither. It is a complete accident.'

Fleur smiled gently. 'Then he won't be angry.'

Colette blinked away a tear. 'Gunther was furious, and that time was an accident too. I don't want Sébastien to hate me.'

'He won't hate you *because* he's a good man,' Fleur said. Her mouth twitched sideways. 'He probably won't be happy, but he's half to blame, isn't he, so he deserves the worry as much as you.'

Colette blinked in surprise. It was the first time she had ever heard Fleur criticise Sébastien. 'I suppose so,' she said thoughtfully.

Fleur nibbled her lip then asked, 'What if Sébastien wants the baby?'

Colette hugged herself, shaking her head. She'd had one brief daydream of them raising the child as a family but when she imagined them crammed into Sébastien's room that became a nightmare. 'I can't imagine for a minute that he would. It isn't as if we were planning a future together; we were just supposed to be having fun.'

'But you'll tell him soon? It isn't fair not to.'

Fleur's face was like stone, her eyes looking past Colette.

'Yes. I will. Soon, I promise.'

She felt a bubble of nausea rising and put her head in her hands. After a moment, Fleur stroked her hair.

'How do you feel?'

Colette sighed. 'Terrible. Every morning I wake up feeling sick and can barely eat. Thank goodness coffee is so scarce because I truly believe that if I smelled it, I would vomit.'

～

Delphine's reaction was to scream recriminations at Colette for a full twenty minutes.

'You stupid little whore! What have I raised? To do this once

287

was bad enough, but a second time! How many men have you gone to bed with?'

'Sébastien is only the second,' Colette answered quietly.

Delphine gave her a disbelieving look. 'If that's true you must be the most unluckily fertile woman in France.'

She flopped onto the chair and put her hands over her eyes. 'What will your father say? What will my friends say? How are we going to dispose of this one? I can hardly send you to England again under the circumstances and who is going to take the little flea this time?'

Colette hung her head. 'I don't know. I'm sorry.'

'I spit on sorry! Do you realise what sort of trouble you have caused? You'll just have to hide in the house until you've had it. I suppose that means I will have to queue everywhere. And how much more do you think you will expect to eat?'

'I don't want to hide,' Colette said. The thought of being imprisoned in the house for the next seven months at least was unbearable.

'Do you want to parade your shame all over the city? Absolutely out of the question. Your father will agree with me. And speaking of fathers: who is responsible? If you've been fucking another German, I'll whip the skin from your back!'

'I haven't!'

The tone of Delphine's voice was appalling, but worse was the implication. Gunther hadn't been the enemy when she had made love with him but Delphine was rewriting the past.

'He is French, and his name is—'

'I don't want to hear his name.' Delphine's hand whipped up like a slap. 'Some champagne-soaked cabaret crawler I suppose.'

'No. Actually he is a student and a waiter.'

She could have added, *and he spends the nights helping people in trouble get to safety*, but she suspected Delphine would not see this as an advantage.

'Does he know about your condition?' Delphine asked sharply.

'Not yet.'

'Then don't tell him.'

She walked, remarkably steadily, over to her dressing table and pulled out a drawer. 'I'll have to sell some of my jewellery and get you to a doctor quickly.'

Colette frowned. 'I don't need to see a doctor yet. I feel perfectly well.'

Delphine's lip curled. She strode back to Colette and pointed a finger at her belly.

'Not to check your health you stupid little girl. To scrape that mistake out of you.'

Colette slapped her across the face.

Delphine yelped like a small dog.

Colette stared at her hand in horror. 'I didn't mean... I don't... *Maman*, I...'

Delphine raised her face. A livid streak branded her left cheek and her eyes were black with rage.

'You little bitch! I should have aborted you but Louis begged me to keep you.'

Colette had withstood the tirade but now her legs wobbled. She staggered sideways and bumped against the chair, reeling at her mother's words.

'That's not true. You're lying.'

Delphine stared at her. 'The choice is simple: either you abort that child or you remain indoors until it's born and we can dispose of it.'

The thought of undergoing a termination was too terrifying to consider. Women died from those. But she could not choose Delphine's other option and become a prisoner. Colette felt vomit rise in her throat. She put her hand over her mouth for fear she would physically throw up.

'There's a third choice,' she said coldly. 'I'm leaving.'

'Ruin your life if you want. But do that and you're no longer my daughter,' Delphine said.

Colette stood. She was taller than Delphine but had never really noticed until now. Her mother was a vain, stupid woman whose life revolved around drinking and clothes. No wonder her father preferred to spend his time at the factory.

'That should make you happy by the sounds of it. It's just a pity it's two decades too late for you.' She walked to the door. She had her hand on the handle before Delphine spoke.

'Where will you go?'

Colette hesitated, not bearing to admit she had no idea. She forced herself to look her mother in the eye. Delphine had turned white; the only colour the mark left by Colette's slap. She looked shocked. Colette felt the same.

'I don't have to tell you.'

'You'll be home by the end of the week.'

'No I won't. Goodbye, *Mère*.'

She walked to her room and looked around. She owned so much. She had never needed to ask more than once for anything. Never gone without, even when she had gone weeping to her parents the first time she had got pregnant. It terrified her to leave all this behind but if she didn't do it now, a part of her knew she never would.

She needed to think straight. This was as bad as the morning Louis had broken the news that they would be leaving Paris. Delphine may not let her back into the house so she filled a large suitcase with clothes then stopped with a shaky laugh. How long would it be before she was too large to fit into them? Well, she could alter or sell them. She put her watch, rings, and necklaces into a sponge bag along with her toothbrush and tooth powder, and a few small ornaments that might be worth pawning or selling. She would need money.

The sound of sobbing came from Delphine's salon. It tore at Colette's heart but she hardened it. Delphine was crying for herself, not for Colette.

Time to face the world. She pulled the front door closed and lifted her suitcase.

Chapter Twenty-Seven

By the time Colette reached the bookshop she was growing exhausted. She thought back with despair to the early months of her previous pregnancy where everything had felt too much effort and all she had wanted to do was lie on the sofa and eat cheese.

To her dismay, the blinds were rolled down and the sign in the door was turned to closed. Colette sagged against the window frame. She had come all this way and Fleur wasn't even there. Her eyes fell on a handwritten notice on a card.

For urgent enquiries find me at Café Morlaix.

Colette pressed to lips together. She wasn't sure if the note was just for her benefit or something Fleur used habitually. Sébastien would be at the café. He had to learn at some point, and as today was a day for revelations and admissions, she had nothing to lose by telling him now.

~

Fleur was sitting alone at a table by the bar, reading a book and drinking a coffee. Colette took two steps forward and then stopped. Fleur looked up, saw her, and walked swiftly to Colette.

'What's wrong? Why are you here? You've told Delphine, haven't you?'

Colette nodded. 'It went badly. I've done something very stupid. I need to tell Sébastien.'

As if summoned by his name, Sébastien appeared from the back room. He smiled warmly upon seeing Colette.

'How lovely to see you.'

Despite her anxiety, there was space in her belly for a flutter of pleasure. She hadn't seen him for a few days and had missed him. It was quickly surpassed by trepidation. She was about to turn his world upside down. In a moment or two his delight would turn to rejection. She couldn't smile back, and his face changed as he reached her.

'What's wrong?'

He placed a hand gently on her upper arm. A spontaneous, loving, gentle gesture that typified him and which Colette had come to value. She opened her mouth, but nothing came out.

'I told my mother that…'

She stopped.

'Colette, tell Sébastien what's wrong,' Fleur said gently, taking her hand and giving it a reassuring squeeze.

Colette looked at Sébastien and took a deep breath. His eyes radiated concern, magnified by the thick lenses. Would their child be short-sighted like its father? She would probably never know.

'I told my mother that I am pregnant. With your child.'

'My child?'

He looked at her as if she was stupid, or he was, or both of them.

'You're pregnant?'

293

She nodded, dropping her eyes and staring at the knots in the floorboards.

'With my child?'

This time she flicked her eyes up to his.

'Nobody else's,' she said coldly.

'No, I didn't mean that!' He looked horrified. 'But how? I thought we had been careful.'

'So did I,' Colette said, giving him a weary smile. 'Obviously we were both wrong.'

Sébastien held a hand out, lowered it, turned away, and walked into the back room. Colette looked at Fleur, feeling helpless. Gunther had shouted and denied it could have been his, calling Colette terrible names. At least Sébastien hadn't made a scene, which was slightly better.

'What did your mother say?' Fleur asked. Her eyes had followed Sébastien across the room and it was to Colette's eternal thanks that she had not gone to comfort him. Colette felt the worst guilt she could recall. Fleur cared for Sébastien and Colette had just ruined his life through thoughtless, selfish behaviour.

'She told me to abort it or to stay in the house until it was born and then give it up. *Dispose* of it.'

She curled her lip in distaste at the ominous sounding phrase.

'I don't want to do either of those things so I told her I was leaving home.'

She gestured to the suitcase. 'I came to ask you to let me live in the flat above the bookshop. I wouldn't need much and I have nowhere else to go.'

She glanced at the door Sébastien had exited through and added in a small voice, 'I'm on my own.'

Fleur followed her gaze. 'It was a shock to him. Trust him. Come and sit down.'

After what had felt like hours, but could have been no more

than five minutes, at most, Sébastien reappeared. He walked to the table where the two women sat and dropped to one knee.

'Colette, will you marry me?'

Her jaw dropped.

Like any other girl, she had dreamed of the day that the man she adored would ask for her hand in marriage, but it had always been somewhere dramatic. In front of or at the top of the Eiffel Tower. On a moonlit beach at Nice. Sailing along the Loire past a chateau – preferably one he owned. Anywhere but a dingy bar in the middle of the day during wartime.

The man of her dreams had never been Sébastien either. She hadn't met him yet and now, thanks to her carelessness, she never would. She burst into tears.

Sébastien looked mortified and struggled to his feet. She realised how cruel to him she was being. 'I'm sorry,' he said.

'No, I'm sorry.' Colette sniffed. 'Of all the things you could have said to me, I didn't expect you to ask me that. Do you mean you aren't angry? You aren't going to leave me?'

Sébastien shook his head, 'Not angry, no. Surprised, definitely. Scared, for certain. But I could never be angry with you. It isn't as though you've got pregnant without my help.'

Her heart swelled and a little of the bleakness she had felt since learning of her condition ebbed away. He was the best man she had ever known. How different her life might have been if Gunther had reacted in this manner.

She realised that silence had fallen over the café. She looked around at the faces of people Sébastien must know. Even the German patrons were looking at them eagerly. She felt as if she had been picked up and dropped in the middle of a film but not one with a happy ending.

'Sébastien, that's the sweetest thing anyone has ever done for me, but you don't have to marry me. Yes, I'm going to have the baby, but after that I will try find a family who will adopt it. It isn't fair on you to change your life. Neither of us want marriage, do we?'

She caught the quick flash of relief flit across his eyes. He wasn't going to argue with her too hard. She leaned down and embraced him.

'Thank you. You are wonderful,' she whispered.

'I know I am,' he said, giving her a weak grin. 'I will do whatever I can to help until the baby arrives. Afterwards too. I suppose I should meet your parents and apologise to them.'

'You'll do no such thing,' Colette exclaimed, aghast at the idea of Sébastien and Delphine in the same room. 'I mean, you have nothing to apologise for. It isn't something you did *to* me. We did it together.'

'I think I had better speak to them,' Fleur said.

She had been sitting quietly, trapped in the corner by the dramatic scenes taking place at the other side of the table.

'To Louis, at least. He has been so kind letting me live with you but now I think it is time for me to leave. The apartment has two bedrooms. You take one and I'll take the other.'

'You don't have to do that,' Colette said. She could feel tears rising, emotions swelling inside her at the way her friends had responded. She was not alone.

'I want to. I'll save hours of not having to cycle all the way there and back.'

Colette gave a small laugh. 'Then it's settled. Thank you.'

∼

If the exchange with Delphine had been harrowing, it was nothing compared with the emotional onslaught that Colette's interview with her father wreaked on her. He appeared unannounced at the bookshop a week after she had moved out, bearing two heavy cases. She led him upstairs to the apartment.

He dropped the cases by his side, put his head into his hands and groaned.

'Why, Colette? When you were younger I might be able to excuse such reckless and indecent behaviour, but now it's shameful.' He raised his head and looked around the apartment. 'And this is where you choose to live rather than accept your mother's help?'

Colette saw it through his eyes. Sparsely decorated and shabby. Old, mismatched chairs and rugs. A double gas ring in a corner that barely deserved the label of kitchen. A cramped bathroom with only a hip bath and a toilet with a cistern that screeched when it was flushed. It didn't look welcoming and Colette regretted that Louis had to see it before she had had the chance to make it more homely. Delphine had stood, granite faced, over Fleur and Colette as they packed their possessions and there had not been much time to gather the furnishings, ornaments and pictures that she liked. She led Louis to the comfortable chairs before the front window, sat on the arm of the chair he sat in and put her arms around his neck.

'I'm so sorry, *Papa*. I did not intend to disappoint you. It was an accident and we thought we had been so careful. Don't you see I had to leave the house though? *Mère* was going to keep me trapped inside for the next six or seven months. I just couldn't do it, I couldn't!'

'Your mother has strong feelings,' Louis said. 'She only wanted to take care of your mistake as she did before.'

Colette hugged him tighter. 'I'm not a child and I don't expect either of you to take care of my mistakes.'

Louis smiled for the first time since he had walked into the apartment. 'A father always expects to take care of his daughter. I want to help you a little. At the very least I will give you an allowance of some of the money we would've spent keeping you at home.'

'Thank you, *Papa*, but I don't want to take your money. I have a little saved and Sébastien says he will support me until the baby arrives.'

'You chose better this time I see. Very honourable of him,' Louis said. 'A man should support his child, and the mother of it.'

Colette sat up and twisted the end of her belt. 'Sébastien asked me to marry him, but I said he didn't have to. The situation is only temporary, after all, and it wouldn't be fair or sensible to tie him to me for the rest of our lives.'

Louis gave her an approving look. 'That is very sensible of you. If by some chance you decide to keep the child in the end, maybe you will reconsider.'

'I won't keep it,' she assured him.

'You say that now,' he answered.

There was something in her father's tone that made Colette think back to the words Delphine had thrown at her.

'*Papa*, did you and *Mère* plan to have me?'

'Why do you ask that?' His brows dipped into a frown. 'Did your mother say something?'

Colette nodded.

He sighed again and muttered something too quietly for Colette to catch.

'No, you were not planned. It was a time of great upheaval and the future was uncertain so people took advantage of opportunities they might not ordinarily have taken. Morals were looser than they had been.'

He huffed and looked at Colette. 'Like they are now, I suppose. Your mother intended to give you up and I was happy for her to do that, but when I held you in my arms, I could not bear to let you go. I swore to her that if she married me and raised you, I would dedicate my life to giving you both the life she desired. I have never regretted a day of it.'

There were tears in Colette's eyes. She blinked them away. Her dear father, who worked so hard and looked increasingly tired and old. She couldn't express the love that swelled in her as he spoke of his sacrifice.

'Whatever your mother might say, she loves you too,' Louis added.

Colette looked away, doubting it was completely true. Delphine had loved the idea of a daughter she could take to lunches and show off to her friends as an accessory. Someone she could form into a woman who could live the life she had wanted for herself. Marry a man she chose rather than one who she was forced together with because of her circumstances.

Louis looked around again and shook his head, sighing wearily. He stood and walked to the door.

'This is not the life we planned for you, but how many plans have come to nothing in the past few years? Take care, my little one.'

Once he had left, Colette sat by the window at the front of the apartment. It was actually quite nice, if she ignored the furnishings, with the front window that caught the sun from late morning and the rear that caught it from late afternoon. As with her previous pregnancy, the nausea passed by mid-afternoon. She would rest in the mornings, and in the afternoons she would make the apartment into somewhere beautiful for her and Fleur to live in. She would cook and clean, work in the bookshop, and think of other ways of earning money. Perhaps Sébastien could find her some hours in the café until she became too heavy to stand for hours.

For the rest of the afternoon she set about unpacking the cases, feeling more positive. Louis had clearly been into her bedroom and stripped it as he had brought her counterpane and fresh sheets for both women as well as her small rug. There were heavy curtains and cushion covers and a couple of metres of white linen that Colette decided would make a tablecloth. She was standing on a chair, hanging pink brocade damask curtains in the front window when Fleur came upstairs from the shop. She stalked straight up to Colette, hands on her hips.

'What are you doing? You could fall and hurt yourself or the baby!' She narrowed her eyes. 'You aren't… You don't want to, do you?'

Colette hooked the last loop over the rail and stepped off, shocked to the core. 'No! I can't believe you would think that I would do that!'

'I can't believe you would do something so risky as stand on a chair!'

'I wouldn't hurt myself if I fell and the chair is stable. I didn't think it was so risky,' Colette said. She sat and fanned herself. 'I've been busy. Look at what my father brought us. I've been making it a home.'

She watched proudly as Fleur took in the improvements she had made, then showed her the beginnings of the tablecloth.

'It looks beautiful. You have such a good eye for this. You could try to make and sell things.'

'That's a good idea. I was wondering how I could support myself,' Colette said.

Fleur poured a glass of water and drank it thirstily. 'Your father came to see me before he left. He gave me this.'

She reached into the pocket of her blouse and drew out two one-hundred-franc notes.

Colette groaned. 'I told him I didn't want his money.'

'He told me that. He told me to keep it and use it without telling you, but I thought you should know. The price of everything has risen so dramatically that turning down money is foolish.'

'You're right, I know, but I couldn't bear it. You should know how it feels, you don't like to rely on other people.'

'I rely on lots of people,' Fleur said, slightly indignantly.

Colette realised she had prodded a sore tooth and said nothing more. She took the notes and put them in her purse.

'I might try to buy some cooking oil. Last time I was pregnant all I wanted to eat was fried eggs with liver. Disgusting, but something Edith cooked well.'

'I'm not cooking that!' Fleur laughed. 'I thought I'd make *pain perdu* tonight. I think if I put a teaspoon of sugar into the mixture it will go further than sprinkling it on top.'

While Fleur soaked slices of stale bread in a little water and milk and added half a beaten egg, Colette continued to work on the tablecloth. When the buttery scent of fried bread filled the room, she knotted her thread and bit it off.

There was a small amount of honey left. Fleur spread it on one piece but not the other and handed the plate with the honey to Colette.

'Aren't you having any?'

'No, it's yours and I'm sure you will want some more tomorrow.'

'Fleur, I insist you have some,' Colette said. She dropped the needle and thread into her work basket and walked to the table. She took the knife and scraped it around the inside the jar until only a smear remained.

'We can share it. Let's sit in the sunshine while we can.'

They took the bread and honey downstairs and sat on the pavement opposite the shop in what remained of the evening sunshine that streamed along the road at an angle.

'You look happier than I have seen you for such a long time,' Fleur remarked. 'I think you seem happier even than you were when you came back from England and before the war started properly. When you were going out dancing with your friends.'

'I think I am happy,' Colette answered. She hadn't given the Lucienne sisters a second thought since beginning her affair with

Sébastien. Almost a year with no cabarets! 'Life back then felt quite meaningless now I look back on it.'

Fleur licked the buttery crumbs from her fingers and nodded. 'I didn't really think there would be much to be happy about during war. Isn't it awful how we have been so accustomed to being occupied that it barely seems to bother us?'

'We are growing up, aren't we?' Colette said, leaning back against the wall and closing her eyes.

It was long past the time, she decided.

Chapter Twenty-Eight

July 1942

Fleur had never experienced pregnancy close up before and if Colette's experience was typical, she never wanted to. From the first announcement, Colette had seemed perpetually tired and vomited for a couple of hours every morning, though usually rallied after lunch, and gradually the period of sickness grew shorter as her condition became evident in her growing belly.

On a hot morning in mid-July, Fleur returned home from another nightly collection of packages to find Colette lying on the sofa. She was still wearing her nightdress even though it was almost ten in the morning. It struck Fleur as unusually slothful until Sébastien walked out of Colette's bedroom with his shirt only partially buttoned.

'I didn't want to spend the evening alone so I invited Sébastien to come over,' Colette said. She gave him a sweet smile. 'He's teaching me how to play *Marjolet*. I think I owe him most of *Papa's* factory now!'

Sébastien laughed. 'I'll call in my debt another way if you like.

Good morning, Fleur, have you only just got back home? Were you rescuing more parachutes with Laurent? I assume that isn't a euphemism.'

'That was supposed to be a secret.' Fleur glared at Colette, who had the grace to look embarrassed. She gave Sébastien an awkward smile. 'No, it isn't a euphemism, and I wasn't with him last night.'

Colette and Sébastien exchanged a glance and Fleur got the impression her relationship with Laurent – or the sorry lack of it – had been the subject of discussion.

'Sébastien, you need to have a word with him,' Colette said. 'He's torturing our poor Fleur.'

'No, you don't!' Fleur glared at her friend. 'We're in the middle of a war and all you can think of is playing the matchmaker. And you really mustn't discuss what we are doing. It could put us all in danger and you don't just have yourself to think about now.'

She stared pointedly at Colette's belly. Fear wrapped around her heart. If Colette was taken and tortured, Fleur would never forgive herself.

Sébastien wandered to her side. 'Do you think you could eat some breakfast yet?'

Colette shook her head and put her hand over her mouth, closing her eyes as she did.

'I don't think she's eating enough,' Fleur told Sébastien. 'She picks at her food and I've never known her to do that before. It isn't as if there is enough to leave.'

Fleur put her hand to her stomach. One of the unexpected consequences of leaving the Nadons' house was losing the opportunity to harvest the fruit and vegetables the girls had nurtured. The Secret Garden would be a carpet of wild strawberries now. Just the thought made her mouth water unbearably.

Sébastien began to boil a pot of chicory and took three cups from the shelf.

'Is there anything that would make you feel better?' Fleur asked.

Colette sat upright. 'Something salty. Or chocolate.'

'If I could get you chocolate, I would,' Sébastien said. He knelt at Colette's side and put his hand to her forehead. 'I think you'll be fine if you rest enough.'

Colette gave Fleur and Sébastien a weak smile. 'I'm sorry. I am being useless. In a week or two I expect this will pass. It's just difficult at the moment. I don't expect you to find me chocolate. I wish I had stayed friends with Josette and Sophie now. I am sure they would be able to get hold of some from one of their German admirers.'

'Could you bring yourself to eat it though?' Fleur asked, raising her brows. It was the first time she had heard Colette mention the sisters' names in months.

Colette grinned, looking a little more like herself. 'If it was chocolate I probably could. But what am I doing talking about this? It isn't helping anything, is it?'

'Not really,' Fleur said.

Colette swung her legs round and stood. 'Enough pity. I brought this on myself. I will go have a wash and then I will go and see if I can nibble some bread. Then I'll go down into the shop. I left my sewing basket there last night.'

She regularly joined Fleur in the shop while she sewed. She had decided to make bookmarks of stiff card covered in her old scarves and embroidered with flowers. Fleur had been sceptical at first but they looked pretty and it seemed that the German customers were happy to buy them to send home to their wives and daughters. The idea of making and selling things for Germans would once have seemed appalling but now the women welcomed a good opportunity to part them from their francs and there were no French customers. Money was tight for everyone, with nothing to spare for luxuries.

She staggered off to the bathroom. As soon as she was gone, Sébastien turned to Fleur. 'I wonder if someone on the *marché noir* can find me some chocolate. I have a suspicion Pierre knows someone.'

Pierre as a contact made sense – he had a slightly devious air to him – but Fleur hadn't seen him for months. Since they stopped writing the leaflets he hadn't been around the café. Having said that, few French could afford coffee these days.

'You will end up paying five times the price if you do,' Fleur said. 'They're as bad as the Germans, if not worse.'

Sébastien looked sheepish. 'Yes, but if it makes Colette feel better it will be worth it. Would you consider stopping what you're doing?' Sébastien asked suddenly, surprising Fleur with the abrupt change of topic.

'Not until every last Nazi has gone from Paris,' Fleur answered. She felt the blood rushing in her veins. 'Don't worry. I won't give up in fear.'

'Would you give up for love?' He looked into her eyes and reached for her hand.

She became breathless. Surely not now? It was what she had always longed to hear, but not when he was soon to be a father and the woman carrying his child was in the next room.

And that was the revelation. She didn't want him to love her. When was the last time she really wanted him to? She struggled to recall. In fact, if he was proposing to abandon Colette right now she would be more furious with him than she could imagine.

'Colette,' she said.

'Exactly.' Sébastien's face twisted with concern.

'What?' Fleur frowned.

'Colette. Your love for her. Would you give up what you do to keep her safe?' Sébastien pressed her hand tightly. 'You didn't see her last night when she asked me to come round. She paced half the night with worry. I've never seen her looking so vulnerable. It kills her every time she thinks of you putting yourself in danger.'

He glanced over his shoulder then back to Fleur. 'And I want somebody to look after her. If I was taken, or had to go somewhere, I wouldn't want to think of her on her own.'

'Oh, Sébastien.' Fleur shook her head sadly. 'You really like her, don't you?'

He dropped her hand and ruffled his hair. 'I know it's hopeless for me. She doesn't love me back, but I can't help it. The very first time I saw her, I was a lost man, even when I thought she was a spoiled little piece. I know that sounds like something unbelievable from a book or movie, but it's true.'

Fleur's stomach clenched. She knew the feeling well enough. She'd felt it about Sébastien for long enough until Laurent had appeared in her life. Now all of her longing had transferred onto him. Another man who she could not have, but at least one she knew wanted her. It was a slight improvement. Perhaps the next man she met would want her and act on it.

'It isn't so unbelievable. Are you sure she doesn't love you?'

'I am sure enough. She is too vibrant to settle down, least of all with someone as serious as I am.'

'Opera would last half an hour,' Fleur murmured.

'What?'

'Oh, just something silly that Laurent and I were joking about a long time ago. It's nothing.'

Sébastien frowned. 'He isn't working you too hard, is he? I really did have reservations about putting you in touch with him. Not him personally, but the Resistance.'

'No. I'm glad you did. Put me in contact with the Resistance, I mean,' Fleur clarified, seeing the light in Sébastien's eyes. 'I feel useful. I'm part of something bigger than I am.'

'But you'll think about what I asked?' He looked at her hopefully.

'I'll think about it,' Fleur promised.

The coffee pot began to bubble and spurt. Sébastien turned the ring off. 'I don't think I'll stay. Tell Colette I'll see her soon.'

'Of course. Are you doing anything at four? Laurent and I are going for a walk along the river to catch the sunshine. The two of you should come with us.'

'As long as we won't be intruding,' Sébastien said. He kissed her cheek. 'Fleur, thank you.'

'For what? I haven't said I will definitely give it up.'

'No, but you said you will consider it. That means a lot. Please don't mention anything to Colette, by the way. I haven't discussed this with her.'

He put his shoes on and left. Colette returned shortly afterwards, wearing a cream linen dress that was starting to look slightly strained around her abdomen. She saw Fleur looking and stopped.

'I know. The little sprout is starting to show already. You'll have to see if Laurent can come by another parachute.'

'Does it bother you?' Fleur asked, ignoring the reference to Laurent.

'It really doesn't. This time it feels different. Feeling the life growing inside me.' Colette sat and tucked her foot under her. She looked thoughtful. 'Would it be a dreadful mistake if I kept the baby when it is born?'

Fleur was silent for a moment. 'I don't know,' she said eventually. 'It feels like perhaps it would be wrong for you *not* to keep the baby. Have you talked to Sébastien about it?'

Colette shook her head. 'No. I'm scared to because I'm not sure what he would answer. I told him about the… the other baby. He was as wonderfully understanding as you would expect but he might expect me to give up this one too, or he might think I would expect him to pay for the upkeep. I think I would have to because I can't raise a child on what I make from sewing and I've nearly sold all my jewellery.'

'Or he might ask you to marry him again,' Fleur pointed out quietly, remembering the love that had shone in his eyes as they had spoken. She was glad Colette had told him about the first baby. She hadn't found a way to ask if Colette was going to.

Colette gave her a bashful look. 'Yes, he might. I'm not sure if that might be worse.'

Fleur sipped her coffee, thinking deeply. She hadn't seen Colette with another man to compare her behaviour with, but she seemed very fond of Sébastien. She couldn't imagine Colette inviting many men round to play card games with. And because the world had twisted and she had stepped into a new one where she no longer wanted Sébastien, she knew that the thing that could make her happiest was seeing her friends recognise each other's affection.

'You do like him though, don't you?' she said. 'When you are together, you both seem very happy. You should talk to him about it.'

Colette's mouth twitched. 'I don't like him as much as he wants me to. I don't want to hurt him by not being there for him.'

That selflessness was the deciding factor for Fleur. She looked at Colette and smiled.

'Being in love agrees with you.'

'I'm not in love. I just said I don't like him enough.' Colette's tone was edged with a finality Fleur recognised. The discussion was over.

~

She spent the afternoon in the shop, but couldn't concentrate on anything apart from Sébastien's request. It was unfair of him to ask her, but she had heard the desperation in his voice. He was thinking of Colette, but doing what she did gave Fleur purpose. She had not so long ago left the Nadons' employment and for the first time in her life was beholden to nobody. If she gave up her work with Laurent to support Colette, then nothing would have changed. And what of Laurent? Would she still see him?

The door opened and, as if her thoughts had summoned him, Laurent walked in. It was half an hour before he was due to meet her. Fleur felt a rush of pleasure at the early arrival, which immediately turned to alarm when she saw his face was contorted.

'Lock the door,' she said.

His hand shook as he drew the bolts. Fleur's stomach tightened.

'What's wrong? Come upstairs.'

He made it upstairs and sank into a chair.

'The stadium. The *Vel' D'Hiv*. A contact heard it was being used to hold people. Busloads were being taken since yesterday. I cycled past and … oh god, Fleur.' He put his head in his hands. Fleur stood helplessly at his side. Colette came softly out of her room.

'Which people?' she asked quietly.

'Jews. Everyone I saw had a yellow star.' Laurent looked at them both, his face grey. 'There were whole families. Women with babies and children. There are guards everywhere. I couldn't get close but I could hear the shouts and the crying as people were taken off buses and pushed inside. The windows are closed. It's horrific.'

Fleur sank onto the chair beside him, feeling sick. The velodrome had a glass roof. In the July temperature it would become a giant greenhouse. She saw Colette's hand move to her belly.

'What can we do?' Fleur asked.

Laurent shook his head. 'I don't know. I'm sorry, I don't think we'll be able to go for a walk tonight. I'm hoping to hear from my contact. He has gone home to send urgent messages to anyone who might be able to help.'

'I don't mind,' Fleur said. She walked to the front window and leaned out to get a lungful of fresh air but there was no breeze and her throat dried. She turned back to Laurent. 'Whatever I can do… If there is anything, tell me.'

He crossed the room to her. 'I will. Wait here. When – if – I get any orders, I'll be in touch. I have to go.'

He drew her into an embrace, arms pinning her tightly to him. She held back a sob and tried to draw comfort from his closeness. Every time she parted from Laurent she felt the same dread it would be their last meeting.

'It's very bad, isn't it?' Colette said after he left. 'What do you think they will do to the people?'

'I don't know.' Fleur looked around the room. 'It's inhuman. What have we become? We only have this flat because of what happened to Monsieur Ramper. We don't know what happened to Michal or his family. I need to go out and get some air.'

'Don't go,' Colette said. 'I think you should wait, like Laurent said. If any Germans thought you were causing trouble you'd be arrested too. It's too risky. I can't bear to think of you in danger.'

'I won't be in danger,' Fleur said. Her throat seized. 'I'm not Jewish.'

'Oh you know it isn't only Jews! What you're doing is dangerous for you.'

Colette burst into tears and Fleur held her friend. She felt sick imagining the families detained in the velodrome. They didn't have the luxury of fresh air. The least she could do was endure the stifling room to keep Colette company.

~

It was a week before she heard from Laurent.

'What happened?' she asked.

'The stadium is empty now. The people have been moved. We were given no orders.' Laurent held his glass out to Sébastien who refilled it. The four of them were sitting around the table in Café Morlaix; the only customers.

'The problem is there are not enough of us to be of any use with something that large.'

Sébastien sat. 'How many people across the city are part of the network?'

'I don't know.' Laurent gave him a steady look. 'That's the point. If one person is arrested it limits the number of names he can give up.'

Fleur shivered. She knew the risk involved in what she did and though her nerves screamed at her to hide away and avoid any more involvement, she couldn't.

Curfew was drawing close.

'I need to finish tidying up,' Sébastien said. 'Laurent, will you walk Fleur home? Colette is staying with me tonight.'

Laurent smiled at her. 'Of course.'

'I'll take the glasses,' Fleur said and followed Sébastien.

'I've made my decision. I can't give up what I'm doing, not even for Colette. I'm sorry,' she said once they were alone.

'I thought that would be your answer,' Sébastien said, dropping his eyes. 'I think you are probably right. Thank you for even considering it.'

∼

'You were speaking about something serious, weren't you?' Laurent said as he left Fleur at the bookshop door a while later. 'You don't have to tell me, of course, but if you'd like to unburden yourself…'

He left the sentence hanging. Now she had made her decision there was no reason not to tell him. His reaction was unexpected.

'He really asked you to give up important work for the war to be a chaperone? Incredible! That girl will have no chance to become the woman she could be if everybody cossets her. You do enough already for her.'

Fleur's cheeks grew warm. 'She's my friend and she's pregnant. Besides, she keeps my accounts in order and sews neater repairs than I do. It's fair. Besides, I said I'm not going to stop.'

He gave a wry smile and leaned in towards her. 'Which makes me happy, of course. But what do you want, Fleur?'

'I want to do it.' She looked at him, loving the intensity in his eyes. 'I've never had the luxury of not working. I can't imagine it. Colette's mother drifts around her salon all day entertaining equally superficial women. Even if I could do that, I don't think I would like to.'

Laurent took her hands between his. 'You are a good woman, Fleur – the finest – and I hope one day you will learn to be a little more selfish than you are. Good night and thank you for all you do.'

He kissed her cheeks and slipped away. She resisted the urge to stand in the street hoping he would look back.

What she really wanted was him, but whatever was keeping him from acting on his clear attraction was a mystery. She had to be patient and hope that mystery would be solved and resolved eventually.

Chapter Twenty-Nine

October 1942

'I'll take the ring and the bracelet and give you the cloth in exchange.'

The woman behind the counter at the Credit Municipal crossed her arms and stared Colette down. Colette bit back her retort that the exchange was far from fair. The bracelet and ring were both silver with small chips of emerald inlaid, and the fabric was thick cotton in a dull mustard colour, but she could not afford to argue.

She was rapidly growing too large for most of her clothes. She had let out what she could, but needed more and sewing from scratch was much cheaper than buying. There was a queue growing behind her of men and women waiting to exchange or surrender their possessions and she heard a couple of irritable comments directed at her.

'Agreed.' She handed over the jewellery and took the bundle of cloth. As she exited the line, she kept her head high. There was nothing to be ashamed of in what she was doing. The system had been going on since the seventeenth century in this very building. It worried her how few pieces of jewellery she had left to sell though. She had given all of her previous maternity clothes away in England, never planning to need them again and not wanting the reminder of her shameful secret. Now she wished she had kept some.

She hoped in vain that Fleur or Laurent would produce another parachute soon. It was one of the jokes that the four friends shared. When one, or both of them, weren't off doing whatever clandestine work they were given, Fleur and Laurent often spent their evenings in Café Morlaix, keeping Colette company while Sébastien worked. They never spoke of what they did but knowing that there were men and women actively working to sabotage or defeat the Nazis gave Colette hope that it would not last for ever.

The four of them had built up quite a repertoire of card games, all played with stakes of imaginary future riches. Colette currently owed Laurent seven thousand francs. Fleur, less cautious in her bids, owed him nineteen thousand.

'I'll collect my winnings one day,' he promised Fleur with a laugh, leaving Colette to speculate what form of payment he would choose. It was blatantly obvious to Colette that they were falling in love, so why was Laurent so insistent that nothing should happen between them? Colette didn't know him well enough to ask and Sébastien flatly refused to become involved.

~

'I hope Laurent doesn't expect you to ever pay the debt with real money,' she commented as she and Fleur walked around the market one morning before the sun had even risen. The earlier they arrived the better bargains they could get, but money was always tight.

'I'll offer to darn his socks and shirts,' Fleur said, grinning. 'I have more time now I don't have such a large house to clean.'

Colette stopped and looked at Fleur. The women never really spoke of their previous life. 'Do you prefer living like we do now?'

Fleur paused her examination of a basket of potatoes that looked green and consequently were cheaper. 'Of course. Even though it's a struggle with money, we have our own lives. I couldn't do what I do so easily if I had to find excuses of why I wasn't coming home some nights.'

'I think I do too,' Colette said, selecting a couple of bunches of herbs. 'Certainly the part about not having to explain to my mother where I spent the night.'

She concealed a smile as her breasts twinged. Sébastien, unlike Laurent, had no reservations about carrying on a love affair. Making love with a large bump in the way was tricky, but they both agreed that accommodating it was a challenge both of them enjoyed.

They never spoke of the baby. It was there, and soon it would be gone … unless she decided to keep it, which was becoming something that increasingly played on her mind. She rested her hand on her belly, feeling a kick, then took it away. During her first pregnancy she had not felt anything other than revulsion or fear when she thought of what was growing inside her, but this time was different. She found herself stroking the odd bumps that rose and fell beneath her skin, and humming songs she remembered from childhood. She was starting to care about the child she and Sébastien had created. It was troubling her and she didn't have long left to broach the subject with Sébastien of what to do when it arrived.

Whether or not Sébastien would leave her once there was no longer anything to keep him tied to her was something she didn't want to dwell on too deeply. There was no reason why they couldn't continue as they were. She was happy to.

She was more than happy.

Apart from the constant hunger, life under occupation had become bearable, and the restrictions that had once felt so constricting had become commonplace. Queues for the meagre rations, showing papers at checkpoints, moving aside on pavements for Germans to pass; all were accepted and endured. Sitting in cafés where German was spoken as commonly as French no longer made her stomach clench with fear.

≈

All that changed on a cold November evening.

Sleet had made the pavements treacherous and Colette had stayed inside for the whole day, feeling at odds with herself. Sébastien was working and Fleur had left to do something or other. The ringing of the bell from below came unexpectedly and Colette tensed. Someone was at the door to the shop. No one calling unexpectedly at this hour could be bringing good news. She heaved herself out of the chair and answered the door.

Sébastien stood there, a grim expression on his face. She smiled but his face remained marble.

'Is Laurent here? I need his help.'

'No, and Fleur is out, but not with him I don't think.' She clutched her belly, feeling a kick as the baby responded to her panic. 'What's wrong? Has something happened to Fleur?'

He took off his glasses and rubbed them on his sleeve, smearing water across the lenses. 'Not Fleur. They want me, Colette.'

She noticed a suitcase at his feet. Her stomach plummeted.

'Who?'

'The STO. I've been selected.'

The *Service du Travail Obligatoire*. French men selected by lottery to be sent to Germany to work in labour camps for the war effort. It was relatively new and deeply unpopular, for obvious reasons.

Colette sank against the doorframe, the strength leaving her. Sébastien swept her into his arms. She clung to him, trembling. 'I'm sorry, I didn't mean to shock you. Are you alright? Do you want anything to drink? I could do with something myself.'

He led her upstairs and helped her to sit on the sofa, then walked to the kitchen, poured a neat brandy for himself and diluted one with water for Colette. He drank it in one.

'When are you going?'

Sébastien replaced his glasses. His eyes glinted. 'I'm not. I'll go to hell before I do anything to help the German war effort. I'm leaving Paris. Laurent has contacts. So do I, but I need help from the network. I'll go into the countryside. Up north, down south, I don't really care. I'm going to join the *Maquis* and fight.'

'Today?' Colette shook her head in horror.

'No. Tomorrow or the day after. As soon as I can make arrangements. I brought this suitcase here now while no one suspects me. Can I leave it to collect when I'm ready to go? I have been given four days to get my affairs in order before I need to report to the railway station. I'm going to spend the next couple of days doing normal activities so they won't suspect I plan to run.'

He sounded so determined. So calm. It was inconceivable to Colette.

'If they catch you, I don't know what they will do to you.'

He shrugged. 'Probably nothing worse than what they will do if they send me to Germany. I can't imagine the work camps are particularly nice places to be.' He took his glass back to the kitchen. 'I have to go.'

A fist squeezed Colette's heart. Her imagination ran wild, and she pictured Nazis round every corner waiting to seize him and carry him off before he had the chance to put his plan into action.

Just the idea made her want to cling onto him and stop him leaving the building.

'Fleur said she would be back soon. Can't you stay a little longer?'

'I can't. I'm supposed to be working. If I don't show up someone might get suspicious, as I said. I have a number for Laurent so I'll try that, but will you tell Fleur please?'

'Of course.' Colette felt tears rising. Of course she would tell Fleur. She would need someone to share her grief and worry with. She wrapped her arms around him. 'Don't go without saying goodbye to me,' she said, hugging him tightly.

He kissed her cheek. 'I won't. I promise that you will be safe here. Fleur will look after you.'

He thought she was worried about her own safety or welfare. How come he did not realise that it was concern for him that brought the tears to her eyes?

She only realised after he had left that it was because she had never told him. She hadn't realised how important he was until the threat of losing him became real.

∽

Three nights later, Colette met Sébastien at the *Les Halles*. It was early morning, and the iron and glass halls of the were bustling with lorries and vans waiting as stallholders set out their produce for the day. Sébastien was dressed in overalls and wearing a heavy coat. Colette had transferred the contents of his suitcase into a flour sack provided by Laurent. Now he blended in with the men moving about everywhere.

Colette and Fleur carried their shopping baskets and the three stood together under one of the archways. Colette and Sébastien had already bid each other a subdued farewell that morning, but the women had decided to accompany him.

Colette ached with the need to kiss him one last time, but in the unfamiliar clothes he already looked like a stranger to her.

He stuck his hands deep into his pockets and nodded at Fleur. 'Will you watch after her?'

'You know I will,' she answered.

He looked back at Colette, his eyes softening the edges. 'You take care too.'

'And you.'

He picked up the flour sack and turned away.

The baby kicked. Colette put her hands to her belly. She was nearly at full term and the immense fear overcame her that her child would never know its father. She would have only tales to tell of him. She hadn't spoken to Sébastien about her thoughts of keeping it, but in that moment, she realised how badly she wanted to. Sébastien had come into her life in the strangest way but now she could not imagine living without him.

'Come back to me,' she said.

He half turned. A brief hesitation brought on no doubt by the suddenness of this display of affection.

'I mean it. I don't want to lose you.' Why had she left it so long to realise how deeply she cared for him?

Say it, say it, a voice inside her shouted.

'I … I think I love you.'

He turned fully round, a crooked smile on his lips.

'You don't have to say that.'

'I mean it,' Colette said. She walked up to him and kissed him. He was motionless. She brushed her fingers into his hair and pulled him closer, savouring the moment when his lips yielded against hers. She drew back and looked at him. 'I should have seen it a long time ago. You're the best man I know. I've been blind and stupid.'

He might not be the best-looking man in France, but to Colette he was the dearest. Sébastien blinked. As always, his glasses made his eyes look enormous. Currently, they were full of passion. He took her face between his hands and held her still.

'You've given me what I need. A reason to go, and a reason to return,' he murmured. 'One day France will be free and I will come back. In the meantime, I will keep fighting and you must keep safe.'

He adjusted his cap to a jaunty angle so he looked as casual as if he was going for a walk by the river. He picked up his sack, hefted it over his shoulder then turned and walked off among the stallholders and delivery men. He did not look back.

'Come on, let's go quickly,' Fleur said. 'We are unfamiliar faces in the queues and we don't want to get caught here either.'

'One moment,' Colette murmured wistfully. 'Just until he turns the corner.'

She felt Fleur take her hand and squeeze it, glad of the support and friendship. When Sébastien had disappeared into the huddle of men carrying sacks, baskets, and boxes, she and Fleur walked home together hand in hand.

'Was that true?' Fleur asked when they were safely back inside the apartment.

'Every word.' Colette sighed. 'I don't know why it took me so long to see it.'

'I don't either.' Fleur's tone was brisk as she poured the coffee into cups. 'I knew the moment I saw him that he was a man in a thousand. I am glad you finally realised.'

She brought the cups over to the table. It was weak and bitter, not at all like the coffee Colette remembered from before the war, but it was welcome nonetheless. She remembered with dismay how in the early weeks of her pregnancy even the smell turned her stomach.

'And I'm glad you've got Laurent.'

'I haven't,' Fleur said. 'We just work well together.'

'Of course. If you do decide you love him though, don't leave it too late like I almost did.'

Fleur twisted the cup in her hands and smiled bleakly. 'I'm not the one you should be giving that advice to.'

Ah, so it was like that, was it? Colette said nothing but promised herself that if the opportunity arose, she would indeed pass on her thoughts to Laurent.

～

Four days after Sébastien left, the bookshop door opened and a man walked in. He was not a soldier but wore a uniform of some sort. An official. Colette gripped hold of her book. The visitor might just be a customer or on another matter but Sébastien had warned her there would be repercussions for his disappearance. The warning meant she had already considered how to respond.

'Good afternoon, may I help you?' Fleur asked politely. 'We are closing in half an hour.'

Just the right combination of politeness and confidence, Colette thought approvingly. After all, what did either of them have to hide?

'I am looking for Fräulein Nadon. Is this you?'

'It's me.' Colette laid her book face down on the table. Knowing Fleur's opinion of people who did that, she thought better of it and inserted a hairpin into the page. 'Is there something the matter? Are my parents ill?'

'I am not here to discuss your parents. My name is Herr Gersdorf. I am looking for the whereabouts of Sébastien Guyon.'

Colette pushed her bottom lip out. 'Well, if you find him, please let me know. I haven't seen him for almost a week.'

'Really?' The man looked unconvinced.

Colette and Fleur exchanged a worried glance.

'We can't help you, I'm afraid,' Fleur said. 'Have you looked at the Café Morlaix?'

'We tried his place of work. A customer said he often spends time with you here. You are his lover, we understand,' he said, turning back to Colette.

Colette flushed. It wasn't a secret, but she wondered which of the patrons had given them up. She couldn't blame them. Under threat from this rather sinister-looking man most people would do what they could to be rid of him. She stood and patted her belly.

'You could say that,' she said bitterly.

'He is the father of your child?'

'Unfortunately, yes.' Colette scowled. 'What has he done?'

'He is missing. He was supposed to report for STO two days ago and he did not. He is now viewed as a fugitive.'

'No, oh no!' Colette sank onto her chair and dropped her head onto the table. Fleur ran over and began to fuss around her.

'Are you faint? Do you need water? This is terrible. How can you surprise her with this information?'

This last question was addressed to the visitor.

'Men are such snakes,' Colette sobbed.

'You did not know this?' Herr Gersdorf hadn't been affected by Fleur's recriminations.

'No, I didn't,' Colette answered plaintively. 'He never tells me anything. We argued last week when he had drunk too much, and I haven't seen him since. I thought he must be sleeping off his bad head somewhere. Have you checked the prisons? Please will you help us find him?'

Now Herr Gersdorf did look slightly taken aback. Presumably he was not used to being asked on behalf of French women to help find missing men.

'Naturally, we investigated all departments for his whereabouts. He is not anywhere in our system.'

A chill ran down Colette's back. *Our system*. Such a mild term for what it represented. Interrogation and torture. She began to cry. It was easy to do. The tension combined with her racing mood in late pregnancy and the loss of Sébastien gave her plenty to cry about.

'Have you checked the brothels? Why am I so unfortunate? I should have listened to my *maman*. She cautioned me against men, but I was too stupid. He promised me that when the baby came, he would marry me. And now he's run off and I'll never see him again. Oh what am I to do?' She dropped her head onto the table again and began to wail. Her heart thumped painfully and the baby rolled over, pressing uncomfortably on her bladder as it had a habit of doing lately. She let out a moan and sat up.

Their interrogator appeared unmoved. 'I would like to search your apartment. I will do it now.'

He walked to the door, clapped his hands and two soldiers walked in. Young men, both with carefully neutral expressions. Herr Gersdorf spoke rapidly to them in German. They walked into the back room, weapons at the ready but returned shortly and gave their report. No fugitive there.

'You, *Fräulein*, will come with me.' Herr Gersdorf pointed at Fleur then looked at Colette and his eyes flickered uncertainly. 'You will wait here. Lock the door and give me the key. No one will leave until I permit it.'

Fleur did as commanded. Colette sat on the chair, gripping the edge of the table while Fleur, Gersdorf, and one soldier went upstairs. The youngest soldier remained. A boy barely out of his teens. Colette avoided his eyes. She listened to the creaks of floorboards from above, heard the closing of doors, the scraping of furniture being moved. It was agonising. They were upstairs for half an hour. Far longer than Colette would have thought possible. All the time, the soldier stood motionless by the door. Finally, they returned downstairs. Herr Gersdorf had an irritated expression.

Presumably he had hoped to discover Sébastien hiding in a wardrobe.

'Thank you for your cooperation. You may unlock the door. Needless to say, if you hear from Monsieur Guyon you will let me know immediately.'

'And please will you tell me if you find him?' Colette replied.

He eyed her coldly. 'We have greater concerns than finding one absent and absentee father. If he contacts you, we expect you to tell us. There is no obligation on us to do the same. Good day, *Fräuleins*.'

He snapped his heels sharply and walked out of the door, followed by the soldiers. Fleur held the door handle. When the sound of boots died away, she closed the door again and locked it. She turned to Colette.

'I think perhaps you should be in the movies after all!'

Colette burst into tears. Fleur rushed to hug her.

'Oh, my dear, you were wonderful. I know that must have been horrible for you. There's no need to cry. They've gone and I don't think they'll be back.'

Colette blew her nose on her handkerchief. 'I'm not crying because it was horrible, though it was. I'm crying because I'm happy. I don't know where Sébastien is, but the Germans didn't intercept him. Wherever he is, he is beyond their reach. It gave me hope.'

She put her hand on her belly. The baby shifted and she felt a lump roll over again. Elbow? Knee? She had no idea.

'He or she will get to meet its *papa* one day, I'm sure of it.'

Chapter Thirty

Colette gave birth at twenty-seven minutes past three on New Year's Eve 1942. In the final weeks she had felt the pregnancy would never come to an end. It was the second labour she had endured, but the first child she had held. A girl. She cradled the tiny scrap against her. Naked and slippery, it felt as if she may drop the child at any time. So precarious. So precious.

The midwife had packed up and left quickly, moving on to another job.

'Shall I take her and wash her?' Fleur asked, reaching her hands out gingerly. 'You're getting covered in blood and…' She wrinkled her nose. 'And whatever all that other stuff is.'

'I don't care,' Colette murmured. Already the baby was nuzzling against her breast and she was reluctant to surrender her. 'Can you put a blanket over us both? I like feeling her against me. I think she is hungry.'

Fleur reached for the blanket. 'Oh, of course she is.'

Colette guided the small mouth to her left nipple and the baby latched on immediately. Colette's breasts swelled and spasmed uncomfortably, but after a few pulls from the tiny mouth she felt them ease. This was nothing like the agony she had felt after the first birth, when she had bound her breasts to force the milk to dry up. She wondered whose milk the first child had drunk and a twinge of guilt shot through her. She rested back against the pillows and closed her eyes. The small mouth pulled determinedly at her nipple.

'You have as powerful a suck as your *papa*,' she murmured sleepily.

'Colette, that's disgusting!' Fleur exclaimed.

'No it isn't. It's natural and wonderful.' Colette opened her eyes and slid a glance at Fleur. 'Haven't you gone to bed with Laurent yet?'

'Of course not,' Fleur replied. She blushed bright red.

'Well, you should. But be more sensible and careful than Sébastien and I were, unless of course you want one of these.' She stroked the back of the baby's head then, without warning, burst into tears.

Fleur dropped to her side. 'What's wrong? Are you in pain?'

'No. I mean yes, it's very uncomfortable down there right now, but that will go. I just … I miss him. I never thought I would miss him so much. And now I've got his daughter in my arms and she might be all I ever have of him again. How could I ever have considered giving her up, even for a second?' She bit her lip, hard enough that she tasted blood. 'How could I have given up her sibling? I just wanted to be rid of the problem. I am a monster.'

She began to sob in earnest. Fleur patted her shoulder. 'Of course you're not. You did the right thing at the time. You were too young to be a mother and the Lord knows you would have resented every minute of it. Sébastien will come back to you, I'm sure of it. And you will be waiting for him with his daughter. Let me fetch you a cup of milk.'

She walked away and returned with a glass, as well as a piece of buttered bread. Colette finished them in a flash. Since her pains began at almost eight in the morning she hadn't eaten or drunk anything. She switched the baby to the other breast.

'You do like him, don't you?' she murmured. She was growing sleepy. Physical exhaustion was being supplanted by mental tiredness.

'Laurent? Yes, I do.' Fleur sat on the end of the bed. 'It's not fair, really. All the time I've been alive, I've never met anyone who has obsessed me so much. I don't think he even knows I exist other than as a courier. I might as well be a carrier pigeon as a woman.'

Colette pursed her lips. 'You're a dove. Not a pigeon. Delicate and beautiful. But if you can't see that Laurent is completely desperate to tear your clothes off whenever he looks at you, then you have got the intelligence of a pigeon. I've seen enough men to know what lust looks like.'

Fleur twisted her hands. 'Oh yes, I know that. I don't want to though. Not if it only means something special to me.'

'You think too much.' Colette sighed. 'Just go to bed with him. It will be fun.'

'He won't, even though he's said he wants to.' Fleur picked at a hole in her skirt. 'He's probably right not to because I think that if I discovered we were compatible in that way and it still didn't mean anything to him it would destroy me. I'd rather not find out.'

Colette sagged back against the pillow. Perhaps Fleur was right. After all, what had going to bed with Sébastien achieved? Far better that she had continued to view him as someone who despised her silliness than realise too late that they cared for each other.

'I wish you could be happy, Fleur. I wish all the happiness in the world for you.'

'I know you do. And I am happy most of the time.' She leaned up the bed and stroked the baby's cheek. 'I'm very happy now this little one has come into the world safely. Are you going to tell your parents?'

Colette's throat constricted. Her euphoria ebbed slightly. 'Why? My mother has disowned me and now I am going to keep her there will be no chance of reconciling, even if I wanted to.'

'Your father hasn't though. Don't you think he would like to know he has a granddaughter?'

Colette gazed at the baby. Louis would have been overjoyed if his grandchild had been the product of a respectable, successful marriage. An illegitimate wartime baby sired by a waiter was a different matter.

Fleur stood. 'I have to go out soon. I have work tonight. I could visit the house and tell them?'

'No, don't do that. If I decide to tell them I will do it myself. But not for a few days at least. Apart from anything else, I don't think I could walk that far. What do you have to do tonight?' she asked innocently. Fleur always referred to what she did as 'work' but never spoke of specifics. Colette had tried to get her to drop hints, but she always refused, as she did now with a smile.

'I'm not going to tell you that, as you know. The fewer people who know, the safer everyone will be.'

'But what if something goes wrong?' Colette was gripped by an intense fear. Panic made her want to climb from the bed and hold Fleur but the baby settled against her breast, preventing her from moving.

'That is precisely why I am not telling you. It is dangerous enough that you know I am involved at all. If something goes wrong, you are safer being able to honestly deny all knowledge, just like when the men came looking for Sébastien. I'll get you the water.'

She kissed Colette's head, bundled up the used towels and left.

Colette drifted in and out of sleep and woke again when Fleur knocked at the door. She held a carafe of water and a plate containing two biscuits. She was dressed in black trousers and a dark grey sweater. Her hair was swept back and caught under a blue headscarf.

'I won't tell your parents if you don't want me to, but someone needs to know you are here and that the baby has arrived in case anything happens. I will tell Mademoiselle Dufroy in the apartment next door so she can check on you in the evening. I'll leave the door on the latch.'

She walked to the bed and kissed Colette's cheek, then stroked the baby's downy cheek. 'I am so pleased for you, my dear.'

She left, and Colette tried to go back to sleep. Drifting in and out of wakefulness, Colette wasn't sure how happy she was. She awoke to the smell of soup. The old woman from the apartment next door was standing over her bed.

'The best thing for after a labour,' she said as she took the baby from Colette's arms and replaced it with a tray holding a bowl of onion soup. The soup was thin and the onions were sparse and it lacked the beefy brandyish depth of the soup that Delphine would make for the girls when they were ill as children, but it had the same comforting associations.

No not Delphine. *Tante* Agnes had made it, of course. Delphine had never actually mothered Colette. When Mademoiselle Dufroy exchanged the bowl for the baby once more, Colette kissed the bridge of her nose just between her downy eyebrows.

'I am going to be the best mother in France to you, my little one,' she swore.

She slept again and awoke in darkness when the baby began to whimper and sniffle.

'More milk? Surely not,' she exclaimed wearily. She had just changed the baby from the left breast to the right one when the front door clicked open and shut. Shortly afterwards, Fleur tiptoed past the doorway, her shoes in her hand. Colette called her in.

'I'm sorry, did I wake you? I was trying to be so quiet.' Fleur put her shoes down and perched on the end of the bed.

'You didn't,' Colette assured her. 'This little mademoiselle appears to have an empty belly again. Did everything go to plan?'

'Mostly. Eventually.' Fleur rubbed the soles of her feet.

Colette studied her closely. Her hair was still neatly tied beneath the headscarf, but there were damp patches on her elbows and knees. 'What happened? Can you tell me anything?'

'I was escorting someone and we almost walked straight into a German patrol. He escaped from a camp somewhere and is trying to reach Switzerland. The conditions he described sounded awful.'

She rubbed at a smear of dirt on her trousers. 'We had to hide in a garden. I need to wash and then go to sleep. Will you be alright tonight? In the morning I can look after the baby and you can get some sleep.'

'That would be wonderful, but only if you don't mind,' Colette said, trying not to sound too eager.

'I don't mind at all.'

'I do love her, you know. I didn't realise it was possible to fall in so much love like that. I'd do anything to keep her safe.'

Fleur laughed. 'I don't think it's that strange. I think you're supposed to feel that way.'

'Do you remember the little girl on the road out of Paris during the exodus? I was shocked at the way her mother asked us to take her but now I know why she did it. I hope they made it to safety.'

～

When Colette next woke it was morning. The baby was gone and the sky was light. Bleary eyed and sleep deprived, she lay for a few moments, not entirely sure the past nine months hadn't been a dream. She discovered Fleur reading in the living room. The baby was lying on the rug with her legs and arms splayed out and a blanket covering her midriff. Fleur put a finger to her lips then mimed washing. Colette nodded and backed out of the room.

She sat in the cramped tub and washed off the blood and mucus, recalling that when she had given birth before, Edith had run her a warm bath and ensured she was well looked after. Lots of English puddings with boiled fruit and thick crème anglaise. She hadn't realised at the time how privileged she had been. She joined Fleur in the living room with a gloomy expression.

'It's nineteen forty-three,' Fleur said. 'Let's hope this year will be the last of the war. You look so sad. Want to tell me what's wrong?'

'I'm thinking about the other baby. I know it was the best thing for it, and for me, but I wish now there had been some other way,' she explained. 'I wonder if one day, when it is possible to communicate freely again, I might write to Edith and ask if she could find out what happened to the baby?'

Fleur squeezed her hand. 'Would you like to see the child?'

Colette gripped the arm of the chair. 'No. Wherever he or she is, they will have a family. No, it would be for myself. It is probably best left alone, but I'll always wonder.'

She gazed down at the baby on the rug and was unprepared for the wash of love that bowled her over. 'That baby belongs to whoever is raising it. This little girl is mine and always will be.'

'Does she have a name yet?' Fleur asked.

'Not yet. I didn't bother to make a list.'

'Ah well, I'm sure you will think of something before she starts running across the room making a mess and you need to shout at her. I seem to recall our names being shouted often enough.'

Colette sat back and closed her eyes. The carefree years they had spent running around the garden seemed like another world. She didn't dare hope her own daughter would be so lucky.

Chapter Thirty-One

March 1943

Fleur had fallen in love, completely and utterly, and the recipient did not care in the slightest. In fact, Fleur noted with some irony, it had been the case with Sébastien. Colette was the only person who mattered and his daughter was the same. Colette was the world and all it contained.

Nevertheless, Fleur treasured every moment she spent with the baby. Now the child was old enough to go for a few hours between feeds, three or four mornings a week she would take the girl out while Colette washed her hair and slept in peace for an hour or two. Often, she was accompanied by Laurent. One bright morning in late March they met at the banks of the river and walked along, watching the stallholders setting out their books.

Laurent had arrived late and unshaven. 'I'm sorry, it was a very late night but never mind. The Germans will have woken up to discover that the railway lines ten miles to the west of the city are buckled beyond use.'

'That's wonderful. Well done.' Fleur had played no part in this act of sabotage beyond carrying a copy of a magazine from Elouard to a woman in an office at the *mairie* of the fourteenth arrondissement.

'I also shan't be able to stay long, I'm afraid,' Laurent said. 'I must meet someone in an hour. Let's walk onto the island. There might be a breeze coming down the river. It's going to be warm today I think.'

He offered Fleur an arm and they strolled side by side. The baby gurgled in the sling wrapped around Fleur, full of milk and content for an hour.

'Does she have a name yet?' Laurent asked.

'No. And I am slightly worried about that,' Fleur said. She stroked the baby's hand. 'What if Colette decides to give her up after all?'

'Do you think she will?'

'I didn't, but I don't know why she hasn't named her.'

Laurent lifted the brim of the baby's knitted hat and made kissing noises towards her. 'It's a pity she isn't a racehorse or a pedigree dog because then there would be a long list to choose from.'

'Did you hear that!' Fleur exclaimed in mock indignation. 'The slug called you a racehorse! You're much more beautiful than that.'

'Of course she is,' Laurent answered, 'and she knows it too.'

Fleur's contemplation of whether the baby knew anything beyond where her milk came from was interrupted by a voice.

'Hello, Fleur.'

Pierre was strolling towards her.

'I haven't seen you for a long time,' she said, giving him a smile.

'You've been busy, I see.' His face was set and he did not look amused. He looked at the baby.

'Oh dear, no! The baby belongs to Colette and Sébastien. She isn't mine.' Fleur laughed.

He smiled. 'I wonder how much like her father she will look. It was good to see you, Fleur. We must catch up again soon.'

Pierre strolled on. Shortly afterwards, Fleur and Laurent parted, he to go to his meeting with his friend and Fleur to go shopping quickly before the baby started demanding food. She hadn't gone very far and had just turned down a narrow alleyway that was a shortcut when Pierre caught up with her.

'I want a word with you.'

She paused. 'Only a quick one. I want to get to the shops. I need to try buy some stockings.'

'Stockings? What have you done with all the ones you own? Gone through at the knees, have they?'

Fleur froze. Yes, she'd laddered a pair the week before when she had had to clamber inside a lorry, but how did Pierre know that? 'I don't know what you mean?'

'I bet you do,' Pierre sneered. 'I bet the mechanic's floor is pretty dirty. Did you rip them getting your lips around something from his tool-box?'

'You're disgusting!' Fleur exclaimed. Part of her was repulsed. A greater part relieved that he didn't know her secret life after all.

'Am I?' Pierre snapped. He folded his arms and glared at her. 'Still the coy little virgin, are you? Don't think I haven't noticed you and him. What is it he can give you that you didn't want from me? Is he a black marketeer?'

Fleur looked at him with something approaching pity. 'Pierre, you are talking complete nonsense. Laurent is just somebody I know.'

She wondered what he would say if she told him the truth. Moonlit trips to isolated fields and smuggling weaponry and explosives around the city.

'You want him, don't you? Was I not good enough for you?'

She hung her head. 'I'm sorry. I tried to like what we did, I honestly tried. You know that.'

It was the wrong thing to say because immediately he reached out and took her by the arm, jerking her close. 'You didn't try that hard though, did you? A few half-hearted kisses and a bit of a grope. You're pathetic. Why don't we try again? I bet I can find something that you'll enjoy.'

Once she might have reluctantly submitted, but not now. She brought a free hand down sharply across the wrist of the hand that held her. Pierre yelped and released her. As he lunged forward, she kicked him sharply in the shin, then again across his kneecap. He swore and swung his fist. She stepped out of reach, giving a shriek and shocked beyond belief that he might strike her, or worse, the baby.

'You little bitch. After everything we have done. All the nights we spent working together, arguing over ideas and pamphlets. I thought we were friends.'

Fleur's ears began to buzz. She realised she was trembling with anger as much as fear.

'We are friends. But only friends. We both did it for France.'

'And if I go to the Gestapo and tell them, what will you say?' There was a malevolent glint in Pierre's eyes. Vomit rose in Fleur's throat. Her legs began to tremble. She bunched her fists, digging her nails into the palms in the hope that the sharp sensation would stop her from fainting.

'You wouldn't. You couldn't without betraying yourself, and Sébastien too. And even if you did, I'd make sure that yours would be the only name I gave them.'

'Fleur? Is everything alright?' Laurent stood at the end of the alley. He strolled towards them, hands in his pockets. 'I stopped to greet a friend and realised I hadn't seen you go past.'

Pierre seemed to shrink. The skin round his eyes twitched. He was strong and well-built but nothing in comparison to Laurent.

When Laurent was halfway towards them, Pierre wrinkled his nose and spat on the ground.

'This isn't worth my time.' He pushed past Fleur roughly, colliding with her shoulder and knocking her against the wall, which she had no doubt was intentional. He walked away with the slightest limp in his step. Fleur gave a sob.

Laurent strode after Pierre but Fleur reached out a hand as he went to move past her and grasped his sleeve. 'Leave him.'

He turned back to her. She'd rarely seen him angry, but his shoulders were tensed and his eyes glinted dangerously. 'Are you sure? Say the word and I'll arrange to have him kneecapped.'

She wasn't sure if he was joking. 'No. He won't bother me again.'

She was reasonably confident that Pierre would leave her alone now. Laurent shook his head.

'You're shaking. I've seen you calmly walk past a squadron of Nazis with a dozen clips of bullets under your shopping, but that little coward upset you.'

'It was a horrible surprise. He's always been slightly erratic, though I didn't think even he could behave that terribly.'

He folded her into a tight hug until she stopped shaking then held her at arm's length and looked her up and down. 'There, that's better. Do you want me to take you home?'

His concern was overwhelming. She wanted to stay in his arms, but he had to deliver his messages in the opposite direction. Moreover, her old inclination to cope alone reared up. She was in the centre of the city and Pierre had gone. She was brave and could manage alone. 'No, thank you. I'm going shopping. There's no need.'

'As long as you are sure.'

He pulled her close and dropped a light kiss onto her brow then left. Fleur walked out onto the avenue and almost collided with a pair of laughing women. She jumped back and they walked round her, chatting in German as they carried on as if she had been a bollard. Fleur gulped in a couple of breaths and went home, the shopping forgotten. Colette was sweeping the floor. She smiled as Fleur entered, then her face dropped.

'What?'

'It's nothing,' Fleur said, then burst into tears. She unwound the baby and handed her to Colette then poured out everything that had happened.

'That bastard,' Colette thundered, holding the infant close. 'Do you want me to go and get Laurent?'

'No. He went to meet a friend. I told him I was fine. I can cope. I'm just shaken and angry. It's all done with now and I expect that will be the end of it.'

She brightened. 'Pierre's face when I kicked him though! I don't think he ever imagined I would do such a thing!'

'I hope so. If he does anything to hurt you, Sébastien will tear him apart when he returns.' Colette put the baby over her shoulder and burped her expertly then laid her on the mat. The baby lurched all four limbs up, attempting to roll over. 'I'm going to take the baby to the fountains in the *Tuilleries*. Do you want to come?'

'No. I think I'll stay here and read. One trip out is enough for me today and I half expect Pierre to come and throw a brick through the window out of spite.'

'Do you think he would do that?'

Fleur remembered the way he had hurled an apple core with real violence when he had been in a bad mood. 'I don't think so really, but perhaps I'll sit by the front window with a jug of water to throw down just in case.'

Colette laughed. 'That's the spirit.'

Fleur watched the baby playing with her feet while Colette went to change her dress. Colette often spoke as if Sébastien would be returning any day now. It was good to see her optimism, but it seemed unlikely to Fleur. Laurent must be better placed than she was to know whether the tide was turning in favour of the French, being in contact with others higher up the chain of command of *resisteurs*. Perhaps she should ask him?

∼

No bricks came through the window and after a few weeks Pierre's unpleasantness was erased from Fleur's mind by something far more concerning. She was returning to the bookshop at Saturday lunchtime when a man fell in beside her.

'Keep walking, Roxane.'

She glanced up, the use of her codename allaying the fear that had immediately filled her.

'Good afternoon, Elouard.'

Fleur had only met Elouard a handful of times. He was a kindly-looking man in his late forties who worked as a teacher. Few people, if any, would suspect that he spent his nights coordinating men and women to carry out acts of sabotage on railway lines or factories, but perhaps handling ten-year-olds gave him the management capabilities he needed.

'Augustin has vanished.'

He announced it with no warning and it took Fleur a moment to associate the name as Laurent's codename. Her legs turned to water. She leaned against the nearest bollard.

'Where did you last see him?' she asked.

Elouard clicked his teeth. 'We spoke briefly at the fountain in the park beside my school at eight yesterday morning. He was to meet Corentin at five to go over the preparations for the factory bombing that is scheduled for tonight, and then was to report back to me at seven.'

Corentin was someone Fleur had heard of but had never met.

She only knew he operated a radio, sending and receiving messages from all over France and across the channel to Britain.

'Corentin says Augustin never made the rendezvous. Did he come to see you yesterday or today?'

Fleur grew cold. Something must have gone wrong in between his departure from the fountain and the meeting with Corentin. That was nine hours unaccounted for.

'No.'

Elouard bowed his head, his face grave. 'No one else has approached you, I assume?'

Fleur shook her head. Her stomach rolled and she felt nausea rising. She had walked along Avenue Foch this morning. If the Gestapo had Laurent, she might have walked straight past where he was being held.

Being tortured. The strength left her legs completely, and she was glad she was already sitting down.

'Have you asked at the workshop?'

'Not yet. That is my next port of call. You are closer.'

'I'll go,' Fleur said. 'I'll see if I can learn anything and let you know as soon as I do.'

'Good.'

'Will tonight still go ahead?' she asked.

Elouard looked thoughtful. 'Yes. It might be dangerous now but too many people have endangered themselves putting everything in place. The factory owner has assured me there will be no one on the premises. If we leave it any longer, we risk innocent civilians being caught up in it. I hope that if Laurent is being interrogated, he will be able to hold out for long enough before revealing anything. Be warned, Roxane, if he gives your name up, they will come for you. Be ready to run.'

~

She walked home, threw her shopping onto the table and collected her bicycle. She was at the garage within the hour.

Laurent was not there but the old man was sitting outside the shuttered doors to the workshop.

'A car took him away yesterday lunchtime.'

The information caught her roughly and it was only because she was holding onto the bicycle that she did not fall to her knees.

'Please let me know if you hear anything, or if he comes back.'

Her voice sounded tinny in her ears. She must have said the words out loud though because the old man nodded. She scribbled down her address on a piece of paper then immediately thought better of it when it struck her that if anyone came back to search, she would be making it easy for anyone to link her to Laurent.

'Never mind. If he comes back, I'm sure he will contact me himself.'

The man shrugged again. 'Are you Fleur?'

She nodded cautiously.

'Thought so. He said you were the pretty one.'

There wasn't much to say to that. Other than the implication that other women visited Laurent, it told her nothing useful. She hoped the other women were also involved in Resistance activities and she had not stumbled on the reason Laurent was determined not to become involved with her. Or perhaps he flirted and shared a bed on missions with every female contact.

Either way, with him gone, it ceased to matter. She thanked the old man and cycled away to share the dark news with Elouard.

~

For two days Fleur could barely bring herself to eat thanks to the sick churning of anxiety in her guts. Sleep evaded her. She heard nothing from Elouard. Either Laurent's disappearance had brought a halt to any activities, or she was deemed too close a contact, and other operatives were being used instead. Her bag was packed and ready beside her bed in case she received the message to run into hiding. She could barely leave the apartment without looking over her shoulder, wondering if she would be swept off the street and into the back of a van, or whether she would receive warning and be able to flee.

She did not share her terror with Colette, reasoning that the less she knew, the safer she would be. The baby was going through a difficult phase and was awake for hours every night. Colette looked haggard and miserable and did not need another burden. Neither woman had much of a temper, but both found themselves snapping in reply to quite reasonable comments or requests. It was the worst time Fleur could remember since Sébastien's departure while they waited for the inevitable visit.

On the third day, just when Fleur thought her nerves could not become any thinner or more fragile, a visitor appeared in the bookshop shortly before closing time.

Elouard.

Fleur reached for the nearest bookcase to steady herself.

'Do you have news?' She could barely force out the words.

'Augustin is back. He's been released. He sent a message to me via one of his workmates.'

'Oh thank the lord!' Fleur let out a gasp of relief. 'Does that mean he didn't tell them anything?'

Elouard frowned. 'I don't know. I have never heard of the Gestapo releasing anyone. Go see him as soon as you can. He might be able to tell you something. I would go myself but I have a large pile of grammar exercises to correct, and I suspect he would rather see you.'

She raced upstairs and poured the whole tale out to Colette.

'You told me nothing of this!' Colette sounded aggrieved.

'I thought it would be safer if you knew nothing and I didn't want to burden you.'

Colette seized her by the hand and glared. 'Burden me? I'm your best friend. Your sister! If you don't tell me your problems, what use am I?'

'I know. I will. I have to go now. I don't know when I'll be back.'

She grabbed her hat and left.

Chapter Thirty-Two

The old mechanic and his friend were sitting outside the garage as always, playing a game of chess. Apparently, the chilly April wind made no difference to them. They recognised Fleur and broke off their game as she dismounted.

'I'm here to see Laurent,' she said without any preamble.

'He's not well.'

She propped the bicycle against the doorway and folded her arms. 'I know. That's why I'm here.'

The mechanic stubbed out his cigarette and led her through the workshop and upstairs. Fleur had never been beyond the garage and was surprised to see the space above it opened into a spacious living area with a balcony that overlooked a small courtyard at the back. Almost every available surface down below was covered with pots and planters. It was an oasis of colours; fruit and vegetables beginning to grow. She longed to go down and walk among the vegetation to see what was growing. There was no sign of Laurent, however, and the garden could wait so she followed her guide up a smaller staircase until she came to a bedroom.

She could not say what this room contained because all of her attention was fixed on the body lying in the bed. She gasped aloud. Laurent's face was swollen. Both eyes were blackened, and it was hard to tell what were bruises and what were shadows under his eyes. He was naked from the waist up – and possibly from the waist downwards, although a sheet and quilt covered his modesty. His chest was an artist's palette of hues in browns, blacks and purples. His eyes had been closed but at Fleur's horrified cry he opened them.

'What the hell! Why did you let her up here, Marcel?'

Fleur cringed. His words were bad enough, but his tone was brutally harsh, not helped by being spat from lips that were swollen and cracked.

'I'll go. I'm sorry,' she said, her words catching in her throat.

'Don't go. I'm not angry with you, but I told them I didn't want you to see me like this.'

The old man shrugged. 'She was not going to go away until she had seen you.'

Laurent's eyes slid to Fleur. He didn't move his head and Fleur was gripped by a terror that perhaps he was no longer able to. She gave a sob.

'See,' Laurent said accusingly. 'Now she is upset.'

'Did you think I wouldn't be?' Fleur exclaimed. 'My god, Laurent, what have they done to you?'

'If you fetch me a cup of wine, I will tell you. Marcel, thank you for bringing her. Now will you leave us alone?'

Marcel cast Laurent a disapproving look. 'Come with me, mademoiselle. I'll show you where the wine is downstairs then you can come back up.'

Fleur followed him downstairs.

'He says it isn't as bad as it looks, but I don't believe him. He's just trying to be brave. Look after him. He may have said he didn't want to see you, but your name was the first thing on his lips when he woke last night.'

Fleur tingled all over. 'Last night? When did he get home?'

'We found him on the doorstep yesterday morning. He's been in and out of consciousness ever since and he hasn't eaten anything. He's drunk some wine and brandy, which I think helped him with the pain. If you can get him to eat that would be good.'

'I'll try.'

She noticed a half-empty glass jar filled with syrup-preserved pear quarters. She put two and a small knife on the tray along with the wine and a couple of glasses. She didn't think Laurent would mind if she had a glass too and she felt a definite need for something strong.

Laurent was asleep again when Fleur entered the room so she put the tray on the bedside table as quietly as she could. His eyelids flickered and he sighed, mumbled something unintelligible, and rolled his head to the left, but did not wake. His sleep did not look peaceful, and Fleur could only imagine what horrors his dreams were inflicting on him after his ordeal.

Fleur had fantasised about being in Laurent's bedroom on numerous occasions, but never had any scenario included him being unconscious. A small armchair with misshapen cushions stood in front of the window. She sat on it and looked down into the courtyard then at the buildings that backed onto the other side of it, wondering if anyone was watching the garage. The idea made her skin crawl, so she looked around Laurent's room instead, feeling slightly guilty for taking advantage of the opportunity to be nosy.

There was one wardrobe and a plain dressing table, upon which stood a shaving kit and toothbrush, Laurent's cologne, and a mismatched bowl and water jug. There were no photographs or ornaments. The only sign that the room was occupied were a handful of paperback books that stood piled on top of each other on the bottom shelf of the bedside table.

Fleur, never able to resist books, tilted her head to the side to read the titles. A cheap paperback edition of *La Maison du Péril* by Agatha Christie, a copy of Charles Dickens' *Paris et Londres en 1793*, and curiously, a copy of the same book in English: *A Tale of Two Cities*. Perhaps Laurent was attempting to learn English, much as Fleur had. She reminded herself to ask him when he was recovered. There was also a slim volume of poetry by Rimbaud and a dull looking textbook on repairing motorcycles. It was a curious selection, but Laurent was a curious man.

Fleur picked up *A Tale of Two Cities* and opened it at a random page, wondering if she would be able to read any of it. Laurent, or a previous owner, had made comments in the margin, underlined words or phrases in pencil and added the French translation, and folded over pages. Fleur smiled to herself. Her own English language books were covered in similar scrawls.

Presently, Laurent's eyes opened.

'I fell asleep. I beg your pardon.'

'No need to apologise. You didn't do it on purpose to offend me.' Fleur closed the book hastily, feeling guilty at having helped herself. She slipped it back onto the pile. Seeing Laurent's eyes following her she continued, 'You weren't asleep for too long, but I never miss the chance to read a new book. I'm sorry for taking it. Would you like some wine now?'

'Please.'

Laurent wriggled himself slightly more upright. He looked to be struggling so Fleur instinctively reached over and slid her arms about his chest to help him lean forward. He paused and looked at her intently. She hadn't considered how he would respond to being touched, but seeing his reaction, she wondered if she had crossed a line. He was half-naked after all, and she had never touched him like that before. When they had shared the bed on their first night mission he had kept his shirt on.

He was warm and slightly clammy. Not unpleasant but it

made her very aware of his body. She wriggled a pillow behind his back with one hand then lowered him down.

While he scuffled from side to side to get comfortable, she poured the wine and gave him a glass. He sipped it gingerly, as if it hurt to drink. Once again, Fleur filled with concern and anger at how he had been treated.

'Will you tell me what happened? I've been out of my mind with worry. I felt sick walking along Avenue Foch thinking the Gestapo had you.'

'They didn't. It was the Gendarmerie.'

'Did they suspect you of being in the Resistance?'

He closed his eyes and grew still for a moment before answering.

'No. Thankfully they didn't, or I doubt I would be here now. They had received a denunciation that I was an influential *trafiquant* of the *marché noir*, selling fuel.'

His eyes were purple and black smears on his face but they were still capable of anger.

'I think if I had admitted to it, they might have let me off with a quick beating and a heavy fine after confiscating my contraband. Sadly, as I had no contraband to admit to, they kept trying to exact a confession out of me. Eventually they decided the information had been unfounded and probably made out of spite. They were furious at having their time wasted so gave me another kicking before dropping me off here at dawn yesterday.'

His eyes dropped. Fleur followed their gaze down to the mess of bruises. There was barely an inch on his torso that wasn't purple. She took his hand and held it tight, wanting to cry but not wanting him to see the effect it was having on her.

'I can't bear to think of you suffering. How did you endure it?'

Laurent sighed. 'I forced myself to think of every school lesson I could remember. My multiplication tables, capitals of different cities. The sonnets of William Shakespeare. Anything to stop me letting slip something incriminating by accident. If I had done that, they would have handed me over to another department without hesitation.'

Fleur squeezed tighter, sure that in his place she would have forgotten every poem or fact she had ever learned.

'Who do you think could have reported you?'

'I don't know.' He licked his lips. Fleur fought the urge to kiss the swollen flesh. 'Someone who thought I had charged them too much for a job? Someone who has a grudge against me? Someone who genuinely believed it? I don't know.'

'Pierre.' Fleur sat back. 'He was angry at me for being with you. That time you found us in the alleyway, it was what we had been arguing about. What if he did it as revenge on me, or both of us? This could be my fault.'

'It isn't your fault,' Laurent said. 'You don't know that is the case. Besides, if he really wanted to cause me harm, he would not have said anything about the *marché noir* but would have accuse me of being a *saboteur* or a *resisteur*, wouldn't he?'

Fleur's mind went back to the bitter words Pierre had flung at her. 'I don't know. He made an empty threat about that to me, but I told him he would be the first person I implicated.'

Laurent's hand tightened on hers, bordering on painful. She had rarely seen him truly angry but now he looked incandescent. 'You should have told me. I would have beaten the living shit out of him for that and saved us both a lot of trouble. As soon as I am well, perhaps I might anyway.'

A hand tightened around Fleur's throat. Her skin felt clammy. 'I'll do that myself when I catch up with him.'

'No, you won't.'

She had only shifted slightly on the edge of the bed, but Laurent's hand moved to her wrist. Not painfully but firm enough that she would not be able to break free and was left with no uncertainty about his opinion.

'If it was him then why let him know his plan worked? If it wasn't him then why give him ideas or accuse him of something so base and cowardly?'

She dropped her head. Laurent did not release her.

'Fleur, I have only ever asked of you things you are happy to do. Now I must order you to let this matter lie. The consequences could be dire for more than just us. Our whole network relies on discretion. It is bad enough that I have caught the eye of the authorities. I don't know what Elouard or his superiors will say, but they won't be happy. Anything else will make matters worse.'

'I don't like it,' Fleur murmured.

'Neither do I,' Laurent answered. 'But right now all I care about is that I am alive and you are safe. We have greater work to do than to settle petty scores. Promise me you will leave it.'

'I promise.' One day, however, she would get revenge, she told herself.

Thankfully, her answer seemed to satisfy Laurent for now because he released her hand and lay back. He winced as his back touched the pillow and gasped between closed teeth.

'Does it hurt a great deal?' Fleur asked.

'It's starting to now. At first the pain was agonising, but after a while it became so hard to distinguish one ache from another that everything blurred.' Laurent motioned to the bottle of wine. Fleur topped up his glass and he took a deeper swig. 'I think I might have cracked a rib or two.'

Fleur tentatively reached out a hand and ran her fingers lightly over his ribcage. He winced and sucked his teeth but gave her a weak smile.

'Mmm, that is definitely helping me feel better.'

'Behave yourself,' she told him. She smiled back though, relieved that he was able to make light of his injuries. 'You're so brave.'

He shrugged, looking a little embarrassed. 'The lack of sleep was the worst thing. That and the hunger. Not that I could have kept food down in any case.'

'Oh, I brought you a pear,' Fleur said. She reached for it. 'I can cut it up if you want.'

Laurent smiled and she took it as a yes. She sliced the quarter into three and offered him a slice. He tried to raise his hand but it trembled and he lowered it, giving a grunt of frustration. She couldn't bear seeing the arms that had held her so securely in such a weakened state.

'Let me help.'

She held the slice to his lips and fed it to him. He sucked it into his mouth and chewed. She held out a second piece. Syrup dribbled down her fingers. This time Laurent gave her a suggestive look and darted his tongue out to lick at them. She almost dropped the slice in astonishment. A craving to be touched flooded her senses. She held up another slice, slipping it into his waiting mouth and running her thumb over his lips. He closed his eyes and gave a small sigh.

'I should allow myself to get arrested more often if this is the result.'

Fleur pulled her hand back. Her eyes filled with tears. 'Don't joke about it. You might have died.'

His lips twitched. 'I know. I expected at any moment to get a bullet to the back of the head. Whenever I close my eyes, I can see their faces as they kept repeating the same questions over and over. The lack of expression as they hurt me. The stench of the room floods back.' His voice was little more than a whisper and all signs of joking melted from his face as his eyes took on a faraway look. Then he shuddered violently.

'Fleur, will you do something for me? Go to the dressing table and bring me the shaving brush.'

She obeyed the odd request. His face was rough with three days' worth of stubble but it hardly seemed a priority.

'It's stiff, but if you push the handle down towards the bristles, it unscrews. Can you manage it? Then you'll have to use a fingernail to prise out the bung.'

Mystified, Fleur obeyed again. Sure enough, the wooden handle unscrewed in an anti-clockwise direction and the two parts separated. She dug her thumbnail around the hair-thin ridge inside the thread. Something dropped onto her knee and rolled under the bed. She knelt and retrieved it then held it out in her palm. It was a thin piece of wood identical to the one the handle was made from. She smiled in delight. The handle of the brush was hollow and there was something inside it. A small paper package. She unfolded it and revealed five small pills. Three round and white, two elongated and pink. She looked at Laurent with a question on her lips. He answered it before she spoke.

'Barbiturates. Sedatives. I need something to dull the pain and give me a dreamless sleep. These will knock me out for a good twelve hours. Give me one of the round ones. The others are amphetamines and would have the opposite effect. Put the rest back and make sure you tighten the handle on the brush.'

'Where did you get these?' Fleur asked. It seemed unlikely he would have had a different number of each, and she wondered under what circumstances he might have used something to force him awake.

He grimaced. 'Best not to ask. What you don't know can't be taken from you.'

Icy hands dragged themselves down Fleur's spine and gripped her heart. She shivered at the thought that someone might do to her what had been done to Laurent. She would never be able to withstand that amount of pain. His fingers brushed against her forearm, causing her skin to prickle and grow hot. She met his eyes.

'You're wondering if you should ever have got mixed up with all this, aren't you?'

She nodded.

'That's understandable. I've asked a lot of you already but will you do one more thing and fetch me a glass of water?'

Fleur obliged. Laurent took it from her. His grip seemed a little firmer.

'I'll be out like a light in ten minutes once I take this. You can go then if you want.'

He swallowed the small pill and handed the glass back to Fleur.

'Why didn't you take one before now?' she asked.

'I didn't want anyone else to know they exist. I trust you, though.'

Did he, she thought wryly. Not enough to tell her what was preventing them being together. She helped him lie down, moving the pillow and easing him back. It meant she had to lean over him. Their gazes met. He licked his lips and Fleur had to resist the strong temptation to kiss them. Not so much out of desire – though that was as powerful as ever – but simply to confirm he was there and alive.

'Fleur, will you stay a little while longer? Just until I'm sleeping.'

'Of course. Whatever you wish, you only have to ask.'

Laurent's eyelids flickered. 'That's a very dangerous offer.'

'Is it?' she asked, trying to keep the tremor from her voice.

She sat on the edge of the bed. She tried to stop her eyes roving down to settle where the sheet was a neatly folded demarcation between the visible and hidden body but couldn't help herself. It was a Maginot Line whispering seductively to be breached.

'I think you're a gentleman, and even if you're not you don't look in a position to demand anything scandalous, or act on it if it was offered.'

He laughed, though it quickly turned into a cough. He winced and put his hands to his ribs. 'Now look what you've done, making me laugh, you wicked temptress. You've probably set my recovery back days. You will have to come every day to nurse me.'

He spoke lightly but there had been real pain in his eyes. Fleur felt a prickle in the back of her throat and the rims of her eyes grew moist.

'Don't cry. I'm only teasing,' Laurent murmured.

Fleur sniffed. 'I was so worried. I couldn't stop thinking about you and wondering if I would ever see you again.'

'Thank you. It's good to know I wasn't forgotten by the world outside those walls. Come here, my girl.'

He tugged on her sleeve until she gave in and lay beside him. There was barely room for two bodies lying side by side so she snuggled against him, taking care not to put any weight on his bruised frame. He yawned loudly, taking Fleur by surprise. His jaw grew slack then and she realised the sedative was starting to work. He murmured something and Fleur had to put her ear close to make it out.

'I thought of you. I didn't want to. I tried not to, of course.'

'Oh.' Fleur couldn't keep the disappointment out of her voice. 'Of course?'

'Of course. Any prospero … pros … prospect that you might spring to mind might mean you were in my … thoughts, and if you were in my thoughts, you could very quickly appear … on my lips. I would rather have died than risk… I couldn't let anyone discover … you are so involved, but we aren't involved and I think I'm…'

He was burbling, making increasingly less sense the longer he spoke. The sedative was working its magic and easing him into sleep.

'Falling…'

Fleur tensed. Falling asleep? Falling in love? She was desperate to ask but his frame had gone limp and presently he began to snore. Fleur lay beside him a little longer until she was certain he was asleep.

'I think I love you,' Fleur murmured.

She hadn't meant to, but the words slipped out before she could stop them.

Exhilaration, exhaustion, intoxication. She could blame any or all of them, but she knew in reality she had been hoping to say the words for months.

Chapter Thirty-Three

July 1943

For six months after her birth, the baby remained nameless. In the absence of a pram, Colette still wore the baby strapped to herself, tied securely in place with scarves and a blanket, though now this made her back ache and she was increasingly worried the infant would wriggle her way out. It was worth the discomfort because the good-natured child with her dark brown eyes and fluff of light brown hair drew comments and praise from women queuing, and even smiles from some of the guards at checkpoints.

'I should be the one carrying secret messages,' she told Fleur as they strolled down the Champs-Elysées one afternoon. 'No one would suspect me and half the time the soldiers barely glance at my papers, especially the older ones who have children back in Germany.'

Fleur giggled. 'If you get the timing right you could stuff her napkin full of weapons and no one would want to go near it.'

∽

After a particularly frustrating week comprised of broken sleep, feeding, and changing disgusting napkins, Colette ventured out into the world to pay some visits.

Firstly, she went to the Luciennes' hotel to see Sophie and Josette. She hadn't been there since she discovered her pregnancy, and the building was looking quite shabby now. Pangs of anxiety rippled up and down her as she walked inside to the reception desk. She had granted her mother's request not to share her pregnancy with any of Delphine's social circle, so the sisters and their mother were not even aware of the baby. She wasn't sure how she would be received but need not have worried. The minute Josette realised who was standing in the foyer, she came round from behind the desk, squealing at the sight of the baby.

Any inclination to condemn Colette's behaviour was clearly overridden by maternal feelings. Colette proudly unwrapped the baby and passed her over for a cuddle.

'Is this why you vanished from the face of the earth?' Josette asked. 'I missed you. I went to your house once or twice, but your mother refused to tell me where you were. We thought you must have been taken ill and were shut away in a sanatorium somewhere.'

Only once or twice! She tried not to feel hurt at how quickly she had been forgotten. Faced with Delphine's unwelcoming behaviour, however, it was hardly a mystery why Josette had given up so quickly.

So Delphine was still furious, she mused. She had made the right choice coming to see the sisters first.

'I'm living above the old bookshop Fleur is minding while the owner is absent. It's a strange life but actually I'm happy.'

The two women retreated into the office behind the reception desk. It was the middle of the day and the hotel was quiet.

'Most of the guests are on leave in the city and out sightseeing,' Josette explained. 'You won't recognise any faces. They come for a week and go again. I preferred it when we had a whole detachment for months at a time. They treated us better but that doesn't happen anymore.'

She frowned and her mouth became a thin line.

'Where is Sophie? I'd like to see her too,' Colette asked.

Josette's eyes dropped. 'She is upstairs in her room. You should go and see her. I imagine she'll be very pleased to see you. I should warn you… No, I won't. You'll see for yourself.'

Josette handed the baby back. 'I'm very pleased you are happy and the baby is beautiful.'

Colette made her way to the private flat on the top floor of the hotel. Sophie was in her bedroom and Josette's cryptic words became apparent as soon as Colette saw her.

She was pregnant. About five months from the size of her bump, Colette estimated.

'Don't!' she exclaimed as Colette opened her mouth. 'I can't bear it. I'm so ashamed of myself. Is that your baby? No wonder we haven't seen you for months.'

She motioned to a chair then eased herself into another. 'What a dreadful pair we are! What is going to become of us?'

'Who is your baby's father?' Colette asked.

'A German officer in the Luftwaffe,' Sophie said, hanging her head. 'He told me he loved me and asked me to marry him when the war was over. Then, when I told him about the baby, he took it all back. Apparently, he already has a wife and two children in Munich and it was a lie from beginning to end. Now here I am, stuck on my own in this position. I assume yours belongs to the man you were arguing with in front of the hotel all those months ago?'

'Yes, she does.' Colette laid the baby down on the bed.

'Unfortunately, he was selected for the STO and has left Paris so he hasn't even seen her.'

Sophie smiled faintly 'I rather hope mine is a girl too.'

'Are you going to keep her?' Colette asked.

'Of course. Why wouldn't I? I expect *Maman* and *Papa* will throw me out. They are already unhappy enough. I think *Papa* was preparing to write to the Governor of Paris himself to complain about the behaviour of the Luftwaffe until *Maman* told him not to be so stupid. She cries every time she looks at me and won't let me even work on the reception desk. Did your parents throw you out or have you been locked in a sanatorium somewhere?'

'Neither. I left of my own accord,' Colette replied. 'I was lucky, of course, that there was an apartment above Fleur's shop that I could move into with Fleur.'

'I have nowhere else to go.' Sophie sighed. 'Did you ever think all those years ago when we were dancing at the Cabaret des Papillons that we would both end up in this situation?'

'Not at all,' Colette answered. 'We were both going to marry rich, handsome men, weren't we, and now look at us. Sophie, if you want a friend then please come see me at the bookshop.'

Sophie looked doubtful. 'What about Fleur? I was fairly unpleasant to her on occasion.'

Colette wrapped the baby back to her chest, thinking what an understatement it was. 'Yes, you were, but luckily she does not hold grudges.'

She hoped she was right because three days later Sophie appeared at the bookshop door. Colette was not surprised to see her, however the large suitcase that stood beside her *was* surprising.

'I decided I would leave. I don't suppose I could sleep here for a night or two?'

Sophie looked so anxious that Colette couldn't bring herself to refuse or question the wisdom of leaving without a destination in mind.

'I'll give you my food tokens as payment and I brought two tins of biscuits, a whole peppered saucisson, and a can of pork fat. The soldiers come and go so quickly that things are always getting overlooked,' Sophie said.

Stolen food! Colette's mouth began to water. She would just have to apologise to Fleur and hope for the best. She picked up the suitcase and invited Sophie inside.

'You can share my room. The bed is large enough for two people and, god knows, I haven't had anyone to share it for long enough.'

They were both sitting on the bed chatting and playing with the baby, considering and rejecting names, when Fleur returned. She peeked round the bedroom door and froze, then walked out.

'Wait here,' Colette murmured to Sophie.

Fleur was in the kitchen. She unwrapped a paper bag of small potatoes and put them on the table beside a courgette.

'Laurent gave me these. Marcel, the old mechanic, grows them. I didn't know you were friends with Sophie still.'

Colette admitted that not only was she friends, but that they had a temporary houseguest.

Fleur's expression became thunderous. 'What were you thinking inviting somebody here to stay!' she exclaimed.

'I didn't invite her to stay. She came off her own accord and begged.'

Colette reached for her hand but Fleur whipped it away.

'But you didn't have to agree.'

'I could hardly turn her away onto the streets,' Colette pleaded. 'You know I've never turned anyone away, and there is no risk like when we sheltered Michal.'

'There's every risk! What if she gets an inkling of what I do?

She's going to wonder where I go. She could endanger us all. What if she lets something slip when she goes dancing?'

Colette sagged onto the dining chair, feeling stupid for not thinking of that. 'She won't be going dancing in her condition and she doesn't have any friends to tell. I'm sorry. Truly. She said she would only need to stay for a night or two.'

Fleur crossed her arms. 'Do you believe her?'

'I don't know. I'll tell her to leave if you want, but I want to help her. Think of what would have happened to me without you. She isn't as lucky as I am. No one could be as lucky as I've been to have you.'

Fleur closed her eyes, looking pained, then gave Colette a weary smile.

'You don't have to flatter me. I know you're too compassionate for your own good, but it is going to make life much more difficult for me. I need to be in and out at all hours and that is going to be hard with somebody who may not be trustworthy. Just promise me you will come up with some explanations for if she wonders where I am.'

Colette grimaced. 'I don't think she will notice or wonder. She is quite self-centred.'

'Just a little,' Fleur said, frowning

Colette hung her head. 'Just like I can be.'

Fleur sighed again. 'That's not true. You do think of others, just not necessarily at the best time.'

Colette told her about the liberated food and Fleur relented.

'We'll make the best of it, as we always do. Just don't go inviting anyone else because I'm certainly not sharing my bedroom.'

Colette readily agreed, knowing that there would be no chance of her next call resulting in a guest.

～

The following day, Colette put on her best blouse and hat and visited her parents. She waited until six in the evening, knowing that by then Louis would be home from the factory. Delphine answered the door. She held a cocktail glass in her hand.

'What is that child still doing there?' she said, looking at the baby.

'Hello, *Mère*.' Colette smiled but it was not returned.

'You had better come inside before anyone sees you,' Delphine said. She turned and walked away, heels snapping on the wooden floor. Colette followed but Delphine whipped round and raised a hand once she was into the hallway.

'This is far enough. When will the baby be leaving? Have you struggled to have it placed?'

Colette raised her head. '"She", not "it". I will be keeping her.'

'Don't you remember what I told you?' exclaimed Delphine.

'You told me lots of things,' Colette said, 'but I've made my mind up. I'm going to raise my daughter and when her father comes home, I hope he will raise her with me.'

The dining room door opened and Louis walked out. His eyes crinkled with delight and Colette was reminded of the baby when she laughed.

'Colette, are you well?'

'Yes, I am, thank you, *Papa*. How nice of you to ask.' She flashed her eyes at Delphine.

'And where is the father?' Delphine asked, as if the exchange had not happened.

Colette began to rehearse the same lie she had used on Sophie and Josette but then changed her mind. She lifted her head and looked at both her parents.

'He is away fighting for France. I don't know where, or if he will ever return, but whatever happens, I will raise his daughter to know how brave and patriotic her father was.'

There was nothing Delphine could object to, without appearing churlish in the least or a traitor to France at the worst. Colette could almost see her mind seeking for something else to criticise. She settled on, 'Why are you wearing the child like a Russian peasant woman from the nineteenth century? Where is its pram?'

'*She* does not have a pram. They are too expensive. This is perfectly comfortable and practical. Obviously Russian peasant women were very wise.'

Delphine made a noise in the back of her throat and spun away. She stalked up the stairs and Colette heard the door to her salon slamming shut. It felt very similar to her childhood.

Louis stood awkwardly in the hall. He'd lost more weight and his hair had thinned. Colette wanted to run to him and hug him as she had done in childhood.

'*Papa*, you look tired. Are you unwell?'

'My heart is tired knowing my daughter and wife are estranged,' he said. 'Colette, are you absolutely sure you want to do this? Think of the future you could have. It isn't too late to come home. We'll find a good home for your daughter, and no one need to know about this. Most eligible men are absent and the whole incident can be cleaned away by the time any return home. We can throw parties and invite people by the dozens.'

Once, it would have been tempting, but those days were over. Colette shook her head slowly but smiled to show him she was grateful for the offer.

'The future you wanted for me has gone. The Paris you wanted for me has gone. I don't know what the future will hold. None of us do. *Papa*, I want you to be proud of me. I am making my way in the world. I've created order out of the chaos that are the accounts for the bookshop, and I love an honourable man. Please be happy for me.'

'Wait here,' Louis said. He walked away and returned shortly afterwards. He gave Colette an envelope. 'I don't want my granddaughter to starve. Open it when you get home.'

'Thank you.' Colette reached up and brushed his cheek with her lips, touched at his generosity. She could refuse help for herself but she was not too proud to accept it if it meant her daughter was well fed.

He kissed her back, then put his hand on the baby's head. He looked as if he was going to say something, but then cleared his throat.

'You had better go and I had better go speak with your mother. I'm glad to see you, my child.'

∼

Instead of walking all the way back, she took the Metro and by the time she reached home the baby was fully awake and making hungry noises. Colette unbuttoned her blouse and latched her on.

'Well, my darling,' she said. 'You have met your grandparents.'

She settled back and opened the envelope. Inside were rations coupons for bread, milk, and meat, and nine hundred francs in notes.

Dear sweet Louis. He must have saved the tokens without Delphine knowing. Tears welled up in her eyes. She did not really care that Delphine was disappointed but felt dreadful at spoiling her father's opinion of her. Perhaps she would be able to meet him again without Delphine knowing. She could even take the baby to the factory.

When Fleur came home later, Colette greeted her with a smile.

'I know what I'm going to call the baby. Her name is Louise. Louise Sébastiene.'

∼

A week later, Colette took a delivery of a pram and a white painted wooden cot with a gauze net around it.

'It's from my father. How generous of him. It must mean he has forgiven me.'

She laid Louise in the crib. The baby looked around, unaccustomed to the space. Usually, she slept in Colette's bed.

'Your mother is bound to forgive you eventually,' Fleur said. 'It would be nice if you could go home, even if it was just to visit again.'

'It isn't a question of her forgiving me, but me forgiving her,' Colette replied. 'I made my bed, and I chose to lie in it with Sébastien. I would not swap Louise for all grandest *châteaux* in France. Though I do miss the garden. Louise would love to play in the grass and watch the fountain.'

'I wonder how long it would take for her to discover the Secret Garden,' Fleur mused. 'I bet there are hundreds of strawberry plants now.'

Colette's heart throbbed. 'Do you think we'll ever go back there? All those books buried in the cold frame. Can you imagine if somebody finds them one hundred years from now? The war will have ended by then, surely?'

Fleur stood from where she was kneeling by the crib. 'I hope so. I need to go see Laurent now.'

'Is he recovering well?' Colette asked. Fleur had gone every day since Laurent had been hurt, coming home late and sometimes staying overnight. She swore to Colette that they had not yet made love, merely shared a bed, which Colette considered a wasted opportunity.

Then again, Fleur, unlike herself and Sophie, was unencumbered with a child, so maybe she was right after all.

~

Fleur returned from her visit to Laurent much sooner than expected. Colette and Sophie were playing backgammon when Fleur walked in and straight to the kitchen.

'I wasn't expecting you back,' Colette remarked. 'Dinner won't be long. It's soup.'

'It's always soup,' Fleur said with a weary smile.

She stirred the pan of white beans and ham bones that simmered on the stove. The apartment smelled of bay and cloves. Sophie had turned out to be a better chef than either Fleur or Colette. She enjoyed shopping and finding bargains and had contacts in the hotel world who she could talk into slipping extra into her bag. She made their rations last longer and even Fleur had admitted she was worth having around.

'Laurent has gone to help a friend with his car. He left a message telling me not to wait.'

She poured a glass of water and drank it. Her hand trembled a little, which could be accounted for by her long journey. 'It was very annoying because cycling in this weather was hot. I think I am going to go for a lie down.'

She went into her bedroom and shut the door. Colette returned to the table, deeply worried. Only someone who knew Fleur as well as she did would realise how anxious she was. The tightening around her eyes betrayed real anxiety and her merry tone had sounded forced. She looked at the backgammon board. Sophie, who was allegedly a beginner, was two moves away from winning. Colette made a deliberately unwise move and Sophie won. While Sophie packed the board and pieces away, Colette took Fleur another glass of water.

Fleur was lying on her bed. She was fully dressed apart from her shoes, with her hands clasped together over her belly. She raised her head when Colette entered.

'You weren't telling me everything, were you?'

Fleur shook head. She pressed her lips together, looking as if she were about to cry. Colette felt a little guilt at having invited Sophie into their household and making things more awkward. They shouldn't have to hide in a bedroom to discuss things in secret in their own flat.

'I'm just worried for him,' Fleur said. 'It won't be like the last time, I know. He had time to leave a message and went with a friend.'

'Then why are you worried at all?'

Fleur sat up and took the glass. 'I don't know. Just a feeling inside me. I can't explain it.'

Colette sat and held her hand. 'I can. Someone you care about went through something horrible, and you're worried it might happen again. But there really is no need to. He'll be back by the end of the day. Unless, of course, it is a mission that lasts longer, or he stays out drinking and gets too drunk to find his way home. Or the car is impossible to fix.'

She was running out of ideas, but Fleur gave a ghost of a smile.

'Thank you. I hope you're right.'

'Of course I am. You'll see. He'll call on you tomorrow.'

∼

But Laurent did not call. Not the next morning, nor the next evening. Fleur walked around the house like a ghost, not even bothering to open the shop or conceal her worry from Sophie.

'I can't concentrate on anything. I just wish I knew what was happening.'

'I understand,' Colette said.

Her heart broke for Fleur It was as bad as when Sébastien had vanished. Worse, even, because then they had not expected to hear from him. Colette didn't often pray and since the start of the war there had been precious little indication that God cared anything for the French, but now she lifted her eyes to the sky and prayed for an end to the war, a future for her daughter, and the safety of both their men.

It appeared at least one of her prayers had been answered when Laurent walked through the door of the bookshop a day later.

'Hello, Colette, how is my favourite little girl? Is Fleur here?'

Colette held Louise up for him to kiss. 'Surely she is your second favourite? Fleur should be the head of your list.'

'She isn't a little girl.' He gave a half smile then his eyes grew serious. 'Is Sophie upstairs or has she gone out?'

'She's shopping,' Colette said.

'I need to speak to Fleur. When I leave, will you check she is alright?'

Colette clutched his sleeve. 'If you say anything to hurt her…'

'I am afraid I *am* going to, but it is beyond my control. If I could do otherwise I would.' He stopped as his voice cracked and when his eyes met Colette's she saw they were filled with pain.

'I think I am about to break both our hearts.'

He walked past her towards the stairs. Colette watched him go, her whole being filled with foreboding.

Chapter Thirty-Four

F leur was reading on the sofa when Laurent walked in.

'Laurent, oh thank God!'

She threw down her book and ran across the room and into his waiting arms. He pulled her close, arms tight.

'Oh, my darling, I thought you must have been arrested again, or worse.'

She began to sob as relief flowed out. He buried his lips into her hair, kissing her head, forehead, cheeks, and finally lips.

'I couldn't come before now. I have had no chance of getting away.'

'But now you are here and that is all that matters,' Fleur whispered. She pressed up against him, desperate to feel the heat of his body against hers. Prove that he was real and alive. 'Where have you been? I got your message and thought about going to ask Elouard but I didn't want to be a problem.'

'No, you did the right thing to stay away. I was being debriefed by my superiors at a location out of the city. They wanted to know what had led up to my arrest and what precisely

I told my captors. What happened to me after I was released. I felt at some points they were harder on me than the police!'

He grinned faintly to show he was joking, but his expression was weary. 'They talked for a long time about the implications, and that is why I have come to see you.'

He looked into Fleur's eyes. His expression and tone sent a chill down her back.

'Let's sit down.'

He unwrapped Fleur's arms from around him and linked his fingers tightly through hers. She nodded, anxiety starting to gather, a crushing knot in her belly. She led him to the sofa in front of the window. It was bathed in warm sunshine but the height of the room let in a gentle breeze. Laurent sat straight-backed and stared at Fleur, unspeaking.

'Do you have something to tell me?' she prompted.

He dipped his head and ran his hand through his hair. 'I do, but I'm just enjoying looking at you in the sunshine.'

Fleur's stomach rolled over. He sounded and looked so solemn. He appeared unhurt – the bruises on his face from his ordeal had faded and had not been replaced by any fresh injuries. Beneath his clothes might be a different matter, of course.

'Laurent, please, don't do this. I've been imagining all sorts of terrors, then convinced myself I was overacting and now you appear and tell me something is wrong after all.'

He took a deep breath and stood. He faced her, hands behind his back. 'You know there are British operatives involved in what we do. You've escorted one or two from location to location. They are men and women hiding in plain sight, sending and taking messages, acting on the information they receive to best strike where it was needed. They've been working with local *resisteurs* such as Elouard. Such as you.'

'And you,' Fleur said.

'No, not me. I say *they* but I mean *we*.' He looked away a moment and then back at Fleur. 'My name is not Laurent and I am not a mechanic. And I am not French.'

'Is this a joke?' Fleur's chest tightened.

He shook his head. 'I wish it was. I have very much liked being Laurent, especially since he led you to me. No, I am British – English, to be precise. My name is Charles Danby.'

As he said his name, his accent dropped. Fleur laughed. She put her hand over her mouth to hold it in. It wasn't at all funny. She stood and walked away, first to the other end of the room, then into her bedroom. She sat on the edge of the bed and scrunched her fingers deep into the counterpane, wanting to rip it in frustration. He couldn't be telling the truth, but as she tried to convince herself, she knew it was pointless. He wouldn't joke about something so serious.

He tapped on the door then entered without waiting for an answer. He stood by the door, hesitant.

'Are you alright?'

'Of course I'm not!' She spoke harshly and he flinched, only momentarily but it was enough for some of her anger to ebb away. She stared straight ahead. From the corner of her eye she could see Laurent standing with his hands by his side, his imposing frame at ease. She let him wait.

'Talk to me,' he said quietly after perhaps fifteen minutes of silence. 'Tell me what you're thinking.'

'You lied to me. I believed everything you said. You are very convincing.'

He tilted his head on one side slightly. 'I have to be. If there was the slightest hint that I was not who I said I was, it could have compromised the entire operation. Lives would be at risk. I couldn't tell anyone.'

Fleur's ears began to ring. Laurent – she couldn't think of him as a Charles – sat beside her on the bed and took her hand. She stared at their linked fingers. Still the same hand. In England, did it fix cars or do something entirely different? She tried not to feel hurt that he had not taken her into his confidence but failed miserably.

'I wanted to tell you. I came close when we were in the hotel bed and you asked why I thought being with you was a bad idea, but I knew it would be the worst thing I could do.'

'That's what is stopping you? I don't care that you are English. I can't believe I didn't realise. The books in English on your bedside table. The fact you know *Jane Eyre.*'

He gave her a long look and she realised she was being naïve.

'I could never have told you because the thought that you might be arrested and interrogated caused me fear on a daily basis. There was too much at stake for you and for me. For the Resistance and the war. For the other men and women doing what I am doing.'

'Does anyone else know? Sébastien?'

'No. Not even Elouard or Corentin. One of their superiors does, but only because he was my point of contact when I arrived. Can you forgive me for not telling you?'

'Of course I forgive you,' Fleur said. How could she not when the secret he was entrusting her with was so momentous. She forced a smile. 'I'm a little relieved, to be honest. I thought you must have another woman.'

He drew her close, wrapping her in his arms. 'There is no other woman. There have been a couple in the past, but the moment I saw you – when you first walked into the workshop brimming with determination and courage – I was certain there never would be again. You mean everything to me.'

He kissed her and the slow intensity of his lips on hers was enough to assure her that he was telling the truth.

'I love you, Fleur.'

She had longed to hear those words, but why now? Why the

sudden confession and declaration of love? Unease began to form in the back of her mind.

'Why are you telling me now?'

'I'm compromised now.'

'But you were arrested for an unrelated matter. I know Elouard was worried, but he needn't have been.'

'It doesn't matter. I've caught the eye of the authorities. If they look too hard at Laurent Renou, they might discover discrepancies. My cover story and papers are first class, but it can't be risked.' He closed his eyes then opened them and looked away. 'I have to go back to England. I don't want to, but I'm being sent.'

A pit opened in Fleur's belly, her heart and lungs dragging down into blackness. She moistened her lips, though her tongue felt too dry.

'When?'

'As soon as arrangements can be made. It may be weeks before I am able to leave, or just days.'

'Are you here to say goodbye?' Fleur whispered. It was too sudden. Too soon. She willed herself not to cry but a tear must have slipped past her defences because Laurent reached out and wiped her cheek with his thumb.

'I'm saying *au revoir*. Or perhaps not. There is a possibility.' He stood and paced around the room then stopped in front of the window. The sun was behind him, silhouetting him in the brightness and she struggled to see his expression. 'Would you come with me?'

'To England?'

'Yes. It might not be possible. I don't know what type of plane they'll send for me, or where I'll have to meet it, but I can call in a few favours with a few people. Life isn't exactly luxurious, what with rationing and the war, but it's a safer place to be. Hitler hasn't managed to invade and he won't.'

No Nazis. No checkpoints. No watching behind her at every turn. No demands for papers.

'What would I do in England?' she asked.

Laurent sat beside her again. 'You can do useful work for the war effort there. I'll be assigned another role at that end of the operation. I have a flat in London that I stay in when I'm not in the family home. Only a small one, but big enough for two of us. When this whole thing is done and dusted, we can move back to the country. There is a piece of family land in the Yorkshire Dales that is ready to build on. I've never done anything with it because I didn't see the appeal of living there alone, but together we could build a home.'

He smiled, inviting Fleur to complete the picture in her mind.

She put her head in her hands. There was so much to take in. To discover that Laurent had lied to her was bad enough, but in the same blow to be offered something she had always wanted, and at the side of the man she loved. It was more than tempting.

He stood. For a large man he was very careful and unobtrusive in his movements.

'I won't ask you for an answer now. It wouldn't be fair. I know I have at least three days' grace before anything can happen. I'll come back soon, or you can find me at the garage fixing engines and swapping tyres. I've been taken off any useful work.'

Fleur raised her head. 'Will you tell me when the date is confirmed?'

He nodded. 'I will. Though I rather hope you will be coming with me.'

He left then, closing the door quietly. Fleur lay on her bed, her mind spinning. Presently, there was a tap on the door and Colette entered. She was carrying two glasses of wine.

'He told me to come look after you,' she said softly.

'Did he you tell you why?' Fleur sat up and declined the wine. She didn't want it. Her insides felt too sour to stomach it.

'No. Only that he was probably going to break your heart, and his with it. Did he?'

Her eyes blurred. 'Yes, I think he did.'

'Are you angry at him?'

'No. It isn't anything he could control. I'm so sorry, Colette. I know we said no more secrets, but he's told me something I really can't share with you. I can only say that he is leaving Paris.' She clasped Colette's hands to prevent any protests. 'Please, you have to trust me. If I can ever explain, I will. I'm sorry, I think I want to be on my own for a little while. I have a lot of thinking to do.'

She turned on her side and faced the wall.

England. She had always wanted to go but not under the circumstances and not during a war. She thought back to the night they had spent hiding in the forest, waiting to collect the delivery. Getting out of Paris would be risky. Getting out of the country could be deadly. She didn't want Laurent to go but he had no choice. What would be here for her once he had left?

The answer came in the sound of a shrill cry of delight from the other room. Louise, and Colette laughing in response. As much as she wanted to be with Laurent, she really couldn't leave them.

~

Laurent left Paris on the seventh of September. The weather had turned wet and Fleur met him under the archways of the Palais Garnier. The once vibrant and brightly lit opera house was, like all buildings, boarded up to prevent any escaping light. The performance would soon end, as dictated by curfew, and then he would leave her. When the audience flowed out, Laurent would blend in among them, making his way to the railway station. He was to go by train from the Gare Saint-Lazare to a destination he would not name, be met by a courier, and escorted to a safe house.

From there, Laurent Renou would cease to exist and another man would travel onwards, eventually to be taken by plane to Britain. He did not yet know the name he would travel under.

He was dressed in a smart suit with a silk tie, beneath a fine wool coat, suitable for a night at the opera. He looked impossibly handsome and Fleur couldn't stop looking at him. If she never saw him again, she knew she'd have this memory fixed in her mind for all time. They held each other tightly, to any observer a couple snatching a few moments of intimacy with nothing better on their minds than keeping out of the rain.

'Are you sure you won't change your mind? It's not too late to come with me,' Laurent said.

Fleur bit her lip. The temptation was great, but it was too late, whatever he said. Only one set of papers would be waiting. One set of clothes. One seat in an aeroplane.

'You know I can't.'

He nodded, not really expecting a different answer to the question he had asked a dozen times. 'I hope Colette realises how much you care for her.'

'I'll make sure she does.' Fleur smiled, though it was forced.

The doors beside them opened and the audience began to leave the building. Chattering and bidding each other goodnight, they could have no suspicion of the farewell that was taking place.

Their time was up.

They exchanged a look of undiluted grief.

'I'll wait,' Fleur whispered. 'When this is all over you could come back.'

'Don't wait.' Laurent took Fleur's hands and clasped them tightly. His eyes were watery. 'I don't know if I'll get back there alive and I won't be able to let you know either way. I don't want you to spend your life waiting for something that might never be able to happen. I want to think of you being happy. Marrying, having children, being happy.'

Fleur's eyes filled. 'I'll never forget you.'

'I should hope not. I'm very memorable,' he said, smiling.

He bent and kissed her softly on the lips. She closed her eyes, savouring the last touch. The pressure of his lips lifted and he spoke quietly, his breath like a feather on her cheek.

'Goodbye, my dearest. Whatever happens to me, I'll carry you in my heart for ever.'

She felt his absence before she opened her eyes and when she turned to look for him, she saw him walking alongside a group, nodding and giving the impression that he was a part of a conversation. He caught her looking and his eye flickered in a brief wink. Her spirits lifted a little. He was clever and brave. If any man could reach safety, that man would be Laurent.

❧

She made her way home. Colette was alone.

'I suggested Sophie should spend the night at the hotel seeing Josette. I thought you would like an empty house. How do you feel?'

'Thank you.' Fleur sagged onto the sofa and kicked off her shoes. 'I feel like I'm lost. I feel like he ripped out my heart and carried it away with him.'

'Will you keep doing what you've been doing?'

Fleur sniffed and wiped the back of her hand over her cheeks. 'Laurent wants me to. Elouard too, especially now he has lost a man.' She looked at Colette through filmy eyes. By now, Laurent would be far away from the city, on a train steaming through the countryside toward an unknown destination. Could there be any harm in telling Colette the truth now, if Fleur did not even know herself the direction he was travelling in? If anyone came searching, they'd lie as they had done when Sébastien had gone.

No, she'd wait a few more hours just to be on the safe side.

~

In the morning, she made coffee and sat opposite Colette at the table.

'Laurent is going to Britain. Because that is where he comes from. I didn't know until the night in July he came here and told me.'

Predictably, Colette was shocked and fascinated. Fleur shared as much as she could, save for the fact that Laurent had invited her to go with him and that she had declined for Colette's sake. That was her choice and not a burden she wanted to place on her friend. She was weary to the bone and heartsore when she finished.

'How have you managed all these months? Not knowing where Sébastien is or even if he is alive? How do you find the strength to get out of bed every day and keep living?'

Colette wrapped her arms around Fleur. 'I do it because I have to for Louise. And I can only do that because you have given me the strength to keep going. I couldn't have done it without you and now I am here for you. I don't know if our men will ever come back to us but we have each other and we always will. We are luckier than some. We have a house, we have food, and we have friendship. That is more than many people can hope for, even without a war going on. We have each other and we always will.'

Fleur leaned against Colette, feeling slightly less distraught. 'You're right. Together we can survive anything.'

~

Months passed and there was no word from Laurent. If Elouard had heard anything he did not share the information with Fleur.

Sophie gave birth to a son at the end of November. She had

never moved out and it appeared she would be making a permanent home with Fleur and Colette. At least Fleur no longer had to worry about explaining her late returns home because Sophie was completely overwhelmed with motherhood and love for her son.

'I'm calling him Augustin,' she announced. 'I heard it over the radio on that silly BBC broadcast where they talk nonsense to annoy the Germans, and I thought it was a lovely name.'

Fleur's scalp prickled. Sophie would have no idea that the broadcasts were used to transmit information. 'What did the radio say?'

Sophie shrugged. 'I can't be expected to remember everything. My brain has turned to wool. Oh yes, actually I do remember. Something about sending flowers to Roxane, because I thought that was a pretty name for a girl. Are you alright, Fleur? Where are you going?'

Fleur didn't answer. She walked out of the apartment and into the street where she leaned against the windowsill of the bookshop. The biting air made her throat tighten but she didn't care. She wanted to scream with delight. The names were too much of a coincidence. It had to be Laurent who had sent the message. He had reached England safely. Even if she never received confirmation, it would be the story she told herself when her spirits were low. He was carrying on the fight from England. She was carrying it on here, and she had fulfilled Sébastien's request to keep Colette safe. It was the best of the bleak situation but it was the light in the darkness of war that she clung to in the lonely nights.

Chapter Thirty-Five

June 1944

I f Fleur still grieved for Laurent, she did not show it outwardly. The chance mention of the radio message by Sophie had appeared to give her hope to cling onto. Colette wished she had something herself. Louise was a clever child and had learned to say '*Maman*' and always that, not the austere, '*Mère*' that Delphine had insisted on. Other children would be learning '*Papa*', but Louise had none. At least she would eventually have a playmate in the form of Augustin who was nearly eight months old. At eighteen months, Louise found the younger child fascinating and Colette held a secret hope that the two would grow up as close as she and Fleur had.

She was watching both children while Sophie shopped when Fleur burst in, her eyes bright.

'Normandy is in the hands of the Allies. The coastal defences have been conquered and towns retaken. Elouard just called into the shop.'

'What? Are we winning the war?' Even behind closed doors, to speak of a possible turn of the tables seemed to be inviting Fate to roll the dice against France.

Fleur dropped her bag on the table and rushed into her bedroom. She emerged dressed in a pair of culottes and a blouse. 'I'm not sure. I'm going with him now. As soon as I know, I'll tell you what I can.'

She rushed past Colette towards the door. Colette seized her by the hand. 'I want to help. Tell me what I can do.'

'I will.'

~

Fleur returned with a bag full of posters and the instructions to paste them to walls and pass them out. This time the message was simple: be prepared to fight. The atmosphere in Paris grew thick with tension but there was an undercurrent of excitement that had been absent for years.

Colette helped distribute the leaflets. She wheeled Louise in the pram through the streets, once again dressed in her finest hat and coat. A beautiful woman with a handsome baby naturally attracted attention, but only of the most adoring nature. Even the checkpoint guards managed to raise an indulgent smile. Little could any of them have suspected that beneath the blankets and mattress were sheaves of leaflets and a pot of glue ready to be handed to Fleur when the road was quiet.

'My baby was born in a war, but she will grow up in peace. One day I'll tell her that she was part of the Resistance before she even knew it.'

It was easy to believe at this point that Colette's prediction of peace might be right. Every day came news on the BBC or the Free French radio that the Allies were advancing. There were other enemies beside the German forces however, as the women were reminded when they came face to face with Pierre. He greeted Fleur with a fawning smile and gave Colette a cursory nod.

'You bastard, I have nothing to say to you,' Fleur snapped.

'Why?'

'Because it was you who made the allegations against Laurent regarding the *marché noir*, wasn't it? Don't try to deny it.'

'What if it was?' He shrugged. 'The arrogant bastard deserved a good beating.'

Colette had heard the phrase seeing red but had never truly appreciated how true it could be until she saw the colour rise to Fleur's cheeks.

Fleur shoved Pierre hard in the chest. It caught him completely unaware, and he staggered back.

'What the fuck? You mad bitch!'

'He could have died! They could have handed him to the official authorities! You didn't even know who he was, did you! He wasn't just a mechanic. He is British. He was sent here to help the Resistance and to try bringing an end to this war. Do you know what they do to spies? They don't just give them a quick beating and let them go!'

Colette put a warning hand on Fleur's arm and Fleur stopped, taking in a long breath.

Pierre stood open-mouthed. 'I didn't know.'

'Of course you didn't,' Colette sneered. 'That is the whole point.'

'Forgive me—' Pierre began.

Fleur cut him off with an angry hiss. 'You ask forgiveness, but are you truly sorry? I have half a mind to let his associates know who was responsible. What do you think they would do?'

Pierre paled slightly. They would see him as a traitor, of course.

'Don't...' he began.

Fleur curled her lip. 'I'm not going to. We need people here.

The fight for France is more important than you. But I don't ever want to see you again.'

She linked her arm through Colette's and they stalked past him, noses high in the air as if they were passing a dirty smell.

'Oh my goodness, did you see his expression?' Colette said. 'You were so fierce. I'm proud of you.'

'I'm proud of myself,' Fleur admitted. 'I'm glad I finally got to confront him. It feels like closing the lid on a box for the last time.'

Colette had her own box to close, though she had not realised it. It began when she opened the door to the bookshop one morning in late July and found herself face to face with Delphine.

An older-looking Delphine who was wearing barely any make-up, which left her eyes shadowed and red rimmed. She was wearing a black hat, tipped back on her head, and a plain black coat that seemed at odds with the summer heat. She looked unsure of herself.

'May I come inside?'

Colette shrugged. 'It's a shop. You don't need my permission.'

'I mean inside your apartment.' A prickle of tension ran over Colette's shoulders. She turned and walked to the stairs, not turning back to see if Delphine was following. When Delphine entered the living room she looked directly at Colette.

'Your father is dead.'

Delphine spoke with her head up, but then dropped it and appeared to visibly crumble. Ever since she had noticed Delphine's clothing, Colette had suspected bad news, but the confirmation pulled her legs out from under her.

'*Papa*! But I only saw him last week.'

Delphine looked at her sharply. 'Did you?'

Colette felt her cheeks redden. As far as she knew, Louis had not told Delphine about the monthly visits Colette paid to his factory but that didn't seem important in the light of the dreadful news.

'What happened?'

'When you told us about your baby's father being in the Resistance, apparently it awoke something inside him. He began to let a group use the factory to meet in the evenings. Two days ago they were discovered and the members ran. Your father was unfit. He suffered a heart attack and died before he could be arrested.' Delphine dropped onto the sofa and put her head in her hands. 'I knew nothing of what he had been doing until the Abwehr came to tell me and ask how much I was involved.'

'Then it's partly my fault.' Colette sat beside her mother. The idea of gentle, devoted Louis becoming involved in the Resistance was incomprehensible. Having said that, the idea that she or Fleur were involved would seem as unlikely to many.

'If you've come here to blame me, you don't have to,' she said.

Delphine looked at her bleakly. 'I'm not here for that. He seemed happier over the past half year but I never understood why. It gave him a purpose. He fought in the Great War, of course. I imagine he was proud to defend his country again.'

Her face crumpled. 'I loved him,' she sniffed through her tears. 'I know I flirted with other men and I told you I only married him because I had to, but I truly did.'

Colette reached for Delphine's hand.

'Would you like…' She hesitated, reluctant to offer Delphine an opportunity to ask for alcohol.

Delphine's mouth curled into a wry smile. 'Only water, please.'

Colette brought her a glass. From the bedroom Louise began to babble as she woke up from her morning nap. Delphine looked up in surprise.

'Your baby?'

A little of Colette's sympathy diminished. 'My daughter. She's not a baby any longer.'

Then, remembering Louise's namesake, the father and

husband she and Delphine had just lost she asked, 'Would you like to meet her?'

Delphine swallowed and nodded. Colette went into the bedroom and brought the sleepy girl out. Louise tried immediately to climb down so she could toddle across to the basket of toys and pulled a face when Colette held her tight.

'She looks like you.' Delphine smiled for the first time. 'She is beautiful.'

'She is called Louise,' Colette said.

'After your father? Oh!' Delphine crumpled into tears again, sobbing and hugging herself tightly. 'I'm so, so sorry, my *chérie*. I was furious with you and distraught for you. I behaved so badly.'

Louise began to wail. Colette jiggled her up and down on her knee. Delphine's eyes were on the child constantly.

'Would you like to hold her?' Colette offered.

Delphine nodded. Her lip began to wobble and she bit it. She held her arms out.

'My granddaughter,' she murmured as Colette placed Louise into her arms. She bent and kissed Louise's forehead and whispered something Colette didn't catch.

Colette smiled. 'Let me make coffee. I think we could both do with some. I have no sugar, but I do have a little milk.'

Fleur and Sophie returned from shopping while the coffee was brewing and Louise clambered off Delphine's knee and demanded to kiss Augustin. Then Sophie corralled both children and took them off into the bedroom. Colette whispered to Fleur what had happened, and the two women hugged tight before Fleur joined Sophie and the children.

Delphine watched the exchange quietly with an odd sort of expression on her face.

'This is where all of you live?'

'Yes. Fleur sleeps in that room, and I share my room with Sophie and the children.'

'This is so small,' Delphine said. 'So cramped. It's not good for a baby. Come back home. The house is too big for me alone.'

Colette gaped at the unexpected offer. 'Home with you? With Louise?'

'Yes. I should never have forced you into leaving. It was heartless of me. I've wasted so many months and now we are both alone and we shouldn't be.'

Of course the offer was made out of self-interest. Delphine needed to be surrounded by people.

'I am not alone,' Colette replied. 'I have Fleur, Sophie, Louise, and Augustin.'

Then Colette paused and considered the offer sensibly

The apartment was cramped and unbearably hot in summer. Louise was growing and would need a room of her own eventually. A garden she could play in. Maybe more than anything she needed family. She heard Augustin begin to cry and Fleur's level tone soothing her.

'If I come, I won't come alone. I want Fleur too.'

'Why?' She could almost see Delphine's internal struggle. Her mother was still the same woman after all.

'You said yourself the house is too big for one person, but really it is too big for three. If you want me then you will have to take my friend too. Both of them, in fact, if Sophie wants to bring Augustin. She can't stay here alone if we go.'

Delphine looked at her and Colette saw something she had never seen before: a growing respect.

'You've changed, Colette.'

'We've all changed, *Mère*. Anyone who has not changed because of the war is inhuman. I think it's a change for the better.'

'You might be right,' Delphine said thoughtfully. 'Yes, your friends can come too. For the time being at least. If that is the price of having you back, then I will willingly pay it.'

She stood and gathered her bag. Before she left, she peered

round the doorway of Colette's bedroom and smiled. 'The crib looks lovely.'

Colette blinked. 'You know about that?'

Delphine smiled slightly condescendingly. 'Your father was a great man in many ways, but he did not know the first thing about how to decorate a nursery.'

She went, leaving Colette staring after her thoughtfully. Fleur and Sophie came cautiously out of the bedroom.

'I have a proposal for you both,' Colette said. She told them of Delphine's request. Sophie agreed immediately. She had always been envious of Colette's spacious house. Fleur was a little more reserved.

'It is very sudden. It feels like the world is upside down enough. Are you sure you want to live with your mother again?'

'It wouldn't be my first choice but it is my home. Our home. Besides, if the Allies are advancing through France, I'd rather be living on the outskirts of the city than in the centre. I don't think anyone will be wanting to buy books for a while. We should board up the shop and go somewhere safer.'

That appeared to be the deciding factor to convince Fleur so the three women made plans for packing and moving. Everything would have to be carried by hand, though Fleur thought Elouard might know someone with a delivery van who could help, and it would take at least two days to ready the bookshop. They set on waiting another week and leaving on the first day of August.

When there was a knock on the door, two days before, Colette assumed it was someone confirming the use of the van. She opened it to find an unfamiliar man standing there.

He wore a collarless shirt, baggy trousers held up by braces and a light cotton jacket. His hair was flattened beneath a peaked cap and his face was obscured by a full beard. The eyes however, peered out at Colette from behind thick lenses. Her heart missed a beat. A loud buzzing filled her ears and the world around her receded.

'Sébastien?'

He nodded.

'Oh my god! I didn't know if you were even alive!' She lowered her voice. 'What are you doing here? What if the Germans find you?' She ushered him inside and up to the flat.

'I am the least of their concerns. They are retreating across France. The Allies and the Free French are gaining ground daily.' His face creased with worry. 'When I saw the windows of the shop boarded up, I wasn't sure you were still here, but then I noticed the door was ajar. What is happening?'

There was so much to tell him she didn't know where to begin.

'My father is dead. We are moving back to the house on Henri-Martin. Thank God you came today. Two more days and we will be gone.'

'That's good. There will be fighting but another day or two and we will have the city. Paris will be ours again. Is Fleur here with you? Are she and Laurent still involved? I can't stay long.'

Colette nodded, then shook her head, not sure which question she was answering. She wasn't even sure he was real and if she reached out to touch him, he might vanish. Fleur came out of her bedroom.

'Colette? Who was at the door? Did I leave it unlocked downstairs?'

She stopped, shrieked, and displaying none of Colette's indecision, ran to Sébastien and flung her arms around him.

'Oh my god, you are alive! How wonderful! I'm so pleased to see you. Where have you been?'

'I've been in Brittany. I went back to where I came from. It seemed the obvious place to go, to get as far away from Paris.' His face darkened. 'There's been a lot more collaboration there than in Paris. Perhaps it is the nature of small towns. Then, when the allied troops landed in Normandy in June, we knew it was not going to be so long before they began to make headway through the rest of the country, so I came back here. If there is going to be a battle, I wanted to fight it here.'

Fleur nodded. 'Yes, I understand.'

'Do you have to go fight?' Colette asked. Her heart began to race at the thought of him being taken from her again. He straightened his back. Behind the familiar glasses, his eyes grew steely.

'Of course I do. Every man and woman will be needed.'

'I know how to fire a gun. I want to help too,' Fleur said.

'Absolutely not. You stay indoors where you are safe. I want you to look after my wife.'

'Your wife?' Colette felt sick.

Sébastien met her eyes and grinned. 'Well, that's slightly premature, but I hope you will be as soon as I can find a time to get somebody to marry us. Perhaps if the British get this far, or the Americans, I'll ask an army chaplain. I've met one or two.'

'Are you proposing to me?' Colette asked. Again, it was not the way she had ever imagined it. Before he could answer, Louise woke up and began to shriek happily in the bedroom. Sébastien stiffened.

'What's that?'

Colette grew tense. Of course he had no idea that she had kept the baby. She had promised to give up the child. He might turn on his heel and walk away and she would never see him again.

Her voice shook as she answered. 'That's my daughter.'

'Daughter?' Sébastien's voice was husky.

Colette swallowed again. 'Our daughter. I'm sorry, Sébastien. I know I said I wasn't going to keep her, but I could not bear to give her up.'

'We have a daughter?' He sounded stunned.

'Would you like to see her?'

He nodded.

Colette rushed to the bedroom and gathered up Louise. She was warm and her thin hair was standing up in wisps all over her head. She smelled slightly milky and slightly soiled. Never mind. Colette walked back to the living room.

'This is Louise,' she said shyly. She held the infant in her arms, displaying her to Sébastien.

He gazed down.

'She's not a little baby.'

'It's been a long time,' Fleur said. 'Why don't you hold her?'

Sébastien looked at Colette. 'May I?'

He held out his hands and Colette placed Louise in them. He held her at arm's length as if she might explode then drew her towards him and bent his head over hers. Louise, ever patient, tolerated the odd behaviour of the unfamiliar man. Colette gave Fleur an anxious look. She could not bear the wait. After long, agonising moments Sébastien looked up at Colette.

'She's beautiful. She's just like you.'

'You aren't angry that I kept her?' Colette asked. 'I won't ask you for any money. You don't have to look after her, but if you want to see her you can come any time you like. You don't have to marry me.'

'I want to,' Sébastien said, almost before she had finished speaking. 'I want to do both. I want to raise her with you.'

His eyes were streaming and tears fell from beneath his glasses, droplets clinging to his beard. 'Colette, you have no idea how happy this makes me. Yes, I want her. I want both of you.'

Colette felt a sob rising in the back of her throat. Fleur reached forward and took Louise from Sébastien's arms. Sébastien's eyes met Colette's. Meltingly soft.

'Do you mean that? If it's for Louise, you don't have to.'

'I mean it, Colette. I mean it for me. For us. I asked you before I knew she was still ours, and I don't take it back in the slightest now I know. Will you marry me?'

'I will.'

And, finally, Colette could touch him. She reached out a hand to his face, brushing her fingers over his beard.

'This will have to go, of course,' she said, smiling.

He reached his hand up and covered hers, capturing it, then he pulled her into his arms and then enfolded her in a tight embrace.

'Oh, my sweet.' He kissed her and as their lips met Colette knew with absolute certainty this was the right choice. The right man. Her veins flooded with heat, her body with desire. She snaked her arms around him, pressing her breasts against his chest. His kiss became more passionate.

She heard Fleur whisper to Louise, 'Come on, little one. Let's go for a walk and leave your *maman* and *papa* to their reunion.'

Colette and Sébastien broke off the kiss and smiled at each other. Then Sébastien took her hand, led her to the bedroom, and closed the door behind them.

Chapter Thirty-Six

The fighting began as skirmishes. Despite Sébastien's instructions, Fleur went into the street to supervise the shelves from the bookshop being taken and used as barricades. Poor Monsieur Ramper would come back to find his shop changed, but for the first time it felt he might have a city to return to.

They retreated to stay with Delphine and once again, the air over the sixteenth arrondissement thundered with the sound of explosions. The four women crowded round the window in Fleur's attic room to watch the sky lighting up, this time gleeful with hope.

Then, on the night of the twenty-fourth of August, a new sound breached the walls of the house.

Fleur clutched Colette's arm. 'Listen. That's *La Marseillaise.*'

The song grew louder and closer. Doors opened and the streets filled. Fleur raced down the stairs and outside. Into the streets poured women and men, carrying children, holding each other and raising their voices in song.

'It's over.' Colette hugged Fleur, then Delphine. Then all the women were in each other's arms, sobbing with joy.

～

Of course it was not over immediately.

Once again military vehicles drove through the streets of Paris. Once again boots marched in unison along the Champs-Elysées, past the War Ministry on the Rue Saint-Dominque, but this time it was a cause for jubilation. Paris had survived.

Over the following weeks, the sight of German uniforms was replaced by those of English, French, and Americans. Uniforms in different livery but all allies. Soldiers laughed with children, shook hands with men. What they got up to with the women was a nobody's business but theirs.

Sophie appeared determined to find a new father for her child. She put on a black hat and veil and carried Augustin on her hip, telling the same thing to each of the soldiers who stopped to speak with the pretty young woman and child.

'It's very sad. His father was a brave man, but he died working for the Resistance. He never met his son.'

One recipient of her tale, a stocky man with sandy brown hair and a sergeant's stripes, looked sorrowful.

'Well, ma'am, he sure is a pretty child. I'm sure his father would have been very proud of him.'

'That's a complete lie,' Fleur said indignantly after the officer had moved on.

Sophie jutted out her chin. 'I don't care. Have you seen what is happening to women who are accused of collaborating with the enemy? They are shaving their heads and parading them through the streets. I'm not going to let that happen to me, and I won't have my child grow with the stigma of being half a German rat. I don't care if you disapprove. I've got a life to live and a son to provide for and he will not grow up in shame.'

She sashayed away, heading towards a group of officers who were sitting in a café, smoking cigarettes and drinking coffee, and asked if she might take the spare chair to feed her child. Fleur walked on, half incensed, but also slightly admiring of Sophie's nerve. It was a cold lie but understandable.

'They aren't shaving the heads of the men who served drinks to Germans or fixed their cars,' she remarked. 'I don't think I blame Sophie at all. She will probably find a husband before the war is officially over.'

'I hope she does,' Colette said. 'I don't blame her either. If Sébastien hadn't come home I'm not sure what I would have done.'

'It's lucky you don't have to. Though perhaps an elopement might have been more peaceful.'

Colette laughed weakly. Although Colette had said she would be content with a quick ceremony performed by anyone who could spare the time, Delphine had decided that if her daughter was going to marry a hero of the Resistance, the occasion would be marked with the most elaborate means available.

~

They compromised on a quiet ceremony in October, followed by a reception in Delphine's salon. The party was slightly more subdued than before the war, but the joy on the bride and groom's face left no one in doubt that the marriage would be a long and happy one.

Fleur sat on the edge of the fountain, a glass of not-exactly-champagne in her hand. The temperature was still hot but the air was scented with flowers. Colette joined her, sitting down carefully so as not to crumple her dress.

'Are you alright?'

'Perfectly but my feet are tired. It's been a long time since I danced,' Fleur said.

'Me too. I'm sorry that there aren't many partners for you. I wish you could be as happy as I am.'

'I am happy,' Fleur said, surprised at the comment.

'You know what I mean.' Colette took her hand. The thin gold band on her left hand was cold against Fleur's palm. 'With Laurent. Do you think he might come back?'

Fleur stared up at the sky. 'I don't know. I'd like to think so but I can't spend my life hoping.'

Colette hugged her. 'You could go to England and look for him. I'm sure Edith would give you a room.'

'I don't even know how I'd go about finding him. A man who did secret work he couldn't talk about for people who probably won't have a sign on the door of their building. It doesn't sound very easy, does it?'

She took a sip of not-champagne. 'No, I'm lucky I had the chance to fall in love even though I can't pretend I wish it had turned out differently.'

'One day you'll find someone else,' Colette assured her.

Fleur murmured a vague sound of agreement. She was not sure, but at that point in time, she didn't much care either way.

~

August 1945

It shouldn't rain in August, but nevertheless torrents hammered rhythmically on the pavement. It reminded Fleur of the relentlessness of jackboots marching. Even though a year had passed since the last regiments of Germans had marched out of Paris, the association was enough to make her shiver. The rain might account partly for the reason the bookshop was empty on a Saturday morning.

Monsieur Ramper would find his business a sad shadow of its former self when he finally returned.

If he returned.

Regretfully, it was becoming less and less likely that he would. Fleur had read the newspaper reports that told of the existence of the death camps where the Nazis had murdered the Jews they had said would be housed safely in work camps. Seen the photos of the emaciated faces, jumbles of limbs, bodies piled on top of each other in a sickening display of callous evil. The true numbers were not yet known but they must be in the tens of thousands, if not the hundreds of thousands. The lies and the horror were impossible to comprehend.

Monsieur Ramper. Michal. The Halevy family. Where were they now? Would they ever be accounted for? The names in the bookshop ledgers would remain for ever with their debts unpaid, a chilling memorial to lives abandoned and destroyed.

It was a grim train of thought and Fleur was glad when the doorbell clanged and a damp wind blew in as a customer entered the shop, forcing her to think of other things.

'Good morning, monsieur.'

She glanced up briefly then went back to her writing. Most customers wanted to be left alone to browse the shelves before making their purchases and so she spent most of her time in the shop writing. Trying to make some sense of her thoughts and memories. Most likely only she would ever read them but pouring out a story was cathartic.

This customer was different. He walked straight up to the desk and cleared his throat.

'Do you have a copy of *Cyrano de Bergerac*?'

At the sound of the voice Fleur raised her head and looked at him properly. Her hand began to shake and she lowered the pen into the inkwell before it dripped onto her notebook.

Laurent's beloved, familiar face smiled down at her.

'Hello, Fleur,' he said quietly.

She stood and wished immediately that she hadn't because her legs began to tremble.

She thought back occasionally to the moment when Sébastien had returned and Colette had stood like a statue in the doorway. She had always wondered what possessed Colette not to hurl herself straight at him. Now she had the answer because her legs refused to move.

'You came back.'

He smiled. 'Of course. Did you doubt I would?'

She didn't want to admit it, though long nights lying in bed wishing he would get in contact had meant with each passing day she thought it less likely.

'I didn't know if you would be able to. Or if you would want to.' Her voice sounded very small.

'I would have come sooner but travel isn't as easy yet as it was before the war. I had affairs to tend to.'

'Affairs?'

His lip twitched. 'Matters, let's say. Certainly not affairs of the sort you're worrying about. I told you before there would be no other women besides you.'

He took his hat off and ran his fingers through his hair. It was longer now, parted at the side so it flopped slightly across his forehead. There was a slight wave to it that suited him.

'Aren't you going to kiss me I've after I've come all this way?'

'Not yet,' Fleur said frankly.

He laughed ruefully. 'There's a wretched greeting for me. Don't tell me you've moved on and met somebody you prefer?' His voice was light but his eyes watched her intently.

'You told me not to wait,' Fleur said quietly.

She lifted her eyes to his and smiled.

'I waited anyway.'

She walked around the table and past him.

'The door is unlocked, you see, and when I do kiss you, I know I'm not going to want to stop.'

She closed the door and drew the bolts across, then pulled the blinds down, taking deep breaths to steady her hand. Her heart sang and she wanted to sing along with it. When she was assured of their privacy, she turned back to him. He was leaning against the desk. He drummed his fingers on the wood then raised his brows.

'Any other preparations?'

Fleur shook her head.

'Good. Then come here.'

She walked towards him and he met her halfway across the room. Fleur stood on her tip toes to reach up to him. He bent and whirled her off the ground until she was level with his face and her feet dangled. The lips met, hard and frenzied, pulling at each other eagerly. Fleur closed her eyes and felt him move around until he deposited her on the desk.

'My notebook,' she said in alarm, pulling her mouth from his.

'I have very much missed your practical nature, my darling,' he said with a laugh in his voice.

She moved the ink pot and notebook to the other end of the desk. There were passages in the book that she would rather throw herself out of an aeroplane than let him read.

'Happy now?'

She nodded.

'In that case, kiss me like you have missed me, my darling,' he instructed.

So she did.

〜

Colette and Sébastien were delighted to see Laurent again.

'I'm not sure I can get used to calling you Charles,' Colette announced.

The rain had dried up and the two couples sat on the terrace enjoying the early evening sunshine.

Laurent described the plans he had for a house on the plot of land he had mentioned to Fleur before. Apparently, it was part of a larger estate that belonged to his family. He had refrained from saying how large that was but mentioned that the original house had suffered damage during the war when it had been used to house convalescing soldiers, leaving Fleur to wonder who exactly he was.

Sébastien and Laurent drank Scotch that Laurent had brought, Fleur had a martini, and Colette drank orange juice. She was in the early stages of pregnancy and, as before, was suffering with sickness. When she announced she was going inside and asked Fleur to join her, Fleur agreed, thinking nothing of it, but as soon as they entered the dining room, Colette rounded on Fleur, a stern expression on her face.

'We promised not to keep secrets but I know there's one you've been keeping from me.'

'What secret?' Fleur wrinkled her nose, confused and unable to think of what Colette meant.

'That Laurent asked you to go to England with him when he left Paris, and that you said no.'

Fleur's hand tightened around the stem of her glass. 'How do you know that?'

'He told me while you and Sébastien were making the drinks.'

'It's not a very big secret,' Fleur said.

Colette rolled her eyes. 'It's possibly the most important one ever. You said no. Was that because of me?'

Fleur dropped her eyes. 'I couldn't leave you and Louise alone. It was before you had reconciled with Delphine.'

'I understand that and I'm more grateful than you could ever imagine but I think you need to go with him. I have Sébastien and Louise and soon I'll have another baby. I have a perfect life.'

'Don't you want me in it?' Fleur asked in a whisper.

Colette blinked. 'More than anything, I do. No, not quite more than anything. Not more than I want you to be happy. Because you have a real chance of happiness now and I am not so selfish that I would prevent you taking it. Laurent clearly can't stay here if he has a job and land in England, so you'll have to go there if you want to be with the man you love. Do you want to be with him?'

Fleur's eyes prickled. Leaving Paris and saying goodbye to her dear friends would wrench her heart from her body, but saying goodbye to Laurent for the second time would do that too.

'Yes, I do. I do so very much.'

Colette hugged her. 'Of course you do. It isn't me you need to be saying that to though, is it?' She glanced over Fleur's shoulder. 'You can come in now.'

Laurent walked through the door.

'How long have you been there?' Fleur asked. She glanced at Colette who had a triumphant look on her face. This had been planned all along. She wondered how much he had heard.

'Decades, I think. At least that is what it felt like waiting.' He glanced at Colette. 'Does this mean your friend has persuaded you to leave her side?'

'Yes,' Fleur said.

His face creased, joy spreading over it. In three steps he had gathered her into his arms.

'Then my darling, everything is settled. Shall we marry here or in England?'

Fleur laughed. 'I don't know. I don't care. Anywhere you choose.'

'Here, of course,' Colette said. 'I'll be too pregnant to travel soon and I demand to be involved, and Louise will make a charming bridesmaid. I will miss you dreadfully, but I expect you to come back and see me as often as you can. I will come to England to see you too and we'll write to each other – and make sure the letters arrive. Every summer we can all travel to Brittany to stay with Sébastien's family there. They live near Morlaix. Like the name of the café, of course.'

Laurent reached for Fleur's hand. He pressed it tightly. 'It sounds like Colette has our lives planned for us all.'

'Oh I do,' Colette said. 'And wherever you are, we'll always be sisters.'

Fleur beamed, tears welling up, but tears of joy. A future stretched before her of love and family. No war. Only brightness.

'Yes, we will.'

Epilogue

I n the summer of 1994, two elderly couples walked along on the promenade at Cabourg on the Normandy coast. The women walked arm in arm, one tall and plump, with steel-grey hair set in an elaborate bun, the other shorter and more delicate, with soft streaks of silver in her chin-length bob. Their husbands were a little way behind, the larger one in a wheelchair pushed by a handsome man in his early forties, and the other steadying himself with a walking frame.

'Fifty years since Paris was liberated,' Fleur said, lowering herself onto a bench. 'I can scarcely believe it.'

'Look at us now. We are old. Louise is getting married again next year to a younger man. The children from his first marriage will be coming to stay with us while they honeymoon.' Colette sighed and took a bite out of her ice cream. 'Can you imagine what I shall do with two almost teenagers running around the house? I don't know why they couldn't go and stay with one of their uncles. What was the point in me having four children if I can't make use of them?'

'Tell them there is a secret garden and let them look for it.'

Fleur laughed, adjusting her sunglasses. The prescription evidently needed updating because the road signs were looking fuzzy.

The two women sat in silence on the bench, contemplating the past and possibly the future. The men drew alongside. Colette shuffled up to make room for Sébastien, grumbling good-naturedly as he tangled his frame in her skirt.

'Are you gossiping?' he asked, leaning over to kiss Colette's cheek.

'Thinking about the past,' Fleur said. She narrowed her eyes and tutted playfully. 'Charles, why aren't you wearing your hat? Laurence, be a dear and nip back to the car to fetch it for him.'

Laurence jogged off. He was a handsome man who had his father's build but his mother's sharp eyes. It had taken seven years of disappointments and heartbreak to conceive him and Fleur loved him dearly. She watched him go.

'I don't think Laurence will ever marry. Did I tell you he is a homosexual?'

'Yes, you did.'

More than once, Colette mused privately.

'Ah. I thought I might have. I do hate not having a sharp memory any longer. He has a "partner", as they call each other, who races vintage cars and they live in the lodge on the edge of the estate. I think Charles is quite happy with the situation as he gets to tinker about under the bonnets, aren't you, Charles?'

'Partner indeed!' Colette said, rolling her eyes. 'Of course they all think this is new and that they were the first to invent the idea. If only they could see what went on in the clubs of Montmartre in the thirties and forties. Their eyes would water!'

Fleur stared out to sea. 'Of course. Sophie. I wonder what happened to her?'

'We lost touch after she divorced the American and moved to San Francisco to live on a women's commune.'

Ahead of them, the pale sands stretched into the distance before meeting the sea. Children built sandcastles and a vigorous game of beach cricket was taking place, accompanied by loud shouting. The official ceremonies to mark the anniversary had taken place a week previously and now the beaches were the preserve of holidaymakers once more.

'Do you think any of them can comprehend what took place here?' Colette asked, eying the families.

'Not really,' Fleur replied. 'I can't myself and we lived through it.'

'Perhaps that is how it should be,' Colette said thoughtfully. 'We made the sacrifices, so they don't have to.'

She leaned against Sébastien. Fleur reached for Charles' hand, and with her other, she linked arms with Colette.

Still friends after so long, they sat and watched as the sun went down.

Author's Note

As much as this is a romance, it is equally about women's friendship and support. I'm fortunate to have a number of wonderful women in my life who I love and admire. I won't name names because I'm bound to leave someone out, but one day I hope you all get to meet each other!

Paris is a wonderful city that I don't think I'll ever get tired of, so it was wonderful to visit vicariously through photographs, maps and books at a time when getting abroad seemed like an impossibility. Many of the locations and clubs mentioned are (or were) real places. The Bois de Boulogne near the house where Colette and Fleur grow up is a great place to escape the heat of the city in summer and now houses the Fondation Louis Vuitton, an excellent art gallery, as well as a fairground and parks.

Among my sources I turned once again to Maurice Buckmaster's *They Fought Alone*, an account of the SOE agents working in France. For the differing attitudes of French women living under German rule I also used Anna Sebba's *Les Parisiennes*.

Some women enthusiastically resisted, some actively collaborated, many tried keep a path of neutrality between the two extremes in order to survive. It's worth mentioning that French women did not get the right to vote until the summer of 1944, weren't allowed to work outside the home without their husband's consent until 1965, and wearing trousers was technically illegal until 2012. With husbands and fathers away fighting, the new opportunities for independence and the weight of responsibilities must have been staggering. I hope I have represented their responses fairly. Who knows how we would react in their place.

Thank you to Charlotte Ledger and Julia Williams for their excellent editing in drawing the book together into something coherent.